NO THIRD CHOICE

AJ. Kohler

Editor in chief: Nik Morton

Publisher's Note:

This is a work of fiction. All names, characters, places, and
events are the work of the author's imagination. Any
resemblance to real persons, places, or events is
coincidental.

Solstice Publishing: www.solsticepublishing.com

Dedication

For Chewbacca and Princess Leia, who taught me about
Long-coat Akitas, and who together, became Sasha for this
story. For Finnegan and Djinni, who taught me about
Belgians and are now waiting at Rainbow Bridge.
And always and all ways, for CEO, who has always
believed.

Prologue

Some days are dull. Some really get your attention, and a few make you wonder what in the hell ever possessed you to get involved. Today is definitely already in that last category.

The sun isn't up yet. I'm standing in the front yard, pinned by something like half a dozen spotlights on what feels like half the police cars in the world. I've got my hands in the air and I'm about to get down onto the ground at the orders of the approaching SWAT team member. Over on the other side of the front walk, Alec is facing another half dozen or so spotlights and going through the same routine, which is anything but routine for either of us.

I'd just had my house shot up with automatic weapons, been shot at personally, and I'd put half a dozen rounds into the truck that had brought the shooters to my front doorstep. Trying to protect me, Alec had added his own. The dogs in the doorway I was desperately attempting to keep safe were upset, to say the least, and if they twitched the wrong way, they were likely to be killed by the cops.

So what in the hell *had* possessed me?

Chapter 1

People talk to me. Sometimes, usually, they do it with their voices, and they always do it with their body language. It's partly a knack I was born with, and partly a skill I've worked very hard to develop. I usually have very little trouble getting people to open up and tell me all sorts of things, and I use that ability shamelessly, I have to admit.

Today, my professional life seems to be taking a serious turn for the better, as I'm expecting Raymond Escarton Fields, the Family CEO. That may not sound like a big deal, but for me, as a Family member, trust me, it's *huge*. The Family is simply that, a family. It's very secretive, but it's not any sort of crime syndicate or the like, simply a family that's hundreds of years old, far older than the Rockefellers or even the Rothschilds. Think of thousands of cousins, all around the world. It's organized as a corporation, so it's got a CEO. He's responsible for investing the Family fortune.

Just the idea of his coming to my office was unsettling for me. The office is in one of these little houses along East Speedway in Tucson, near the university. It's a handy place to be, because I'm in the same neighborhood with a bunch of lawyers who, fortunately, utilize my services. The sign out in front says A.M. Youngston, Investigations—that's me. A.M. stands for Alannah Meav, which personally, I can't stand. To my friends, at least, I go by Amy, from my initials. Have ever since before I started kindergarten.

Fields was due at two o'clock. By a quarter of, I was in the bathroom, checking the details of my appearance in the mirror; for the third time, no less. I wasn't going to change my usual wardrobe for him. I wear jeans and plain, oversized T-shirts virtually all the time. The outfit is nondescript enough in appearance to let me fade into the background most anywhere in or around Tucson, and the T-shirt is big enough to conceal the pistol that's my constant companion, nestled under my left arm. I took a moment to run a comb through my hair. It's dirty blonde and not quite down to my collarbones, with no particular style. The last person who called it dishwater blonde is buried out in the back yard. Well, not really, but I do have a major objection to that description. The length and lack of style is so I don't stand out, all part of that 'fade-away' thing. No lipstick or anything like that. Makeup and I don't have any acquaintance to speak of. I could have wished for more height, but I've been five foot six since I was in high school, so I doubted I was going to grow taller in the next several minutes. This is me, and it's what he was going to get. He could damn well live with it.

The clock in the front room began to strike the hour just as the doorbell rang. One last pat for my hair and I headed to the door. Right on time.

I hadn't laid eyes on Raymond Escarton Fields since we were kids. He had been around fifteen, and I must have been, what? Ten? Eleven? He wanted to read the Wall Street Journal, every page, every day, and I wanted to go out and run around in the woods. But I had to stay nearby, which really cramped my style and threw us together no matter what I wanted. In my opinion, which I'd formed back then in our very brief acquaintance, he's an overbearing, self-righteous prig. Those are his good points. I won't get into his bad ones. But he's at least fair to middlin' honest, so far as I know, and he manages the Family finances very well indeed, despite his relative youth. As a result, he's highly respected in the Family for his investment judgment and abilities, even if his personality leaves something to be desired.

I hadn't had any reason to change my opinion, at least not yet. Oh, he was older, yeah, but he didn't seem to have changed that much otherwise. Still much the same sort of clean cut, preppie look. Still the same bright blue eyes, which are probably the only real outstanding feature he has—he'd never be picked out of a crowd as one of the richest men in the country. His suit had clearly never been on a rack in its life, and the overcoat probably hadn't either.

"Good afternoon, Ms. Youngston."

"And a good afternoon to you, sir. Won't you come in?"

He stepped inside the door and looked around the room. I didn't miss the disdainful expression that flashed across his face for an instant before he controlled his reaction and shut it down. That didn't get our meeting off to the greatest start. Of course, it didn't exactly make me want to change my opinion of him either, and it certainly didn't do anything for my unease at this meeting.

After he turned down my offer of coffee, tea or whatever, I ushered him into my office. Bruno, my Belgian Malinois, hadn't moved from his bed in the corner. It had taken me several years of hard work to stop him rushing the door whenever the bell rang. He's my guardian angel in the office, among other things. Very handsome, in my eyes, with his tan body and black mask, but I wasn't worried about Fields attacking me. Just like the Malinois the police have, he's built like a fine-boned, long-legged German Shepherd. No sign of Sasha, so she was probably still curled up in the footwell of the desk, looking kind of like a medium-sized white and brown bear hibernating there.

Fields took a seat in one of the chairs before the desk as I went around behind it. Yep, there was Sasha at my feet. I started the computers recording and we passed a couple of minutes in small talk—his choice—before he got down to business.

Finally, he gave his head a short, sharp shake. "Well, I suppose I may as well get started telling you what this is all about."

That would be a pretty good idea, I thought, but said nothing, simply watching him. He seemed a bit tense. I wonder why?

"Someone is trying to kill me, and I want you to find out who's behind it."

That could certainly explain the tension, although it struck me as an odd choice of words. Shouldn't I be trying to put a stop to it? He had originally made the appointment to come see me over the phone yesterday. I was sitting in my office killing a certain amount of time because it was a chilly February day, chilly, at least, by Tucson standards. Today isn't a lot better. It was in the low 50s and overcast. I was wondering which divorce lawyer would be the next to call with a job for me. This definitely wasn't the sort of phone call I'd been expecting.

By the time his call was over, he told me that he'd see me at two o'clock the next day. It almost escaped me that he didn't ask whether that would be a good time; he just told me when he was arriving at my office. There was more to it, but that was the gist of his side of our conversation. My, my, my, I thought. Raymond Escarton Fields himself, here, in my office.

Of course, we weren't kids any more. Now he was the Family CEO and rich as hell—richer than that, actually, I suspected—and I'm only a reasonably successful private eye. Should I be panicked or not? I decided not. At the time, I'd wondered why he needed a private eye, specifically me. Now I knew. Did I like it? Well, it's a job, and probably a pretty good one, financially, but...can I get back to you on that?

Yesterday had started as a most ordinary day. I'd just finished one case and done a couple of service-of-process jobs. Before I got back into the marketing, I was relaxing for the day, waiting for what would come in next. Raymond Escarton Fields wasn't what I'd ever imagined, to say the least.

5

And now here he is in the flesh. I suppose I should be flattered. On the other hand, he doesn't have a lot of choice, unless he wants to bring in an outsider, because as far as I know, I'm the only private investigator in the Family. I don't think he'd do that, especially since this job is an intra-Family investigation. It's going to be interesting to see whether there's anything more going on here than the investigation he's come for. Shut up, girl, you're yammering. Listen to him the way you look like you're doing. Even if he doesn't know you're good, you do. Really listen to him and prove it.

"I'm not sure exactly when it started," he said. "It was probably sometime shortly after, well, around the time that Greg Casaday suggested that I involve the Family in shorting the yen. Forex isn't an area I have all that much familiarity with, and I've tended to avoid it. But more importantly, neither he nor Jim Parkinston had any evidence that I thought was adequate to suggest an upcoming devaluation of anything Japanese at all, so it made no sense to me."

I nodded sagely, like I understood everything he'd said. Truth be told, he could have said it in Japanese and I wouldn't have understood it any better.

I'm not normally used to murder mysteries, or attempted murder mysteries, other than written ones. Juicy divorces, errant spouses and hidden assets, separately or together, are more my usual sorts of cases. But there was certainly no reason to pass up a chance to get Raymond Escarton Fields indebted to me. Maybe I could even get my profession accepted by the Family. Yeah, right. And pigs might fly. He was going on, though.

"Everybody on the board was putting forth their investment ideas and analyses, pressuring me to invest in whatever...scheme they were pushing." He leaned forward, like he was trying to involve me in what he was saying, and began gesturing with his hands. "Understand that on the

6

one hand, all investing has a degree of speculation, of risk. Some investments have a little, some have a lot. I can do whatever I want with my own money, but I can't risk Family resources like that. My duty is to increase the Family fortune, not gamble it. As I see it, that limits the ways I can invest, and I felt that everything they were pushing me to get into was much too risky. Some of them I wouldn't even have put my own money into." He leaned back.

Well, the Family fortune is pretty big. Make that huge. I think there are whole countries, and not necessarily poor ones, that are worth less than whatever the actual number is now.

Despite these little mental detours, I actually was listening to him.

He continued. "All the proposals were put forth in ways that made them seem superficially very reasonable. Since they came from different board members each time, I couldn't figure out who was actually behind them. Perhaps if I'd been able to see how a proposed investment would have been to someone's personal benefit, I might have had more of a clue. In most cases, I couldn't, and even where I thought I could, it didn't seem worth the risk if only because the potential benefit to the board member wasn't going to be all that great. Each of these proposals would have meant a drastic reordering of the Family's investment direction, and I felt that I had the appropriate investment mix as it was. Changing it like that would have been...a really bad idea, in my opinion."

I agreed, for what little—nothing—I knew of such things.

"Then the attempts on my life started."

I sat up a bit straighter. Even if this was something outside my past experience, it was something I understood. Right up my professional alley, so to speak.

"One time, it was some sort of fireworks under my car. You know, some small explosive. A cherry bomb or the like, if you know what they are."

I do. Daddy enjoyed them and got some occasionally.

"Another time, there was a whole string of firecrackers that went off when I started the engine."

I had to interrupt here. "Were these simply tossed under the car, or were they wired into the ignition?"

"Didn't I say? They were connected so they'd go off when I started the car. It wasn't kids. Couldn't have been, they'd never have come that far up the drive. The police...I called them at first, but they weren't really interested. They just filled out their reports and said they'd get back to me. Another time, I was sitting in my study, and as I got up from my chair, somebody shot at me." He pulled a tiny plastic bag from his shirt pocket and handed it to me. Inside was what was still pretty obviously a .177 air rifle pellet. I suppose it could have hurt him, but judging from the minimal amount of deformation, it wouldn't have done him any permanent injury unless it had hit him in the eye. It wasn't even one of the pointed hunting pellets, but rather one of the flat-nosed target jobs.

"When the police made it pretty clear that my calls were regarded as nothing but nuisance calls, I quit calling them."

Of course, you don't explain the Family to the police, even if it would have made a difference to them. For something like this, it wouldn't have. But there's a different 'feel' to such things when it's kids playing pranks than when it's someone serious, someone trying to send you a message. If nothing else, repetitious or circular as it sounds, there is a professionalism to what's happening when it's being done by professionals, and that was the impression I was getting here. Everything that had happened to him, as he related it, was, I thought, carefully tailored to send a

8

message: We have your number. We can do this for real and kill you any time. We have not decided to kill you...yet.

Now, it's probably pretty unnerving to be sitting on ground zero. I figured I was about to find out as soon as I became involved in this case. My back itched where my target was going to be. A lawyer acquaintance—not Alec—some years back, once described his job to me as having people come in and dump their garbage on his desk, expecting him to organize and fix everything. Now I know exactly how he felt, and why he didn't like it.

There was another side to the coin too. I figured that if I could pin this on someone, or even several someones, potentially, with enough proof for Raymond Escarton Fields to bring before the Family board, he could, at the very least, boot his opponents off the board, and then he'd owe me big time. If I couldn't, or if they decided to quit making thinly veiled threats to him and actually carried out one of them before I got to them, then I'd probably be history along with Raymond. If I died, it probably wouldn't matter much to me whether he was killed with me or not. Oh, brother. That's way too much thinking at this point.

The back of my neck was starting to itch as well, the way it does when I'm being watched. I was suddenly inordinately grateful for the pistol nestled under my left arm. Normally, I no longer noticed it, but now, I surreptitiously pressed it with my arm to reassure myself: a 40 caliber security blanket. At the same time, I'm not half as excited about this venture as I had been when Fields first called me. Somewhat excited, yeah, but more the kind of excitement that could lead some people to consider anti-anxiety medications. Not me, though. I'm tough.

These are a whole lot of lovely thoughts, especially the ones about someone trying to kill me. Regardless of my feelings about the afterlife, I had no interest in pondering it and I definitely wasn't interested in facing it any time soon. Sasha seemed to catch my disquiet; she looked up from where she was lying. She liked it there in the footwell, all close, unless it was too hot and stuffy. I glanced at her and she laid her head down again. Bruno was still over on his bed, against the far wall of the office. His head was down too, but his eyes had been fixed on Fields the entire time. No other reaction, but then, Bruno was, among other things, trained to detect drugs, and Raymond Escarton Fields was hardly likely to be carrying cocaine, or heroin, or anything like that. If he'd had marijuana, Bruno wouldn't have cared, which was why he was mine, instead of working for the police, but I couldn't imagine that, either. Not Raymond Escarton Fields. His recreational drug of choice was green, folded in the middle, and had pictures of dead presidents on it.

At the same time as one track of my mind was running around like this, another was keeping a close eye on Fields' body language. Not only is body language a serious part of the whole listening thing, but being able to pick up on what people aren't really telling you can be very valuable in my line of work. He was showing a bit of uneasiness, first and foremost. Big surprise, I thought sarcastically. Other than that one time when he had leaned forward, he was also closed, pulling away from me with his arms folded loosely. Why?

You'd think that if anything, he'd be more likely to be leaning forward most of the time, trying to convince me of what he's telling me. Instead, he's protecting himself, guarding himself, apparently against me. And he's not comfortable about meeting my eyes. This is not the best sign of honesty. No signs of indecision, but there are some serious suggestions that he isn't giving me the entire story, or perhaps isn't being entirely honest with me.

A couple of careful questions from me along the way made it clear that he wasn't going to give me any more than he already had. What he was saying about the investing itself was, to some significant degree, going right over my head, which is why I'm not putting it down, but since I was recording it, that gap in my understanding could, and definitely would, be fixed. Was there something going on here beyond what he was telling me? Likely. What was it? Damned if I knew. But it was going to be interesting to find out. Maybe like in the old Chinese curse about 'May you live in interesting times'.

Fields finally stopped his explanation and looked at me. "Aren't you going to take notes?" he asked.

I gestured at the microphone on the edge of my desk. "I'm recording it all, as I told you before we started. That way, I have the exact things you've told me, in your own words, not simply what I thought was important now." Actually, I was recording it twice, one copy on each computer. Suspenders and belt, so to speak. But he didn't have to know that. And my security system would have a complete record, audio and video both, of this as well as everything else that happened in the house. That was something else he didn't need to know. Three times, all told. Am I paranoid? Perhaps. But just because you're paranoid doesn't mean that somebody isn't really after you. And just because that's a well-worn cliché and an age-old joke doesn't mean it isn't true, as I suspected I'd probably confirm all too soon. That goes to show how little I knew.

Finally, his narrative came to an end. I actually didn't have any more questions for him at that point; his account had been quite complete with very little prompting on my part. Like I said in the beginning, people talk to me, and Fields proved to be no different.

Then he asked, "Can you handle this?"

He didn't ask me that, did he? Yes, he did. I thought an unkind thought about him. Even worse than what I'd already been thinking. Then I thought another one. I didn't let either of them show.

"I'd be a sorry excuse for a private investigator if I couldn't," I replied. "Besides, unless you want to go to some outsider, I'm the only one you've got." I smiled slightly simply to seem polite. He didn't return it, so I continued. "We do have the matter of my fee. I need an advance retainer of,"—I named a figure I thought would set him back a bit, but he didn't flinch at all—"for my expenses. There's obviously going to be quite a bit of travel in this investigation, and ancillary expenses as well. I'll need you to keep it up to that level monthly, as I use it. At the end, I'll apply anything left over to my fee. For my fee itself,"—thought quickly, although I'd gamed this out in my head several times since yesterday—"I can do this for my hourly rate of $250." My heart pounded. I'd never asked anyone for anywhere near that amount of money per hour in my professional life. Of course, I'd never had an assignment like this before, or such a client. "Or, we can lower that substantially, but it would depend on another consideration after I've found who's after you and, hopefully, why."

I've got to hand it to him. He took it all deadpan as could be. Finally he spoke. "What 'another consideration' did you have in mind? I'm not really interested in buying a pig in a poke."

Well, he hasn't blown me out of the water on this. Here was my big chance. Mentally, I crossed my fingers. Amy, step very carefully, but go for it. Just don't blow it. I had it all ready in my mind. I'd been working on this ever since he first made his appointment to see me, even before I knew what he wanted. I had all these ideas if whatever he needed was big enough. It was. His life? Oh, boy, was it ever. Now it only remained to see if I could deliver it as smoothly as I could imagine it.

"One hundred shares and a seat on the board."

He looked at me for a long moment. One hundred shares—an accomplished specialist doctor with advanced certifications and several years of practice, might hold a hundred shares, I figured. Raymond, as the CEO, probably had several hundred, if not more. I had under twenty. It wasn't bad as these things go.

I own both my houses free and clear, thanks to the shares I have and a gift from Daddy. Not money, directly. He assigned me the rights to one of his books—his newest, actually, at the time. A couple of months later it had not only been sold to a publisher for a nice advance, but the movie rights were optioned as well. Nothing came of the option, but it was a very good deal for me and quite lucrative by my standards. A decent car, two dogs to keep me warm at night—at least some small part of the year—as well as letting me know of threats and helping me deal with them, a business that kept me off the streets and out of mischief, so to speak. I could have done lots worse. But if someone is going to voluntarily put himself in your debt, there's no reason to let it slide completely.

I could see the wheels turning in his head. I could also feel my heart still pounding. I was asking for a lot, but I guaranteed that nothing would escape about the Family. If I could indeed find the real culprit, or culprits, it might be worth it to him. If I couldn't, well, he probably wouldn't be worrying about it anyway. I might not be, either. His expression got a bit sour.

"I can get you the shares. I...the seat on the board might not be that easy. You know, the board members. You understand that they would probably not agree to giving you a seat. And there's never been a lot of turnover."

I looked at him for a several seconds before responding. "I understand that." I didn't, not really. It felt like the right thing to say. "But it seems to me that if I find whoever is behind all this, then there should be at least one opening on the board. Maybe more than one." Being on the board of directors was almost certainly additional shares each year, maybe a serious number, not to mention the prestige within the Family, and I saw this as my chance to make a serious move. "If I start digging into this, I'm probably painting as much of a target on myself as you have on yourself. Maybe more. If neither of us survives, I think it's going to be, shall we say, somewhat irrelevant. But bluntly, I think I deserve to be paid something extra for choosing to make myself a target, and I feel quite certain that whatever is pointed at you will be pointed at me too as soon as I take this case on."

He grinned momentarily. I don't think he did that very often. I had no idea how prophetic my comment would turn out to be.

Finally, he exhaled deeply. "All right. I'll get you in. If you succeed." He sighed. "And I'll get you the shares, even if I have to give you some of my own. *If* you succeed. Bill me directly. Don't send this to the Family business office." A deeper sigh. "It's not the money, you know. It's not any of it. It's only...I can't do it myself. I haven't any idea where to start."

"Not to worry," I said. "That's my job. And if I don't succeed, then there's a good chance that neither of us will be worrying about any of it." I waited.

I was beginning to think that he must have liked or appreciated something about me when we were kids. Maybe it was just my imagination. Maybe he really didn't like me any more than I liked him. Did it matter now? Nope, not at all. He had a job he needed to have done, he was here and he was hiring me to do it. That was all that really counted.

He stood up and shook out his overcoat. "You're probably right. Do you have a written contract?"

Again, that slight smile. Just to look pleasant, not like the canary that ate the cat, even if I did feel a bit that way.

"Of course. I'll have it for you in a minute. Would you like to sit back down? Or..." He remained standing. "Give me a second." Luckily, I'd already drawn up the hardest part, the payment clause, before he came, just in case. Some cut and paste, then I quickly typed in the remaining necessary information and sent it to the printer. "Sign here, please."

He signed with his usual flourish. I'd seen that signature often enough, but never saw him make it before. It looked a lot simpler as he did it than the finished product suggested. I added my own signature and turned to the copier on the other side of the office near Bruno. He noticed the dog for the first time.

"Don't you think it looks a bit unprofessional to have a dog in your office?" He actually looked a bit snooty as he asked.

"Bruno is my assistant, my bodyguard and my friend," I replied. "Here, he does several things I couldn't do for myself. If I left him locked up in the house, he'd only be a pet." I hoped I didn't sound as annoyed by his question as I suddenly felt. Bruno hadn't bothered him one bit; Bruno was none of his business. How I ran my business was none of his business either.

His right eyebrow arched. I'd never been able to do that and it irritated me that he could when I couldn't. "Assistant? He's just a dog."

I leaned down and gave the dog a quick pat. "I'm sorry, Bruno, he doesn't know what he's talking about." Bruno lay there, watching both of us. He didn't care what Fields thought of him. Smart dog. I turned back to Raymond and handed him a copy of the contract. "Bruno is a walking detector for hard drugs as well as a trained guard dog. Damn right he's my assistant. If you'd been carrying cocaine, heroin, or any of several other drugs, he'd have alerted me the moment you stepped inside the door. Quietly, but clearly. Because some people who come in here are carrying drugs, and when they are, I need to know. If you tried to attack me, he'd beat you to it and keep you far too busy to continue or even *think* about continuing to attack me. Because sometimes, people who come in here do try just that. And he also guards things, like my house when I'm there with him." I picked up the fanny pack I use as my purse, walked over and set it on a table about two feet in front of Bruno while I shut off the copier. Quietly, I said, "Bruno, watch!" His head came up.

I stepped through the door. Looking back over my shoulder, I asked Raymond if he'd bring me my purse. I heard him take a step or two, then I heard Bruno start to rumble. Not a growl, just a rumble deep in his chest. Hm. That put Fields probably not less than four feet from the pack. Bruno didn't start to actually growl until the subject was about three and a half feet away from whatever he was supposed to guard. Then he stopped. Fields must have stepped back.

"I think you better get it yourself." He didn't sound pleased. "But I guess I see what you mean." He appeared in the doorway shrugging into his coat. Sasha was now out from under the desk, but he had his back turned and hadn't seen her. "I've got to get back."

"Very well, sir. It's been a pleasure meeting with you, and I hope our relationship proves to be productive for both of us." I shook his hand. "Can I offer you a lift to wherever you're going from here?"

"No, thank you. I've got a car." And sure enough, he did, waiting out in the parking area in front of the house. Not a rental; he had a limousine waiting outside, so help me God. Mentally, I shook my head. Must be nice to have that kind of money. Perhaps if I could solve this mess, I could find out for myself. At least a bit, but I'd pass on the limo. Maybe, for now. Though a part of me did like the idea. The rest of me figured it was overkill. My car gets me places just fine.

* * * *

16

TO: D
FROM: HB
Primary target, Youngston, acquired. REF seen to arrive at primary location, Youngston's office, at 1400 local, remained inside until 1707 local before departing. Youngston left her office for secondary location, her residence, at 1718 local. Will emplace surveillance devices in Youngston's office after nightfall.

TO: HB
FROM: D
Very good. Continue with plan.

Chapter 2

Closing the door behind him, I looked at Sasha. She smiled and waited for a pet, but I knelt down and gave her a hug instead. "If I get through this one, it's going to be prime steak for all of us, pretty girl," I said as I straightened up and plucked a dog hair from my lip. Long-coat Akitas have a *lot* of hair, and it was way too early in the year to clip her. I mean, even without shearing her, I get enough hair from her every spring to weave a couple of puppies.

The day that Fields had called was also the day of my weekly date for drinks and dinner with my best friend. Becky Swan is a psychologist professionally, but we've known each other since we were both knobby-kneed girls with freckles from too much sun and scratches all over ourselves from running around in the woods together. Well before that, actually. We've been very best friends as long as I can remember—she's my fourth cousin—and since we lived near each other growing up, it's probably been even longer than that.

My parents enrolled me late into school and she took a whole bunch of courses in high school, so we graduated together and then roomed together all through undergraduate school. We're really more like very close sisters than simply friends, however good ones. She's tall and outwardly willowy, at least at first glance. I'm more compact and solid. She's still got a stunning figure, while I've got enough of a figure to show when dressed as female. Don't let appearances fool you. She and I sometimes go to the gym together, and while I can outdo her, it's not by a lot. She's also a lot more formal than I, at least on weekdays. When we go hiking or camping together, we're both in jeans and T-shirts, but when she's working, she's always beautifully dressed. I normally don't need to when I'm working. I'm told I clean up nice, but I don't do it very often. No real interest, and other than occasionally with Becky or Alec, nobody to do it with or for. Looks and style aren't my issues.

Becky and I are probably the only two Family members in Tucson, as far as we know, other than maybe a doctor or two. Being the sort of long-time friends we are, we like to get together every week to catch up, talk and be with each other: dinner, drinks or, usually, both. It's so *nice* to have someone to talk to with whom you don't ever have to be careful of what you say.

We sat down together last night and I must have looked like I was about to bust. She got the first words out.

"Okay, Amy, you look like the cat that ate the canary. Out with it. What's going on that you can't wait to tell me and astonish me with?"

I leaned back with exaggerated casualness and a slight, but insufferably smug, smile. "I got a phone call today." Long pause. I should really stop it. Being insufferably smug from time to time is one of my worst habits. But Becky loves me anyway.

"I presume there's something special about this phone call? Something you intend to tell me so I don't have to come across this table and shake it out of you?" She smiled as she said it.

"Well, *duh*. It was a very *special* phone call. I mean, you'll *never* guess who it was." Another long pause. I definitely need to quit this.

Becky leaned over the table toward me and reached across it. I leaned forward and she took my chin in her hand. "Amy, if you don't quit playing games with me, I am going to become very angry with you. You don't *like* me when I'm angry. Now *give*." She wasn't exactly smiling now.

I was. "You are *not* going to believe this. His imperial highness, Raymond Escarton Fields himself, called me for an appointment."

Now she was the one to lean back. "Come on, Amy, you can find a better way than that to pull my leg." I shook my head slowly. Her eyes got even bigger. "You're *not* pulling my leg. Calling you? Calling *you*? For an appointment? Not to give you an audience?" I was nodding now. "Holy... oh my God!" At which point we both broke down and giggled uncontrollably.

She and I rarely talked about the Family to each other anymore. We'd pretty much talked ourselves out about it back when we were kids and first found out about it. Back then, of course, it was all so very new and exciting, but now it's just something that's part of our lives. Oh, well, at least I *could* talk about the Family with Becky. I couldn't do this with anyone else in my life, not ever. Well, Daddy and Becky's mom, sure, but they weren't here and I rarely saw either of them anymore.

Anyway, back to the present. With Fields gone, it was time to close up the office and even a bit beyond. I sent a copy of the security system record of his visit to the house computer before packing up the laptop, lowering the shades and setting the alarm. It's not the simplest procedure; the keypad inside the back door is a trap, and trying to use it actually triggers the alarm. There is another keypad in a concealed location, and there are two different code numbers, depending on whether or not a special key is used in the process, to arm and disarm it. It's probably overkill, but I designed and installed the system and it was fun as well as a challenge.

As the system beeped toward its final activation, Bruno, Sasha and I headed out the back door. Bruno trotted off to his favorite grass clump to water. Sasha moved off in the other direction and stuck her nose in the corner of the yard wall.

"Sasha." Nothing. "*Sasha!*" Still nothing. "*SACHIKO!*" I think that for dogs, their full name is kind of like a child's middle name—it lets them know when they're in real trouble, or at least cruising on the edge. She looked up at me and, unconcerned, strolled toward me, squatting halfway across the yard. I opened the gate for them and closed it behind us.

Alec was in the kitchen when I came in. The dogs' dinners were sitting on the counter, ready, and he was watching something on the stove. I gave him a quick peck on the cheek—he's about six inches taller than I am, so it's a stretch—brushed a lock of hair off his forehead and made the dogs sit and wait while I put their dishes on the floor. Then I released them and they dug in.

"So how was your day?" he asked. "I figured you'd be here pretty much on time since you didn't call." Alec and I are kind of like a very comfortable married couple without some of the window dressings, like sex or sleeping under the same roof. We'd tried the first—once—and never got to the second, except occasionally when we had no choice. Both of us agreed that we didn't need to further complicate our lives by stressing our relationship. It was just fine the way it was. Well, I thought so anyway.

"Alec, glad as I am to see you and have dinner with you, if it's not on the table in five minutes, I'm going to have to send you home. I picked up a huge case and I need to work late tonight. Really huge, really work, really late."

"Not a problem. It's ready; I've just been waiting for you." He uncovered the pan and started dishing up. Yum. I love paella, almost as much as I do chili. "Does this job have anything to do with the limo I saw out in front of your office this afternoon? And I could stay if you like. Rub your back, or maybe your feet."

Don't push. Oh, God, don't push. "Are you trying to escalate, Alec? I thought we had this situation settled a long time ago."

"Ah, well, just a thought. And it's an honest offer just the way it sounds, nothing more. Thought perhaps you could use the relaxation."

I touched his arm lightly. "No, thanks, Alec. It's a lovely thought, and you're a very special friend, but let me take a rain check, okay?" Relaxation was not on the agenda for the evening.

The table was already set, wineglasses and all. The wine was open and breathing, so I poured as he served. "All right, Amy, what's it about?"

I looked at him over the rim of my wineglass. Nice wine tonight. "I can't tell you, Alec. Not one thing. If I did, I'd have to either marry you or kill you."

He grinned. "Do I get a choice?" I grinned back at him, but said nothing. I figured I knew what he'd choose. Having me kill him likely wasn't it. And I really didn't want to go there, either way. So why did I even bring it up in the first place? Idiot me.

I took a moment as I cut up a shrimp. "No, seriously. I need to work and do some major research and planning. I can't do that if we sit around and talk or watch the tube. And this is a case that I really can't talk about. Not to you, not to anyone. I'm sorry, but that's just how this one is. Utterly confidential. That was one of the conditions of the case. If I could share it with you, I would, absolutely. And no, you don't get a choice. Not now."

"You're keeping secrets from me? We've known each other...how long?" He was grinning. It was probably a rhetorical question, but I answered him anyway.

"It was the third day of first-term Torts. You pushed your coffee cup off the edge of your desk with your notepad, and if I hadn't caught it, it would have spilled all over my notebook, my jeans and my backpack. Probably all down your leg as well. Simple self-defense on my part."

He laughed. "Has it really been that long? Good lord, yes, it has. What secrets have you kept from me in all those years?"

Now it was my turn to laugh. "If I told you, then they wouldn't be secrets I'd kept from you, now, would they?"

Sasha came over to the table. I gave her a quick pet. "Sasha, you know better. Go lie down."

She walked over to Alec, who looked at her mock-sternly. "You were told to go lie down." Reluctantly, she did, although first, she went to get the lone squeaky toy she'd kept since she was a puppy. Funny dog.

We finished dinner in silence. I think he wasn't happy about being booted out so early. No, actually, I knew he wasn't. I know him much too well to overlook or misinterpret that. He was hurt, and I was very sorry to have to do that to him. Not that he hadn't tuned me out whenever he was going into court the next day, but when he had to do that, we were still together, just not talking and not watching TV. No problem; I liked to read. This was definitely out of pattern. We normally spent our dinners and evenings together about every night except when I was out with Becky, and when we were together, we never broke up early. He put on a good face, but he was sending out some very unhappy and sour vibes. I couldn't blame him.

Without any further discussion, he helped clear the table, pack up the leftovers and began putting dishes in the dishwasher.

"You really don't have to do that," I said.

"I know." He kept on, making more noise than the activity required. He was definitely unhappy and also being a bit passive-aggressive, which is very unlike him.

"The sooner it's done, the sooner I'm out of your hair. My place tomorrow night?"

"I honestly don't think so. Or at least I can't make any promises. I don't know where this one is going. I'll call you, okay?"

"Okay." He sounded as unhappy as I figured he was. A quick kiss, a pet and hug for each dog, and he was out the door. This was the first time in ages we hadn't spent any time together after our evening meal. I did wonder what confused and hurt thoughts must have been going through his mind. Of course, that kept me from wondering what thoughts should have been going through my own mind, and that was fine with me. I think.

Well, it wasn't that simple. I'd been married right around graduation from college, and it wasn't something I'd planned out and spent time on. I should have. Daddy didn't approve of him—Becky didn't either, but I don't take hints well—so we snuck off and did it on the quiet. His name was Robert, but now I think of him—when I bother at all—as 'Robbie', which he hated. Getting to that point in my mind was quite a triumph for me. Alec and I started off well, and all through law school, it was a platonic relationship. We were simply study partners, very close, inseparable, actually, in that regard, but nothing more, then.

After law school, when I was trying to start my own investigation business, Robbie started getting...abusive. Not physically; that I could have fought. Would have. Instead, he got psychologically abusive. Long story short, his sexual demands started to get further and further out there. The last straw was, well, way too much, almost...no, it *was* repulsive. Let's leave it at that. The first time I called him Robbie to his face was that night on my way out the door. My business hadn't really taken off, so I slept on the couch in my office, then spent the next two days packing up and getting a divorce lawyer. When I left, I came to Tucson and found the place on Speedway almost immediately.

Becky had just finished with her internship, so she came too, and we moved in together. We often slept in the same bed early on, like we had as kids. Nothing more than being a comfort for one another. It's not sexual, never has been, but we're very tactile with each other, and I really needed some serious comforting then. About two years later, both of us had going practices, and we decided it was time to move out. She bought her place up in the Catalina foothills, and I managed to get the house right behind the Speedway house, so my commute was nonexistent. I liked it that way.

Six months or so later, out of the blue, Alec called. He'd left his firm in Portland, gotten divorced and moved to Tucson. Was I free for dinner? Three dates later, we wound up in bed.

God, what a mess *that* was. Neither of us could get anywhere. I was too wound up in my own failure to help him through his, and far too terrified of what he would do to me, for my failure and his. He wouldn't have done anything at all to hurt me, not Alec. I know that now, intellectually. He was just reacting, as I was, to a truly horrid marriage. But at that point, Robbie and his awful, cruel reactions were really all I knew. I was terrified of going through that again, and especially with someone I was responding to as strongly as I was to Alec. So I simply shut down.

We both dated around a bit after that. I had a couple of...well, the blunt term would probably be friendly screws, if not something even cruder. Simply making sure the equipment still worked, hadn't rusted, that sort of thing, you know? Nothing worth a replay, or even spending the night. But without the emotional attachment, everything functioned like it should. Over time, though, something kept pulling Alec and me back together, so we gradually settled into the relationship we have now. Very close; we spend most of our free time together. Neither of us dates, although we sometimes go out together. Just no sex—I'm still terrified of that sort of thing with him, I have to admit—not to another living soul, other than Becky—and he lives a couple doors down Helen Street. His office is next door to mine.

And sometimes I regret not being closer to him. When I can bring myself to look at it, which isn't often.

I stretched and looked at the clock. Good lord, it was after eleven. I still hadn't done my exercises and the dogs needed a last spin outside. Sourly, I looked at the laptop. I also still hadn't finished taking notes on the account Raymond had given me. Eight board members besides Raymond, scattered round the world, although most of them were in this country and those, in fact, were all in the western U.S. Each of them was, according to his account, trying to push the Family's investing in different directions. I'd finally gotten down at least the basic essential information on them from what he had given me, so I guessed, I could knock off for the night.

"Okay, guys, let's go out."

Bruno came at a brisk trot; Sasha moved at a somewhat slower pace. I usually refer to her normal gaits as 'stroll' and 'amble'. Tonight, she was set on amble. When she finally got to the door, we all went out and the motion lights came on.

The ones behind my office were already on. Odd. Was there a tree or bush moving in the wind that had set it off? Not that I could see. No alarm yet. Maybe someone had driven up the alley, although I usually hear when that happens. Maybe a bicyclist out late? I pressed my left arm to my side, feeling the pistol nestled securely in its holster under my armpit. Bruno looked alert, but unconcerned, as he did his business. That reassured me. His senses are a lot better than mine. After Sasha had finally relieved herself, we went back in and I set the house alarm. It's less complex than setting the one in the office.

A half hour of draw and dry-fire drills later, I could go to bed with a clear conscience. I must have been tired, because I don't think I was awake more than five minutes after my head hit the pillow. As deeply as I was sleeping, I almost wouldn't have heard the alarm go off. Either alarm; they were connected. If one was set off, both would sound.

* * * *

TO: D
FROM: HB
Primary target Youngston and secondary target Trevethen met in her residence; separated after meal. Surveillance devices emplaced in Youngston's office. It has an impressive security system, but no trace of our efforts remains on it. Will attempt to cover her residence and additional locations as indicated in immediate future as circumstances allow.

TO: HB
FROM: D
You appear to be doing an excellent job. Continue.

Chapter 3

I woke up around six or so the next morning, which is late for me. After taking care of the dogs, I fixed my first cup of coffee and headed to the computer to catch up on the news. The last thing I was expecting was to find something going on in my life right this moment beyond what had been dumped in my lap. Well, all right, I'd been delighted to get it. But I still thought I'd be able to ease my way into the case over the course of a couple of days. Do some basic research, set up my files, take my time...

Yeah, right.

About 8:30 or so, we went across the alley to the office. Bruno went on high alert as soon as we walked through the back door, but when he didn't seem to find anything in any of the rooms he raced through, I figured it had been a false alarm. It happens from time to time. Maybe some rodent had gotten in or something. They're too small for the motion sensors to notice.

The next thing that gave me pause was when I booted up my desktop computer and it said that it had been last accessed at 02:43:37 that same day. What the hell was this? I'd been sound asleep in bed at the time.

That made me more than a bit suspicious. I ran some spyware checks, and when they came up blank, I tried reinstalling and running them again. This time they caught a spy program that hadn't been there yesterday and wasn't supposed to be there now. I left it alone for the time being, but now, I was really becoming concerned. My next order of business was to check my security system. I shouldn't have been as surprised when I found the night record blank. Not just empty, but blank, as in *erased*. I certainly should have been as annoyed. No, make that *angry* as I was by now. In fact, I was furious. At least I'd saved the record of Fields' visit.

Then I started going over my desk with a fine-tooth comb. I even got a hand mirror from the bathroom and looked underneath it. That's where I found the bug. Short range and sound activated—I recognized the model—which meant a rebroadcast hub somewhere in the house. I'd never find it; there were way too many places in the house to hide something little bigger than a pack of cigarettes even if it were hardwired into the electrical system. I ought to have Aurelia come in early and vacuum the office for a couple of hours, that'd serve them right.

Then I put the wiseass ideas aside to look at the situation more analytically. Now what? I sat and thought. Sure, I could erase the program, remove and stomp the bug. Of course, if I got rid of what I knew was there, as fast as it had been put in, I figured it was certain that something new would be installed right away and almost certainly better hidden. Besides, there were probably others already in place. I looked around the office, trying to analyze it as though I were bugging it myself. Yes, under the desk was probably one of the first spots I'd try. Easy to get to, good sound pickup. Almost optimal, in fact. But I could see at least half a dozen other places almost as good and harder to find a bug in, and another bunch even less accessible, but still usable. As fast as this had been put in and as easily as they'd gotten through my security system, there was no advantage to be gained beyond the personal satisfaction I'd get from yanking and stomping this one bug. If it was the only one in this room, which was unlikely, there'd be another one in here by tomorrow anyway. I'd just have to live with it.

Okay, then. Nothing of import goes onto the office computer and nothing of import gets said here. The house was safe, wasn't it? Probably. They could get around the alarm system, but they couldn't get around Bruno and Sasha. I hoped. Oh, wait a minute. The dogs are here with me and nobody is in the house. Oh, shit. Could they tap into my Internet connection? Hey, I'm supposed to be the one who does this, not who has it done to her. I'm not used to being on this side of things, but if I can do it to other people, I have to presume that they can do it to me. I had to completely reorder my thinking, figure out how to frustrate them. Without letting them know I was on to them.

Confession moment. I've been known to bug people and even tap phones, tap cellphones and Internet connections on occasion. On *rare* occasion. Yeah, I know it's not legal. I don't like to do it. Any time I don't have to, I won't. But there are times when it's the only way to get the information I need, and when it's done, I can get more information faster than any other method I know. Most of my work is entirely legal stuff, like talking to people, checking public records, surveillance in public areas or from public areas and so on. But I get paid for results, not for sitting around moaning about what I can't do. I'm good at what I do. End of confession.

Worrying about being the subject of someone else's surveillance, that was the way to paralysis. I had to be able to work, and my basic assumption was that they couldn't get past the dogs, wherever the dogs were at any given moment, without leaving some sort of trace or making some sort of fuss. At least I'd be fairly safe when we were all together, so I'd go with that for now. I guess I couldn't have everything, although nobody had ever explained to my satisfaction why not. Enough of this. I'll feel sorry for myself next Tuesday, or some other time. Not now. But anyone who could get around my overdone security system and bug my office was damn good, too good for me to be taking on alone. I needed some help, and really, there was only one person I could turn to.

It hardly needs to be said that I didn't want to. Alec, wonderful friend that he is, is not Family. There's no way around that fact. I'd had it drilled into me from the time I first learned about the Family that you *do not* talk about the

Family except to other Family members. Yes, you can tell your spouse, if you choose. Nobody is going to make you do that. I certainly didn't tell Robbie. But that is *it! Nobody* else. No other outsiders. Period. End of story.

But if I followed that rule, then the only person I could ask to help me was Becky, and let's be fair here. She's a lovely friend, and if I needed some sort of mental analysis, I'd turn to her in a heartbeat. What I have here, though, is people breaking into my office, bugging me and, I expect, either trying to kill me or at least tell me that they can. That's not anything that Becky can help me with.

So, in all that running around, I keep coming back to the same starting place. There's only one person I can possibly turn to, even if it means telling him about the Family...out of school, as it were. Shit. But if it's got to be, it's got to be. And if I hire him as my attorney, then he's bound by attorney-client privilege, isn't he? So even if I tell him, it can't go any further. What the hell, that ought to work. Can't think of anything better anyway, and I do need the help. Let's do it.

I picked up the phone, when it occurred to me that it was almost definitely tapped too. I'd certainly have done it if I'd been putting bugs and spyware in. I set the handset back down and tried to think it through. If I cut off everything they got, they'd know I was on to them, whoever the hell 'they' are, as surely as if I ripped out their bugs and spyware, although without the personal satisfaction. I simply had to live with it and order my life accordingly. This wasn't anything I'd be concerned about their hearing, so I picked up the phone again and called Alec.

"Hey, Alec, it's Amy. Dinner tonight's good after all. Your place?" He seemed a bit puzzled after the way we parted last night, but willing. Then it was time to get to work and earn my keep. How, with some party or parties unknown watching over my shoulder? Well, hell, I can still

31

do net research; any idiot would assume I would be doing that, so it wouldn't tell them anything. I spent the rest of the day doing just that, continuing to chase down the board members and their records on the Internet. Let whoever was watching see me stumbling through the immense amount of garbage that's out there, trying to separate the wheat from the chaff. I spent a lot more time than I would have expected making written notes instead of taking them on the computer the way I'd usually do. I didn't think they had a video bug here.

Yet. Wait for next month's model. And what were the odds they were bugging my house while I was here with the dogs?

Probably pretty good.

* * * *

Dinner—my turn to cook—was better than usual. I made a fresh pasta sauce with heirloom tomatoes from a nearby market, roasted chili peppers, ground pork, onion and garlic. I also took a few extra minutes to set up Alec's pasta maker and produce some homemade spaghetti to pour it over. Not all that difficult and fairly impressive, even though Alec had seen it before. And done it too. A nice bottle of Pinot Noir sat open on the counter breathing while I assembled a small salad to complete the meal. More involved than I usually get, but I needed a big favor and wanted Alec in the mood. He was surprised when I suggested a walk to settle our dinners. He seemed to be even more surprised when I steered us down Speedway toward the university, with all the traffic. But traffic noise would make it even harder for anyone to catch our conversation, if they were trying, so I started talking as we walked.

"Alec, I need your help. And I want to hire you." I took a deep breath. Even with all my earlier rationalizing, this wasn't easy. In fact, if it had been any harder, I couldn't have done it at all. It was *so* ingrained that you *do not* talk about the Family with outsiders. "It's that case I picked up yesterday. I...I've got to have someone else helping me with it. It's bigger than I thought. A *lot* bigger. And I'd like you to help me handle it."

He was silent for a moment. "As a lawyer, at which I flatter myself that I'm better than decent, or as an investigator, about which I know little or nothing? And by the by, is this you killing me, or marrying me?" He chuckled.

"Oh, shit." I tossed a couple of smart-ass retorts around in my mind and discarded them. "Neither. I really need your help, and I'm willing to pay you. I need your confidentiality as well as your help. I'm not entirely sure how to characterize it between lawyer and investigator. I probably need some of each. Mostly, I need help."

"Confidentiality, confidentiality...there was something about that in one of our courses, wasn't there?" He was grinning from ear to ear.

"Listen, turkey, I really need you on this case with me. Will you help me with it?" I corrected Sasha a bit more strongly than she probably deserved. She ignored me. Maybe it wasn't too strong after all.

"Sure. One dollar and all expenses."

I looked at him sideways. "A dollar an hour?"

"No, a dollar. Flat fee for everything. Expenses on top. That's my fee for you, Amy."

I stopped in my tracks as Alec stood there. Bruno stopped too and looked back at us. I turned toward Alec and put my hands on his chest. "Thank you, sweetie. You don't know what it means to me." I leaned my head against his chest for a moment, savoring the comfort. "I've got a problem."

"I rather gathered that. So tell me about it. Should we do this at your office, or mine?"

"Um, that's part of the problem. My office is bugged. My computer is bugged. My phone is almost certainly tapped. By now, my house is probably bugged as well, and for all I know, so is your house and your office."

He stopped dead. "Bugged? No way. You've got to be kidding me." I shook my head slowly. His eyes widened. "You're not kidding." Another step or two. "So that's why we're talking business out here in the middle of town, huh?"

"Yeah. Let's find a nice bench and I'll tell you all about it."

"How about we go get a hot cup of coffee first? There's a coffee shop a block back."

And they had tables out on the sidewalk where all of us could relax. Coffee is our weakness, so that was a no-brainer. I began explaining, and once I got started, I couldn't shut up.

"Okay, this case I got yesterday. The man who came to see me, the one with the limousine, was Raymond Escarton Fields. He's the CEO of the Family. Let me start by explaining what the Family is. It probably sounds like the Mafia or something, and it isn't. It's not anything illegal, and we don't do anything that's against the law, or at least not that I know of. It's not any sort of organized crime family or the like.

"The Family is sort of like the Rockefellers, or the Rothschilds, or any of the other old, large and very rich families, except that our ancestor didn't set up a business or a trust the way they did. He set up a corporation, and he did it a long, long time before old John D. or even Mayer Rothschild were so much as gleams in their father's eyes. Well, to be honest, I don't know that he himself did it, but it's that way now. Since it's a corporation, Family members get shares, and they earn more shares along the way, so they wind up with different sized holdings."

I told him all of it. Not just about the Family, shares in the Family and Raymond Escarton Fields, but also about the board, the pressures reportedly being put on Fields, the threats, the spyware, the bug under my desk—everything. When I finally did come to the end, we sat in silence for what seemed like an eternity. It was definitely long enough for Bruno to get up and come check on us. I guess Alec was digesting what I'd told him. Finally, he turned toward me and grinned lopsidedly.

"Get a lot of bang for your buck, don't you?"

I looked at him for a moment and then said, "Want to raise your rates while you still can?" He smiled and shook his head.

"It's not the money, Amy. I'd do it for free for you, but charging you makes you realize that I'm being serious."

I snorted. "Somehow, a dollar doesn't seem all that serious."

His expression grew grave. "Remember back to our contracts course, and the difference between a dollar and nothing? Besides, if you really need to pay me big bucks to know I'm serious, I'll let you do it. Do you need that?"

I shook my head. "No, it's not that. I...I'm really in a pickle here."

"I can see that." He seemed far more calm than I felt. I can definitely handle stress, but Alec is usually totally unflappable. Like now. It's part of his charm. "So what's the problem?"

I gave him a wan smile in reply. "It's just...I thought it was going to be a bit more straightforward, a bit more gradual. This case is getting to be a *lot* more complex than I had figured on, and it's doing it a lot faster than I expected. I mean, I understood, at least intellectually, that if they were sending Fields messages like that, I'd be getting them too. And they might not be merely threatening me. But I sort of expected them to wait until I got going. I certainly didn't expect them to do anything this fast. And that suggests there's a lot more going on here than I thought initially, which is why I figure I need help."

"Okay. Remember the old law school line about drinking from a fire hose. Let me ask you some questions, just to help my own understanding. How many people are in the Family?"

I had to think about that one for a minute as I shouted down my internal instinctive reaction to shut up! Say nothing! I'd brought him into this, so I had to answer his questions. Only fair. Among other issues, some of which I really didn't want to address within myself.

"I don't know the number for sure, but it's thousands, at least. It could well be ten thousand or so, I suppose. Probably not significantly more than that." I looked around. There was a solitary person on the far side of the patio area, but by and large, it was too cool for most people to sit outside. The dogs may have helped keep some people away as well; Bruno has a patented menacing look when he wants, and Sasha looks rather like a medium-sized bear. Thank God for small favors.

He mulled that over for a moment. "Doesn't seem like all that many people for a family that's half a millennium old. Where is the Family located?"

"The Family doesn't produce a lot of children; we tend to be singles or occasionally doubles, and with so many first-borns, there are a lot of go-getters. As for where— we're scattered all round the world. We tend to concentrate in North America, Europe, well, the UK, and, I think, Australia, the English-speaking world, but there are some, at least, on every continent."

"Antarctica?"

Smiling, I slapped his arm. "Don't be an ass."

He laughed, even though he was shaking his head. "I'm sorry, I was clarifying your answer. And I wasn't clear. Where is the Family headquartered?"

36

Now I understood what he wanted. "It's a little dot-on-the-map, or dot-not-on-the-map, country called Golondrino, in Europe."

He looked thoughtful for a moment. "Are you a citizen of this Golondrino?"

I smiled. "As a matter of fact, yeah. I was born here, so I hold dual citizenship, of course. Daddy explained it all to me during The Conversation." Alec looked puzzled. When I realized what he thought I meant, I had to laugh. "No, no. Not *that* Conversation. Daddy never told me about sex. Well, not directly. Another story. No, this was The Conversation about the Family, my initial shares, how I'd get more and so on. And most importantly, first and foremost, actually, that I needed to keep from telling other people about it. Make that first, last and always, for that matter. That sort of thing. I could show you my Golondrino passport sometime. I never use it."

I could see his brain working a mile a minute. "Are all the Family members citizens of this Golondrino? And vice-versa?"

I thought back to The Conversation. I had asked Daddy much the same sort of thing. "Well, if I understood what Daddy told me, and if he understood things correctly, yes, all Family members are citizens. Non-members may be tourists, or if they're connected to Family members, like spouses, or if they work there, I expect they can be what amounts to resident aliens. Well, I don't know how many people actually live there. But every citizen is a Family member and the other way around."

"Does the Family have a name?"

I had to think about that one. "Honestly, I don't know. I expect it does, or once did, at least. But everything that comes out from them now is simply labeled 'Family'. A statement of Family shares. The cover letter for the Family dividend check. The Family financial statement. Ballots for the Family board. And so on. It may officially be simply 'the Family' now. That's the only way we ever refer to it nowadays, and it's really the only name I've ever known for it."

"How do you increase your share holding?" I started to feel as though I was being deposed. Well, I suppose I was. He was good at this. He should be, it's his job.

"You get five shares simply for being born. You get more—I'm not sure of the exact number, I wasn't paying attention at the time—for finishing grammar school, for finishing high school and college. There may be a differential for graduating with honors, but you'd have to ask Becky about that, because I just missed the dean's list cutoff and she made it. You get more for finishing graduate school, for getting a professional license and so on. Then you get more shares if you can show net positive income derived from an occupation or business, whether it's related to your education or not. Family dividends don't count, but other investment income does. The way Daddy explained it, the Family rewards work and success, and while it doesn't directly penalize laziness, it refuses to reward it. Shares bringing what they do in dividends, that failure to reward is punishment by itself. Oh, and the number of shares or fractional shares you get for that income varies according to the amount of net income you show."

Alec looked off into the distance for a moment, apparently gathering his thoughts. "How does the Family handle members who aren't able to work?"

"You mean like disabled?" He nodded. "The Family supports them, as far as I know. The Family probably takes back their shares, but then it takes care of them for the rest of their lives."

"What about entrepreneurs?"

"What do you mean?"

"Well, will the Family fund your business? Loan money and so on?"

38

I had to think about that for a moment. I'd run into it when I opened my office, but I'd decided to go elsewhere—that arrangement with Daddy that had paid off better than either of us had expected—and I tried to remember what I'd found out then.

"For businesses, they will make start-up and probably expansion loans. Those generally aren't as good as what you can get commercially, or at least they weren't when I looked at them. In fact, I'd have to say that the payback terms are pretty stiff. For something like manufacturing, or anything else that can be publicly held, they take an ownership share. They don't, as far as I know, exert a lot of control, but they do take a goodly chunk of the ownership of the company. The advantage of going to the Family for a loan is that they will always loan to a member, regardless of credit, even if the terms may not be all that good. The real problem with taking a loan from them is that your shares are pledged as collateral no matter how good your credit is, or what your other security is, and if you get into arrears, your dividends will be attached as soon as they're paid to bring you current or pay it off. Same problem with mortgages. The Family says it isn't in the business of lending money, and it usually won't go after whatever other security you've pledged unless your shares are simply completely inadequate to repay the loan, or at least make it current. They do the same thing with mortgages. And even then, they actually take all your shares first, although you can still get more in the future."

"So when I see a sign that says a business is family owned, at least once in a while it'll mean 'Family owned'."

"Well, yeah, I suppose so."

He seemed a bit skeptical. "Does Golondrino tax you?"

"No, but I have to file a copy of my tax return with them each year as proof of my income for the year."

He raised his eyebrows. "And you really do this?"

"Absolutely. A positive income gains me more shares or fractional shares. Of *course* I send it in. If I don't, there's a presumption that I haven't had any net income for the year and I get no additional shares for the year." I drained my cup. "I need a refill. You?" Alec handed me his cup and I took them in for fresh coffee. When I got back, the grilling continued. I stayed leaning forward, hunched over the table so I could keep my voice that much lower, even though the fellow at the other table had left long ago.

"You mentioned mortgages and business loans. Does the Family make other loans?"

"Not as far as I know. They won't lend discretionary money, that's definite. Like I said, they don't like to loan money at all. But mortgages, business start-ups and expansions aren't really discretionary, and they're all activities which are encouraged under the Family mindset."

He nodded thoughtfully, drank some coffee, leaned back in his chair and was silent for a minute. "What's the Family worth?"

I shook my head. "I honestly don't know. I get the financial reports every year, but they're not easy to read and I really haven't paid much attention to them. I've been somewhat concerned with how many shares I had, and more concerned with whether and how I could get more. The total net worth of the entire Family has never been any issue for me. My best guess off the top of my head would be billions, and likely a whole bunch of billions. Maybe a trillion, but I can't say for sure. Let's say that if the balance sheet showed a trillion, I wouldn't be at all surprised. If it showed half that, I also wouldn't be."

He looked impressed. "And it probably varies with the market. Let me think for a moment. Let's say half a trillion or so and a five percent return, that's $25 billion. Divide that by, say, ten thousand shareholders averaging what? Say fifty shares per person? Will that work?" I shrugged.

"So let's call it half a million shares outstanding. That's about fifty thousand per share per year. Accurate?"

I shook my head. "Oh, Lord, no, that's way too high. I mean, I *wish*." I wanted to stop right there. What Family shares pay isn't anyone else's business. I'd had secrecy about the Family, *everything* about it, drilled into me since I before I was a teenager. Well, just about the time I became one. "Uh," I hesitated. I reminded myself that I'd started this. I had nobody to blame but myself here, and I'd already given him the basics anyway. If I refused to answer, he'd keep looking, and since I was the one who'd brought him into this, it was my fault. Finally, I lost the argument with myself, which was a most unsettling feeling. He acted as though I hadn't hesitated at all. "I'd have to say that at least as long as I've been watching, I've probably averaged around six to eight thousand per share each year. Occasionally, a bit less. I suppose it might go a bit higher in a real banner year, but probably not much."

His lips turned in briefly, a sign that his mind was working hard. "So, either their investments are extremely safe and conservative, or else they've got an awful lot of expenses and retained income. Or a bit of both. Either way, there's a whole lot of money floating around here. Well, it's nothing but supposition until we have the financial statements in hand. What does the Family do with all its money?"

"I'm not entirely sure. I presume they fund some charities, and they run Golondrino, of course. But...so you have the whole story, we're supposed to use Family members for whatever we need whenever we can. The Family pays for all our education, which is why there are a lot of doctors of every kind, lawyers and other professional people in it. That's why so many of us go to private prep schools, like Becky and I did. I mean *all* our education. If I wanted to take a basket-weaving course at Pima Community, they'd pay for it.

41

"The Family also pays for our utilizing other Family members professionally. If, and this is only an example, you understand, I went to see Becky, the Family would pay for it. That creates some real pressure to keep things within the Family, but that's another drain on the Family money."

"So you and Becky are...that's right, you told me she was your cousin."

"Fourth cousin, actually. She and I have the same great-great-great-grandmother. Being Family tends to keep people in touch when they're distantly related more than otherwise, at least judging from what I've seen, although she and I are a lot closer than you'd probably expect otherwise. But what's really drummed into you from the moment you first hear about the Family growing up is that you never, ever talk about it to outsiders. You can tell your spouse, if you choose, but as kids, Becky and I used to snicker over the idea that there were even couples where the non-member never heard about the Family from his or her spouse. Probably just a kid's tale, although I have to admit that I never told Robbie about it, so maybe it isn't just a tale. Daddy wasn't like that. He told Mom everything. And vice-versa, although she didn't have any earth-shattering secrets to share with Daddy. Or at least not that he's told me about."

"How old—no, you already said the Family is about five hundred years old. Who started it?"

"I don't remember the Founder's name, if I ever knew it. He may have been a pirate who went straight, I'm a bit fuzzy on that too, although that's what Becky and I used to think when we were kids. But he definitely had a whole bunch of money, and I mean a *whole* bunch, which he wanted to keep in his family. I guess somebody told him about the Rule Against Perpetuities, or the like, so he set up a corporation instcad. And a country to boot. I presume he could have set up a trust there and abolished the Rule, at least for his own trust, but I'm not sure. It's not like I can dig him up and ask him." I grinned.

He grinned back. "Yeah, that would be kinda pointless. Although talk about getting the dirt on somebody. Five hundred years, though...not the Rule itself; it isn't that old. But perhaps some predecessor rule of equity. And five hundred years or so? I daresay the corporation has undergone a lot of changes, but that would make it one of the oldest corporations in existence, probably with a royal charter originally. Having a corporation may...no. It clearly does give you options that a trust wouldn't. Anyway, so what happens to your shares when you die? Can you leave them to anybody, or does it have to be a Family member?"

"Neither one. You can't leave them to anyone; they revert to the Family. They're more on loan than they are actually given to you. They always belong to the Family. The founder was a great believer, apparently, in everyone making his or her own way. You can leave the money you've accumulated from those shares to your kids, but even there, Family members are encouraged to give heavily to charity, especially from their estates, or else return most of the money they die with to the Family. Some do. If I die tomorrow, my estate goes mostly to the NRA and the Desert Museum." I paused and thought. "Actually, I don't know of anyone in the Family who's rich because of what they got from their parents or grandparents, not that I know all that many of them. Some are better off than others, but that's going to happen in any group. You just grow up in that sort of mindset, I guess. Parents usually help their kids, but they don't leave the kids enough to live in luxury without working. The ones who are rich because of the Family all earned it themselves. The Family rewarded them for being successful and made them richer."

He digested that. "Okay, so you have a beneficial interest, not actual ownership of the shares. I can handle that." He drained his cup and crushed it in his hand. I guess

43

he'd had enough. "Last question. I know I've asked you this a couple of times before and been put off, but you're in a mood to answer questions now and I want to get as much as I can. Don't you think you're a bit old to still be calling your father Daddy? I mean, if you were some magnolia blossom from the deep South, it might be one thing. But you grew up in Denver, for Pete's sake."

Now, having moved on from the Family as a topic, I could chuckle. And he was right; I was in a mood to answer questions.

"It's a bit of a story." He waited patiently until I continued. "I began to call my parents Mom and Dad when I was...oh, I don't know, somewhere around nine years old, give or take. Then when I was twelve, I came home from school one day to have Daddy tell me that Mom had been killed in a traffic accident. A stupid goddam traffic accident." I wiped away a sudden tear. It still hurt, more often than not. "We spent the rest of the day literally crying on each other's shoulders, sometimes alternately and sometimes simultaneously. Well, actually, I climbed into his lap and we sat like that for hours. I was so upset, I guess that I reverted to calling him Daddy instead of Dad for a while. He seemed to respond to it; he was probably at least as upset by the whole thing as I was. I know he still misses her terribly. And he still calls me 'Baby'.

"Around a year or so later, I began trying to call him Dad again. He was actually a bit hurt by it. He really liked being 'Daddy' to me, so I figured I'd continue calling him that. By now it's habit, but it makes him feel better, and to be honest, it still helps me on some level too. Like Mom's not completely gone in some sort of fashion." I surprised myself. Becky knew, but she'd been there. I was also aware that she didn't think it was completely healthy, but...tough. It was our business. I'd never told another living soul about it, and would have bet I never would have. Now here, I'd spilled it without a thought. For some reason, I didn't worry about telling Alec. Hm. Another thought to shove down into the depths.

He smiled gently. "Where is your father these days?"

"He's back in Denver. He tried coming down here for a while, and got one of those houses out west of Casino Del Sol, so he could get to the range and the trap club easily. We shot together every Saturday morning at the trap club while he was here. He's better than I am at skeet, and I can kick his butt at trap. But his current squeeze—whom I cannot *stand*—hated the heat, hated the lizards, hated the snakes and hated even the *thought* of the heat, the lizards and the snakes. One day, she found a tarantula sitting on the newspaper when she went to get it. She immediately went back into the house and demanded that he move back to Denver, or else *she* would, and he could do whatever he wanted. Oh, and he had better go get the paper himself, since there was a spider on it the size of my dog, and he would continue getting it until they got back to Denver.

"I got the full report. Of course, she's never run into a wolf spider around Denver. She may be in for a shock when she does." I shrugged. "Anyway, so he went. We talk from time to time, but only when he calls me. I will not talk to *her*. If he comes this way alone, we get together. But he's rarely away from her, so we don't see each other much any more." I swallowed the last of my coffee. "Daddy seems to like her, but for what it's worth, Becky thinks she's a jerk too. I think her purpose in life is to control him. One way or another, he responds to her and keeps her around. I don't get it and I don't care to."

He smiled. "She should know. Smart woman, Dr. Swan. Okay, I think I've got a bit of a handle on this now. The first thing we need is some better security. I don't trust your laptop any more, since it's been sitting in my kitchen while we've been out here. I haven't half the security you do, and if they've gotten into my place to install their bugs and spyware while we've been gone, whoever the hell

45

'they' are, then it's probably just as compromised as your desktop. I also have to assume that so is my laptop, and my desktop, and as you said, probably my house and my office as well. I've no reason to believe that they don't have access to any of our phones, including our cells. We need some new equipment." He checked his watch. "It's getting a bit late. No, it's way too late. How about we fix this in the morning? I don't think it's going to get any worse tonight. You want to pick me up around nine? And, uh, do you think this is going to be dangerous? Are you armed? Stupid question, you're always armed. Gun and knife, right?"

"Three knives, actually." I patted the holster under my armpit. "Gun here, knives here, there and there." I tapped the Hideaway knife hanging below my bra and indicated the ones in the back of my waistband and above my ankle. "Frankly, I have no idea how dangerous this could turn out to be. Last night, I would have said not at all, at least not until I got more into this. Tonight...I have no idea. But it seems kind of stupid, now, for me to assume it's going to be at all safe in any way. Whoever these people are, whatever they want, they've already told Fields, by his own account, that they're quite able to take him out, not once, but several times. If I'm lucky, they'll be telling me the same thing.

"However, I've got no reason to think I'm anywhere near as valuable to them alive as he is, and I'm probably going to be a lot more of a threat to them. Logic suggests that at least compared to Fields, they won't hesitate to take me out if they think I'm causing them a problem. My job in that regard is to either beat them at their own game or else make them realize that I'm not easy to kill. Failing that, I intend to take a bunch of them with me and make them pay big time for their efforts." As I heard myself, I realized that was exactly the sort of resolve I felt. I intended to survive this, just as I had been taught at Gunsite, and everywhere else I'd taken any of my many practical shooting courses. Everybody needs a hobby, and that's mine.

Alec took a deep breath. "Somehow, nothing that my father ever told me about Vietnam included how to adjust to being on the bull's-eye. I don't even know if you do, and I'm not sure I want to know. Which may not keep me from finding out anyway. Nobody's asked for my opinion." He looked me in the eyes. "You aren't asking, are you?"

I simply shook my head.

* * * *

TO: D
FROM: HB
Surveillance devices emplaced at Youngston's and Trevethen's residences. IMPORTANT: Youngston aware of surveillance devices at her office, but has left them in place. She has also engaged Trevethen to assist in investigation and has disclosed extensive sensitive Family information to him.

TO: HB
FROM: D
This disclosure is not entirely unexpected given the relationship between them. Continue as per instructions.

Chapter 4

I'd been right about one thing. After Alec and I had split up for the night, Bruno went on high alert as soon as we walked into the house. He dutifully checked all the rooms before coming back to report all clear. I gave some thought to trying to find the bugs they had undoubtedly planted before dismissing it as wasted effort since I was going to leave them in place anyway. I'd simply have to assume they were there and act accordingly. I did my exercises, grabbed the big gun to slip underneath the pillow, dropped into my bed with the gun where I could touch it with my fingertips and slept like the proverbial log. Having a nice big pistol under my pillow didn't bother me a bit. Maybe it even helped me sleep better.

I like to think I can handle whatever life throws at me. Lord knows I've tried almost all my life to work at being that way. Daddy was the one who first taught me to take care of myself, and that means I go armed at all times, even when I'm reduced to carrying nothing more than a reinforced pen that functions as a...well, let's call it a martial arts weapon that's somewhat better than bare hands. It writes well too. The truth is that I feel naked as hell now without a pistol, which Daddy taught me to shoot well before I ever got into my teens.

It was a damn good thing he had too. One evening, a couple of months after Mom was killed, I was home alone watching TV in my bedroom. I'd only been allowed to stay alone without a sitter for, oh, less than a year at that point, I think. When I heard the glass break in the living room, lots of adrenalin aside, I knew exactly what to do, not that I had ever expected to *really* have to do it. But here it was.

I took my .45 from my nightstand—the same one I shot in competition—and racked the slide. The magazine was already full, eight shots in all. I got down on my knees on the side of the bed away from the door. When the two of them got to my doorway, I didn't give a shit about the comments like, 'Oh, look at the little girl with the great big gun'. Or even 'Better put it down, little girl, you might hurt yourself'. But when the one in front started to point his own gun at me, I started shooting. Five shots in all. He dropped like a rock and started bleeding all over the carpet. The other one ran, leaving a blood trail.

Damn it, this was *Mom's* house. Sure, now it was only Daddy and me living there. But there were still enough things there that she had put in, and I could still feel her; her touch, her things, even, sometimes, her *presence*. He had no *right* to come in, he wasn't supposed to be trying to take her things, and if that weren't bad enough, he had to try pointing his gun at me. Just the thought of him being in the house was creepy enough and insulting to her, but I had to draw a line somewhere.

I sometimes wondered if I'd drawn it in the right place. Everybody told me that I'd done just fine, that everything was great—it wasn't—and that I couldn't have started shooting them for simply being in the house and trying to take Mom's things. Even when it was still and quiet in the middle of the night, lying awake in bed, I could almost— almost!—feel Mom telling me that too. And I knew it. But they had to push too far. So I guess it doesn't really matter where I drew that line. Once they did what they did, that was enough.

Anyway, after it was done and I'd managed to calm down enough, I called Daddy's pager and put in our emergency code. He called back within minutes, and I told him everything that had happened. I also apologized for messing up the hallway. I was...a bit messed up myself, I guess, to be worrying about that right then. After making sure I could handle it, he told me to give him five minutes by the clock, then call 911. That way, he'd be home before the cops got there. Oh, and don't worry a bit about the hallway or anything else. He'd take care of everything. Thank God for Daddy.

Waiting that five minutes, alone in my room, with the body of the man I'd just shot lying like a pile of used laundry in the doorway wasn't easy. I could have burst into tears several times, but at that point in my life, I had tears every time I thought of Mom. I wanted to cry for her. I've missed her for years and still do. This...it was upsetting, it was traumatic, to say the least. But my tears, like the ones I cried for Mom, would have been for me. He didn't deserve them, and I wouldn't give them to him. Just her. So I held them and simply sat on my bed facing the other way while I waited. I wanted to get out of the room, but then I'd have had to step over him, and I couldn't do that. Not alone.

Killing a man, even when it's justified, well, it makes you grow up fast. I had to learn to be tough. Daddy worried that I was becoming hard, not tough, and he and Becky's parents talked to me about it. Several times. Finally they figured out that I was handling it as well as they could ask for and we let it drop, at least as a topic of conversation. I wished I could have talked to Mom about it, sat on her lap and cried on her shoulder. But without her, I *had* to learn to be tough, because it was the only choice left. Sometimes I talked to her at night, when I was lying in bed and couldn't get to sleep. She never answered me, although once I felt her, or thought I felt her, caress my cheek the way she used to do, like she was telling me without words that she loved me. It helped. It would have to do.

Everybody else seemed to think I should be a lot more upset than I let on, and other than with Daddy and Becky's parents, I probably got a bit of a reputation for being harder than I was because I showed so little of what I was feeling. I figured, rationalizing it, that those clowns didn't have to come into our house and didn't have to point a gun at me. I was still around and healthy, they weren't. No reason for me to feel too terrible about that. Defenses are amazing things, aren't they? I did get to watch the detectives at work. Really neat. Also the crime scene techs, which was almost as neat. It gave me something to watch and think about, which almost kept me from missing Mom. Almost.

Daddy found a fancy lawyer to keep me from being grilled by the detectives at the station. He was Family, as I later learned, when Daddy told me all about them a couple of months later. Since the corpse still had his gun in his hand, and there was gunshot residue all over my comforter, the DA wasn't inclined to say much about it. Oh, I had some lasting upset, sure. Still do, sometimes. I expect that killing is never an easy thing to do, for most people anyway. There were some unpleasant dreams, but nothing like nightmares. Just...not nice dreams. Certainly nothing like the nightmares I probably would have had if I'd been defenseless, assuming I'd survived. Becky was more concerned about it than I was. Come to think of it, that may have been part of the reason she went into psychology.

By the time I went back to school two days later, since Daddy had managed to keep our name out of the papers and nobody at school told the rest of the kids, everybody naturally knew at least generally what had happened. Most of the girls had even less to do with me for a while, but I had more attention from the boys than I'd had in all the previous years put together. That, I found, was annoying. It was simply notoriety, not like they had any real interest in me. Finally one of them came right out and asked me what was it like to kill a man? I told him that I hadn't really been paying attention at the time, and I'd probably have to do it again to see. Was he volunteering? I tried to sound serious, and it must have been a good answer, because he got a real nervous look on his face and decided he had business elsewhere. That was the only time anyone ever asked straight out. They also quit hanging around me, which was fine.

I cut classes that afternoon and took a bus to the Police Department downtown. When it turned out that the detective I asked for, the lead detective who'd been at the house, was off-duty, an older one came out and kind of took me under his wing. He insisted on calling Daddy first. Oh, he knew who I was, all right. Seems at least half the department knew who I was by then and was very impressed. I'd apparently saved them a bit of work by taking that clown out. But I asked him to teach me how to be a detective, very determinedly. He gave me a tour of the labs, told me some of what they do and how they do it, but explained that he couldn't do more than that; departmental rules or some such. Before taking me home, he took me to meet a former partner of his who was now a private investigator. That fellow let me come in to watch him work and even let me do some minor things with him for a month or more after school, until he had to go do a job that I couldn't tag along on. But by then, I was hooked. I probably would have gone back after he was done with that job, except that I got my first guide dog puppy to raise. Daddy thought it might help me over losing Mom. Going back to work with him would have made my life too complicated, although Lucy and I did go see him from time to time. He liked dogs. But I definitely had the bug by then, and I knew I was going to be a detective when I grew up.

Back to the present. I spent some time dawdling over my coffee the next morning. What did these unknown people want? Well, obviously, they wanted to know what I was doing, who I was talking to and what I was saying. I suspected that they'd be just as happy if I would keep out of their way, which suggested that they probably wanted me to stop investigating whatever they were trying to accomplish. I had to presume that some, and probably most, of the people Fields had told me about were playing their own private games. If the entire board, outside of Fields, was in on whatever was going on here, he was likely screwed already, and they wouldn't need to be playing at threatening him. He would be voted out and they'd be done with him. Could they do that? Probably. I didn't have my copy of the bylaws handy to check. Maybe Becky had hers. Another mental note—my brain was rapidly getting covered in imaginary sticky notes.

The private players could be ignored, but I had to know who they were first. Whoever was involved was clearly playing in a very big game, if, as it appeared, they were willing, even if not eager, to leave some very dead bodies in their wake. Just like I'd told Alec, I didn't know exactly how much money the Family had or controlled, but I knew it was a whole big bunch. Probably enough to make it a *very* big game indeed. I also had to admit that I wasn't half as concerned about Raymond Escarton Fields' body as I was my own. I'm kind of attached to mine. Like I said, I expect to go sometime, but preferably a long time from now.

At the local big box store, Alec and I started through the computer section. I finally settled on the smallest thing I could find, a little netbook smaller than a pad holder. Alec steered me to a large capacity thumb drive as well.

"Keep your working files here, not on the netbook. We'll disable the wireless net access so you have to change that or hardwire it to connect, which will let you control when it's online. But keep your files on this little thing. Never have it plugged in when you're online. Then even if someone ever does manage to plant some spyware on the machine, it'll be that much harder for them to get anything. And the netbook never leaves you. When you need to take a shower, let Bruno watch it. Sleep with it, or let him do it. But never leave it unguarded."

"Sleep with it? Seems a bit drastic, doesn't it?" Actually, I probably would, unless I stuck it under Bruno's bed. It might be safer there, although I suspect I wasn't as susceptible to some doped hamburger. Well, not raw anyway. Grilled on a bun with green chilies and cheddar cheese might be a different thing altogether.

"Bugs and spyware, remember? Let's try real hard not to let this one get infected." He was right, of course.

Alec snagged a pair of prepaid cellphones on the way to the register. "Just for the two of us." He'd mentioned our phones last night, but truth to tell, they'd slipped my mind. My dollar was paying dividends already. And I should have known better. I worked with other peoples' cellphones without their knowledge on a regular basis. I simply never thought about it for my own. Like I said, I should have. I certainly would now. He turned back to me.

"Don't take your own phone out of your fanny pack unless you're willing to have whatever you say near it overheard."

I smiled back. Now he was playing in my court. "Trust me, Alec, I know. And keep your own in its case. Or off."

We retrieved Sasha and Bruno from the car and headed for a different place for some coffee. I wanted to go someplace with a patio where we could sit outside and have the dogs with us. It was still a bit chilly, which wouldn't bother them, but would give us more privacy. Coffee for us, some pieces of bread for the dogs, and everything seemed very peaceful. On the surface.

"Once your files are on that thumb drive, treat it like the computer. Either wear it or let Bruno or Sasha wear it, but never ever leave it unattended. And encrypt everything on it."

I smiled. "Alec, I may be stupid, but I ain't *dumb*. Of course I'll protect it *and* the data on it."

He smiled back. "No, Amy, I know you're not dumb. I'm not suggesting you are. You've hired me for my counsel and I'm giving it to you. And yes, I am taking this very seriously." He flipped his jacket open slightly; he had a pistol on his hip. I was surprised. I don't think he'd ever used his permit before.

"Is that still a 9mm?" He nodded. "One of these days you're going to learn to carry something bigger. If you have to shoot somebody, you don't want to make them mad. You want to make them cease their activities forthwith." I shook my head. "What have we gotten ourselves into?"

He looked off into the distance for several moments. "I suppose I could say that you got us into this, or that you got yourself into it and then dragged me in after you, but the most honest response is that it really isn't all that important. To some degree you were born into it, and for the rest, you do remember that I asked to be involved, and then you needed me and brought me in. So? We're both in it now, whatever 'it' is, and that's the hand we've been dealt. You going to need any help putting your software on the netbook?"

"No, I don't think so. I'm not installing much. Some basic word processing, expenses and maybe my checkbook, and I think I'm about done. I don't believe there'll be a problem playing solitaire on my other machines. If they want to watch me do that, more power to them."

He grinned. "That's my Amy."

I smiled back. "Where shall I drop you?"

"I think...back at the house. My afternoon's free and I'm going to get some range time. I haven't been shooting as much as I should have been and it occurs to me that I may need to be as good a shot as possible."

"I'll go too. I have that same feeling that I may definitely need the practice. A couple of adrenalin drills?"

He thought for a moment. "Oh, sure. Why not?" He had a bit of a sour look on his face. He didn't like them the way I did, but I already knew that.

Adrenalin drills are neat—afterward. They're my own invention. What they amount to is a randomly varied course of fire that can include a rifle and/or a shotgun, but always includes a pistol, and is intended to be as stressful as I can possibly design. They're hard—they're supposed to be—but they're the best training I can devise. It takes a bit of time for the heart to settle down once you're done. Then you can say they're loads of fun. When you're in the middle of the action, well, you're much too keyed up to say or even think anything so silly.

Later that afternoon, I cleaned all the guns. The rifle and shotgun were no big deal. The pistols required more work. I'd needed the practice with my carry gun, a little Kahr PM40, and shooting the big .45 was always enjoyable. I've loved shooting .45s since Daddy got me started.

He'd been shooting in the Colorado Pistol League for about two years when he started me in it. That was probably, oh, about a year or so before Mom was killed. Anyway, all these guys—a whole bunch from the Jefferson County Sheriff's Office, a number of civilians and God knows who else—thought it was so touching and so damn *cute* to see this little slip of a—well, I *told* them I was a girl; I was even flatter-chested then than I am now and looked sort of androgynous—trying to compete with a big .45. That lasted for about three months, which is how long it took me to start winning and moving up in class. By the time I was shooting in A class, and racking up some very competitive scores, they didn't find me cute any longer. Their problem. Daddy and I quit shooting IPSC with them when it became too obvious that the gamers had taken over and winning became more a matter of athletic ability and tricks, not shooting ability.

Alec and I spent much of the evening talking about inconsequentials while I was putting files onto the netbook. We, then walked to the coffee shop for more serious discussion. By the time I fell into bed, I felt a lot better. The next day would be worse, although hopefully for the other guys, not for us.

I was almost asleep when the sound of breaking glass brought me and both dogs wide awake, very quickly. The alarm never went off, but it shouldn't have. The motion sensors in the house weren't armed at night, in case the dogs wandered around the house—just the door and window alarms, and I only had the sliding windows alarmed. Both dogs ran barking into the living room. I followed, dressed in my .45 and flashlight. 'This' turned out to be a brick thrown right through my living room picture window, the one I'd had put in where there had originally been three double-hung windows. Talk about movie melodrama. There was even a note tied to the brick. This was too Hollywood for words.

The note was blank. Okay. I'm no psychic, but I definitely knew what that meant. Luckily, I had some heavy plastic sheeting and duct tape in the house. I didn't sleep all that well that night. I was in a constant state of alert, and yes, some alarm. I envied the dogs. Their senses and reactions were good enough, and their imaginations limited enough, that they could sleep soundly, secure in the belief that they could handle whatever arose and they would wake up fast enough to do it. I didn't have that sort of faith. I suppose the plan was to tire me out or maybe stress me out. To some degree, it was working. Both were working, in fact. I looked forward to being able to turn the tables on them. If I could.

* * * *

TO: D
FROM: HB
Youngston and Trevethen have foiled computer/email surveillance; it may not be possible to completely overcome this target's awareness of surveillance. Youngston is more heavily armed than originally believed. Trevethen is now armed as well. Plan A has been initiated.

TO: HB
FROM: D
Everything is proceeding as expected. Your work so far is excellent. Continue with Plan A.

Chapter 5

It was obvious that I needed to learn a lot more about investments, even to understand what Raymond Escarton Fields had told me. I didn't know much at that point—just enough to buy some decent, if unspectacular, mutual funds with my leftover money and let it alone to hopefully grow while someone else worried about what specific stocks to buy within those funds. From what Fields told me, he had people pushing various mutual funds, common stock, preferred stock, bonds and God knew what else on him. He'd also mentioned one of the board members pushing to get the Family involved in Forex, whatever that was. I needed to bone up and quickly. I figured I might need to present at least some semblance of understanding to Fields at some point in time, and even if I didn't, I still needed a lot better understanding of what was at stake, as well as what was going on between him and the board members.

This was easy. I could do this on my desktop. Again, it was nothing that would surprise anyone to find me doing. In fact, it would probably look more suspicious if I *didn't* do something like this on my computer. Most people would use their computer for checking and working on their investments, and if I didn't do this sort of research where they could see it, whoever was bugging me might get suspicious. It was important to keep them thinking that I was unaware of them looking over my shoulder whenever I was doing something that I didn't mind showing them.

As I continued, I could feel my spirits drooping. Fatigue does that to me. I fortified myself with several cups of coffee during the course of the day. They kept me going, but only barely. They also kept me *going*, and that helped keep me awake almost as much as the caffeine, which doesn't affect me as much as I might sometimes like.

Easy, my ass, I told myself. By suppertime, I could only lean back in my chair and pinch the bridge of my nose. Mutual funds I now understood—far better, at least, than I ever used to; different kinds of funds, different classes of funds, different sorts of investments within various funds. On the one hand, the more I learned, the more I realized that I was only scratching the surface. Lightly. I could spend weeks—years, perhaps—on nothing but mutuals and still not know everything there was to know. Or even the greater part of it. But I thought that I might now have enough of an idea of what I was facing in that particular arena to be able to move on. So why did I have this nagging feeling that what I had done so far was the easy part? Of course, given the assets the Family had to invest, it was really a very large mutual fund all by itself. But Fields had said that two of the board members were pushing specific mutual funds on him. Didn't I have to understand what that meant somehow?

Tuesday night with Becky was, well, interesting. Of course, I had to tell her about Fields' visit and the job he hired me to do. Then I had to tell her everything that had happened since, like the bugs, spyware, taps—well, I presumed there were phone taps, I'd have used them if I were using bugs—hiring Alec, everything. She was by turns fascinated, aghast, supportive, skeptical and just plain silent. She was also playing with her flatware, which was unusual for her, to say the least. Finally, she responded.

"I've been wondering if I should tell you this, but it seems I have to. Alec and I have been having lunch together from time to time, and he...told me about you hiring him and telling him everything about the Family."

Watching her expression and body language, I couldn't be sure. Was that disapproval or just nerves?

So my two best friends were having lunch together. Nothing to concern myself with. Was it? "Do I need to be worried about you and him?"

Becky smiled. Wistfully, I thought. "Oh, no, no. Just as friends. We talk." I watched her expressions. She was good, damn good. But I knew her back when. I don't think anyone else in the world could have picked up on it, including, probably, her mother. I also knew she'd die before she gave in to it, or voluntarily let it show to anyone else, including Alec.

"You're interested in him." I smiled to take any possible edge off it.

So help me, Becky blushed! I don't think I'd seen her do that since she went to graduate school. She shook her head. "In that regard, I'm not sure he knows I exist. Amy, I..."

I reached across the table to pat her hand. "It's okay, dear friend. Sister. I know you're not poaching, and I'm not worried. If he decided he wanted you, well..." Would it be okay? Oh, lord, let's not go there. Maybe it won't even come up. "Let's not even worry about that. We're all friends. Good friends. We'll let it be like that, okay?"

She gave me a sharp look. "Amy, sometimes you simply astound me. You read people incredibly well. *Unbelievably* well. You do it at least as well as I do. But you don't have any idea what makes people *tick*."

"What do you mean?"

"Look. You ask what it would be like if Alec decided he wanted me. You don't seem to understand that I'm the *last* woman he would ever turn to. If he wanted some sort of solace, some relief while he waits for you, he'd never turn to me, because you and I share everything—not that you leave him any time, because the only time he'd have to do it is when you and I are together, unless we did something over lunch, and neither of us would spend our time like that. No, he'd go to someone who's a stranger to you. And if he decided to quit waiting for you, trust me, he'd never turn to the one woman who would *never* let him escape you, because you and I are so close."

If he quit waiting for me; that brought up a whole host of interesting emotions. Emotions I didn't really want to look at, so I shoved them down into the dark. "So what do the two of you talk about?"

"Mostly you." Oh, God, it would be, wouldn't it? She was reluctant to admit it. Of course, she may have thought that holding back would sound lots worse. It probably would have.

I crossed my arms on the table in front of me. Yeah, I know I'm guarding myself. Reading body language doesn't mean I don't use it myself or that I'm not aware of my own. "About me?"

"Yes. He's...quite taken with you."

How to react to that? Intellectually, I knew it, of course. I'd been aware, after our abortive effort at more of a relationship, that he dated around for a while. So did I. I also knew, when I bothered to think about it, that he and I both then, by unspoken mutual consent, let it go and sort of concentrated what efforts we made on our relationship with each other. The sorts of things we did together, innocent as they were, didn't leave much time for anyone else. Any time, actually. Mostly, I admit, I didn't think about it. Didn't really want to. Didn't let myself.

"Mm-hm. Is there something more I should know about?" That seemed safe.

Becky was silent for a long time. "He wants to have sex with you. In the worst way."

Well, there it was, right out in the open. I leaned back into my chair. Yep, reluctant as all hell and not hiding it at all.

"Yeah, I know. We tried that once, and that's just how it was. The worst way."

She looked at me, waiting for me to say more. I looked back, declining to do so. "Jokes aside, Amy, you asked. I should, though, to do him justice, say he really wants to make love to you. It's way beyond simply wanting to have sex. To put it in the vernacular, he's got it bad for you."

And in my professional opinion, giving in to him might be good for you. No, she didn't say it. She's far too good to do that. I heard it just the same.

"We seem to be managing as is."

She simply nodded. When she realized that I wasn't going to go anywhere further with it, we moved on to different topics.

By the time we split up to go home, I was beginning to question whether I'd been smart to involve her in all this. I mean, yes, it was a Family affair, so to speak, and as my best friend and the only other Family member I was close to, sure. But if it was dangerous for Fields, and it was going to be dangerous for me, and likely Alec as well, was I doing her any favors by bringing her into it? Or was I painting another target on her? I had a certain amount of confidence, not enough, which I'd never admit to a living soul, but some, in my ability either to defend myself or to at least cause some serious difficulties for anyone trying to take me out. Alec might not be up to my level, but he had a decent basic understanding of the issues of self-defense and a certain ability to, well, shoot back.

Becky...didn't quite live in the same world I did. Her world was safe. Emotionally, at least, violence happened to other people, ones she wasn't close to. Certainly not to her or the people immediately around her. The concept of going armed at all times would probably never occur to her. I feared for my friend, but at the same time I knew I needed her. The whole sex with Alec thing...that could be tabled for a later time. It wasn't anything I wasn't already intellectually aware of. Or anything I really wanted to think about right now.

By the time I'd been at it for a week, I'd had a far more extensive course in investments than I had ever expected to need, sketchy as it was so far. And it definitely was that. By now, the baristas at the coffee shop knew all four of us—five, actually, as Becky sometimes came with us—far more than they had when we first began coming there. They'd bring out pieces of stale bagels or other treats for the dogs and always made sure we had fresh coffee. They'd begun to offer us refills instead of waiting for us to ask for them.

I had started to run my hand underneath the table when we sat down, even though we never took the same table two nights running. Somehow, never finding anything hidden under the table didn't make me feel better. Luckily for me, I'd had no more late night surprises after the brick through my picture window—yet. I'd also taken no chances. I'd replaced the window with one of those plastic windows that would bounce bricks instead of shattering. I was even thinking of redoing all my windows that way. Maybe.

I continued to remain in my constant state of mild alert, and I never quite shook that itch at the back of my neck while we were sitting outside at the coffee shop, the one that tells me someone is watching me. Us. On the other side, however, my eyes were beginning to cross over my course in the length, width and depth of investments. Yes, I was learning, but it had become a massive project. The more I learned, the more I realized that there was to learn, and the part that I knew I didn't know grew far faster than my knowledge. Definitely drinking from a fire hose.

I needed a break from my study. "I'm going to run up to Sedona for a couple of days," I told Alec one night. "One of the board members lives up there and I need to get some on-the-spot investigating in. I think it's time I began to earn my fee. Besides, I need to get away from this studying for a bit."

"What are you going to do, tap his phone?" He was smiling. Let him. What he didn't know wouldn't hurt him. I smiled back.

"I need to be there to do my investigating. Can you come?"

He pulled out his phone to check the calendar. "I've got a hearing day after tomorrow. I can come up Wednesday, if that works. Where will you be staying?"

"I thought I'd find a little out-of-the-way B&B. If nothing else, whoever seems to be trying to watch me will probably find their job a bit harder that way. I'll get you another room, if they have one. Call me and I'll tell you where we're staying once you're on the way." I nudged Bruno with my toe. "Come on, lazybones. We need to get home. You're going to stay with Aunt Becky in the morning." He looked up at me, glanced at Alec, and slowly got to his feet. Sasha got up, butt first as usual.

I drove to Sedona the next day. The scenery didn't develop until I was almost in town, but when I got close, some of the most incredible red rock formations emerged from behind hills covered with scrub vegetation. What I found, though, when I got past the exquisite red rock views, was nothing more than a golf course community. Was this what everybody was so excited about? I vaguely recalled going through Sedona many years ago, when Daddy took me to Gunsite for my high school graduation present. Somehow, nothing here seemed the least bit familiar other than the colors of the rocks. I followed the road out the other end of town as my GPS directed me toward the B&B, and after another couple of miles, I found the real town. Even better views too, and it, at least, seemed faintly like something I'd seen before, although it had obviously grown a lot since. It nestled in the valley between incredible formations of red rocks, and I could have spent an hour or more enjoying the scenery were I so inclined, but business beckoned. I spent the remainder of the afternoon checking in, exploring the town and finding out where my subject lived. It took me a while to determine which house in the gated subdivision off Dry Creek Road belonged to Mr.

Gregory Casaday, Esq. I couldn't get into the subdivision—at least not without risking making someone curious, and that was something I definitely didn't intend, want or need. There was no listing for him under attorneys in the phone book, and the state bar association didn't show him, so I presumed he was retired. It also didn't seem like the sort of area where I could sit in the car and watch the house, even if I'd had my telescope with me. This time, though, I didn't expect to need it. I'd even left my camera in the B&B. Visual surveillance didn't seem like it was going to be productive in this case.

Gregory Casaday had gotten his start, professionally, as a compliance officer at a major currency trading firm. As I understood the job description, that made him the person responsible, or one of them, for making sure that everything the company did was done correctly, by the rules and so on and so forth. From there, he'd become a trader and was apparently one of their stars until he retired. That, perhaps coincidentally, was just about the time he got his seat on the board, back during the tenure of the previous CEO. He must have been good at what he did, or else Fields would have dismissed him and gotten someone else. Casaday was the person on the board who had, according to Fields, been pushing Fields to get involved in Forex, which turns out to be currency trading. When two different currencies are shifting their values relative to each other, then holding one that is going higher is going to make money when converted into the one that is lower than when the original purchase was made. Clear? Mud? Yeah, that's sort of where I am. Suffice it to say that it treats money like another commodity. You take one and buy the other with it, hoping the other will become worth more in terms of the one you started in, at which point you can cash in. That's simple enough that I could understand it. Just.

I had some problems at first seeing how this could benefit some unnamed third party until I realized one vital fact. The Family has a number of brokerages scattered round the world. They actually own the brokerages, and in most cases, although the brokerages are small, or perhaps because they are, all the employees are Family too. It appears that Family business is all these brokerages do. Or maybe they sit on the exchanges; I'm not exactly sure. My terminology may not be completely accurate here, but I only found this out after I was digging around in a Family-only site and had been working on it for a half-hour or more. The point is that none of the brokerages, or whatever they are, the Family operates is engaged in currency trading. If the Family did get involved, it would, at least initially, have to go to an outside broker. If cousin Casaday could steer the Family's business to a specific currency trading firm, then somebody stood to benefit handsomely, at least until the Family set up its own. Okay, I can understand that. Of course, cousin Casaday might simply feel that becoming involved in currency trading was in the Family's best interest.

Time to find out. The first thing I did was call his cellphone. I had my phone hooked up to my computer, and as soon as he answered, I downloaded my nifty spyware into his phone. A bit tricky, and definitely not legal, but as long as I made sure that I left no traces, nobody needed to know—and it let me hear what he said anywhere near his phone, whether he was using it or not. And after a week and a half or so, it would disappear of its own accord and leave no trace. At least that's what the author of the software promised for quite a bit of money and no names. It had also tested as doing what he'd claimed when I tried it on my own phone to check. What more could a girl ask for? I apologized to Casaday and told him I'd called a wrong number. Sorry, cousin. But I'm on a job and you're it. You wouldn't know me anyway.

Now understand, this isn't the sort of thing I do as a matter of course. Yeah, I know I've said this before. Bear with me. It bothers me on some level, so if I say it more than once, it's because it matters to me. Most of my investigations are simply matters of going places, seeing things—I'm more observant than the average bear—and talking to people, sometimes sitting in the car for hours waiting to photograph someone or even playing some sort of role to get to hear what people are saying. Sometimes it's a matter of poring over public records.

I really prefer not to cross the legality boundary. It could get expensive and might mean I'd have to find another way to earn a living. But when I have to do it, well, results are what matter. I don't advertise what I'm doing. I produce results, and on this case, I *really* need results. In this particular case, I saw no other way to get those results in anything like the sort of timeframe the people pursuing me were likely to let me have—or at all. The only way I could figure out how to discover whether someone was in league with the bad guys was to put them in a position to contact whoever they were working for, or with, and that meant the sort of surveillance I was doing here.

Out on the road, it took me only minutes longer to run down the phone pedestal. That's the narrow green thing, about two feet tall or so, that holds terminal blocks to access the landlines that run through it. You probably see them all the time and never notice them. In my business, I always notice them. Naturally, it was right by the street in plain view of God and everybody—they usually are—so I couldn't do anything more in daylight than note where it was. Under other circumstances, I've posed as a phone company repairperson to do things to pedestals in the middle of the day, but that was out of the question this time. They don't drive BMW SUVs, and this was not the sort of area where I'd had to go to some rent-a-wreck to get a car that would fade into the background. In fact, in Sedona, BMWs faded into the background. A rare and fancy sports car like a Z8 probably would have been noticed, but a mid-sized SUV like my X5 was utterly unremarkable. It just faded into the Toyota ForeRunners, Porsche Cayennes, Mercedes M350s and everything else in four wheel drive running around town. Not standing out is important in my business; how you accomplish it is less so. I was satisfied.

I'd given my hosts at the B&B a cock-and-bull story about doing research on bats that would justify my coming and going at all hours. It also gave me a way to explain away the expensive camera and my electronic equipment if anyone got too snoopy.

The bats weren't too active when I got to the phone pedestal shortly after midnight, although I'd seen one or two soon after sundown. At least I thought they were bats; they fluttered a lot more than any bird, and that was always how I'd recognized them in the past. I'd parked about a half-mile away and walked up the road to keep from drawing any attention to what I was doing. I didn't expect to be there long. I was in luck; there were only about a half-dozen or so lines in the pedestal. I made my connections, closed the pedestal and spent a few moments piling rocks over the box I set behind it. The box itself was already covered in some epoxy to break up its outline and colored like a chunk of granite, but most of the rocks here were really pinkish to brick-red and black, and I didn't want it to draw attention. It was likely to be there for several days, perhaps as much as a week, before I went to get it back—if I did.

I didn't want to lose the unit, but I could if I had to. Being able to walk away from everything when it seemed advisable had saved my bacon more than once in the past. I'd never had to do that with a unit like this, which was far more complex than most of what I'd used before. But to be safe, I had never handled it, inside or out, with bare hands, and this was no time to start. I stripped off my gloves as I walked back to the car. Damn, but it got dark here. I stumbled over rocks at least twice and almost turned my ankle once before I got out my little flashlight. By then, I figured I was far enough away not to be noticed, and the light wasn't all that bright anyway. I probably wasn't either, or I'd have started using it sooner.

* * * *

TO: D
FROM: HB
Youngston and Swan have discussed her assignment. Swan and Trevethen appear to have a relationship independent of Youngston. Should that be pursued further? Youngston has initiated active investigation, conducting direct surveillance of board member Casaday. Plan A will continue when Youngston prepares to leave area of surveillance.

TO: HB
FROM: D
Progress so far is excellent. I see no need to explore any relationship between Swan and Trevethen at this time. Keep me apprised and we may reevaluate later. Continue.

Chapter 6

I drove by early the next afternoon and triggered the download of the recordings to my computer in the car. A couple of miles farther on, I found a place to pull off the road where I wouldn't be too obvious and started playing them back. I hit the jackpot on the third line, and the fourth had DSL tones that could be Casaday's, so I set my program to disable the other line recordings when I drove back. Now with any luck, he'd call whoever he was fronting for, if any, or email them. I didn't really expect to get lucky. He could do things by snail mail, and that would definitely be harder for me to access. But this was a good place to start, and anyway, snail mail is *so* yesterday. I also suspected that if he really was fronting for somebody, he wouldn't want to put any more in writing than was absolutely necessary. Besides, there were eight board members, and the likelihood seemed very high to me that no more than one or two of them were actually acting for some unnamed outsider. With that sort of odds, I had no reason to think I'd hit the jackpot on my first time out.

* * * *

Alec drove in late Wednesday afternoon. For all that it felt a bit strange not to have the dogs with us, we managed to have a very pleasant dinner and evening. Sedona has some very fine dining. Afterward, we drove by the development so he could see the task in front of me. He raised an eyebrow when I downloaded the current recording, but said nothing.

However, when we got back and I began listening to the voice line recording, he all but went ballistic.

"Do you know how illegal this is? You think that summers in Tucson are bad, think about spending time in

71

Leavenworth. You can't *leave* Leavenworth. I mean, you're probably in violation of at least two or three federal statutes, not to mention a whole bunch of state ones." He kept on, repeating the illegality of what I was doing, how much trouble I could get in, how much trouble *he* could be in for not stopping me, and so on.

Nothing good, so I erased the recording. Not simple erasure, either. I used one of these programs that deletes, overwrites and then deletes again to make it completely unrecoverable. The DSL tones confirmed that I had the right line, and showed me nothing of interest otherwise. I deleted that too. The cellphone recording was equally worthless and met the same fate. In all honesty, Alec was right about the danger, and there was no reason to tempt fate by keeping evidence I didn't need. I waited for him to run out of steam and quit talking.

When he finished, I looked at him and said, "Is that all?" Hm. I'd never seen quite that shade of puce before. I think that's what they call it. "Okay, look. You're right that I shouldn't do it. I know that. But I've left no fingerprints at the scene, there's no DNA there that I know of, and I can walk away from every bit of my equipment if I have to. There's no fingerprints or DNA *inside* it either. All the components are off the shelf, purchased for cash from walk-in places, some here and some there. It's as utterly untraceable as I can possibly make it. What really matters, though, is that if you know a better and quicker way of getting the information I need, I'm all ears. I don't. This isn't some case where I can go snoop through public records, or hang around outside his house with a telephoto lens and snap pictures of him with his girlfriend. I have to have exactly this sort of information and I know of no other way to get it. Until I do, this is what I have to do, so just let me be."

I could see him wrestling with everything, and it was clear when he reached his decision. It was also clear what it was.

"All right, it's your baby. I have to admit that I don't really know anything about what you have to do. I do know that I don't like it. I mean, I *really* don't like it. But you certainly know that. How long do you have to keep doing it?"

And for this, I was paying him a dollar? Should I offer him more money? Nah. As good a lawyer as he was, he wouldn't be tempted by more money, although a dollar was extremely low wages. But even that lone dollar meant that I was his client, and as such, I trusted his silence, even though the point where I let him know I was going to continue breaking the law put him in a more difficult position ethically. Much more difficult. I'd make it up to him. Somehow. Let's not think about how. Back to business.

"Tomorrow, I'm going to have Fields call Casaday and blow off his investment suggestions. If anything will get him to call his backers, if any, that should."

"And if he doesn't?"

"Then I move along, for now. At least some of the board members, probably the majority of them, are pushing their investment proposals, I presume, from honest, even if misguided, feelings of their own. I'd have to guess, which is all I can do at the moment, that no more than one of them, or perhaps two, are really fronts for someone. He might be one. Statistically, I figure he likely is not. But I'll come back to him later if I have to."

Alec got a sour look on his face. "That's a relief, I suppose. Let us by all means minimize our criminal activities."

I patted his cheek and then kissed it lightly. "Yes, by all means let's do." I smiled.

Sleep didn't come too easily. I'd done my usual draw and dry-fire exercises after Alec left for his own room, but without the dogs and their usual evening routine, I was thrown off. I was also conscious of Alec on the other side of the wall. Too much so. I don't know why, since we'd decided that we were much better off being best friends than being lovers. I'm repeating myself, aren't I? But I certainly didn't want to be the one to ruin an already good thing. A very good thing, yet I couldn't shake my awareness of him. Or my recollection of what Becky had said about him. And me. And what she didn't say as well. Finally, I drifted off into a restless and unsatisfying sleep.

I wasn't at my best the next morning. I do better with a bit more sack time. Oh, well, I'd get over it as the day progressed. After breakfast, I went back to my room and called Fields on my cellphone. My regular one; there'd been no sign of whoever was trying to spy on me. Even if they had the line identified, I was here, not in Tucson, which was probably where they'd be listening. And if it was tapped, nothing I was saying would be a surprise anyway. If anything, Casaday was operating on his own and they wouldn't care. Or he wasn't and they'd have to contact him to give him instructions about how to respond. A win-win situation for me, or so I figured. The prepaid cell, I mostly save for discussions with Alec when I needed them.

Fields answered promptly. Apparently this was either his own cell or else his private line. Mentally, I upgraded my opinion of him a notch. I'd been ready to have to fight my way through a receptionist or secretary to get him directly.

I explained where I was and who I was watching, although not how I was doing it. I asked him to call Casaday and tell him in no uncertain terms that Casaday urging him to get the Family into currency trading was not going to bear any fruit, that his suggestions were being rejected—and be as forceful as he could. I needed to shock Casaday enough to have him contact his principals, if any, for further instructions. Fields seemed to understand what I wanted, so I left him to it.

It was almost suppertime when I retrieved the next batch of recordings. I have to say that I wasn't all that impressed with Fields' phone call. In fact, I'd have to describe his style as more conversational than confrontational. He thanked Casaday for the report that Casaday had done and simply said that he didn't feel this was the time for the Family to become involved in the currency market. Well, he knew cousin Casaday and I didn't. Perhaps this was simply how Casaday had to be handled.

After that, at least on the voice line, there was nothing. Nothing, that is, except for Mrs. Casaday setting up a tennis date and then inviting some friends for dinner next Saturday. Hardly anything of interest to me. I checked the other line for his email and found nothing more interesting there either, if you don't count a couple of websites that Casaday visited; the sort of things I first saw on Daddy's computer many years ago. Of no interest to me, although I thought Alec might be reacting to some of them. File that away for future reference. Casaday is entitled to his private activities.

The cellphone came up dry too. Alec and I looked at each other, puzzled. Finally, I closed the laptop and said, "Maybe he's simply making an honest recommendation." Alec muttered something I didn't catch, but it probably amounted to an agreement. I pulled out the netbook and set up my notes on the thumb drive as we sat there. Finally I spoke up. "I'll retrieve my stuff this evening and we can leave tomorrow."

"How about the day after? I'd like to take you out for a really nice dinner, and it's a bit late now." He was right, I realized with a start. It was already close to eight o'clock.

"Fine. Surprise me." I finished packing everything up. "Let's go pick up a quick supper and then I'll get my stuff."

I slept better that night. Of course, it was after midnight when I finally fell into bed, so I may just have been bone tired. I can certainly do covert things at night, but wandering around all in black, especially in such a dark area as Sedona, is not really my idea of fun. If nothing else, it's a high-stress activity, because not only am I very hard to see, I *need* to be unseen. Any time a car goes by, I have to see it before the driver can see me and play boulder until they're gone. Luckily there wasn't a lot of traffic on Dry Creek Road at almost midnight. But 'not a lot' is not the same as 'none'.

Alec and I spent some pleasant time the next day seeing the sights of Sedona without spending much money on purchases I really didn't need. Well, not very much. I did pick up an exquisite Indian bracelet in gold with turquoise, coral and fire opal, which struck me as unusual. I love unique and Alex gave me a pair of matching earrings, which rated him a *very* nice kiss. Once in a great while, I do like to dress up, although not for work, and maybe I'll get my ears pierced again. Or have these remounted with clips.

I also got a nice pin for Becky and another for Carol, one of Daddy's former girlfriends and the closest thing to a mother I ever had after Mom died. Becky deserved something special for watching the dogs, particularly since, unbeknownst to her, I figured she'd likely be keeping them a lot more before this was all said and done. Carol just plain deserved it.

I don't remember the name of the place, somewhere up Oak Creek Canyon with a big silver deer out front. I got a nice snapshot of Alec with the deer. Any good excuse to take the Leica out, although I only had the M8 digital with me on this trip. For serious pictures—fun, not work—I prefer real film. I call myself a photo Philistine because I

76

refuse to do serious photography in digital. I got it from Carol, who had been a photographer. Still was, as far as I knew. Some freelance, some sports, but her real loves were wildlife and scenery/landscape. We spent plenty of time together skulking around the mountains for hours, or occasionally even days on end, living in our down jackets, armed with long lenses, motor drives and heaps of patience. Carol taught me so many things. I'm deeply indebted to her and I love her dearly to this day.

I also picked up some ruddy-colored T-shirts, purportedly dyed with local red dirt, in matching designs for Becky and me. I avoid printed shirts in favor of plain pastels when I'm working, because they're yet one more identifier, and I need to be as nondescript as possible. On the other hand, I love them when I can get away with them. After all that, Alec treated me to a very spectacular dinner. I made a mental note to do something more for him than just a good kiss. I'd think of something. No, not *that*. As I've said, we had that out years ago.

The next morning, I met with a major surprise when I finished tossing my stuff into my car and hopped in. Perhaps thirty seconds after the engine caught, a string of firecrackers went off underneath it. By the time the explosions ended, I was already out of the car and a good ten feet away, crouching behind a far-too-small rock with my pistol drawn, eyeballs frantically scanning the area. Alec came running, gun drawn, out of the front door to find me squatting down and hyperventilating, but with no danger in sight. I stayed where I was and tried to get my heart down to no more than about twice its normal rate. I knew I was appropriately covered and positioned behind shelter, wearing jeans and a T-shirt. But some part of me felt as though I was standing on the highest point around, stark naked.

And unarmed.

* * * *

TO: D
FROM: HB
Youngston and Trevethen leaving area of surveillance on board member Casaday. Plan A still in operation. She appears to be reacting as expected.

TO: HB
FROM: D
Excellent. Continue with Plan A.

Chapter 7

Driving home was all sorts of fun. I have to admit that I hadn't been watching my back as closely as I might have been—should have been!—driving up to Sedona. Surprise, as the old maxim goes, is most often the result of failing to see what is in plain sight, although judging from how long they left me alone, they might not have been in plain sight because they weren't watching me closely at all. Or they might be tracking me electronically, in which case all my efforts to watch my back trail would be worthless. On the way home, though, after my little good morning greeting, I couldn't take that chance. Alec initially followed me about a quarter-mile or so back on the way home.

We agreed to meet up at a place on the south edge of greater Phoenix, since we were going to split up and go in opposite directions at the first I-17/I-10 interchange. The Interstates meet up again where I-17 feeds into I-10, but the whole idea was that we'd both make random lane changes and occasionally get off at an unexpected exit and then back on. The split was more of the same. Whoever was in back at a given time would be watching for someone reacting to the front car. Also having the harder time, because the rear driver had to watch anyone potentially following the front car, but also for anyone following him—or me. Zipping off at random exits let us swap places with ease. It also gave me the chance to give a quick scan of the sky from time to time to see if there was an aircraft watching me. I never saw any circling around, although I did think that one of the turkey vultures soaring over the undeveloped desert of the reservation south of Phoenix looked rather suspicious. But our new cellphones got a workout. And of course, if anyone was tracking my regular cellphone, or not tailing either of us, then we were also wasting our time.

One way or another, we were.

By the time Alec and I got together again in Tucson, he seemed to have come to some sort of terms with my activities. He never mentioned the possible legal penalties again and, for that matter, never brought up the surveillance again, even when he was helping me with it. I hoped I hadn't set up too much of a conflict within him. I worried a bit about that, but what the hell, he's a big boy. If it gets to be too much for him, he can say so. I don't take hints well. Never have, and he knows it. On the other hand, my vital signs were finally back to normal. I didn't have the heart to tell him that I'd only used the units once or twice before this job. I'd actually made them more because of the challenge than because I really needed them—until now, of course.

It was the second night after we got home. Becky had come over to return Sasha and Bruno, and I prevailed on her—it wasn't hard—to stay for dinner. I was in the process of fixing a large pot of chili. I've been accused of being a one-trick pony in the kitchen, not by Alec, or Becky. Contrary to popular opinion, I am a decent cook. It's just that chili is not simply a dish, to me; it's a food group. At the same time, I was preparing a stir-fry for supper. It too would generate plenty of leftovers, and it's my most common spur-of-the-moment meal.

Becky tasted the chili, fanned her face, gulped some water and decided to have the stir-fry instead. Wuss, I thought, smiling to myself. Afterward, the three of us, well, the five of us, walked to our usual coffee spot for a private discussion. Two other tables were taken, so we leaned in close to keep our conversation private.

"I've been going over the articles and by-laws of your Family," Alec began as we sipped our coffee. "It's an odd corporation, to say the least. The board functions, as nearly as I can tell, simply as advisors to the CEO, who doesn't get to his position by being a board member. By that I mean that he's not elected from the board, or by the board, at least not normally. It seems that each CEO picks his or her own successor, and his word is law. The board is more like his private fiefdom than it is any normal board of directors. Or you could look at it as his royal court, if you prefer. The board members are elected by the Family at large, but he can dismiss any member at his own discretion, regardless of how much time they have remaining in their term, and nobody can stop him. The only time, and I mean the *only* time, that the board can choose a CEO is if the office becomes vacant without a named successor. I find that whole setup strange and also a bit unsettling."

I reached down to pet Bruno. "Truth to tell, I hadn't paid any particular attention to it before now. I've let them have my proxies when it came time to vote, since I basically didn't know any of the candidates, much less what they did or were qualified to do. I'm learning a hell of a lot more about them now, of course. And since the only way to leave the Family is to die, I always figured there was no point in my worrying about it. I mean, if I'd wanted to live on the shares I got for being born, finishing high school, college and law school, and just put my feet up, nobody would have said anything to me, and I'd still be a member. I've bettered my share holding by working at improving my own position, so I really haven't concerned myself with the details of the Family organization. I've been a lot more concerned with *my* job."

Becky spoke up. "I'd have to agree with Amy here. I admit that I don't have the legal education the two of you have, but for me, it's been a fact of life. It's been a nice advantage not having to worry about the costs of college and graduate school, and letting our parents send us to private grade school without having to pay for it, but it's not like we can do anything about it one way or the other. We were born into it, we've been living it, and we'll die in it. It's gone on quite well for centuries without us, so neither one of us has really had any incentive to concern ourselves with it."

I suspected from the expressions that played across his face, that Alec wasn't really thrilled with that sort of attitude. Of course, if I'd been the sort of person to concern myself about such things, I'd probably have become a lawyer after law school instead of a private investigator. I did have a certain amount of sympathy for him; he is and, I have to admit it, at least to myself, has always been very dear to me. But I can't be someone I'm fundamentally not. Finally, he seemed to steady himself emotionally and looked at both of us.

"Well, first, that's not entirely true. You can be removed from the Family. If you're convicted of a crime of violence, fundamental dishonesty, or moral turpitude—that's a direct quote from the by-laws—your shares and dividends are suspended for ninety days pending an automatic appeal to the CEO. Unless the CEO rules otherwise, at that time your shares revert to the Family and you're out. Any children you might have after that are out as well, although any children already born will keep their shares and membership. But beyond that, don't either of you think it's kind of odd?

"I mean, here you have what is purportedly a corporation, but it's essentially set up to be run as a private kingdom by one person who's not answerable to anyone. The only way that a CEO can be removed against his will is by a supermajority vote of the Family, and the only way to force such a vote is by a supermajority of the board—*if* you can get such a supermajority before he dumps the board members that would rather see him out. Even if you're not into social consciousness, or any of the other politically correct buzzwords that go with it these days, this is still a totally archaic sctup. I mean, you might as well be in a medieval kingdom."

Becky broke in. "Fundamental dishonesty? Moral turpitude?"

Alec leaned back in his chair and stretched out his legs. I glanced around, but the other tables were now empty. And the back of my neck still itched.

"Think of things like theft, embezzlement, bribery, prostitution, there are plenty of other things I could mention, but I think you get the drift. Violence, of course, is obvious. But what it boils down to, in the simplest plain English terms I can think of, is that if you run afoul of the law while doing that which would generally be considered 'right and proper'"—I could hear the quotes—"you should be in good shape. If you're doing something that any normal, moral person would realize is wrong, you're probably out on your ear. Now if we were in a court here, I could probably make a whole bunch of arguments to tie up any such determination, and if I could show a good reason, I could probably get a plea deal that wouldn't show that. Of course, since you can't mention the Family to outsiders, it's a bit difficult to justify coming up with some other reason to be allowed to plead to a charge in court that wouldn't show as dishonest or immoral. If you want to challenge it within the Family, you have one appeal, to the CEO, and that's that. The CEO's decision is final. Like I said, quite medieval."

I hauled the conversation back to the basic topic. "Alec, is there any way to change it? In the articles and by-laws, I mean. Remember, it's not an American corporation. American law doesn't apply." I leaned back and waited. I could see him going over everything in his mind before he responded.

"I really don't think so. At least, if it were an American corporation, there wouldn't be any way, simply by the clear terms of the documents themselves. It's a 'four corners' issue. You remember." He glanced at me. "But for Becky's sake, the answer lies entirely within the four corners of the document." He checked his notes. "There is no way that it can be changed simply by the Family members at large on their own. The CEO can propose changes, as can the board members. It takes a supermajority of the board to enact them, or they can be proposed to the Family as a whole by the decision of either the CEO alone or by a simple majority of the board, and then it only takes a simple majority of the Family members to put them into place. The Family members at large, on their own, have no say. The only say they have is through the board or to remove the CEO, and as I said, they can't remove the CEO themselves without having the board bring it before them. And you're right about the law. You'd have to bring any action in...where in the hell is that place anyway? It's almost like the Duchy of Grand Fenwick."

Grand Fenwick, Grand Fenwick—something with Peter Sellers. Oh, yes, *The Mouse That Roared*. Becky recognized the reference too. She laughed. "Alec, you're dating yourself. Listen, for all we know, the pirate who started this family, and while it may only have been what two silly kids thought when we were younger, for all we know right now, he may really have been a pirate who decided to live honestly for a change and probably started the country too. I'd also suggest to you that he did it for the primary purpose of putting the Family seat, or whatever you want to call it, in a place he controlled. In fact, I'd say it probably *is* a Family-controlled if not wholly Family-*owned* flyspeck of a country, since although it calls itself the Republic of Golondrino, it never has any elections that I know of. I mean, being citizens, if they have elections, we should be able to vote."

I added my two cents' worth. "Becky's right. Nobody ever asks us if we want to use our vote or tells us how or when to cast it, except for the board members. If the CEO isn't the ruler *de jure*, then he certainly would be *de facto*." Becky looked a bit lost, so I turned to her. "If he isn't the ruler according to the law, then he certainly is in fact, in practice." She nodded, understanding now, and I turned back to Alec. "So the likelihood then strikes me as overwhelming that there isn't going to be the proverbial snowball's chance in hell of changing anything about the Family through the courts. The Family will *own* the courts, if there even are any. So why should we worry about it?"

I don't think that thrilled him. If I thought about it to any degree, it probably wouldn't thrill me either. But he didn't have any way to argue with it, so he changed the subject. A bit. He looked at me. "Didn't you say that Fields was being pressured by board members to invest differently?"

Where was he going with this? "Yes, that's what he told me. You've heard it too." Becky nodded.

Alec looked almost triumphant. "He *cannot* be pressured by the board members. He holds the power of, figuratively speaking, life and death over the board members. He can pressure *them*, if you can find anything they can do individually. But there is just *no way* that any of them can exert pressure on him. If one tries and the CEO doesn't like it, he's history. If the whole board is putting pressure on him and he wants to, then the Family needs a whole new board, end of story. It would simply be a case of telling them 'don't let the door hit you in the ass on the way out'."

Becky and I exchanged glances. If he was telling us the truth, and I didn't doubt him for a moment, he was a good lawyer and he'd taken the time I hadn't, but should have long ago, to go over the articles and by-laws, then this job was beginning to feel a bit hinky.

Alec was going on. "And he said that the board members might not agree to giving you a seat on the board, right?" Becky and I both nodded. "What's that about? The board members are elected by the Family members at large, so they have no say about who else gets to sit there, except for their one vote, the same as any of you. And *he* can toss any of them out on a whim, so the only one they have to satisfy in order to stay is, again, him. Frankly, Amy, unless I've missed something, if you do manage to get a seat on the board out of this fiasco, you better get what you can while you can, because there's only one seat really worth sitting in, and that's the one that his ass is warming."

By now, I was really perplexed. Becky broke in. "How do you figure that?"

He turned toward her and leaned forward, putting his elbows on the table. "It's very simple. The CEO holds just about *all* the power in the Family. He can't put specific people *on* the board, true, but that's about the *only* thing he can't do. He can take anyone *off* the board, at any time, for any reason. That forces a special election, but so what? He can name as many candidates for a seat as he likes, he can even stack the ballot. He makes all the investment decisions and the board is simply his formal advisors."

Becky raised her hand. I guess she felt she had to interrupt him formally. "One question here. If he can't name anyone to the board, how does he give Amy a board seat if she successfully completes this investigation?"

That seemed to give Alec some pause. After a moment he said, "I guess he calls a special election to fill whatever board seat her report empties and has her alone on the ballot. That should do it."

Becky and I nodded. That seemed reasonable, although I was beginning to wonder what I'd wind up doing as the only board member who hardly knew anything about investing and knew diddly about any industry worth investing in. I could be a pretty quick study, but I sure hoped I'd get cut some slack while I came up to speed. Otherwise, I'd better take Alec's advice and get what I could while the getting was good, because I'd probably have the shortest tenure on record.

Alec continued. "Like I said, the board is only the CEO's formal advisors. They can research, they can recommend, but he's the only one who makes the choices, unless, I suppose, he delegates that power. In any event, he's still responsible for the choices and the results. He even fills his own seat when he retires, and nobody else has any input into that decision except as he chooses to ask them and he then decides to listen. So when you look at it like that, what is the real value, other than prestige and shares, of any of the other seats on the board? And as secretive as the Family is, how much is that prestige worth?" He hoisted his coffee cup. "All that prestige, and a few of the many bucks you'd get by virtue of being a board member, will get you a cup of what we're drinking. And the same number of bucks will do it without the prestige, too." He drained his cup.

"I mean, I've seen some strange things since I started practicing law, but this one really takes the cake. And speaking of cake, would you ladies like to split a dessert? I'm still a bit hungry."

I nodded absently as I considered what he'd been saying. Becky continued to look puzzled. When he came back, chocolate layer cake with three forks—he knows our weakness—I had to stop him as he went for a forkful.

"Hey, wait a minute. Do we all just dig in, or are you going to divide it equally first?"

He shook his head. "No, we dig in. I don't have separation issues."

Becky looked at him. "Separation issues? Alec, that is really *bad*."

He simply nodded, unconcerned, and again went for a piece of cake. After his first bite, he resumed speaking, punctuating his remarks with his fork.

"And one more thing. If someone's trying to tell him that they can kill him anytime they want, there's a major question that all this raises. *Why?* He has the power, they have none. I mean, he has *all* of it. They cannot make him invest any way they want. He can ignore them or even boot them any time he has the whim. I suppose that sure, someone might be trying to knock off the king, so to speak, but *he names his own successor.* There is no established line of succession here to let any particular someone else step into his shoes if he's gone, except by the entire board's electing a replacement, and if that's what's going on, then it seems to me that you need to have at least five members of the board involved or you've got a crapshoot. That means, at least as I see it, that you had a better than even chance of having this fellow in Sedona be one of the problems. Check three more and I'd say it's an absolute certainty that you've got at least one. If none of them are dirty, then there's got to be something else going on."

Becky and I stared at each other. She spoke first. "From where I am, Alec, professionally probably more than personally, I'd have to say that given what you've described, then if the board really is doing something, I frankly wouldn't be at all surprised if every one of them were in on it. I absolutely agree with you that it must be a majority, and likely an overwhelming majority, if not every single one. I'd even suggest thinking of it as being the next best thing to a *coup d'etat.*"

Alec shook his head. "Becky, I don't think you've quite gotten the thrust of what I've been saying. If the board is trying to oust the CEO, it isn't 'the next best thing' to a *coup d'etat.* It *is* a *coup d'etat,* pure and simple. He is the ruler of an independent state, and they are trying to overthrow him. QED." She looked at him.

I don't like being at a loss for words. It's a most disquieting feeling. But when Alec laid it all out like this, not only did it make a certain amount of sense in terms of what both of us knew of the Family, it didn't make *any* sense at all in terms of what Fields had said in my office. And I had his words recorded; I'd listened to them several times. I'd played them at least once for Becky and two or three times for Alec. He had even watched the entire video recording once.

I knew *exactly* what he'd said, and Alec was right. I was wrong a few moments ago. This case wasn't feeling a *bit* hinky, it was beginning to feel *totally* hinky. And I had a sneaking feeling that I'd been lied to and set up in every regard in this case, and that is definitely *not* a way to get on my good side, if I have one. Was I being used? If so, why and for what? By whom, at least, seemed to be obvious: Raymond Escarton Fields. It was time to say something carefully thought out and reasonable, so I did.

"Oh, *shit.*" Then I thought of something else. "But none of this answers one major question. It may not make any sense for someone to be sending 'we can kill you' messages to Fields, and the truth is that we don't know if it's even really happening. But what about *me*? The brick through my window might be somebody's idea of a prank. Conceivably, although I strongly doubt it. I don't believe in coincidence. Not to that extent anyway. But the bugs? The spyware? The burglary of my office in the middle of the night that bypassed the alarm *and* the security system? And how about those firecrackers under the car in Sedona? That's *exactly* what Fields reported having happen to him. And while *he* could be lying, you know *I'm* not. You were there."

He leaned forward and put his elbows on the table. "That's all true. And the only way to get to the bottom of what's happening to you at the moment may be to keep on with the current investigation. Unless you have a better idea, because as God is my witness, I have absolutely no other ideas at this point. I'd say it would be more productive to backtrack the people running surveillance on you, *if* we could get some sort of handle on them. As it is, they're ghosts for all intents and purposes. Which leaves this investigation as the only route I can see. So where do we go from here?"

Keep my mouth shut and watch how this plays out. I was not appreciating Raymond Escarton Fields at this moment. Or his job. Or the board. Or the Family itself, for that matter. Screw all of them and the horses they rode in on. What was this really all about? Time would tell. With luck, I'd still be around to find out. If not, well, I probably wouldn't care anyway.

But I'd miss Alec.

I pulled out my little netbook and plugged in the thumb drive after it booted. I found the file I wanted and turned the machine so they could both see the screen where I had the locations highlighted on a map.

"There are eight board members in all. Five of them live in the western continental U.S.: Sedona, Albuquerque, Santa Fe, Denver, and Jackson Hole. One lives in Hawaii, and the last two live in Europe, one in Scotland and the other in Germany. Fields himself lives on the east coast, in Greenwich, Connecticut. I've already looked at Casaday in Sedona. I figured I'd work my way from here to New Mexico next and check out the two there. I'll probably swing up to Denver from there. Jackson is a haul from most anywhere, unless you fly in, and it doesn't have a lot of flights. I'm not sure how I'll handle that one, but I should be able to hit the two in New Mexico and the one in Denver in one trip without leaving these two for too long, although they do fine with Becky and she loves them." She was nodding and petting Sasha. "Judging from what happened that last morning in Sedona, I'm probably better off not becoming as publicly visible as I'd be if I flew unnecessarily. I already know I'll have no choice with the one in Hawaii unless I want to swim, or with the two in Europe either. And I'd be really upset to have something like that happen to me with the dogs in the car."

Alec looked over the list. "You're probably right." He gave Bruno a pet. "Don't worry, big fellow, I'll take good care of Amy for you." He turned back to me. "Let me shift my cases to some friends of mine and I'll join you. Nothing on my docket is all that important to me, or all that pressing at the moment. It's about a seven-hour drive just to Albuquerque, and you may need an extra pair of hands along." He looked sideways at me, seemingly still standing on ceremony. "If you want me along, I mean."

I touched his arm. "Of course, I do. Becky, can you take them back tomorrow night?" She nodded and reached to pet Bruno as well.

"And we'll leave early on Thursday. Okay?" She looked like she had some things to say, but thought better of it at the moment.

I wished I could spend more than a night with the puppies, but business calls.

* * * *

TO: D
FROM: HB
Youngston has become more cautious while driving on highways. Trevethen has given Youngston and Swan extensive explanation of Family organization and procedures. Recording and transcript attached. Youngston is making plans to investigate board members Mouleton, Barnsfather and Morristone next, all in one trip

TO: HB
FROM: D
IMPORTANT. EFFECTIVE IMMEDIATELY terminate Plan A, go to Plan B. It is more important than ever that you disrupt investigation and keep all parties off-balance if at all possible.

Chapter 8

I was checking my accumulated mail in the office the next morning when the phone rang. I waited for the machine to pick up, remembering when Raymond Escarton Fields had been the caller, and wondering what sort of surprises this call might hold. Nothing so earth shaking, but it did hold at least one.

"Ms. Youngston. This is Family member James Briteman, in Paradise Valley, Arizona. I have need of your services. Please call me back at your earliest convenience." As he began to rattle off a phone number, I picked up the phone.

"Mr. Briteman? This is Amy Youngston. What can I do for you? You said you're Family?"

"Yes, I am. I am a former board member, retired for about fourteen years now. I live in Paradise Valley in greater Phoenix, and I need the services of an investigator, or so my lawyer tells me. I insisted on calling one myself before I let him engage one, and when I contacted the Family business office, they gave me your name. When may I come see you to tell you what I need?"

I thought quickly. I really didn't want to have him spilling everything in my bugged office, or over my tapped phone either.

"Sir, I'm right in the middle of something at this moment. Let me have your phone number and I'll call you back in about five minutes, if that would be all right with you." I could return his call on the prepaid cell and nobody would be listening. I hoped.

I figured that the chairs out back of my house were as comfortable and convenient as anywhere else that wasn't bugged. When I got there, Sasha collapsed at my feet while Bruno checked the recesses of the yard for something, anything, interesting.

"Mr. Briteman? Amy Youngston here. My apologies for the interruption. What can you tell me about your need for my services?"

He paused for a moment. "I'm in the process of obtaining a divorce from my...second wife, who is not aware of the Family. I have accumulated a substantial estate, from the Family and on my own, which I don't wish to share with her to any particular degree. She is quite a bit younger than I am, and she is...this is most uncomfortable for me to relate."

"Sir, anything you tell me is completely confidential. Please be assured that nothing you tell me will be repeated to anyone." Mentally, I crossed my fingers. Becky and Alec would hear something and probably hear almost everything that he told me. But I knew I could depend on their silence. Both of them were experienced, professional secret keepers.

"I presumed as much. It's just...oh, very well. I suppose it will have to come out in any event. She is being unfaithful to me. I know all the particulars, but my lawyer tells me that I need hard evidence. Specifically, I need photographic proof, or so he says, in order to exert sufficient leverage against her to gain a good settlement without having to expose everything to the court."

Oh, wow, I thought. Most of my work seems to have been done here. "So why me, sir?"

I heard nothing but his breathing for almost half a minute. "Let me be blunt, Ms. Youngston. We are both Family. Inasmuch as the Family will pay for my using the professional services of other Family members, I can call on you and have your charges paid by the Family. Were I to permit my attorney, who is not Family, by the way, to engage an investigator himself here in the Phoenix area, I would be at his mercy for his charges. He is very good at what he does, but his fees are quite high enough already. Being able to obtain the photographic proof I need, complete with a witness who can, should it be necessary, testify about those photographs in court, while the Family pays for it, someone who understands the need to maintain Family confidentiality, is a very attractive proposition for me."

Well, that made sense. There were no Family attorneys in Arizona that I knew of. I'd have had more work if there were. I'd never done a job for another Family member before, so I'd have to figure out where the bill went and in what form. Fields's job didn't count; he'd told me specifically to bill him directly. But figuring those out should be comparatively easy. Fields and Briteman had both mentioned the Family business office; I could start with that when the time came.

And this was either the greatest stroke of luck in history, kind of like hitting the lottery jackpot, or else it was still more setup. I wasn't sure how to check on that, but I'd certainly take advantage of it to whatever degree I could. Into every life a little sunshine must fall, or something like that.

"Again, Ms. Youngston, what would be a convenient time for me to come see you and give you the information you need?"

Seeing him in my office was out of the question, thanks to parties unknown. "Sir, I have to be in Phoenix in the next day or so. Would there be a convenient time when I could come meet with you there?" Well, why not? If some God who watches over fools is willing to drop this in my lap just when I need it most, then I should certainly use the opportunity while making a suitable offering to said God. Driving to Phoenix is not the worst thing in the world, although at certain times it's in the running.

"Well, hm. I suppose you would prefer to be able to avoid the rush hour. Would eleven tomorrow morning be convenient?"

Oh, boy, would it ever. Eleven tomorrow night would have been plenty convenient, under the circumstances. I'd have made sure of it.

"Certainly, sir. Where do we meet?"

He gave me his address—we were going to be meeting at his house—and a gate code. I worked at balancing my pad holder on my legs while I took down the information. My, my, my. If this was for real, could there possibly be any better way to check Alec's assessment of the board and what it does or could do? And retired for fourteen years, that meant he would have left the board shortly after Fields took over the Family reins. It seemed somewhat unlikely that he was part of any setup, not that I should completely ignore the possibility. This could be another one of those coincidences I don't believe in. It was definitely awfully fortuitous, and I've never won a lottery in my life. I could have papered my house with my semiweekly two-dollar tickets, but all I'd ever gotten was a couple of bucks here and there. Was my luck changing?

I seemed to remember wondering that same thing when Fields came to see me. Was this a sign? If so, is it good or bad? And even if it is a bad sign, can I afford to turn my back on it?

Hell, no.

Well, plans change. Alec came through the back gate from the office where he'd gone first. "What's up? I didn't expect to find you here; you said you'd be at the office."

I grinned like the canary that ate the cat. "Once again, Alec, providence has smiled on me. Well, maybe it didn't before. But I got another job, one that looks like a real quickie. And it's from...are you ready for this? Here, sit down." I motioned him to one of the other chairs. When he was seated, I continued. "It's from a fellow up in Paradise Valley who's a retired Family board member. He's been out for almost as long as Fields has been CEO. What do you think about that?"

Alec looked bemused. "Well, if it's genuine, then he offers us a chance to check out what the board really does and how the Family functions on the inside. Or at least how it did. We don't know whether things have changed and if so, how much. But it's quite likely that the basics haven't."

"Exactly. So what you and I have to do is put our heads together and draw up a list of questions for me to try to ask him. We won't be leaving for Albuquerque tomorrow after all. If I can wrap this up as quickly as I hope, then we should be out of here in a week or so. And it's not like we're crunching a deadline."

Three hours and a light lunch later, when Alec and I were finished setting up questions for cousin Briteman, we had more than four pages, single-spaced. I looked at them.

"This just won't do. He's hiring me, not being deposed by me. We've got to boil this down."

Alec nodded. "I realize that. But I'd rather lay out all the questions we can dream up together and then cut the list down. If we only try drawing up a short list, sure as hell we'll forget something vital."

By the time we had to leave for Becky's place, we'd distilled the list down to just over a page and a half, double-spaced, large type. Alec said it was a trick he used when going to court.

"The more easily you can see the questions when your papers are on the lectern and you're standing up straight, the better off you are. And the more prepared you look. In this situation too, you want to be able to read the question with a glance. Just be your usual self. Pay attention to him. You know how well that gets people talking to you. Take advantage of it. If he answers questions you haven't gotten to yet, cross them off. If he answers questions we've taken off the list, no problem. We wanted to ask them anyway. The first several questions are the most important. After that, everything you can get is so much gravy."

Becky wasn't too upset when we showed up with the dogs and pizza, but I told her that they were coming home with us. The idea of being able to ask questions of someone who had actually been on the inside seemed to really pique her curiosity. She did have a couple of suggestions for ways to approach Briteman, and told me how to rewrite two of the questions to make them less off-putting.

The drive to Phoenix the next morning wasn't too bad. I did my by-now almost usual tricks to make a tail reveal itself. Nothing. I even had my cellphone—my regular one—turned off and sitting inside a little homemade Faraday cage that would block any signals to or from the phone on the seat beside me. For once, I was utterly certain it wasn't sending information to anybody. It wouldn't have been easy to hear it ring from outside the cage, but since it wasn't even turned on, that wouldn't be a problem. That was the least of my concerns. I would have left it behind, but I needed to check on missed calls periodically without using the prepaid, which would potentially allow someone tapping the office line to get its number. And it's hard to track me if you only get one or two locations during the entire day.

Pulling up to Briteman's driveway, I found a large, ornate steel gate. Well, that was why I had the gate code, I presume. Yep, it worked. I drove up a very long driveway between a corridor of saguaros, obviously put in rather than grown there, and every one a large, blooming size cactus with arms—plural, in most cases. They don't bloom until they're something like seventy-five or eighty years old, and once they get to the size of growing an arm, something around eight feet, if I remember correctly, the price—and the delicacy of moving and replanting them—increases geometrically. If these had been planted, say, five years ago, they probably cost him several thousand each. There had to be at least thirty or more; I wasn't counting. Good Lord. I hadn't even gotten to the house yet and I was already floored by the cost of this place. Well, he'd been on the board for a number of years and, from what he'd said about his fortune, I guess he could afford it. Must be nice to have that sort of money. I'll never know.

When I finally reached the door, cousin Briteman was waiting for me on a chair outside the door.

"The gate sends a signal to the house when it's opened, so I thought I'd come out and welcome you."

I smiled. He was probably in his mid to late seventies, tall, generally slender although with a barely-noticeable paunch, solid white hair and plenty of it. Clean-shaven, with a very pleasant baritone voice. A very courtly manner, and I was glad I had dressed a bit better than my usual T-shirt and jeans.

"Mr. Briteman." I stuck out my hand.

He bent over it and kissed it! I was so surprised, I almost snatched it back, but I managed—with difficulty— to hold still. "Please, call me Jim."

"And I'm Amy."

He looked a bit puzzled. "Amy? I thought that was what you said on the phone, but that isn't the name they gave me."

I smiled. "Officially I'm A.M. My full name is Alannah Meav Youngston. I...don't especially like to be called Alannah, and if I go by Meav, then people think I can sing. They're sorely disappointed when I try, although they rarely throw things. I've gone by Amy, from my initials, since I was very young."

He smiled back. "That would explain it. I shan't ask you to sing. I am unfortunately somewhat tone-deaf these days, so I would have difficulty appreciating it anyway. Please come inside."

Wow. I mean, like *wow*. If *Lifestyles of the Rich and Famous* ever wanted to change to *Lifestyles of the Rich and Utterly Unknown*, here was a place they could sure start with. I managed to overload on expensive beauty in record time. When he indicated where I should sit, though, I almost hesitated to plant my butt on the couch; it was so gorgeous and immaculate. It looked as though nobody had ever sat on it. I gritted my teeth and sat. Gingerly.

There was a picture on the mantel of him and a much younger, very attractive woman. I gestured toward it. "Is that your wife?"

His wry smile and body language both suggested some deep pain. "Yes, I'm afraid it is. That is Karalynn. She is, I would have to say, what would be called a trophy wife. We've been married for eight years, and I've had my...suspicions of her for about the last six of those years."

Carefully, I relaxed. I should have done this already. "Sir, do you mind if I record this? It saves me taking notes and allows me to keep all your words, not just those that seem important at the time. I've found on occasion that something that seemed unimportant during the interview turned out to be very important later, and in that event the recording has proven invaluable." He waved his assent and I set up my tape recorder. I also started the solid-state recorder hidden in my pad holder, the one that would have the real record. The tape was real and I could replay it, but I depended on the solid-state recorder. I hated to advertise it, so I carried the little tape machine primarily as cover. It was also a workable backup when I needed it. Of course, the tape had limits, so I had to feed it repeatedly. And it missed things when I was changing the tape. The recorder in my pad holder could record for eight hours on a memory card, and it held three of those. Changeover was automatic and instantaneous.

He really did have most of the particulars on his wife's lovers. That's plural. She spent her Tuesday afternoons with one and all her Fridays with the other. He had names, phone numbers, hours, and while he didn't have exact addresses, he did know that one was in Scottsdale and the other near central Phoenix. That was fine; I could work from that and fill in the blanks. It wouldn't take all that long, and if I could, I'd have one set of pictures taken tomorrow when Karalynn visited her Friday squeeze. Piece of cake.

Assuming that my unseen and unknown nemeses would let me alone while I was doing it. I couldn't avoid working because they were trying to make my life difficult. Difficulties exist to be overcome—I heard that once.

Now for the tricky part. "Sir, would it be possible for you to talk about the board a bit? I've got several questions I'd like to ask. I mean, I've never met a board member before, either current or former, and I'd really like to know more about how the Family operates." A bit of...what? hero worship, perhaps, in my tone? Couldn't hurt.

I think he was lonely. Lovely, too, but that was a different issue. I didn't get out of there until almost four o'clock. Well, if I had to work my way through rush hour traffic, so be it. I'd gotten every single question on our original list answered and more besides. It seems that the greatest part of board meetings most closely resemble some of those Saturday morning business shows like you see on cable. One person will present a report on a company, or a group of companies, or an industry or sector, and then all the other board members try to tear the report apart. The CEO, well, David Brixton, the preceding CEO anyway, sat back and listened. He would occasionally guide the discussion, but mostly, he sat quietly and took it all in. Then he would take a hard copy of the report at the end of the session and move on to the next board member. During Fields' first year, the format continued unchanged, although Fields wasn't quite as quiet.

And this was the board I wanted a seat on? Hell, from what Briteman said, the only seat I could handle would be the CEO's. I could certainly sit quietly while the board members argued in front of me. But to deliver a report that could spur the investment of huge amounts of money? And defend the report against seven other people, all very well versed in investment analysis and at least fairly well acquainted with the industry? Of course, the CEO is the one who has to decide what to do with the huge amounts of money based on those reports. Hooooh, boy. I was starting to think that everything about the board was way over my head. If it weren't so bloody repetitious, I'd ask what the hell have I gotten myself into here? Shortest tenure in history, my ass. I'd be out of there so fast, I'd be going through the door I'd come in before it even had a chance to close.

I called Alec as I was leaving. "Remember the God who watches over fools? He kissed me today. I got all the information we wanted. Every bit. I'm leaving now, so I may be a bit late."

"Okay, no problem. I'll feed the dogs and hold dinner. Leftover stir-fry or burgers?"

"Surprise me. See you soon."

There are plenty of exits in south Phoenix, so zipping on and off the freeway was no challenge. It also failed to show me any tails, but by now it was getting to be a bit of a habit. I couldn't go zipping through the rest area, though. Jim Briteman had plied me with iced tea, and while I'd availed myself of his gorgeous powder room before I left, my bladder was protesting loudly again by the time I got to the only rest area between Phoenix and Tucson. I swung in and parked as close as I could to the rest room.

Where do these people come *from?* There'd been no sign of anyone following me. I was as certain of this as I could possibly be. But when I came back to the car, both tires on the left side were flat. Damn! A call to AAA and I could get them taken care of, so I started that process. It was going to take an hour or so for them to get to me. Lovely. Just one flat and I'd have put the spare on and driven off. But two? No chance. Oh, and my little recorder—the tape one—was missing. I was unhappy about that; I'd had the machine for several years and knew its foibles. But the tape in it wasn't any of the tapes I'd used recording Jim Briteman. Those were tucked safely away elsewhere, and when I checked, they were still safely in place. And my pad holder hadn't been touched, either. Not a big deal, as these things go. At least a new tape recorder would be loads cheaper and easier to get, than, say, a new picture window.

Actually, even if the pad holder had been taken, it wouldn't have mattered all that much in the greater scheme of things, since I had another one. The memory cards in it didn't include the one I'd used this afternoon either. And I'd also copied the data from it onto the flash drive I was wearing around my neck. It wasn't entirely comfortable inside my bra, but it kept it out of sight. And safe. Which was how I wish I felt right about now.

Alec was very understanding, even when AAA took almost two hours to get to me. Then it turned out that some joker—I didn't offer any ideas about who, it wasn't the driver's business—had simply pulled my valve stems, or cores, or whatever they're called. They unscrew right out, apparently. The bright side was that it was a simple replacement. The other side was that he had none of the little buggers in his truck, even though he had a compressor, so I had to be towed back to his shop in Casa Grande before I could get re-inflated and be on my way. Alec may have been patient, but I was major-league pissed, which seemed to be happening way too frequently on this case. Fields' case, not Briteman's. I didn't get home until a little after nine, and with absolutely no appetite. Poor Alec. He'd held dinner all that time and wound up with a frozen meal. I told myself I'd make it up to him. I tried to put a down payment on it when I kissed him goodnight.

* * * *

102

TO: D
FROM: HB
Youngston had extended discussion regarding Family board and procedures with retired board member Briteman. Unable to record conversation. Unsuccessful at retrieving recordings from Youngston's vehicle. Vehicle disabled in rest area. Uncertain of impact of our actions on investigation.

FROM: D
TO: HB
No major problem. Inconvenience, to some degree, serves the purpose. Would prefer to know what Briteman told Youngston, but if we cannot, we cannot. Continue with Plan B.

Chapter 9

The late arrival home the night before cut seriously into my ability to get back to Phoenix to photograph Karalynn Briteman with her Friday squeeze. I wouldn't have to get a more beat-up car to drive for that one; moving around the Scottsdale-Paradise Valley area in the BMW would be fine. Almost like Sedona, there were plenty of expensive vehicles on the road. I might have to do something for Tuesday, and I fully intended to be on her trail then.

In the final analysis, it was almost a letdown. I picked her up with absolutely no problem whatsoever and she never noticed that she was being tailed. I did notice, and I wasn't. Not, at least, any more than I'd seen before despite my best efforts. Both of her partners came out on their front steps to greet her and the way they swapped spit on the doorstep shouldn't be done except behind locked doors. And the Friday one! I mean, public displays of affection are one thing, but my God, girl. Get some self-respect. Letting yourself be pawed like that in public should be against the law. Actually, I believe it is in at least seventeen states.

I'd also have to say that I think one or both were somewhat body-proud, not that they didn't have adequate reason to be. Lord knows they couldn't be bothered to pull any shades. I got some very nice shots, including several *in flagrante delicto*, as they say, without needing any special equipment or tricks. I had plenty of time to switch the Visoflex between the M6 and the M8 bodies, so I had a whole bunch of film as well as a lot of good digital images. I know there are plenty of people who look down on my camera gear as being all but antique, but it works very well for me. Do I have to say that I love my Leicas? I'm not even going to rave about them, other than to say that they're in the same sort of rarified quality bracket as my Ed Brown pistol is among .45s. And yeah, part of talking them up is so I don't have to think about Alec and me in such a...position.

It took two weeks, in all, before I could return to Jim Briteman with the photos he needed. I delivered the first set directly to his attorney, leaving him my business card, and then at Jim's request, another set to him. I dropped his off in sealed envelopes. Whether he opened them or not, I don't know. He's such a nice guy, I'm not sure I want to know. It would have to hurt him and he deserved better. Much better. Even though he already knew intellectually, seeing it caught on film was entirely different. Inescapable. I'd seen it happen before and didn't really need to see it again. He was indeed lonely, but I stopped at only one glass of iced tea and stayed around long enough to hit his powder room for the last time before I took my leave. Taking no chances this time, I drove straight home and didn't stop anywhere along the way. Just in case.

Sticking around Tucson for two weeks more gave me time to get together with Alec and Becky to give them a report on my initial meeting with Jim Briteman. Neither one was more than casually familiar with the sort of board meeting format I related, and I wouldn't have been either except for this investigation, but both of them could at least understand it. However, when I mentioned that every board member Jim had ever known or known of had been in some fashion an investment analyst or a major trader before getting his board seat, they both looked quite bemused. Becky was the one to ask the obvious question.

"Can you manage in that sort of situation? I mean, can you really pull together the sort of information and experience they seem to have and be able to make a report that they can accept? And what industry would you be looking at?"

She'd put her finger right on what was worrying me. A lot. Of course, I'd gotten myself into this. Nobody tied me up and made me ask for a board seat. I could say that it wasn't greed so much as it was a craving for the acceptance within the Family that I'd get for being a PI *and* sitting on the board. But I also had to admit that the idea of getting the extra shares that board members got—I didn't know how many I could wind up with, but I presumed it was a whole bunch more than I'd ever see in a lifetime as a PI—was awfully attractive. Oh, hell, call it greed. I can handle that.

But I would be thrown into a very shark-filled pool, or so it felt. For some reason, like I couldn't figure it out, I was now a whole lot less certain that I even *wanted* to get onto the board. Not when I still was learning about securities and investing, had barely scratched the surface of the subject and had no idea how to research an industry.

"What industry? Honest truth is, I haven't the foggiest. Oh, I figure I can learn, *if* I've got the time. But if I find a dirty board member, then I presume I'll be taking over the responsibility for his industry or sector, whatever that might be. I guess...I guess I don't know enough to really have an answer for you."

Alec simply looked sour. "Like I said, get what you can while you can. You may not be there long. One good expensive mistake and I'll bet you're out on the street again."

I could outdo his sour look. "Yeah, I know. I'd already figured that. But...does the expression 'having a tiger by the tail' mean anything to you?"

Damn. He could outdo me in sour looks.

"Yes, it does. All too well, and like you, I think that's exactly what we've got. Oh, well."

Then I remembered something else. "Here's a piece we didn't have before. There are some rules that are specific to the board—to all nine members. And the board members don't even get those rules until they're seated on the board."

"Eight members," Becky said.

"No, nine. The CEO functions as a part of the board, remember? Anyway, yes, the CEO can dismiss any board member. But he has to do so one at a time, not as a group, and any dismissal only takes effect after the meeting is adjourned and all pending votes have been taken. It's possible to table a vote until the next meeting under their rules, and if that happens, any dismissed board member continues serving until the vote is taken. So let's say that someone on the board moves for a vote of, well, let's call it a vote of no confidence in the CEO. Sure, the CEO can dismiss the board members, but he can't do so *en masse*, and as soon as the motion is seconded, then even if it hangs there for a month, the board continues in office until the motion to remove the CEO is voted on. He can't defeat such a motion by dumping the board the way we thought."

Alec was nodding. "That makes sense, actually. He has power over the board members individually. They have power over him as a group. And if the board members— six, not five, for this kind of a vote—can't convince at least sixty percent of the Family members that the CEO needs to go, then there's probably going to be a special election shortly thereafter, because I strongly doubt that he's going to keep a board that voted so strongly to get rid of him and then couldn't make it fly with the Family."

Becky and I were both nodding. She spoke first. "That actually does make sense. I don't try to read the financial statements any more than Amy does, but if the balances started dropping precipitously, without the market tanking or some other reasonable excuse, then I expect I'd know about it. If I didn't see it myself, then I'm sure that Mom, or Amy's father, would tell us, even if the dividends held steady, and I'd be awfully inclined to boot a CEO who was supposed to be preventing that."

I couldn't add anything. "What she said."

We broke up shortly after that and headed home. Me to do my exercises and give the dogs their last spin before

107

bed; Becky to drive up to the foothills, and Alec to head back to his house, each with our own thoughts. How lovely it would have been to have no more involved thoughts than whether there was a handy lizard to chase. Or to have a nice strong pair of arms around—stop that! Stuff that thought down into the depths. Humans have it rough.

But how nice it had been to spend more time with Bruno and Sasha. Even if I wasn't especially enjoying spending more time with my thoughts and discoveries. However, Alec and I had a job to do, and having finished with my spying on Karalynn Briteman, it was time to leave.

It's possible to go from Tucson to Albuquerque by heading north through Phoenix to Flagstaff. Take a right, then straight on 'til morning, as the old line goes. The very first problem with that, of course, is heading north through Phoenix. Phoenix has, according to rumor, a rush hour. Since I've seen traffic jams in Phoenix at 3:30 in the morning when going to Sky Harbor airport, I think that it's simply got constant heavy traffic that sometimes gets even heavier.

I avoid Phoenix at almost any cost, and going through it on my trips to and from Sedona, or to see Jim Briteman and to tail his wife, hadn't changed my mind in the least. The alternate route goes through Lordsburg, New Mexico, where we stopped for a late breakfast, and then—I found this out quite by accident—cuts northeast from Deming to the center of the civilized culinary world: Hatch, New Mexico. You know, where they grow all those lovely chiles. Oh, to be able to pick up a bunch. Make that a big bunch. Maybe on the way home. What's the next biggest size after the bushel-plus burlap sacks? I had to stop in at least one place in town just to take in the atmosphere before we continued on and rolled into Albuquerque around mid-afternoon. It's not much of a town, and less enlightened persons would deny that it has any atmosphere at all. But they don't appreciate the finer points of food. Or they have no soul.

Albuquerque seems like a pleasant enough place if you aren't a real Sonoran desert rat like I am. The locals call it high desert, but high? Schmigh. The only cacti I could see were some prickly pear, a few barrel cactus and hedgehogs, and the ubiquitous and horrid cholla. I accidentally kicked a cholla joint once. Teddy bear cholla. Very pretty. Dangerous as hell. Yes, I remember it well. Oh, boy, do I. The spines went through my shoe, my sock and into my toes. Those little suckers are *barbed*. I had to limp to a chair on the front porch and pull their claws out with pliers. Painfully. One at a time. Then my toes still hurt for hours. That's something I will *never* forget. The next morning, I had the gardener yank out all the teddy bear cholla in my yard and replace it with less unfriendly cactus.

Here, there are no saguaros towering over everything, the barrel cactus are small or even tiny next to what I'm used to, and what cactus they do have is scattered, not almost wall-to-wall like it is around Tucson. The hedgehogs and prickly pear were already setting buds back home, but here everything was still dormant. Ugh. They do have the Sandia mountains to the east, and we took the tram up to the peak once while we were there, simply so we could say we'd done it. I don't think I've ever seen quite such a view, with the entire city spreading out below us spectacularly and the vastness of the open space beyond it. I'm certain that it's truly magnificent at night, if you're into that sort of thing. Personally, though, I'll still take Tucson Mountain Park and Saguaro National Park West. *That's* real desert to me, and that's where my heart is. When I die, I want my ashes scattered there, like it'll matter to me then. Preferably not anytime soon. Anyway, once again I digress. Bad habit, I know.

We stayed in a bed and breakfast north of downtown that looked as if it had been around since the Spanish were here. They claimed it was built by the Spaniards centuries before anyway, and I couldn't argue. It had the thickest adobe walls I'd ever seen and a bunch of redesigned rooms around a central courtyard. They had a pool too, but March in Albuquerque isn't exactly my idea of swimming weather. Not theirs either, apparently, since the pool was empty. I figured that staying in a little out-of-the-way place might keep whoever was watching us from finding us, at least as easily as they apparently had in Sedona. I suppose I could have pointed out to myself that the B&B in Sedona had been a little out-of-the-way place too, but I saw no need to beat myself over the head with the obvious. No more than I usually do anyway.

Touring the city, of course, took a back seat to work. Roger Mouleton had formerly been a securities analyst for a major New York brokerage house, working primarily on the transportation industry. He had apparently predicted the demise of a major industry player at a point that most people thought it was still a good investment, and his opinion had saved a certain number of people a lot of money. Definitely a star in his field. He'd had a couple of other relatively minor coups over the years, but I can probably summarize it as 'he was very, very good at what he did'. According to what Fields had said, Mouleton was strongly pushing investing in a new enterprise trying to use airships for passenger and some freight use, which Fields thought would be a poor move at this point. This was one that sent me back for more background information. Airships, it turns out, are what I always used to think of as blimps. In this case, they're more like Zeppelins, and there is a difference. I'd never known this, but a Zeppelin has a rigid body and a blimp is either non-rigid or semi-rigid. Huh. Learn something new every day, I guess.

Cousin Mouleton lived in a part of the city, actually a distinct political entity, called Los Ranchos de Albuquerque, northwest of downtown. Take Rio Grande

Boulevard north from around Old Town and you'll go right through it. In fact, you'll go right past his house, although you'll have to look quick to see it. It's a fair ways back from the roadway and the landscaping doesn't exactly leave a lot of exposure for the house. This is definitely the high rent district, not that I expected to find him anywhere else. A very nice area, to tell the truth, with lots more trees and other vegetation than, say, Tucson. More like a drier version of Denver.

Alec didn't say a word about my intentions when I began to set up my equipment, although I didn't think he was any happier about what I was doing than he had been the last time. Again, I dressed all in black, but this time, Alec drove. We managed to find an interval when there was no other traffic, but without any handy side streets to pull into, he had to let me hop out as we drove by.

The damn phone pedestal sat right off the roadway in a patch of grass, with no rocks around to help camouflage my unit. Just like in Sedona, I only had a few lines to worry about. In an area like this, it came as no surprise. Twice, cars went by on Rio Grande while I was working on the pedestal. I hunkered down and froze each time. Most people won't notice a black shape by the side of the road late at night when the shape is still. I could only hope that those drivers were most people. Apparently they were. Thank God I could clip onto eight wire pairs at a time; it was lots faster than doing each pair separately. I arranged the fake-rock box at the base of the pedestal as best I could and hopped back in as Alec made his third trip past me. Mission accomplished.

We stopped for a late coffee on the way back to the B&B. I removed the black hoody and pulled a red T-shirt over my black pullover. Brilliant red; it was a Chinese New Year shirt, a giveaway from one of the Tucson casinos. As cool as the weather was, it probably wouldn't look as suspicious wearing layers as it would to be out late at night all in black, and it wouldn't hurt to stand out when I wasn't doing anything I worried about. I make a lousy Johnny Cash. Can't sing a note, can't play the guitar and I have curves in places he didn't even have. Not a lot of curves, but I'm reasonably satisfied with what I have. Haven't gotten any complaints lately either. Not that anyone has had the opportunity. But that's another story.

Oh, hell, this is for me and maybe I'll let Becky see it, but nobody else. I think. Truth to tell, I've been leading a mostly celibate life for some time. Of course, even without the sex, Alec and I have made a lot more of our relationship in all sorts of non-sexual ways. What we had was very special to begin with, and fortunately, even with the horrid sexual experience, has remained so and incredibly, gotten even better over the years. To be honest, I'm thrilled to death to have Alec as such a close friend. If he were Family, he'd be as close to me as Becky is. Who am I kidding? He is. Just...differently.

Alec and I were comfortable enough that we could even share a room when we needed to without feeling compelled to hop into bed together when we did, kind of like we were doing now. Just very good friends who happened to wind up sleeping in the same room once in a while. Or so I had thought for these past five years. Still did, I convinced myself. Well, I had convinced myself. Some of the thoughts I'm having during this investigation are...disturbing. No, let's cram those down into the dark recesses and worry about them some other time.

Truth is, I was never allowed to be a prude about sex. Daddy didn't let me become one, although he had no idea about this for the longest time. He was absolutely mortified when he found out, although that's a long time ago now.

Daddy was an author. Mostly, he wrote science fiction. It was fairly unremarkable stuff, I thought, but decent, and it sold dependably enough. What I wasn't told growing up was that he also wrote pornography. I asked him about it years later and he said something about 'whatever pays the bills' and 'whatever comes to me is what I have to write'. Anyway, Mom had always been his first editor and proofreader as long as I could remember. No, I never figured out what she thought of *that*, and I've tried. Who can actually believe that their parents are sexually active? Beyond their own existence, I mean. Besides, Mom was, I have to admit, a bit prudish about sex, or so it seemed to me. Anyway, when she died, he didn't write anything for about a year. When he began again, I had to step into Mom's shoes and do his initial editing.

The science fiction was no big deal since I'd already read everything he'd written in the field. Then one day, he came out of what I thought of as his writing trance and didn't give me what he'd written to edit. I thought that was a tad strange, so as soon as I could get to his computer without him in the house, I had to find whatever he'd been working on. That was my first real exposure to the sexual side of life. I learned to recognize the signs—not hard, since I always edited his other writing—and had to check out everything else he wrote. Actually, it was the only sort of education I got from him on sex. No big talk, no explanations. Mom could have, but she wasn't comfortable talking about sex with me. So she explained about my period when it started, but mostly just put me off and told me she'd 'talk to me about it later'. When there was no more later, well...

Soon after Daddy resumed writing, he hooked up with Carol, the first, and in my biased opinion, the very, very best, of a series of live-in girlfriends. I love Carol dearly to this day, although she was no replacement for Mom. Closer than anyone else ever could be, but not completely. Well, that's not quite accurate. She was a second mother to me, and all the mother I had while she was with us or since. She'd been living in the house for, oh, two or three months when I walked in on her and Daddy one time. It was pretty obvious what they were doing, of course. Daddy sort of gasped, but Carol took it in stride. She said, "Amy, honey, could we have some privacy, please? I don't much mind, myself, but I don't think your father's comfortable with having you here." She looked down at him—she was on top—and said, "Colin, don't you *dare* lose that erection." Then she calmly turned back to me—I'm not sure she ever broke her rhythm, which in retrospect I now find most impressive—and simply said, "We'll talk about this later, okay, honey? And please shut the door behind you."

So it was Carol who gave me my sexual education— beyond the things Becky and I would talk about or snicker about, the porn Daddy wrote and the pictures on Daddy's computer that he thought I didn't know anything about—he still thinks that—and of course, I just *had* to show Becky. What is so fascinating to men about such pictures? I have to say that I really don't understand, because they don't do a thing for me. Neither did the porn he wrote, most of which struck me as either highly improbable or completely impossible. But it sold. Maybe Becky could explain it to me now.

Anyway, Carol explained everything about sex to me, and I mean *everything*. Probably far more than Mom ever could have and certainly more than I think Mom ever would have. Actually, she really helped me put Daddy's writing into proper perspective and let me consider it as writing and nothing more, although with her help, it also gave me quite an insight into what turns men on. When I was concerned about my comparatively small endowment, she was the one who taught me how much of a problem large breasts are—she's quite well endowed—and helped me to eventually learn to appreciate what I had and not regret what I didn't. All my thanks go to Carol. She was really a dear, and she was and is very special to me to this day. We still keep in touch, but she was a bit of a gypsy at heart, so she left Daddy and me after a couple of years to move on.

As I said—or maybe I didn't, but I'm doing so now—Alec and I were sharing a room at the B&B, since they only had one available. Responding to Alec sleeping in the same room with me, I did have a fleeting thought of who was I kidding? I let the thought go, but my feelings didn't disappear with it. If I'd found it hard to sleep with Alec in the next room back in Sedona, I found it far worse here with him in the next bed wearing his shorts, and me wearing nothing but one of these over-long T-shirts, since I didn't think that sleeping nude in the same room with him was a particularly good idea, and I don't even *own* a nightgown. The damn thing clings to the sheets, binds on me and twists every time I turn over. Then it rides up to my waist, making getting out of bed far more of a production than it would be were I simply nude in the first place. Nudity wasn't half so much the issue for me—I'm not especially shy, and he's seen it before—stop that!—as linking it with beds was. I think of myself as good at sublimation. I was, perhaps, not as good at it as I once thought I was. That was an idea I firmly stuffed back into the dark and unplumbed depths of my mind where it had come from. Fortunately for me, I was finally able to drop off by listening to the rhythmic patterns of his breathing. I wished those thoughts would stop coming up, as it were.

We went up to Santa Fe the next day after I made my adjustments to the equipment I'd set up for Mouleton. Again, I'd gotten the right line pair to cover his voice line. There were no DSL tones on any of the lines, though, so he was apparently on cable for his Internet. I couldn't tap his email. Damn. But he kept his cellphone turned on all the time and the charger was apparently right by his computer. And wonder of wonders, he even talked to himself! So I figured I wasn't going to miss too much with him.

When we got to Santa Fe in time for a light lunch, I found it was entirely different from Albuquerque. Almost the entire area was blanketed in scrub vegetation. It really looked sort of green from the highway, and the highway doesn't actually go through the city proper. But John Barnsfather doesn't live in the city, either. His place is out to the southeast of the city, well south of the freeway. He actually lives on a ranch, although it looked like the ranch was going to come under pressure from developers before long. Oh, well, that would be his problem, not mine, and he certainly has enough money to hold them at bay as long as he wants to stay there. Cousin Barnsfather isn't hurting. None of the board members are.

John Barnsfather hadn't been hurting even before he got onto the board either, and like Jim Briteman, he would, I suspect, have been very nicely set up even without the Family to bolster his fortunes, so to speak. He'd been an oil land man for a number of years—his first job after college, in fact—and had done a very nice job during the oil shortages of the 1970s and, as far as I could glean from my research on him, made an absolute killing at that time. Then he moved into a mutual fund specializing in energy companies, with emphasis on oil and gas, as an analyst. It seemed like it would be a perfect fit, and it pretty much was, apparently. Just the fact that he owns this huge ranch—it stretched as far as I could see, and even the house was a long, long way from the road, plus the horses. I don't know much about horses, but that sort of beautiful horseflesh means very good and expensive lines, I bet. And the vehicles I could spot with my binoculars that were up by the house: two Mercedes SUVs and one car that I couldn't identify for certain but it looked to be Italian, very fast and very expensive, all suggested that he had a *lot* of money to spend. Far more, I expect, than he ever got from the Family.

116

Although having one hell of an income outside the Family certainly didn't hurt his yearly share accumulation while he was still working either. Now he was the board specialist in energy issues, and was, according to Fields, trying to get the Family involved in some arcane use of nuclear energy. I don't know the details; conceptually it seemed like a decent idea to me. But as Fields had related it, there were nuances to what Barnsfather was pushing that made it otherwise. Well, that's why he's the CEO and I'm only a PI, I guess.

Luckily, one thing about conducting surveillance on people who have lots of money is that they generally don't live crowded together as a rule. Finding the right lines in a phone pedestal with six or eight line pairs in it was a whole lot easier than trying it on the phone line panel of a large apartment building, or even a small one, for that matter. We were on our way home, with my second surveillance unit in place, by eleven. We'd skipped supper. Instead, we stopped at a casino in Bernalillo for a bite to eat. Making our way through the jungle of noisy slot machines dinging and donging, clinking and clanging all around the casino floor toward the café, I stopped to drop five bucks into a likely looking video poker machine. My third deal came up with four eights, so if nothing else we had our supper covered. And we'd found another sort of place we could talk with relatively little risk of being overheard. It was probably after 1:30 a.m. when we finally dropped into bed, and by then, I was far too tired to consider the myriad of...possibilities...made available by having Alec in the same room.

The next morning we drove up Rio Grande to get the previous day's recordings. The back of my neck tingled as we drew near. Something had triggered my personal alarm, even though I didn't consciously know what, yet. I slammed the laptop closed and quickly began stuffing it back into its case. I told Alec to keep driving by so I could scan the neighborhood. Something had to have set me off. Then I saw what my subconscious had already noted.

In an area where cars were *not* parked on the street, the presence of a drab vehicle by the side of the road perhaps a hundred yards from the phone pedestal had clearly been what set my internal alarm bells ringing loudly. Way too drab a car for the neighborhood, and were those lights I saw behind the grille? Everything about it screamed police. As I was zipping up the computer case, I gave a quick glance at the pedestal as we went on by, and my fake rock was gone. I hoped I hadn't turned my head too much and given any cop in that car a reason to look more closely at us. Fortunately, he didn't seem like he was making a move. Maybe we'd gotten away clean. Alec noted my alarm and began to look worried, at least for him. Glancing at the mirror, he paled a bit.

"That car that was by the roadside is pulling out. Now what do I do?" He glanced at the mirror again. "Shit! He's got his lights on and he's coming up fast. Can that unit be traced to you from what we have here?" Well, I guess Alec isn't completely unflappable.

I felt a chill run down my spine as I jammed the case into the back seat, trying not to show anyone outside the car what I was doing.

"Software in the laptop activates the rock's circuits and they're linked on a short-range wireless connection. If they can make probable cause, they can get into the computer case and find that out. If not, we're golden. I hope."

If the police could connect us to the wiretap rock, I had absolutely no reasonable way to get us out of it, and I doubted that I could justify trying to get Fields to pay whatever penalties the two of us might face as expenses of the investigation, although I'd certainly try. Assuming too, that we weren't simply tossed into the clink, that is. We could also definitely both kiss our licenses goodbye.

There was a four-way stop about a half-mile from the house. Alec slowed for the intersection and the cop did too. Oh, *shit!* He sat behind us with his lights going until Alec pulled around the corner and slowed by the side of the road. He lowered his window while I dug my registration and insurance card out of the glove compartment. I felt as though the adrenalin was pushing all the blood out of me, I was so keyed up. By the time the cop came to the window, I had also gotten my own driver's license and CCW from my wallet. Alec simply sat there with his hands carefully on the top of the steering wheel.

* * * *

TO: D
FROM: HB
Extended discussion between three targets shows specifics of the conversation between Youngston and former board member Briteman; recording and transcript attached. Youngston and Trevethen have commenced simultaneous surveillance of board members Mouleton and Barnsfather. Requirements of Plan B prevent foiling both investigations. Will do everything possible to stop investigation on Mouleton and attempt to further disrupt investigation when they begin targeting Morristone. Query: should surveillance devices be emplaced in Swan's residence? It is presumed that targets will hold discussions there from time to time.

TO: HB
FROM: D
Excellent. Continue with Plan B. Devices may be placed in Swan's residence if feasible. Do not, repeat, do not place any surveillance devices in Swan's place of business without specific permission, and only upon proven need.

Chapter 10

"Good afternoon."

Oh, goody. A polite one. Come *on*, Amy, he's just doing his job. Even if it does interfere with yours.

"Could I see your license, registration, and proof of insurance, please?" I tried to hand over the registration and insurance card, but Alec ignored me.

"Officer, I need to inform you that we are both armed under Arizona CCWs. I understand that New Mexico recognizes Arizona permits."

The cop stepped away from the car a foot or two, to clear his gun hand, I suppose. He looked at both of us carefully.

To Alec, "Step out of the car, please, sir." Alec took the registration and insurance cards from me as he stepped out. I unlatched my door, but the cop, never taking his eyes off Alec, said, "Please remain seated in the vehicle, ma'am." Ma'am? Hmpf. Shut *up*, girl, this is some deep shit. Very deep shit. Pay attention to what's going on. Back to Alec. "Where is your weapon located, sir?"

"On my right hip, in front of where I keep my wallet."

The cop thought about that for a moment, and then asked Alec to slowly draw his jacket back and remove his wallet. Alec did so, very carefully, took out his license and CCW, and handed all four items to the cop. He then put his wallet and hands on the top of the car as instructed. My heart was pounding so hard the cop could probably hear it. Alec's was likely to be racing too.

"I see that this is not your car, sir."

I leaned down to see the cop and tried to hand him my own license and CCW.

"Please sit still, ma'am. Are you the owner of the vehicle?"

I said yes and nodded, perhaps a bit too vigorously, as I sat back up and folded my hands primly in my lap. It was all I could do to hold still. After several minutes, he walked Alec around the rear of the car to my side.

"Please exit the car slowly, ma'am, keeping your hands in sight and put them on the roof."

I was all but shaking. I have a certain number of encounters with police in my work, but they're usually fairly innocuous and easily resolved. I've never had a cop accost me while I was so blatantly violating the law as I was here. Hell, I've never done anything quite this illegal, to be completely honest. Wiretapping on this scale? There goes my license, my career, and since it probably qualifies as 'fundamental dishonesty' as well, my Family membership and shares. In short, everything I've worked for my entire life and everything that gives my life meaning and structure. If that weren't bad enough, I've involved Alec and this could cost him *his* license and career. Bad as it would be for me, I could at least rationalize it to the extent that I went into it with my eyes open, but I never meant to put him into such a situation, too. Shit! This could turn out to be *lots* deeper than I ever expected it to be. Fields, if I don't get out of this in one piece, I swear, you are going to pay!

I managed to get the door open and stepped out carefully, making sure that both my hands stayed visible to him. I handed the cop my two cards with one hand already on the car. He took them at arm's length.

So here Alec and I are, out in what feels like the middle of nowhere, holding onto the top of our car while the cop steps back eight or ten feet and, never taking his eyes off us, calls in on his radio to check us out. And all the while, his unmarked car is sitting behind him with all its flashing lights going. Shit, shit, *shit!* I'd bet that everybody in all the houses around us was watching us. Probably filming us for Internet videos. I had itches I'd never had before, but I was *not* going to take my hands off the car to scratch them, not while we still had the chance at a clean bill of health, so to speak. I fidgeted.

Every time I twitched, the cop's attention focused on me like the proverbial laser. Most of the time, he watched both of us, eyes flicking from one to the other. Finally, I guess he heard something over his radio and seemed to relax slightly. I couldn't blame him. It's not every day when a minor traffic stop—I hoped it was nothing more than a minor traffic stop!—offered the potential to become a deadly confrontation in the middle of the street with two armed opponents. Finally, he stepped back and handed us our licenses and CCWs, the registration and insurance card.

"Everything seems to be in order, sir." He hesitated. "Would you mind if I looked in the vehicle?"

Alec responded smoothly. "Yes, officer, I would mind. Unless you have a warrant, I'm afraid I'll have to refuse."

I could imagine the sweat dripping down his spine. I didn't have to imagine the sweat dripping down mine and between my breasts.

The officer stood there for what seemed like an hour or so, but was probably no more than a minute, perhaps two. Finally, he simply said, "Very well, sir. Have a nice day." He turned on his heel, got into his car and drove off. Alec and I didn't move for the longest time. A few cars went by, but it felt as though it took us close to five minutes to exchange glances, and even longer to get back into the car. It couldn't really have taken that long. Could it?

"Let's go," I said. "Turn around, head north on Rio Grande and then turn left when you get up to Alameda." Alec looked puzzled. I pointed to the streets on the nav system map. "Look. It's a T intersection, so we have to go one way or the other anyway. In case you don't remember, there's a coffee shop, a café and a whole bunch of fast food and not-so-fast food joints a little ways up Alameda from where we are now. We just got away with this, but if he sees us again, we don't want to look like we're running away from him. We're better off making like innocent babes and letting him think we've got nothing to hide. And I think we both need to calm down. I know *I* sure do. Shit. I didn't want to lose that unit; I only brought two. Shit, shit, shit!" It was now time for me to compose myself. What to do for this surveillance?

As he turned onto Alameda, Alec asked, "Did you notice what that cop didn't do?"

I was perplexed. "Huh? No, what?"

"He never asked if I knew why he was stopping me. That, at least in my thankfully limited experience, is a standard part of the litany for a traffic stop."

"God, you're right. I was too worried about losing the unit and whether he could justify getting a look at the computer."

"At least we don't have the other unit sitting on the back seat," he remarked dryly. "So, if this wasn't an ordinary traffic stop, why *did* he pull us over?"

I had no answer to that.

"Oh, lordy. I hadn't even thought of the other unit being here. If he'd seen that, it would have given him probable cause for sure."

We pulled into the parking lot off of Alameda. After Alec had the car parked, we both took deep breaths and just sat for a few minutes, letting the stress bleed away. As we walked from the car, Alec stared into my eyes.

"You have more units? How many?"

We ordered our coffees and found an isolated table on the patio. There weren't a lot of other people out there; it was probably too cool.

"Well, I had four units. I guess I only have three now. Not to worry, Alec. It's like I told you before. They're all made from off-the-shelf components, paid for with cash, and most of the parts have never been touched with my bare hands. I buy blister-packed parts as much as possible and make sure to thoroughly clean any that I actually touch when I buy them. I don't order any and I never pay with a charge card. I've even driven to Phoenix rather than order them, and I've always assembled them with as close to 'clean-room' conditions as I can manage, with gloves, mask and hairnet or hood.

"I've got the vital parts to build two or three more and could probably pick up the rest for additional units in a day or two, at least back home. They're as untraceable as I can possibly manage to make them. You're right, getting caught with another unit in the car would be a serious problem, but tracing one to me without that would not be easy, if it's even possible, and I can't see anyone putting in the extreme effort to *maybe* do it for something as minor as a wiretap on a private citizen. Conceivably, and only as a remote possibility even then, for a murder. Nobody's been killed here. They're not going to get back to me on this, much less to you."

Alec stared at me. "What about the design? Can they trace you through that?"

I looked insufferably smug. Like I've said, it's a bad habit of mine.

"Not a *chance*. I developed that sucker entirely on my own. It took me more than two years, including the time I spent breadboarding it, building a test setup of terminal blocks and a signal generator, and then making sure I could operate it remotely. I've kept the design updated since, but it's all mine. I'm kind of proud of it, or at least I would be if I could ever tell anyone about it, other than you, of course. But there's no way that anyone can run that one back to me unless they pull in most of the electronics buffs in Tucson and maybe, probably, not even then." I took a drink. "No, what I'm really pissed about, besides missing the surveillance on Moulcton, is that I only have one other unit with me on this trip, the one we put up at Barnsfather's place. If I lose it, there's no point in going on to Denver.

124

We'll have to head back home before we can go anywhere else."

I traced the pierced metal of the tabletop with my fingertip. "I don't want to go home now. I want to finish this job. I've already established that Fields, whatever his game may be, will live by the rules and pay my bills as he gets them. No matter what he's doing, as long as I don't know what's actually going on here, and as long as I can't find the people who are pulling all this crap on us so I can turn the tables on them, then I really have to keep at this. Having to go home in the middle and pick up more equipment, well, it's a hassle I don't need. Sure, it comes with the territory, but I simply don't *need* it right now."

Alec was nodding. "You're right, of course. I hope you've got some extra work for me. If I'm caught at this, my license will be yanked so fast the frame on my wall will self-destruct long before it ever hits the floor."

"My license will be right there with yours." I patted his hand. "Don't worry. If anything happens, I got you into this and I'll take care of you. That's a promise."

He snorted. "Some comfort. If there's any taking care of to do, *I'm* supposed to do it for *you*."

I couldn't help it. I laughed out loud. "Oh, my God, Alec. That is just too chauvinistic for words! Tell me you're kidding." I looked at his expression and my amusement evaporated instantly. "You're not kidding. You're serious. I'm so sorry, but it really did strike me as funny. I'll tell you what. We'll each do what we can do for the other, will that work for you?"

I was so impressed with what character he had. I'd reflected upon this many times in private, far too many for my emotional comfort, and I'll probably continue to do so. What a fine man. He'd be quite a catch for some lucky woman. Whups! Let's not go there. I hoped he was mollified by my response. I think he was. At least he didn't look so hurt any more. Not much, or so I believed.

125

Later that afternoon, we went back for the initial download from the other machine. It was still in place and nobody seemed to have noticed it. Yet. I made my adjustments before we drove back into the city. Then I pulled out my cellphone and looked at it.

"What do you think? Should I call Fields and have him call Barnsfather? I'm less certain of his ability to do what I need him to do after the experience of having him call Casaday."

Alec looked thoughtful. "Go ahead. And have him call Mouleton too. You've still got his cellphone, right?" I nodded. "It may not be as good as having his line tapped, but you know by now that he is likely to be on his computer at seven in the evening. That's only nine where Fields lives. If he calls then, and you can certainly tell him you need him to at that time, then even if he's on the landline, you'll probably hear Mouleton's end of the conversation over the cell. And if we're lucky, he'll talk to himself about it. And what he's going to do about it, if anything."

I nodded. He was right, as usual.

It was a trickier call than the last one. I tried to stress that Fields had to be stronger on his calls without letting him know that I had tapped Casaday's phone and had listened to his earlier call. I think I managed it well. I certainly hoped I had. I knew Fields had come to me, and if I didn't know what he was playing at, I at least believed that he needed me. Or wanted me to think that. But I still felt a bit...humble, I guess, about talking to him. I kept that feeling firmly in check. It wasn't going to do me any good.

Since we were already in Santa Fe, we waited around for a couple of hours so I could take a quick download from my unit before heading back to Albuquerque. Strolling around the old town was fascinating; it's something like the oldest state capitol city in the country. Business called, though, and I went back to work. I hesitated to trigger the

126

replay, but finally started it before we began the real descent into the lowlands.

If nothing else, I did have a clean recording. Fields still didn't sound all that strong, but he did a bit better than he had with Casaday. Just a bit. Barnsfather seemed to be puzzled by getting the call at all. I filed that away for future consideration. But like with Casaday, there was absolutely no reaction after the call. Alec glanced at me as he took the sweeping curves on the highway going down to Albuquerque.

When we replayed the cellphone tap from Mouleton, once we were back in our room, it was a lot more difficult to make out what Fields had said. He'd called on the landline, as he'd said he didn't have Mouleton's cell number, and I didn't feel I could safely give it to him. Damn. But at least Mouleton's cell was nearby and we could get one side of the conversation clear as a bell. Half a loaf and all that. After he hung up, though, something quite different happened. He started typing. Not frantically, but steadily for maybe five minutes. I didn't time it, but I could hear the clacking of his keyboard. And he wasn't talking to himself. This worried me. Or excited me; it all depended on how I looked at it. The most interesting part was that we finally seemed to have some sort of reaction. The least interesting part, the part that was most frustrating, was that he wasn't talking to himself and I had no handle on his email. In his case, of course, I wouldn't have even if my unit had still been there, but this made it doubly troublesome.

Now I had to hack into his computer and see if I could find out what he was sending. Damn! But if there were one certainty, it was that I didn't want to do it from here. I'd much rather do it in some nice, anonymous wi-fi hotspot where I could be long gone before anyone noticed what I had done. Not here, where there were, at best, a limited number of possible people who could have done such a thing if it were ever traced back. Not on my cellular Internet connection either, where it was obviously me doing it. Which meant I was done for the night. I got up from where we were sitting hunched over the laptop and stretched.

"Screw coffee. Where's that bottle of Scotch? I need a drink."

Wordlessly, Alec retrieved the bottle and poured for both of us. Stiff ones. As we sipped, I thought furiously. And to no avail.

"Okay, that's two definitely down with nothing to show and one possible." I swirled the liquor in the glass to buy a couple moments of time. "If we find something worth tracing in Mouleton's email, then we have an entirely different trail to pursue. I'm sort of inclined to think there will be, if only because if there is a majority of the board opposed to Fields, then it has to be five people. Six could oust him directly, or at least get a removal motion before the entire Family, right?" Alec nodded. "What are the odds that we'd check three at random and only find all three who weren't involved?"

Alec took a long sip before responding. "Essentially zip." Another pull at his drink. "You're right. It beggars belief that the first three we'd check would be the only three who are clean, but it also beggars belief that under the Family setup, less than five of the board, or at the very least four, would be plotting anything. That argues strongly that Mouleton is at least one of our players. So where do we go from here?"

I took a moment to look into the bottom of my glass. Yep, it was still empty. Alec took the hint and removed it for refilling.

"Tomorrow we go to someplace with a wi-fi connection and see if I can hack into cousin Mouleton's computer. If he's using any sort of email program, then I may be able to lift a copy of the email he sent this evening. If he's using hotmail or anything like that, he may be saving copies of sent messages. If not, then I'll have to see what I can find by poking around his files. And I'll have to snatch it quickly before he notices that somebody is snooping around his machine, so I'm going to get a copy of everything he's created on his machine from six p.m. tonight to about midnight."

Alec looked at me over the rim of his glass. "That isn't exactly legal either, is it?"

I waved his concerns away. "I strongly doubt it. But once again, if you've got any better ideas, I'm all ears. Until then, this looks like what I have to do. I leave as few tracks as I know how, and I'm in and out as fast as possible. You're going to call cousin Mouleton in the morning and lure him out of the house, or at least away from his computer. No, I don't know how. We can sleep on that. But I need him away from the machine for a while."

Alec shook his head. "I don't know why I concern myself with such things. I guess I'm just an old fuddy-duddy."

I laughed, not unkindly.

The next morning after breakfast, I found Mouleton's email address and set up my programs on the laptop. All I had to do was get within range of a wireless hotspot, log onto the net, and punch a short series of buttons. The software would do the rest while I sat tight for three to five minutes. It took me about two hours to set it up the way I wanted it.

Luckily, finding hotspots is becoming easier and easier. A number of coffee shops, cafes and such all around Albuquerque advertised their connectivity. What I was going to do wasn't exactly what they had in mind. It was almost harder to find a table where I could set up the laptop without showing the screen to passers by than it was to find a hotspot in the first place. Then it was Alec's turn.

We'd spent much of the morning while I was working tossing back and forth different ways to get cousin Mouleton away from his computer, but every one we'd found had some serious problems. Luring him away from the house was probably out of the question. Not only would it be harder, but it could arouse suspicions I really didn't want to raise. Finally we settled on one that still seemed to be a stretch, but with any luck, it might work and shouldn't set off too many internal alarms. Or not until later anyway. It all depended on how good an actor Alec was.

Hopefully the background noise wouldn't ruin everything. Alec dialed Mouleton's landline and I tapped into the cell connection. I could have listened on earbuds, but decided to pass; I'd settle for listening to Alec's side of the conversation. Faintly, I could hear the phone ringing and then Mouleton picked it up.

"Good afternoon, sir. Is this Roger Mouleton?" After making sure he had the right party, Alec proceeded to set the hook, such as it was. "Sir, according to our records, you have a particular toilet installed in your home..." He rustled some paper near the phone for a few seconds. "Here it is. According to our records, you have a Kohler WetJet toilet installed in one of your bathrooms. Sir, we are urgently recalling all those toilets. We've had reports of reverse flushing." Pause. "Sir, that is what our records show. Would it be possible for you to check for me? If our records are in error, I'll gladly apologize for wasting your time, but it's vital for our customer service that we replace all the toilets as soon as we can locate them... That's right, sir, reverse flushing...Oh, you are correct, sir, that is a major problem. Just think if it should happen while your wife is...Oh, definitely, sir. Without question...No, sir, you probably wouldn't hear the end of it. Well, sir, if you could check your house for any toilets labeled with our name, I can describe the offending unit and if that is indeed what you have, then we can schedule you for immediate

130

replacement. I have a slot open late tomorrow afternoon...Yes, that's right, after three p.m...Oh, very good, sir, but no, we're not the cable company. We can schedule this in much less than a six-hour block."

I wanted to snicker in the worst way. But I could hear the chair creak and imagine the footsteps as cousin Mouleton got up from his chair and walked away from the computer. I hit my buttons and waited.

Mouleton must have been on a cordless phone, because Alec kept up a stream of patter almost non-stop. I was so proud of him I could have...well, I could have kissed him. When we were done, that was exactly what I'd do. He kept Mouleton occupied for eight minutes before concluding that, "Well, sir, then I shall have to correct our records. I simply cannot believe that we could have made such a mistake. You're sure that every single one of your toilets is an American Standard?...Oh, no, sir, I'm not doubting you at all. I'm simply at a complete loss to understand how our records...Well, sir, I certainly thank you for your effort on our behalf and I, uh, I wish you luck with your plumbing... Thank you, sir, and good day to you." At that, he snapped his phone shut, leaned back in his chair and simply closed his eyes. My program had been finished for four minutes.

"Oh, you magnificent man, you." It certainly couldn't hurt to build him up a bit, could it? "You were absolutely wonderful. Does he suspect anything do you think? And, 'I wish you luck with your plumbing'?" I snickered out loud. It wasn't quite as bad as giggling.

Alec shook his head and opened his eyes. "No, I don't think so. He seems like a very accommodating fellow. I was sure glad that he didn't have any Kohler toilets, though. I'd have had to make sure that the one I was looking for was of a very different design." Then he sighed.

I got up to get both of us some fresh coffee before seeing what my software had retrieved.

131

It took me longer to figure out what he'd been doing after his phone call from Fields last night than it had taken to get it off of his machine in the first place, but I finally located it. Apparently, Mouleton was busy writing a novel. He had written part of what he'd labeled as Chapter 4 minutes after he and Fields had ended their phone call. I skimmed what he'd written and concluded that he needed a good editor, or at least an extensive rewrite. But I've only done Daddy's stuff. What do I know? Alec was bemused by it.

We were almost halfway back to the B&B before Alec spoke again. "So we're skunked once more. What now? Are we going to keep going?"

"You bet we are. I'm tired and frustrated, but I'm not a quitter, most especially not now." I nodded slowly. "I still don't see that I have any other options. I can't simply brace Fields and demand to know what's going on. Well, I suppose I *could*, but before I can do that, I think I have to check all of them out and find zilch. Unless something else changes, I figure I'm locked into this...this...wild goose chase."

I hated to drive back up to Santa Fe again after suppertime, but there was no need to leave that unit in place any longer, and in case somebody might take an interest in it, I really didn't want to lose another one. I especially didn't want to have to touch base back in Tucson before heading to Denver when we were better than halfway there already. Once again it was well after midnight before we fell into our respective beds exhausted, and like the night before, I have no idea which of us fell asleep first.

We were pulling out for Denver the next morning when there was a sharp report, accompanied by the passenger-side window, *my* window, fracturing into a spiderweb of cracks. I shifted the transmission into park, almost stalling the motor, and we both rolled out through the driver's door. I literally vaulted the console and if Alec hadn't gotten out as fast as he did, I'd probably have gone right over him. Or wedged both of us in the door, which would have been a major problem. I hit the ground in a tuck and roll and came up with my Kahr in my hand, scanning for the shooter. I presumed Alec was doing the same behind me. When nothing was evident, we duckwalked around the car to check the rest of our surroundings. Still nothing. When we calmed down a bit, we stood up and looked at the window. Completely cracked, but with a deep pockmark, not a hole. A frangible bullet apparently, designed to break up on impact with the target, in this case my window glass, and not penetrate. And judging from the angle of the indentation, which was deeper toward the windshield, carefully aimed to miss both of us even if it had gone through. Another warning, in other words, not a serious attempt. Somebody tell my heart that it doesn't have to race like this when whoever is doing this isn't *really* trying to kill me. Please?

* * * *

TO: D
FROM: HB
Youngston completed investigation of board member Mouleton despite best efforts under Plan B. Continuing to exert best efforts under Plan B. Youngston and Trevethen completed investigation of board member Barnsfather and appear to be increasingly puzzled by lack of any positive reaction from board members investigated so far. Youngston and Trevethen proceeding to Denver to investigate board member Morristone.

TO: HB
FROM: D
Matters are proceeding according to plans and expectations. You are doing very well. Continue with Plan B.

Chapter 11

We pulled into Denver approaching suppertime the next day. Even when you pay to put a rush on it, replacing a car window takes a certain amount of time. I know I was on the clock even when I was sitting and waiting for the car to get fixed, but it was annoying to say the least. A certain amount of time, of course, was spent wondering what sort of nasty surprise was going to be coming next. Other than the incredible amount of growth the greater Denver area had posted since the last time I was back, that is. That wasn't too nasty, but my word, it's grown. From what I could see as we drove in, Denver was going to hit Castle Rock one of these days. The growth on the southern end, say around Highlands Ranch and south of the Tech Center, had to be seen to be believed.

If there was one thing we could safely conclude about the places where we'd been staying, it was that going to little off-the-beaten-track bed and breakfast places certainly gave us no assurance that we'd be harder to find. That, combined with the comparatively late hour we arrived, made us figure we might as well hit a motel. There are a bunch of them on Colorado Boulevard from around Cherry Creek south. We got rooms at a likely looking one and dumped our bags.

"Come on. Let's leave these in our rooms and grab dinner. I know just the place."

Alec looked like he was ready to crash right now, but he gamely asked whether it was anywhere nearby. I had to tell him it was all the way across town, but well worth the trip. He dragged himself up.

"You know the town, you know the way. You're driving. Mind if I snooze?"

I laughed. "Do whatever you'd like. Let's go."

I got quite a shock when I walked in. They'd expanded like mad since the last time I was there. I was thrilled for them; they used to have a single storefront with about ten or twelve tables and a line stretching down the shop fronts next door, regardless of the weather. That, at least, was fairly decent at the moment, if you weren't a convinced desert dweller like me. Personally, I thought it was chilly. They looked like they had doubled their space and now had around twenty tables with a reasonable amount of room to wait inside.

If the food—marvelous Italian—was still as good as it had been, it looked like a win-win situation to me. We went up to the hostess and gave her our names. Probably about twenty minutes, she told us. I got quite a different shock as I looked around the room before sitting down to wait, and I wasn't alone. Daddy was seated at one of the tables at the rear, and he'd seen me too. He smiled and waved, motioned us over. I shook my head sharply. *She* was there with him. Damn it, he should know better. I turned to Alec.

"You remember I told you about my father? See the fellow in the Hawaiian shirt in the back of the restaurant waving? That's him."

Alec peered over my shoulder. "You mean the one coming up here? He's motioning us to come on."

I went rigid. "No! I am *not* eating with *her*. No way, no how. I will *not* sit at the same table. Preferably not in the same room." I grabbed his arm. "Come on." I was too late.

"Amy! What a wonderful surprise! What brings you to town? Come sit with us. We've got two extra seats and we haven't even ordered yet. Who's this with you? Should I know him?" Daddy turned to Alec. "Hi. I'm Amy's father, Colin Youngston." He stuck out his hand.

What was Alec to do? He shook Daddy's hand. I grabbed Alec's arm again before he could speak. "Excuse me, Daddy. We're just leaving."

He seemed completely at sea. "But, Amy...you can't. We'd love to have you—" Then it dawned on him. I could see comprehension come over him as he understood what was going on. "Baby, it's not her. It's an old friend of yours. Come on. Please?" When I still hesitated, he took my arm. Lightly. "Please? Trust me."

I turned toward his table and saw his companion had turned in her seat to see what was going on. I was stunned to see it was Becky's mom. Well, he was right, she is an old friend. And relative too, naturally. Of course we'd eat with them. Aunt Lori was standing by the time we got to the table. After a quick hug, I made introductions all around. Daddy seemed impressed by Alec, especially after confirming that this was the same Alec I'd studied with through law school. Aunt Lori—Dr. Swan, like Becky, except that she was an MD, for Alec's benefit, until she told him to call her Lori, and that took her about thirty seconds—seemed to know about him already. Interesting. I'll bet Becky's been telling tales out of school.

"Daddy, I'm really sorry about causing a scene. I thought you were eating with *her*."

"Not to worry, baby. I know. It's not a problem. Anyway, she and I probably won't be together much longer. Assuming she's still there when I get home. If I'm lucky, she won't be. It's just the way things go, I suppose."

I made a wry face. "You'll understand if I don't say I'm sorry."

"And I could say I'm sorry the two of you never got along better. But..."

I could see that this wasn't going to get any better as a conversational topic. Aunt Lori rescued us.

"So what are the two of you doing here? Are you an item now? I thought you were simply good friends from what Becky's told me."

136

Yep, Becky had been talking. Oh, well, she was entitled. It was certainly no problem for me if Aunt Lori knew about Alec.

"Well, that much is true. We're not an item. Truth to tell, I'm on a job." I leaned in and spoke more quietly. "It's a Family investigation given to me by the CEO himself." Daddy and Aunt Lori looked at each other, then at Alec, before looking back at me with a certain amount of shock. I kept my voice low. "He's my lawyer, guys. I hired him *as my lawyer* to help me with this investigation. I needed help. It's too big for me to handle alone. Yes, he knows. I had to tell him everything about it as part of my briefing. It's all *confidential*. He can't tell anyone else. Okay? I mean, I couldn't exactly ask Becky to help me. If nothing else, somebody has to watch the dogs. And she has patients. What other choice did I have?" Somehow, I wish they looked like they had more confidence in my judgment. Oh, well. That seemed to throw the conversation for a loop for quite a while. Again. Damn.

Alec finally broke the strained silence when he asked Daddy why the Hawaiian shirt in Denver in March? Daddy hesitated a moment before responding that it kept him from printing. Alec didn't ask for a clarification, but then, he understood. He and I had discussed printing ever since he first knew I carried concealed weapons. Aunt Lori spoke up, though.

"What do you mean, Colin? What's 'printing'?"

Daddy leaned forward and spoke quietly. I was a little impressed in spite of myself; his voice normally carries very well. Too well.

"When you're carrying a concealed weapon and it shows by its outline through whatever you have over it. That's 'printing'. The design of this shirt breaks up the possible outline. Wearing it out like this also makes it easier to get to the piece should that be needed."

After that the conversation seemed to flow better, even if it avoided talking about much of any consequence. It did, though, give us a topic we could milk for quite a while. Aunt Lori knew, at least intellectually, that Daddy and I went armed as a matter of course, but we wound up discussing theories of going armed, self-protection, police effectiveness, the gun store around the corner in this very shopping plaza, and so on. Like I said, nothing of any real consequence.

We were driving back across town when Alec finally said, "Correct me if I'm wrong, but I don't think they really approved of your telling me about the Family."

What could I say? "Yeah." Then I got my back up. "Damn it, I can make my own choices here. I'm an adult, and anyway, it's my responsibility, not theirs. I never asked for their help or their approval."

He seemed amused. "The first I'd agree with. The second, well, you sort of did ask for that, I thought. Didn't get it, for what that may be worth. Not that it matters. But if nothing else, trust me, I now have a much better appreciation for what you faced back when you said that if you told me, you'd have to either marry me or kill me. Jeez."

I had to chuckle. "Hey, I don't think either of us knew what we were getting into here, that front included. Personally, I want to get back to my room. I want to do my exercises, have a nice hot bath, then try to catch another chapter in my Forex book before I fall asleep. Or fall asleep during the chapter. It's awfully dry stuff."

Alec seemed like he wanted to say something, but then didn't. What was that about? I turned my thoughts back to my learning curve. I was starting, I hoped, to get on top of it, at least in a very general sense. I could discuss a lot of investment choices and areas with what at least sounded like a lot of knowledge, if in a not too detailed fashion yet. I understood worlds more than I had back when Raymond

Escarton Fields had walked into my office—what, only about six weeks ago? No, more like seven by this point. By now, I was probably in about the league he'd been in at fifteen or so. Maybe.

I heard a sound, glanced over to see that Alec had drifted off. He didn't wake up until I turned into the motel parking lot from Colorado Boulevard.

Breakfast the next morning was interesting. I had one hell of a time convincing the waitress that I really, honestly wanted salsa and cheese on my oatmeal instead of brown sugar and milk. Brown sugar and milk? Simply awful. Kiddie food, in fact. The waitress had to consult the manager to see whether she could even do that, even though there were omelets with salsa and cheese on the menu. I was strongly tempted to order the oatmeal *and* the omelet, everything on the side, and just leave the omelet. Being able to bill everything through to the client and know he'd pay it promptly, all of it, is *so* nice. But instead, I just waited until the manager apparently reminded her that the customer was always right, and anyway, it was my stomach, not hers. Such an ordeal! And for nothing more than oatmeal.

Afterward, we sat over some very average coffee—free refills—and planned out our day. I knew of the house—mansion—where William Morristone lived. Had he owned it when I lived in Denver? I couldn't recall, and I may not have known in the first place. I'd been gone for the best part of twenty years, other than a very few visits, the last being when Becky and I had been back for her father's funeral several years ago. We had flown in together then. I really missed her father. He'd always been more than willing to treat Becky and me as sisters. Whenever I was at their house at dinnertime, Uncle Jack was actually glad that I was there and always offered me a place at the table or even just set one for me without bothering to offer, probably to show that I was a member of their family as well. Not to disrespect Aunt Lori in any way, it was just that Becky's father was the one who did most of the cooking in their home. Aunt Lori used to say she could burn water—not true. She could follow a recipe quite well, although her cooking wasn't exactly inspired. Daddy never treated Becky that way. Oh, she ate at our house plenty often, but I always had to arrange it, except when Carol lived with us. But again, another story, and not germane. I need to stop digressing. Tend to business, girl. Woolgather on your own time.

Anyway, cousin Morristone and his house...

Morristone himself had been one of the Silicon Valley whiz kids, so to speak, although he was hardly a kid. He'd been at the top end of the age range, or so it seemed to me, to qualify for that characterization. He made a bit of a name for himself in a relatively arcane area of electronics even by my standards, and he then left the active arena to become an analyst at a mid-sized mutual fund that specialized in technology stocks.

He'd done quite well at that, and shocked everyone in the industry, or so it seemed, when he announced his retirement at a time when he was riding quite high. I understood, of course; his retirement coincided with his election to the Family board. He was still doing very well indeed, just not in the public eye any more.

His house was known in the neighborhood as the von Richtofen mansion, at least among us kids. The original owner was actually some sort of relative of the Red Baron himself, and the house itself, built around a century and a quarter ago, is said to be modeled after the Richtofen castle in Germany. His wife is buried on a street corner not too far away with a perpetual light over her grave. Neat stuff, lots of back story there.

* * * *

TO: D
FROM: HB
Youngston and Trevethen have arrived in Denver. Met,
apparently by chance, with Youngston's father and Swan's
mother. Conversation not available. Will attempt to disrupt
investigation of board member Morristone.

TO: HB
FROM: D
I am sure that your efforts will not be degraded by the frustration
of your inability to disrupt the investigations. Continue
nevertheless with Plan B.

Chapter 12

I wasn't here to give a tour, or get one. I had a job to do. It was the kind of residential neighborhood where I could park the car a couple of blocks away and the two of us could walk, hand in hand around the neighborhood, coincidentally checking the street frontage of the property. Not one, but several phone pedestals in the immediate area, and no easy way to be sure which was the one I wanted.

This was hardly comparable to huge properties in fairly new neighborhoods. I'm sure the age of the house and the surrounding neighborhood were working against me, as well as the density of houses on the blocks around the mansion, most of which looked to be on hundred foot wide lots. Oh, well, difficulties exist to be overcome, right?

We went around again, petted and made friends with a couple of people's dogs in the process while I made some careful mental notes of pedestal positions and tagged them in my mind from the most likely to least likely. With only one unit, I couldn't double up to improve my chances of getting the right one first time out. One thing I noticed on our way by, it was hard to make out for certain through the trees and brush that grew just inside the walls, but it looked like there was a Fokker DR-1, brilliant red just like Manfred von Richtofen's own triplane, inside the grounds. It's got to be a replica, if only because there aren't any real ones still around as far as I know, and it can't have much of a runway in there, so I expect it's simply a display, or maybe a toy. Either way, cousin Morristone can afford it.

The neighborhood was quite dead late at night, although we had to wait until about one a.m. for the traffic to die down completely. Now as long as some cop didn't come by when I was out there working. I admit to being worried here. The pedestals were all on the grassy strip between the sidewalk and the street, right where you wouldn't expect to find a chunk of granite unless it was sunk halfway into the ground. I'd have been a lot happier if they'd been in un-landscaped areas. You can't have everything, although I still don't know why not.

We drove by the next afternoon to pick up my recordings. Finding a quiet church parking lot several blocks away to sit in while we listened to them, I was annoyed—make that *very* annoyed—to find that none of these lines were the ones I was looking for, that I *needed*. We drove back by the house on our way out, by the pedestal I'd figured was the next most likely. There was a cop writing out a ticket for some guy standing there. What was the ticket for? I can't help it. I'm just naturally a busybody, I guess. Certainly not for anything I could see, unless—yes! If that's his car, he's parked going the wrong way. That'll do it. I looked at him as we drove by, memorizing his face. Another habit of mine. It's been known to come in handy, once in a while. Most of the time it's just something I do.

There were times I was unhappy with this investigation, and there were other times I was *very* unhappy with it. At least the usual sort of investigation I did offered plenty to keep me busy. Even sitting in a car watching for someone to show up and be photographed was better than simply being at loose ends for hours. It did leave me ample opportunity to take care of my friends, though.

There was a very nice jewelry store in Cherry Creek— so amazing how that place had changed since I lived there—that had the most interesting pair of butterfly wings cut from multicolored tourmaline. I had the jeweler make them into a pin for Becky. It was fairly expensive, especially getting it done quickly, but she'd done some real above-and-beyond-the-call-of-duty work with the dogs while we were gone and would be doing more before this was all said and done. Besides, she loves butterflies and custom jewelry. She deserves it. I also got some special

143

cookies for Bruno and Sasha. Not at the same shop; they really weren't dogs who would appreciate bling. Something more appealing to their appetites was likely to be a lot more to their taste, no pun intended.

Alec didn't look as though he was thrilled at the idea of another late night. Too bad. We can sleep late on this particular job, but when the work needs to be done, that's that. Not that I didn't feel much the same way, I simply didn't talk about it or give in to it. There was a certain amount of luck this time. I saw the cop patrolling his way through the neighborhood while we were still moving, and he went on his way before we pulled over to park. Unhooking the unit is faster than putting it in. I designed it so that I can take all the connectors with one quick yank. The two pedestals were only a fairly short distance apart, so I slunk, camouflaged by the dark, from one to the next and went into my crouch to set up the unit again. No surprises, no problems, and we were back in our rooms before two o'clock.

The same waitress was on duty when we walked into the coffee shop the next morning. I took pity on her and simply ordered the omelet. Was it me or did she look appreciative? At least, as I found out when we went by to retrieve the recordings, this time, I had the correct pedestal. And I had the DSL tones, so I was golden. I already had cousin Morristone's cellphone loaded with my special software, so I was all ready to go. A phone call to Fields and once again my traps were set. I waited.

And once again, Fields didn't take as strong a tack on the phone as I would have liked. What would it take for him to be really assertive with these people? Would I have to spell out for him what I was doing? Not a good idea. In addition to what I could call professional secrets, there are some very good reasons not to put out explicit statements that one is freely breaking the law. I also figured that quoting what he'd said would tell him what I was doing

144

just as certainly as if I gave him chapter and verse. Why wasn't he listening to me? He hired me to be in charge of his case, dammit. I filed these thoughts in the nearer recesses of my mind. If nothing else, I didn't want them getting lost in the pile of imaginary sticky notes littering the bottom of it.

At the same time, cousin Morristone didn't seem in the least concerned about being turned down. He didn't write, he didn't call, he didn't talk to himself. He just took it in stride and went back to whatever he was doing, which I couldn't make out from nothing but a soundtrack. Probably reading.

We adjourned to a small coffee shop on Colorado Boulevard, a little ways south of Alameda. The weather didn't look promising, or rather, knowing Denver weather from experience, it did, but we weren't going to like what it was promising, so we sat inside. Our conversation was a bit circumscribed, but by now there really wasn't much that needed detailing anyway. We got a table by the window and put our heads together.

"Okay, another one down. And I do mean down. We've struck out on four out of four. So, what's going on? Are we really dealing with just one or two board members? Or is something else going on that we're entirely ignorant of?"

Alec hesitated for quite a while before responding. "Frankly, I don't know anymore. I'm just as much at a loss here as you are. Do we keep going?"

"I still don't see that I've any choice at this point." Aimlessly, I doodled on the tabletop with my fingertip. What *was* going on here? It wasn't making any sense, which still told me first and foremost that I didn't have the right angle to look at the problem. When it started to make sense, then I would know I was on the right track. Until then, I'll keep going. What other choice do I have?

Alec's lips were turned in. I knew him; that was the most dependable sign that his mind was working hard.

145

"If it were up to me, I'd say we're done here. I don't want to keep beating our heads against the wall like this. Let's go home and get Becky involved. She's got some distance from this. Maybe she can see something that we're just too close to see."

I shrugged. "Might as well. You're certainly right about beating our heads against the wall." I stood up. "Come on. Let's go." Outside, just as I'd expected, there were snowflakes beginning to fall. Oh, joy. In March? Thank you, God for reminding me why I live in Tucson now.

There was about an inch on the grass and more falling heavily by the time we went to retrieve my unit. The roads were just sloppy. It was a heavy wet snow and I was soaked to the skin by the time I got to the pedestal. Black fleece probably wasn't the best camouflage I could have chosen for the weather, but it was what I had. Opening the pedestal, I quickly yanked my wires loose. Then I pulled the wire harness the other way and it came loose in my hand. What was this crap? I swept the snow away behind the pedestal. My unit was gone! Shit! I took a few moments to sweep around the pedestal. No luck. I risked a quick look with my dim red flashlight, still nothing. Cursing, I stood up and walked back to the car. Alec was surprised when I got into the front seat with only the wire harness.

"Something wrong?" He was pulling away from the curb with his lights off; he turned them on once we were in the traffic lane.

"My unit's gone. *Again.* Shit!" I was one unhappy camper, I can tell you.

Alec said nothing for a while. "Well, at least it happened now instead of in Albuquerque. I mean, we're done here, right? Even if we still had the unit?"

I guess he was right to see the bright side, such as it was. "Oh, hell. Let's go back and get a good night's sleep. I don't know about you, but I am just about dead on my feet.

Besides, you're probably right. At least there was no cop waiting for us here."

He snorted.

The next morning, all of my nerves were on edge as we started the car. Nothing happened, except that the car ran like a top. Nothing out of the ordinary. When was the shoe going to drop? And what would it be?

Past experience suggested we weren't going to like it when it happened.

* * * *

TO: D
FROM: HB
Removed Youngston's surveillance equipment, but too late to disrupt investigation of board member Morristone. Increasing efforts in accordance with Plan B. Will intercept on road outside Denver.

TO: HB
FROM: D
Excellent. Continue with Plan B.

Chapter 13

The snow must have stopped around six a.m. or so. We didn't get out of Denver until closer to eight. The streets in the city were for the most part simply wet and sloppy. There were a few icy patches on I-25 south of the city at higher altitude where the highway went through the pines, but there was more than enough vehicle traffic to have pretty well cleared off the roadway itself. Even then, the worst spots in the traffic lanes were merely wet, not snowy.

The trip was going smoothly until someplace south of Castle Rock. Alec was driving. He suddenly glanced into the mirror and said, "Uh-oh. Hang on. This could get interesting."

There was a horrid jolt as the pickup behind us slammed into our rear bumper. At least I hoped it was the bumper. It might have been the body; that truck looked awfully high.

"What the hell was that?" I was louder than I needed to be.

"Hang on. Here he comes again."

How could Alec sound so calm when all hell was breaking loose? Wham! And again the entire car shook. And blam! There were cars around us honking their horns, and although I tried to see who was doing this, every time I tried to turn in my seat, we were being hit again. I couldn't begin to say how long it went on, or how many times we were hit, but suddenly the pickup just swerved into the next traffic lane and roared off. All I could see was a muddy smudge where the plate should be. The only thing I could tell was that it was a jacked-up white pickup with two men in it wearing sunglasses.

Alec slowed down and steered us onto the shoulder. Traffic accidents—anything going wrong in a car—are a major weakness of mine; it's probably got to do with losing

Mom in one. At any rate, I unbuckled, opened the door and tried to get out. I couldn't make my legs obey. When I was finally able to move, I got my feet on the ground, only to find that my legs were shaking so much it was all I could do to stay upright holding onto the car. Alec came around the car to find me standing there, trembling like an aspen leaf in the wind. He wrapped his arms around me and held me without speaking until I could stop shaking. He murmured soft noises into my ear, but that was all.

Dear, unflappable Alec! I was more like a terrified animal than a rational human being for a bit. And furious to boot, which is an interesting combination. I tried, not very hard, to shake his hands off. He held on. Finally, I thought I had myself together again.

"Okay, I can make it now. Thank you, dear." I kissed his cheek. "Let me go see what the car's like."

"You're not going to like it."

I looked at him sourly. "I already don't like it. But I need to see the damage." I wasn't really surprised to see that the entire lower tailgate below the window was a mess, as were the ends of the bumper where it turned upward. The taillight lenses were all broken, although the light units looked like they'd just been pushed in and might still work. Just for grins, I tried the latch. The upper tailgate with the window opened fine. The lower part wouldn't move. Gee, big surprise. Alec and I checked the lights before going further into the damage, and I was right, they still worked.

As I was standing there with my hands on my hips, trying to find words that would express how I felt, a Colorado Highway Patrol cruiser pulled up behind us. The cop who got out was taller than Alec, at least as broad, and looked like he was trying to be helpful. Little did he know what he was intruding upon.

"Is there a problem here?"

Well, no, officer, I just decided to trash the back of my car for fun.

Alec stepped in. Thank God. I was not at my best. "We've just had a...bit of a problem."

The cop appeared understanding in a professional sort of way. Yeah, sure, buddy.

"So I see. May I be of assistance? And while I'm at it, could I please see your license, registration and proof of insurance?"

Alec stepped forward, carefully holding his hands clear of his body. "Officer, I need to inform you that we are both armed under Arizona concealed weapons permits, which I understand Colorado recognizes."

Oh, thrills, here we go again. At least this cop wasn't suspicious that we'd been involved in perpetrating some sort of skullduggery. I've always loved that word. Right now it seemed appropriate—for our adversaries' actions, not ours. He was probably just as cautious as the cop in Los Ranchos, but less immediately concerned with us. I was far too aggravated about my car to get too far into the issue with the cop. Damn. I didn't want to leave this car in the body shop. I hadn't wanted to do that even before all this crap started on general principles. Now that we'd established that things could happen when it was left unattended, I got even more uncomfortable about leaving it. Was I paranoid? Sure. Did I have good reason? You betcha. No help for that, I guess.

We'd finally driven off and were almost into Colorado Springs before I realized that I'd never given the cop my license and CCW. I looked at Alec for a long moment before mentioning it.

"No, you didn't. I retrieved them from your wallet for him. I don't think he wanted to disturb you more than you already were. A very nice fellow. He even offered to call us a tow if we needed one. I just figured that since the car was completely driveable, we were better off getting home to have it taken care of there rather than spending time in the Springs, or back in Denver."

"And my gun?"

"Well, he never completely took his eyes off you, but since you didn't seem to be paying any attention to him, and you checked out from your license, I think he decided I could take care of matters." He hesitated. "I have to admit to a bit of a lie. I told him I was your husband."

I snorted. "Killing you would have been simpler." He just laughed. At that moment, I could have very cheerfully killed him. The feeling passed almost instantly. Oh, God, what would I have done without him? Crazy armed woman on the interstate! Lovely, just lovely. Thank you, Alec. I can always depend on you, can't I? Don't say that out loud. In fact, stop thinking it. Stuff it back into the depths of your mind where it came from. I pride myself on not being dependent on anyone. I never view myself as a needy person. Utterly and completely self-reliant, that's me. Sometimes I slip. Sometimes I lie.

We got off the freeway in Colorado Springs and picked up some red tape to function as temporary taillight lenses before stopping at a handy coffee shop. Remember Juan Valdez, the supposed coffee grower? I'm sure that we were financing a whole fleet of burros for him. Personally, I needed something to help calm me down. Some part of me was absolutely convinced that the only thing that made this case move forward was coffee. I should buy some stock. The rational part of my mind began listing different investment types by company for investing in coffee. I turned it off by sheer force of will. Not *now*, you little idiot! By the time we left, I was up to driving for a while. I finally broke the very lengthy silence somewhere around Trinidad. With my usual brilliance, I opened the conversation.

"So now what?"

I think Alec was almost asleep. He responded with an equally brilliant reply. "Huh?"

"Well, we've now checked out four board members and lost two units in the process. But if any of them are involved in any dirty deals in this...this...whatever the hell it is, frankly, I'll eat my hat."

"You don't wear hats," he said and I slapped his leg. "Okay, I'll try to be serious. You're right. At the very least, I would think *one* of them should have acted, or responded, or done *something*, if there was anything underhanded going on. At the same time, I feel entirely safe in saying that there *is* certainly *something* going on here, if only because of what's been done to you. And me, although I tend to doubt that I'm the target here. I'd be quite perturbed if anything happened to you. To either of us."

I had to chuckle. "Yeah. Me, too."

"In all honesty, I'm really at a loss for ideas at this point. I suppose it's entirely possible that only one or two of the board members are involved in some sort of shady business. But damn it, it just wouldn't make any sense based on what I know of the organization of the Family."

"No, it wouldn't. It *doesn't*. So what are we left with? Either we're not seeing this from the right angle, because if we were, it *would* make sense in some fashion, or we are, but we can't see the forest for the trees, to jump into a new metaphor. Which is it?"

Alec pursed his lips. "Frankly, I have no idea. And I'm fresh out of suggestions as well. You want to get a different viewpoint. Like I said in Denver, the only person we can ask is Becky."

I thought that one over for a moment. I did have her presents, and we needed to get the dogs. They wouldn't really enjoy having to get in through the back seat, but what the hell, it wasn't like I had any choice to offer them. Alec seemed to be reading my mind.

"Let's keep going. We can stop for an early supper in Albuquerque and I'll drive from there. We should be home sometime in the wee hours. We'll call her in the morning, drop off your car at the body shop, and we'll go get the

152

dogs in my car tomorrow evening. That'll save her a trip to our part of town."

"Not much of a trip," I reminded him. "She usually takes the dogs to her office with her, and her office is closer to our houses than it is to hers."

"Yeah. Well, we'll leave it up to her, then."

"Deal. Except I'll call her this evening while we're on the road."

With the dearth of ideas, we didn't have a lot to talk about for the rest of the trip. Whoever was driving listened to radio the rest of the way without conversation. I'm afraid I let Alec do most of the driving while I slept. Probably recovering from some of the stress, though not enough. Still very conscious of Alec's proximity. Too much. Think about something else. Please.

I, for one, was getting sick and tired of the walk to the coffee shop in the evening for our discussions. I could make coffee myself, I had plenty of dog treats—way too many, in fact—and the only thing we didn't have was some assurance of privacy.

Thinking about going up to Becky's had given me an idea. She has one of these big Soleri wind-bells at the edge of her patio. Huge bell, multiple clappers, very pretty tones. Lovely, at least if you like skeletons. The thing looks like it's hanging from a backbone complete with ribs. I suppose some people like that sort of thing. Actually, I know they do. Becky for one, since she seemed quite miffed the one time I mentioned the resemblance to her.

After we dropped my car off, I spent two hours having Alec run me around town while I bought a bunch of wind chimes: big ones, little ones, multiple pipe ones, even a nice Soleri that I ran across, smaller and without a backbone attached. I even found one huge bell that had been made out of some kind of tank: acetylene, oxygen, whatever. I don't know. But it was huge. Alec and I spent another couple of hours hanging them all around my patio.

153

Believe me, they made one hell of a cacophony. Exactly what I wanted. After we had everything hung—the tank was a real challenge. It took one of us to hold it up while the other drove in the lag bolts—I just stood on the patio and grinned as a breeze blew and it became almost impossible to hear myself think. Perfect!

Sasha was very glad to see us. Bruno's attitude was more 'oh, it's you. Hi.' I presumed that meant he'd had a good time with Becky. She loved her Santa Fe T-shirt, and there were multiple 'Oh, you shouldn't have' over the butterfly pin, even worse than the pin from Sedona. I reminded her of everything she did for us and that I damn well should have. Shortly after that, she turned to Alec and said, "My mom likes you. She says she thinks you're a good influence." She nodded her head in my direction.

Alec rolled his eyes and groaned. "That sounds like an epitaph. Here lies Alexander Trevethen. He was a good influence." We both laughed.

I looked at Becky. "I see you've been talking to your Mom about Alec."

Her professional face suddenly appeared, the one that could have made her a superb poker player. "Should I not have? Would you prefer that I didn't?"

I smiled. "Oh, no, it's fine. I'm just amused, that's all." She seemed skeptical.

After supper, I made a large pot of coffee and led the way outside. Becky all but grabbed her ears as she stepped onto the patio.

"Amy, what on earth have you done?"

I proceeded beyond the patio to the chairs and table out on the dirt. It wasn't quite as noisy there. "Becky, you've got a white noise generator outside your office, in the waiting room." She nodded. "That's to keep anyone from overhearing what's said in the offices. This,"—I waved at the wind chimes—"is my white noise generator. I don't think any bug in the house or even on the patio is going to

154

be able to hear anything going on out here as long as there's even a little breeze." Maybe I'd overdone it. Just a little bit.

I think Alec muttered something about even us not being able to hear what was going on out there. I ignored him.

We'd told her over supper what had happened to us. There didn't seem to be any reason not to; whoever was bugging the house ought to know what they'd done, after all. And if there were two or more groups involved, well, then we were well and truly screwed anyway, bugs be damned. But we held off any substantive discussion about strategies, tactics and general ideas and plans until we were safely screened by all the wind chimes. A brilliant idea on my part, if I must say.

Before we could even start, a gust of wind stirred up the chimes. When the noise dropped to a level where it was merely difficult to hear each other, Becky looked at me and asked, "Amy, do you think you might have overdone it just a bit?"

I gave her my best patented innocent look. "Who? Moi?"

"Vous."

I shrugged. Some of them would have to come down before I went to bed. And I'll probably hear from the neighbors before long anyway. Becky went on.

"I may want to borrow Sasha from you next week. You recall hearing that some of my patients really like the dogs? Pet them, say hello to them religiously and so on?" I nodded. "One of them just lost her own dog a few days before her last session. When she came in, Sasha walked slowly to her even while I was telling her to stay. Then Sasha just sat down right by her side. The patient put her arms around Sasha and literally said nothing, simply cried her eyes out for her entire session, with Sasha just sitting there and occasionally licking her face. I guess it was an important thing for my patient, something she really had to go through. It was truly poignant, but I have to admit that I'd never really imagined Sasha as a therapy dog."

I had to smile. "Neither had I."

Then Becky added, "She must have been a very sweet puppy."

Alec looked at her sideways. "A sweet puppy? You mean Destructo, the Terrycloth Terrorist?" Becky looked shocked. He went on. "I don't remember the exact date, but it was when Sasha was a few months shy of a year. I came in early one Sunday morning, figuring to fix a nice breakfast before we watched the Sunday morning news, and I found Amy and Sasha sitting in the middle of the living room floor. It looked like a storm had dumped cloth bits and threads all round the room. Amy was holding Sasha by the collar with both hands and explaining forcefully to her that her hair was on the verge of being used to weave the next set of nice towels, and she wouldn't have any more use for it anyway, as her hide would be used to upholster something just before it was given to Goodwill. It seems that Sasha had gotten into the bathroom and removed all the towels and washcloths, taken them into the living room and proceeded to chew and shake them to bits. She managed to hit a few things with the bath towels, I suspect, but luckily, nothing breakable beyond a light bulb or two. I spent an hour or so that afternoon hanging a couple of towel bars and working on the bathroom door latch, making sure that it could be closed securely."

I was quite disgusted. It was not a nice memory. "And she so enjoyed herself doing it that all she did when I found out was sit there and grin hugely at me."

Becky looked at Alec. "Terrycloth terrorist?"

Alec lifted his cup in Sasha's direction. "Had to have been her. Bruno was lying in the kitchen out of the line of fire. He lifted his head when I stepped in, stared me for a moment, then laid his head back on his paws. He was *not* going to get in Amy's way. Smart fellow." Alec gave Bruno a rub to emphasize the remark.

Becky looked at me a bit reproachfully. "Amy, you never told me about that."

I shrugged. "You weren't here. You'd left for vacation the day before, and then you had a conference when you got home. I think it was three weeks before we got together again, and we had lots of other things to talk about by then. Besides, I was just so damn pissed when I thought of it that I didn't want to go through it again if I didn't have to."

* * * *

TO: D
FROM: HB
Increased efforts to disrupt Youngston's investigations according to Plan B. Made brief attempt to access Swan's residence for surveillance devices, but Swan was present and accompanied by Youngston's dogs, which reacted in a protective manner. Effort postponed for a later date. Targets, in particular Trevethen, appear to have concluded that danger from team's efforts is more apparent than actual. This will be changed to the best of our abilities, considering our instructions.

TO: HB
FROM: D
Excellent. Matters proceeding as expected. Continue with Plan B.

Chapter 14

"Oh, that reminds me," Becky responded. "Twice now, Bruno has lifted his head for one of my patients and kept it up for the entire session. The same patient, both times. Normally, he just stays in the corner behind where my patients sit and sleeps while they're there, or at least stays with his head down on his paws. But with this patient, both times, he kept his head up for the entire session, just staring at the patient."

Alec looked puzzled. I understood. "Drugs. Your patient was holding, or at least smelled of drugs. Not dope, but hard drugs, something like cocaine, heroin or meth. That's how he was trained to alert. As long as the person behaves, that's all he does. I didn't want a dog that would attack someone or even just bark at them simply because they were holding, but I wanted to know."

Becky looked thoughtful. "Actually, I don't believe I've ever heard him bark before last night. I had some man come to my door after supper, and when I opened the door, Bruno got in front of me and began barking at him in the most menacing manner. Sasha was beside me and also barking. The fellow said he was looking for an address, but he'd obviously come to the wrong house, excused himself and went back to his pickup."

Alec and I exchanged looks. "Pickup? Describe it."

"Oh, I don't know. Big white truck. Seemed higher than normal, and it looked like the front end had been banged up a bit."

I couldn't help it. "Shit. *Shit.*" I looked at Alec again. "It's them. Sure as God made little green apples." Alec was nodding, wearing a scowl on his face. Becky looked worried. I sighed. "All I can say is that you're probably safe, if only because they're after me. Or us. You should be entirely incidental to all of this crap. I hope."

Becky, now that she's a professional, is far too genteel to swear. Normally. I wasn't entirely surprised to hear her now.

"That son of a *bitch*! Pardon my French."

"Yep. That too."

Alec interrupted. "While I'm thinking of it, what was Bruno like as a puppy?"

I had my mouth open to speak, but Becky laughed. "He was a little devil! Amy and I were living in the house on Speedway, and when we were out, he'd pull over the hamper in the bedroom, pull out all of the contents and take Amy's underwear—never mine—to his bed and lie on it. He'd make quite a nest out of it."

I had to add my two cents worth. "He never did anything to them other than lie on them. No chewing, clawing or anything like that. Just smoosh them around and lie on them. I guess he simply wanted to feel closer to me."

Alec shook his head as he poured himself some more coffee. "Okay, all this is very nice, but I need to remember that we're here for a reason. This is our problem. We've now investigated half the board members. As I laid out for you ladies before we left on this trip, there is no reason to believe if what Fields claimed is actually going on, it is being done without the connivance of a clear majority of the board. In other words, at least five board members. Not that one or two members alone couldn't be doing it, but since they couldn't control the succession, it would seem to make no sense. None of the four we've checked out so far seem to be involved. That only leaves us four more, which we have figured is not enough. We have no idea where to go from here, other than to keep on doing what we've been doing and investigate the others, pointless as it may be, unless some break gives us a handle on the people who seem to be harassing us.

"But we were also considering that we might not be seeing the forest for the trees, that we're too close to the problem to see something important. That's where you come in, Becky. You've got more distance from the problem and you haven't really been threatened. Not, at least, as we have been. We wanted all three of us to put our heads together and see if we could come up with any better ideas, or any ideas at all. Now, before we get going, let me recap." He held up a hand before either of us could say anything. "Not to say that either of you have forgotten anything. This is just to make sure we're all on the same page." He held up a finger. "Raymond Fields"—Becky and I chorused, "Escarton!"—"came to see Amy and hired her, giving her an account of what was allegedly being done to him, by the board and by parties unknown, but presumably connected with one or more board members." He added another finger. "Fields has promptly paid all bills submitted to him and has not contested any of the charges, whether for hours or for expenses."

"That's right," I said. "Not one quibble at all."

Alec glanced at me and held up a third finger. "If, and I say again, *if* the corporation is being run in accordance with its articles and by-laws, and as we've been told it was being run before Fields took over, then the board members don't have the power or authority that Fields' account suggests they do. Of course, with the amount of money at stake, I tend to think that they are still observing every jot and tittle." A fourth finger. "The only way that board members can even begin to exercise sufficient power is with a majority of at least five to be acting in concert." His last finger. "Having put pressure individually on four board members so far, pressure which should have been, shall we say, at least reasonably persuasive at causing them to consult with whatever principals are behind them, if any, we have found none who did so, causing us to at least tentatively believe that none of those four are acting for any hidden principals. If so, that clearly obviates the possibility

160

of a majority of the board doing something underhanded and in concert with each other." He paused for a moment.

"That, I think, pretty well sums it up in broad strokes. There are certainly plenty of details, but none, I believe, which would add significant factors or change what I've said. To sum it up, the choices seem to be that Fields is giving Amy a straight story, he really has been getting the same treatment she is now getting and there is something very fishy going on, whether it's driven by board members or by some unknown outside party. Alternatively, he has sent her on a wild goose chase for reasons unknown, and just about everything he told her about what's happening to him is a lie. There is *no third choice*, at least none that I can imagine. Comments?"

I shook my head.

Becky merely nodded slowly. "Question? Are you sure that what you're doing with the board members is enough to make them do something? What if you're not putting enough pressure on them?"

Alec's lips turned in as I sat silently, thinking. What more could I do? Alec broke the silence.

"I don't know what else we could be doing. The only person who has the power to invest is Fields himself. He's the one who is calling the individual board members to tell them that he won't be investing as they're purportedly urging him to. Perhaps he could...no, he *definitely* could be more forceful about turning them down, but if they're acting for some other party, then simply being told that their efforts aren't going anywhere should be enough to get them to at least inform their principal and let him or her know so as to be able to make other plans. At the very least. And we can't exactly give Fields a script to follow here. We're really at his mercy for these phone calls. So I'm kind of at a loss as to how we could step up the pressure even if we wanted, just as I can't really see how what we're doing could fail to elicit *some* sort of a response

161

from some of them, even if not all of them, and we're getting absolutely none whatsoever."

"That's probably right." Becky was nodding slowly. "I agree that more pressure would be nice, but you're probably correct that the basic refusal should, I think, provoke at least some reaction. There's a piece missing here."

I spoke up. "At the risk of sounding insulting, which is not at all my intention, well, duh! Of *course*, there's a piece missing. Hell, the whole damn box for the puzzle is missing, which would at least show us what the puzzle should look like when we've got it all together. We're banging around in the dark here, literally."

Becky normally leaves by ten o'clock or so, but tonight we were still at it until somewhere around midnight. In addition to Alec's recap, we went back through all of the events, everything we'd been through, and I replayed the germane parts of Fields' account for everyone. We had no new ideas. While we were going through our experiences, though, I made some reference to the pickup trying to run us off the road.

Alec objected. "They weren't trying to run us off the road."

I was flabbergasted. "What are you talking about? Look at the back of my car! Of course they were trying to kill us!"

Alec simply shook his head. "No, they weren't. Think about it. There were plenty of curves north of Castle Rock. If they'd hit us there, we'd have gone sailing off the road and off the edge of a mountain or fallen into trees, still going close to seventy-five miles an hour. Instead, they waited until we were on one of the straightest stretches of road around. Had they really wanted to take us out, they could have hit us from the side and run or pushed us off the road even there. At that sort of speed, I'd have given even money we'd have turned over in the ditch along the road;

probably more than once, unless we impaled the car and ourselves on fence posts. Instead, they hit us straight on from the rear. All that does, besides messing up your bodywork, is push us straight down the road. That was a terror attack, pure and simple. Its only aim was to scare us to death, not kill us."

"Damn near succeeded at that." I had to stop and think about it. Damn it, he was right. I didn't want to admit it, but everything he said was true. I couldn't say there was no way they could have killed us doing what they did, but I had to admit they picked the one thing that would absolutely scare us while creating as little danger to us as was humanly possible.

"Damn!" Becky and Alec looked at me. I shook my head. "I don't want to agree with you, but I have to. Well, maybe they can terrorize me when it happens, but now that it's past, I am *pissed. Royally* pissed."

When I looked at Becky, she simply said, "Under other circumstances, I'd suggest trying to remain on a more even keel emotionally. But here, I can't. I don't know what's going on either, but I'm at least as much at a loss to understand it as you are, and I absolutely cannot blame you for feeling as you do. Not one bit. I think I'd feel just the same were I in your shoes."

I had to smile at her. "No, you'd feel worse. Trust me."

"How so?"

I smiled even more. "I wear smaller shoes than you do. Your feet would hurt on top of everything else." That worked to break up the somber mood. Even the dogs seemed to notice the difference. Both of them came over for attention and got plenty. I stood up. "I hate to break this up, but since we're not getting anywhere, I, for one, need my beauty sleep. Tomorrow, I'm back to my studying. But I've made a decision. I am not going to Jackson Hole next. Denver was cold enough. Jackson Hole is too far north, and driving be damned. I'm going to Hawaii next where I can be warm!" They both laughed. "Laugh away, you two. Alec, you're coming along. Becky, you'll have the dogs again; thank you ever so much, dear. We'll be there by the weekend if I can get some decent tickets."

The next two days were uneventful: dinners with Alec, one walk to our coffee shop and one evening in the back yard. Life seemed almost to have returned to what I would have cautiously called normal, at least for someone who had been bugged in numerous places. The third night was different.

* * * *

TO: D
FROM: HB
Youngston has largely blocked efforts to overhear conversations outside her residence. Lengthy conversation between Youngston, Trevethen and Swan. Initial portion of conversation took place inside house, recording and transcript attached. Remainder of conversation took place in yard of residence, and Youngston has utilized noisemakers to create sufficient acoustical screening to prevent picking up most of the conversation. Partial transcript attached. Recording nearly worthless, but can be sent if needed.

TO: HB
FROM: D
Excellent work. Unfortunate about the acoustical screening, but Youngston is resourceful and it was not unexpected. Transcript alone, such as it is, is adequate. Continue with Plan B.

Chapter 15

We'd settled quite nicely back into our routine. We had dinner at Alec's that evening and walked once more to the coffee shop where we found, unsurprisingly, that there was nothing new. I'd have liked some sort of change, but nobody ever asked me what I wanted.

I'd had my nose buried in books and my bugged computer for three days. I could by then have talked to Alec for hours on various investments, but I understood that he wanted, at most, the Reader's Digest version, not the James Michener version. Hell, even I didn't want to stand for that one. Nobody ever asked me what I wanted. That seemed like it had been the pattern in my life recently.

Some time in what I would have called the middle of the night—the clock called it 3:27—Sasha barked and woke me up. Just one bark. The room was quiet as I lay there, and I finally decided it was nothing. Occasionally, she barks in her sleep. Then there was a slight noise from the direction of the living room. Both dogs jumped up abruptly and rushed out of the bedroom. I heard another slight noise from the same direction.

Okay, something was definitely going on. I grabbed the .45 that I slept with under my pillow every night, the flashlight from the nightstand, and headed out nude, flicking off the pistol's safety as I went. I had a problem and I was going to see what it was, skin be damned. Besides, I was going to be behind the light, not in front of it. And the curtains were drawn anyway.

I heard one more repetition of the noise, which turned out to be a click from the picture window, the one I'd replaced after the brick through it, much as though someone had thrown a pebble at it. I shined my light on the curtain. Big mistake. I should have sprung for the blackout curtains.

165

Blam! Blam! Blam! Blam! The dogs were going crazy, barking and running around the room. It was probably good that I'd taken them to the range regularly. It kept them from completely freaking out when some clown—I knew who, at least in the sense that I'd bet it was the same clowns who'd been in the pickup and had probably been the ones pulling all these stunts—fired four shots through my all but brand new picture window, my less than brand new curtains and into the far wall of the room.

I probably should have taken *myself* to the range more, because I was freaking out. I was also trying to scrape a hole in the carpet with my body. Then I heard a large engine roaring off. What do you bet it's a jacked-up white pickup? Shit! *Shit!* Cautiously, I stood up. I looked down at myself with the flashlight and was unsurprised to see rug burns up and down my front. Well, expect Alec in five minutes and the police in fifteen. Better go get a robe at least, if not jeans and T-shirt. Nobody needs a show, or the distraction. Least of all me.

It took Alec less than five minutes, although he arrived without socks and, I'd bet, without underwear, if it mattered. Why was I even thinking about such things? Table that for later. I had called 911 as soon as I'd thrown some clothes on. The police had already been called—no surprise—and they showed up about twelve minutes after Alec. Close enough.

They wrote out their reports, took what information I had, told me a crime scene tech would be along to get the evidence—bullets and what else? What was left of my picture window?—in the morning and that I shouldn't disturb anything, but yes, I could use the furniture if I did nothing else in the room. They finally left us alone.

Alec looked at the holes in the curtain and window, the holes in the wall, and said, "How about some coffee?" Without waiting for an answer, he headed for the kitchen.

I could hear him banging around as he got the coffeemaker going. I swear, this case would never go anywhere without coffee. I had become an advertisement for coffee, lots of coffee. And lots of bladder control, but let's not even go there.

I walked into the kitchen and sat down heavily in one of the chairs. As Alec set the mug down in front of me, he said, "You know this was just another terror effort."

I looked at him. He sipped his coffee as he leaned against the counter. "Just how do you figure that?" This case seemed to be making both of us use the word terror more often than not. Was that a good thing? Probably not, but it certainly was apt.

"Amy, I know how tall you are. I'm quite sure they do too. You could have been standing at the window and those shots would have been well over your head. And the impacts on the wall were higher than the entrance holes. They were shooting *upward*. They weren't trying to hit you. To be honest, I'd have to say they were deliberately trying not to."

I picked up my coffee and walked back into the living room where I'd left the lights on. Damned if he wasn't right. Standing by the window, I had to crane my neck to look up at the holes in my curtains. Then I set my cup down on an end table and just looked at the impact holes for a couple of minutes. Alec was right; they were almost in the ceiling.

I sat down heavily in a chair and just sat there, sipping my coffee and staring at the holes. Alec wandered in a few minutes later and sat down across the room from me. After a while, I broke the silence.

"Why? I mean, why are they trying to terrorize us and tell us—quite explicitly, thank you—that they can kill us whenever they want? Especially when no matter how far we go, at least up to this point, they escalate their technique, but never move for the kill? It doesn't make sense."

Alec had his elbows on the arms of the chair and his coffee cup in front of his mouth, so I couldn't read his expression real well.

"You'll understand that I don't question my good fortune?" he remarked dryly. "Not just that I don't think I'm a primary target here. However much they work at terrorizing you, they don't actually do anything to harm you. Yet." He sipped and thought for a while. "And I'd like that...restraint...to continue. Honestly, I don't understand it either. You're right. It makes no sense. None whatsoever." He looked round the room and tapped his ear. Oh, yeah, the house was almost certainly bugged. I'd all but forgotten about it in the excitement. "Of course, that is exactly what you, Becky and I have concluded. On multiple occasions. If this case made sense, we'd probably be done with it by now."

I had nothing to say to that, so I said nothing beyond a minimally expressive shrug. I stood up, stretched and looked at the time on the cable box under the TV.

"My God, it's almost seven. Hardly worth trying to go back to bed, is it?" I looked at the dogs flaked out on the floor. "Come on, guys, let's go out."

Sasha was a bit less than cooperative that morning, to the point that I was tempted to leave her outside from sheer frustration. Finally, she went and we came back inside. She can be *such* a witch when she wants to, especially in the morning. Alec had already gotten their breakfasts, made new coffee, squeezed fresh juice and was waiting to find what I wanted for breakfast. My usual: hot cereal, salsa and cheese—extra cheese today, I needed the protein. He smiled.

"I don't know how you can eat like that. But it's your stomach, so I guess I'll humor you. At least it's not a bowl of chili, but it's about as close as you can get."

I didn't want to talk about breakfast. I'd been thinking furiously while outside with Sasha and I was angry. *Very* angry.

"I'm done being terrorized," I announced. Alec just looked at me and waited for more. "I mean it. I am fed up to *here* with all this shit." I waved my hand over my head. "I have been pissed on, shot at, banged up, blown up, and I am *done*. I am *over* done. They can piss me off even more, but I am *done* with being terrorized." I looked up at the ceiling and raised my voice. "Do you hear me, whoever you are? Wherever you are? Do your worst. I'm done fearing you."

I looked at Alec and went on in a more normal tone. "No, I'm not giving up the case. I'm going to finish this or die trying." I stopped him as he was about to speak. "Alec, I cannot quit. First, 'quit' is not in my vocabulary. Certainly not my professional one." He glanced at the ceiling, but I waved that concern away. I really didn't care who heard me. "Second, I took the case. It's a matter of my professional honor as an investigator, as well as my personality, to see it through to the end. Third, I will *not* be frightened off a case. Wuss and private investigator are never synonymous. I'd be thrown out of the Professional PI's Guild, or whatever organization would be appropriately insulted at the idea. I'm sure there is one somewhere, and they'd probably make me a member just so they could boot me out in righteous indignation.

"Finally, and this is perhaps the hardest one to say, but also the most important, this case is my financial deliverance. If I find whatever Fields hired me to find, then I will have no more money worries, ever. Another hundred shares plus a board seat? I know I won't ever be as rich as Fields, but frankly, I don't give a damn. Even if I don't last long enough on the board to get one more share, I know that I will not have any more money worries, ever, given my sort of lifestyle. I could even close up shop, put my feet up and stop working entirely if I wanted to. And live very well indeed while doing so. Or I could, at the very least, turn down the flakier cases that come in the door. Our licenses get yanked? No worries. For either of us. None. Got me?"

Was that an unhappy look or a worried one? And worried for himself? Or for me?

"Oh, yes," he said. "I get you. Loud and clear. And while it was never my intention to suggest that you give up, insofar as you may have thought I was doing so, my apologies." He took a deep breath. "So, when do we leave for the Islands?"

I could only slap myself on the head. I'd forgotten to make any arrangements. Well, that I could fix, and quickly.

I jumped up. "Bring me my breakfast. I'll be on the computer."

I was actually surprised to find that I could get to Lihue on the island of Kauai with only one stop. Not a huge array of choices with only one stop, but the long and short of it was that we either caught a hop to Phoenix or Los Angeles, and from there it's a direct flight. We could have our choice of when to arrive, from early afternoon to well after dark. Neither Alec nor I have ever been to Kauai—I had to ask him—so let's rule out late arrivals. I'm not fond of trying to find my way around strange places after sundown if I don't have to. It's a professional duty way too often, so let's not do it by choice.

I stopped for some of my cereal. Most people I know shudder at the thought, like that waitress in Denver. But since my four food groups seem to be coffee, chili, salsa and cheese, emphasis on the coffee nowadays, breakfast always seems like an ideal meal to me. Alec busied himself setting up a tray table so I could set things down and use both hands on the keyboard. What a darling, thoughtful man! Stop it, girl. Back to business.

170

"Okay. We can leave on Thursday at 8:30 in the morning and get into Lihue just before two in the afternoon, local. That gives us plenty of daylight to find our way around and get to wherever we're staying."

Alec sipped his coffee unconcernedly. "Sounds fine to me. That has us getting to the airport when? About 6:30?"

"Yeah. I'll call a cab for us. That'll keep us from having to leave the car in long-term parking."

"Are you going to carry your unit? What if they x-ray the bags? I've heard they do that on all overseas flights."

"Yeah, I heard that too. I guess I'll overnight it to wherever we're staying. Those, at least, don't get x-rayed."

Alec looked thoughtful. "Let me suggest that you send both units, and send them separately. Preferably with different carriers. Just in case."

My goodness, what a concept! He was right, of course. I doubted that anyone was likely to be able to hoist one from FedEx or UPS. By all means, let's double up. I'd also, suitably encrypted, take copies of the schematic for one on my laptop and on my netbook, just in case I did lose both units and had to scrounge parts to build another.

Let's see...I could take a pre-made circuit board; that would be the worst part to get anyway, and by itself, wouldn't be too suspicious. The remainder of the parts I could get off the shelf fairly easily. A couple of pairs or so of gloves, just in case. A ballcap for my hair and perhaps a surgical mask or two, Or at least a scarf. Soldering iron and solder would be easy enough to pick up anywhere if I needed one. It's only money, and for a change, it wouldn't even be mine. Yes! Let's by all means work at frustrating the clowns, whoever they may be.

And just maybe, what is the next shoe to drop going to be? Not to mention when and where? Forget about them trying to kill you. They've been telling you they could for some time. That message you've gotten, loud and clear. They haven't tried seriously yet. If they change their mind, you'll be the first to know. Or else, more probably, you'll never know until it's too late. Nor, for that matter, in all likelihood will Alec. So quit worrying about it. Operate as though they won't. You've already told them that's what you're going to do.

Besides, if they do kill you, then your worries are over, aren't they? Well, yeah, but I don't want it to end that way. There might be a lot more to the story, and I'd kinda like to see how it ends.

* * * *

Kauai is called the Garden Isle, presumably because it is so blasted *green*. Personally, I think the gardener ought to be fired. I've been to the northwestern U.S. several times, and once or twice even as far north as Victoria, BC. Daddy loved to travel. Victoria is a beautiful city, but the entire area around it is way too green and overgrown for my taste, at least for anything more than a visit. But I mean, come on! Victoria looks like *Tucson* next to Kauai. And I've seen gardens. Butchart in Victoria and Washington Park in Portland come to mind. Kauai definitely needs a new gardener, because the whole bloody place needs weeding. Badly. But as usual, I digress. I was here on business. And I wouldn't be staying all that long. Hopefully. Okay, so I'm a desert rat. I'm entitled to my opinion.

Let's ignore them, get the car and get the hell out of here.

* * * *

172

TO: D
FROM: HB
In accordance with Plan B, shots fired into Youngston's residence during the night. This produced responses by Trevethen, police and Youngston. During conversation between Youngston and Trevethen afterward, she specifically informed 'whoever you are', directed at the surveillance team, of her refusal to be frightened, as well as explaining her thoughts and motivations to Trevethen. Recording and transcript attached. Youngston and Trevethen departing for Hawaii to investigate board member Parkinston. Copy of targets' itinerary attached. Leaving tonight to be in place prior to targets' arrival.

TO: HB
FROM: D
The reaction was considered possible at this point, if unlikely from the beginning. Continue with Plan B, increasing efforts as previously discussed. Continue to disrupt investigation whenever possible.

Chapter 16

We seemed to have hit Kauai while it was still part of the tourist season. I wanted to be somewhere on the north side of Kapaa, as James Parkinston lived in Kilauea, pretty much on the north shore of the island. I didn't want to be too close, but I also didn't want to have to drive all over the bloody rock going to and from our hotel. Nor did I want to have to go through one of the most developed and heavily traveled parts of the island every time I did.

There were no cheap rooms to be had anywhere we checked. Finally, I figured that if Fields was going to be paying, we could damn well take what was readily available instead of driving all over creation trying to get some cheap room in order to save his all-but-unlimited money. Once again, Alec and I shared accommodations, but this time it was a luxury suite and we each got our own bedroom. Neat. And *so* nice. I could really get to like luxury.

Cousin Parkinston had a most interesting history. Born in Hong Kong, he had worked in brokerages all over the Pacific Rim. Mostly as a trader, but with some analytical work as well. Rather than covering an industry or a sector of the economy, he primarily knew Pacific Rim investments across a wide range of industries. From what I could find out, that was pretty much his expertise on the board.

Finding his house, though, wasn't all that hard. Not, at least, if you're willing to drive halfway to the sea, take a dogleg and then drive the rest of the way and a bit beyond, or so it felt. Huge estate, way up high—I guess hurricanes had proven to be a problem for Kauai—and with a view that looked from the street like it went all the way to the Aleutians.

Suffice it to say that cousin Parkinston is doing quite nicely for himself, thank you very much. For just a moment, I tried to imagine having a house similarly situated in Tucson that would overlook Tucson Mountain Park on or just below the crest on the western slope of the Tucson mountains. Heaven on earth.

Aha! I see a phone pedestal ahead. That has to be it; there isn't another one anywhere within sight. We'd swung by the FedEx and UPS points to pick up the units before we left Lihue, and one of them had arrived, so I was all set. Except for the machete I'd probably need to get to the pedestal and place my wires. Damn. And also except for the other unit, which seemed to have disappeared in transit, and they had absolutely no record of the tracking number. Didn't I say that nobody was likely to be able to hoist one from the shipper? I was wrong. The end result is the same. I'm now down to one unit. Again.

On the bright side, the fake-granite box, set behind the pedestal, would never be noticed because it would never be seen under all that greenery.

"Okay, I've seen all I need to see for now. Note the location and let's get back to the room and unpack." Dutifully, Alec headed back to our luxury suite.

Unpacking didn't take long. We'd only brought some casual clothes and we needed to pick up some more, something local that would let us fade into the woodwork better. Aloha shirts or something. Tomorrow. Right now, I was still fighting jet lag, three hours' worth, the fatigue of a long flight with no sleep worth mentioning and lack of food. But I got a lot more of my investment reading done. The food problem we could remedy easily enough.

My nighttime excursion promised to be difficult. I've already mentioned the plant life, which I fervently hoped wasn't carnivorous. I put on my usual black outfit, then pulled off the hoody and donned an off-white T-shirt with the Tucson Trap and Skeet logo on it. I wrapped up the hoody and stuffed it into a bag with the unit. There was no need to wear it quite yet, and I could put it on in the car. If Alec enjoyed looking at me in a bra, more power to him. I was working and had better things to concern myself with. And he very carefully kept his eyes averted once he saw what I was doing. Such a gentleman. Even though he's seen them before and even—stop that!

Finding the street in the dark of night was loads of fun. Once on the road, finding the pedestal was fairly easy. Getting to it really wasn't as bad as I'd expected; the plants for the most part just draped over it, they didn't actually cling. Except to me, but that was something I had to put up with. I set my connections and we left, the only car on that road the whole time. I love that sort of privacy for what I do.

Exactly as had happened so many times before, they were still way ahead of us. As we found out the next afternoon, they still were. We were almost at the pedestal when I noticed a distinct change in the foliage. There hadn't been anything like a path behind the pedestal yesterday and I feared the worst.

My unit wasn't gone. Might as well have been; it looked like somebody had driven over it. Several times. From the width of the path, it had to have been a motorcycle, like that mattered. What mattered was that I was now entirely out of units. I gave some serious thought to having a screaming fit out there on the roadway. I gathered up the biggest of the remaining pieces as best I could, yanked my wire harness free and trudged back to the car where Alec waited. Wordlessly, I showed him the wreckage. He simply shook his head.

We were halfway back to the hotel before he spoke. "So now what?"

I was really, really pissed by now. I'd had four units taken or destroyed, I'm not exactly in the electronics parts capital of the Pacific, and I have to do this surveillance, especially since Parkinston has no cellphone. How you live nowadays without a cellphone, I don't understand. Of course, people tell me the same thing about not being on Facebook, or MySpace, or wherever, but there's no need to go into things like that. Suffice it to say that he didn't have one and let's leave it at that.

When I calmed down a bit, I let my scowl relax. "First, I'll see if there's anything here worth salvaging. From the looks of it, probably damn little. The memory cards are still there, I think. I may be able to salvage my initial testing and see which lines I need to connect to next time. Once I find whatever is worth salvaging, you and I will go get the parts for a new one and I'll build it in the hotel room. Then we come back here."

Alec's face went blank. "Both of us?"

"Well, sure. I can't just walk into Radio Shack and buy all the parts at once. We're trying to keep this untraceable, remember? I can break down the list of the parts I need into several lists and we go from place to place, alternately, and buy them. Cash. Break the list down far enough and nobody can tell what we're constructing, which is exactly the way I want it."

He looked a bit concerned. "Amy, I don't know a resistor from a transformer. Just how in hell am I supposed to buy stuff like that?"

I patted his leg. "Not to worry, Alec. I'll give you the easy stuff and a shopping list that shows exactly what I need. You simply hand the list to the clerk, tell him you're buying for a friend, and he'll get the parts for you. Just make sure you get the list back." That must have been all he needed, and he nodded.

We were just about over our jet lag, so we got up at a fairly normal hour the next day, considering how late we'd gotten in. Unfortunately for me, it was Saturday, and other than the only Radio Shack on the island, the few electronics parts places were closed for the weekend. Astounding, I thought. But it's their business, not mine. I knew Radio Shack would not have all the parts. But it was a start.

It's possible to kill a weekend in what most people consider paradise and be bored and aggravated, but I have to admit that I had to work at it. Well, maybe not work, but it's true that my tastes don't run to hiking in rain forests, windsurfing and lying around on beaches, which doesn't leave me a hell of a lot to do here. I also hadn't brought a bathing suit, and I didn't think that trying to find a nude beach, if there was one, with Alec would be the smartest thing I could do.

We managed to kill the weekend and, as these things go, found it enjoyable enough. We even spent time in the gym together. Alec can press more weight than I can. I'm impressed. Not surprised, but impressed. I work hard at doing it. By the time we got off the stationary bikes, though, I was still functional. He was out of breath and kind of tottered for a bit. Not long, but it helped me feel better. I was very careful to not notice his difficulties where he could see me.

Monday morning, I hit the phones. I knew which would be the hardest parts to find, so they were the ones I asked about. I used all four of the cellphones we had: mine, Alec's and both of the pre-paid ones. Anything to make my efforts harder to track. Naturally, there were integrated circuit chips I needed desperately that just weren't available on the island. I checked with a couple of places in Honolulu and located them. That sort of established our schedule for Tuesday.

I wanted to make a day trip out of it and hoped I didn't run into Auntie Jo. I really didn't want to get into trying to explain how I'd come to the Islands without calling her and arranging to get together, much less have to decide whether I told her about how Alec knew about the Family, or have him play dumb and simply let her think we were just friends on vacation. Oh, come on, just how likely is it that you'd run into the one person in Honolulu that you know in one very short in-and-out trip? It's a big city!

Uh-huh. How likely was it that Raymond Escarton Fields would have been sitting in your modest little office on East Speedway?

Well, while Daddy and I had never been to her home, I at least knew she lived on the far side of the city. Would be just my luck to run into her, though. Oh, well. I'll worry about that if and when.

Never mind. Alec and I spent the rest of Monday hitting the few places on Kauai that had some of what we needed. On a sudden impulse, I added a small pack of file folders, a hobby knife and two cans of spray paint. I was far too conscious of not having the modeling putty I used to make the boxes look like chunks of rock. A stop at a thrift store yielded an old bed sheet.

Honolulu was uneventful. We went in, hit the stores we needed and left. Bang, bang, bang. No sign of Auntie Jo; maybe some other time. We did see the Battleship Arizona Memorial while on final for landing, and I made another mental note, this one to come see it first hand some day. Daddy always liked to tour battle sites when we were on vacation, but we'd never been to Pearl Harbor. Some day...

Tuesday evening as we sat in the suite watching TV, I worked over every loose component with my little bottle of bore cleaner. It's neat stuff. Non-toxic, not smelly and it removes grease and oil like nobody's business. The company's literature actually claims you can drink it. No, thanks. But I did ask one of the company reps at a show one time what it tasted like, and he proceeded to tell me. What it did, most importantly, was remove any oil I could have left on anything that might form fingerprints. That's why I always have some when I travel any real distance, even on those rare occasions when I don't have a gun with me. I left everything spread out to dry overnight.

The next morning, we ordered room service and set the Do Not Disturb sign as I plugged in my soldering iron and waited a few minutes for it to heat up and burn off its coating. I worked on the hotel's information book to avoid letting anything burn the desk—I didn't expect them to thank me for my thoughtfulness. By about lunchtime, I had the unit finished, except that it was in a plain black box. I took the thrift-shop bed sheet into the bathroom and hung it in the tub. The latest newspaper underneath it took care of any possible seepage.

A couple of shallow paper cups from the tops of the drinking glasses sufficed to hold the box a little elevated. I sprayed it with a light green paint, and while it was drying, went back to the desk. I swept the excess components— sometimes you have to buy certain quantities no matter what you need—into my hand and dropped them in a compartment of my suitcase. Loose, they shouldn't arouse any suspicion. Then I sat down with the phonebook, the file folders, a pen and my razor knife. In about ten minutes, I had an acceptable stencil of the telephone image that screams 'phone company' to all and sundry, at least on older equipment. When the green paint was dry—Alec was getting horribly bored, but insisted on staying—I took the stencil and the white paint. One good shot each on three sides and viola! The box looked for all the world like an official piece of phone company equipment. Why hadn't I done this in the first place, I wondered? Who cares? Done is done.

On the way back to Kilauea, I had another brainstorm. We stopped by the side of the road and I found, after a brief search, a chunk of local lava rock that was just about the size of my original units. I put that in the back of the car.

The memory cards from the destroyed unit had given me the basic information I needed, so I knew to hook up to two particular terminal sets. I had decided that on such a deserted road, I could take the chance of setting it in daylight. The box I secured to the pedestal with two big cable ties; the rock I carefully set behind it and draped a spare wire harness from inside the pedestal and underneath the rock. I gave the rock a farewell pat and we left. Elapsed time, about four minutes. No traffic at all. Good job.

Once again, I tried to impress on Fields the need to be strong and forceful. When we went by the pedestal again, I picked up the recordings with no trouble. Nothing seemed to have been disturbed. We pulled into a roadside park off the main highway and listened to our take.

What *would* it take for Fields to push one of these guys? I didn't understand half of what Parkinston had been urging on Fields for investment, but the half I did understand suggested that if there really were something underhanded going on, Parkinston was likely one of the principal suspects.

Except he didn't appear to be concerned. Once again, absolutely nothing. No calls out, no frantic emails, and no discernable reaction at all. I wished—fruitlessly—for the cellphone tap that would have let me listen in on his non-phone activities. Alec and I just looked at each other as the recording ended. He seemed a bit puzzled. I probably did too. Finally, I broke the silence.

"Screw it. I'm getting the unit right now and we're going home. We're done here."

"Now?"

"You see enough traffic along that road to be worth worrying about?"

Alec nodded, looking thoughtful. "Okay, you're right. Hang on."

As we approached the pedestal for the last time, there was a motorcycle approaching from the other side at a pretty good clip. Out here? That seemed suspicious as could be, given the amount of traffic we'd encountered on this road before, like none. Then he swerved behind the pedestal and ran over my rock.

I said, "Hey! That's the clown who ran over my unit!" Brilliant and observant, right?

He never slowed down, but kept accelerating and roared by us on the shoulder at what seemed like a good seventy mph or so. Alec could have stuck out his arm and hit the guy. Breaking his arm in the process, of course. By the time we reached the pedestal, he was long gone.

But my rock and my brainstorm had done the job. The rock was knocked awry, off the wire harness, but the unit box was unmolested. The rock was unharmed, naturally, like it mattered. I quickly snipped the cable ties and opened the pedestal momentarily to retrieve my harnesses. I had just gotten back into the car when another car came behind us on the road traveling at a much more sedate rate than the motorcycle had been. The person inside waved at us like she belonged here and thought that maybe we did too. We waved back. Let's not look too conspicuous.

I thought that this surveillance was not going to produce any more terror attacks than we'd already gone through. Foolish me. We'd gotten back to the hotel and were just getting out of the car when there was a loud blam! Accompanied by something going through the front windshield and the back window of the car. I guess it lodged in a coconut palm or something, or else simply kept going, as we saw no damage beyond our car when we eventually got looking.

At the moment, we were both checking out the parking lot surface very close. Finally, I looked at Alec underneath the car and said, "One of us has to get up sometime." We both started to laugh. Bullet holes! Shit! How am I going to explain *this* to the rental company?

They obviously could have shot us if that had been their intent. At least one of us. Me, in other words. Instead, they put a bullet between us when we were at least a foot apart and going the other way. Just another annoyance. Just another perfect day in paradise.

182

Alec stood up. "Well, I thought we handled that with real aplomb."

I snorted. "Not me. I left my aplomb in my other jeans." Once again, he laughed at my lame joke. What a guy!

Actually, explaining it to the rental company turned out to be easier than changing our tickets. Apparently wild pigs were in season, or some such, and when the fellow at the rental company asked us if we'd been in some part of the island I didn't recognize, but probably where there were hunters active, I just mumbled. He took that for a yes and went on filling out his form. Since I was spending Fields' money, I'd even splurged on the extended insurance coverage, so we were literally able to walk away from the car. Something we were *very* glad to be able to do on several levels.

* * * *

TO: D
FROM: HB
Made attempt under original Plan B to divert targets, but due to unavoidable equipment limitations, effort unsuccessful in the extreme. One surveillance device diverted in shipping and second surveillance device destroyed before completion of Youngston's investigation of board member Parkinston. Youngston was apparently prepared to construct another surveillance device while in Hawaii and did so. This device similarly destroyed, but not before completion of her investigation.

Full Plan B action later taken at hotel. Targets returning to Tucson earlier than planned. Team will attempt to return at the same time, but may have to delay return for one day in order to avoid being on same plane as targets. Board member Parkinston does not exactly live in a major transportation hub.

TO: HB
FROM: D
Well aware of the limitations imposed by Parkinston's location.
Please refrain from such comments in the future. Otherwise you
are doing as well as can be expected. Continue with Plan B.

Chapter 17

The flight home was uneventful, at least in terms of malevolent influences. We'd had quite enough of those already, thank you very much. Alec snoozed for some of it, and I had more investment reading to do. I could probably call it quits. Actually, I could have done that some time ago, but I'd never found a natural stopping place, and it just got to be really fascinating on some level. I've always loved reading and almost always responded positively to a challenge. I was no longer charging for simple study time, as I felt that I could not, in good conscience, still claim to be trying to understand the basics of the proposals Fields had told me the various board members were pushing on him. I understood, for the most part, just why they were, in Fields' opinion, bad ideas.

I was well into a book on the subtleties of option trading when Alec said out of nowhere, "You know what they're doing to you, to us, is really horrible." I stuck my finger in my book and looked at him. "That's it. Horrible is the only word I can come up with to describe it all," he added as he shook his head. "Damn. That's not me. I ought to be able to handle this better. Sorry, Amy. I'm way too tired and I'm not sleeping well."

I couldn't help it. I snorted. Daddy would have reacted far worse, at least with someone of Alec's age and his seeming lack of understanding of history. When I had last made some similar ill-thought-out remark, I was a lot younger.

"Yeah, we're both way too tired, but nasty as it is, no, it's not horrible. As these things go, it isn't even all that bad." I stuck my bookmark in and closed the book.

I could see Alec take a deep breath and pull himself together. I waited patiently, and after another moment or so, he spoke. "Okay, I can accept that you say I shouldn't think it's all that horrible, and under better circumstances, I'd probably have a more reasonable outlook. But you seem to have a different understanding of what horrible really is. Care to explain it to me?"

At least he seemed to be open to learning. Hell, we were both way too tired, and as he said, he wouldn't have brought it up in the first place if he weren't. Besides, I was grateful for the opportunity to take a respite from my book. On some level, I was realizing that I was more willing to open up to Alec to a greater degree than I had ever done before. I also realized that I had become more open to him in the course of this investigation in areas and ways I had never been open to anyone else, even Becky. Not just telling him about the Family, although that was certainly a part of it, but in terms of my own perceptions of him and my willingness to talk to him about things that really mattered to me. Was that good? Was it right? Enough ruminating, girl. Worry about those questions some other time. To use your own words, talk to him about something that really matters to you.

"It's difficult, yes. But...let me explain 'horrible' to you the way I learned about it." He had his mouth open, but I gently put my fingers to his lips to keep him from responding. I shuddered. This was a really...difficult memory. "Look, this is something that Daddy put me through a long time ago. I've buried it way down deep, but I want to dig it up and give you the benefit of my own traumatic experience. Daddy had some very firm opinions. Looking back, I understand that a lot of them coincided with things that some of his favorite science fiction author colleagues used to write. I don't know whether they'd fostered those opinions in him as he grew up or if he just agreed with them, but that doesn't really matter. The upshot of it is that he had very little patience with things he referred to as either muddled thinking or historical illiteracy. Your comment would mostly fall into the second category, although it's really both."

From there, I told him about the time I'd brought up the oh-so-horrible issue and wound up getting one of my occasional assignments from Daddy, one to go over some really horrible things from the World Wars. It was a very traumatic experience, but it definitely taught me the difference between horrible and merely bad. God, did it ever. I shuddered again. By the time I finished telling him all about it, I was in tears. Lots of emotion bottled up there, obviously. So much so that I'd never told anyone about it before and would absolutely never show that sort of emotion to anyone else.

When I was done, Alec said nothing. He put his arm around me and gently pulled me to him. I huddled against his warmth, his solidity, and just let the tears continue to flow until eventually, the sobs began to rack me. I needed to cry over it. Badly. I love Daddy dearly, and I understand his choice and don't blame him for doing it. But it was a horrible thing to do to a teenage girl. Oh, hell, it was a horrible thing to do to anybody. I lost track of how long it was before I had control again. Dear, sweet Alec.

When I was done with the tears, he produced a tissue and wiped my tears away ever so gently. Damn. What would I do without him? Well, not think of such things, for one. But in so many other ways...I shut that track down. I did *not* need to be thinking in that direction.

Finally, he spoke softly. "You never cease to amaze me, Amy. I don't think you've ever told me that much about your life with your father before."

Probably not, I thought. Even Becky doesn't know that one. "You're right. I haven't." I inhaled deeply. "I've never told anyone. I don't think that even Daddy has any real idea how much it upset me. I've just kept it packed away inside for so long." And it felt good at some level to have told somebody, in all honesty. Or at least it would when I could stifle the discomfort I could feel building. I sat up. This emotional turmoil would *not* do. I would get beyond it. By myself, as I always had. "So is this when I say, okay, now it's your turn?"

He spoke very softly. "Do you need to?"

Did I? "Yeah, I think I do." Was that another catch in my voice? I hope not. I had begun to open up to Alec. Subtly. Yes, I was becoming aware of my inclinations. I also wasn't comfortable with them. Or entirely uncomfortable either. I needed to think about this ambivalence. Another time.

"Okay." His turn to take a deep breath. What a lovely chest. So nice to lean against. Stop it! Just listen and quit letting your mind ramble in awkward directions.

"There's really not a lot to tell. My usual line—you've heard it—is that my family puts the 'fun' into dysfunctional. My mother was emotionally distant, or vacant, take your pick. My father, well, to be as honest as I can be and give him the benefit of the doubt, he simply didn't have any idea how to raise a son. The older I got, the less he had to do with me. I buried myself in my schoolwork, got really good grades, did well in athletics, and wound up with several offers from various colleges. I chose the one farthest away from my parents and took as many classes as I could over vacations so I wouldn't have to go back there. It wasn't 'home' to me by then. Not sure it ever was. I think I only saw them two or three times after I began college.

"Then they and my two sisters ate in a wrong restaurant one day. Or maybe they simply ordered a wrong dish. Either way, it was the last choice they made. The restaurant made their estates a very nice settlement, and as the sole heir, it all came to me. Just after my divorce, which was helpful. As well as being very good timing, since it let me clear my student loans and put something aside while not having to share it with my ex." He looked awkward.

"I honestly can't say how many of their opinions I picked up. I'd done my best to tune them out for years, and we didn't exactly have a lot of discussions about anything substantive when I was with them. I doubt that I would have been listened to if we did. I suspect I would have been ignored in favor of my sisters, although that could simply be my bitterness talking. Most of my opinions I've come by on my own, and I've really very little idea how my parents thought. I fancy myself to be mainly a self-taught sort of fellow." He grinned at me. "Anything more you'd like to know?"

Was there ever. Anything that I dared to ask?

"Well, uh..." I snorted. "You know, this is really amusing as all hell. Neither of us really, deep down, wants to open up to the other, and yet we're probably the only people we ever talk to. I've now opened up to you twice. Once on the Family and just now on things I would have sworn on a stack of bibles that I'd never tell a living soul. In the case of what I told you today, I never have." Which was true, but it didn't feel like it had been wrong at all. He just smiled gently and said nothing. He leaned over and gave me a nice gentle kiss on the cheek before putting his head back on his pillow and going back to sleep.

At least I thought he was asleep. It took me a long time to go back to my book. I'm not sure whether I was more upset by my opening up to him or by my persistent awareness of him. Although neither was really all that disquieting; at least some of my discomfort seemed more like habit. Was having him with me so constantly a good idea? The tiny, always rational part of my mind responded with 'Got anyone better?' The less rational part simply said, 'Yeah!' And the part that had been so horribly hurt in my marriage sat in the corner and cowered, whimpering softly.

* * * *

189

TO: D
FROM: HB
Unable to arrive at Tucson prior to Youngston and Trevethen.
Will continue with Plan B as soon as feasible after arrival.

TO: HB
FROM: D
Difficulties are sometimes inevitable. Continue with Plan B.

Chapter 18

I wish I could sleep on airplanes. Really sleep, that is. When I can sleep at all, it's fitful and unsatisfying. We got home around mid-morning and I called Becky before I dropped into bed. She'd be by after her patients were done for the day and bring the dogs.

By the time I woke up, I could hear Alec in the kitchen talking to Becky. Bruno and Sasha were sitting by my bed, staring intently at me. I must have really been asleep for them to come in without waking me. I looked at the clock. It was almost 5:30. I could hardly believe it. I threw on my robe and walked toward the kitchen, trailed by both dogs. I'd passed on the fuzzy bunny slippers that always broke Becky up, opting for flip-flops instead. Anyway, it was getting a bit too warm for fuzzy slippers, at least until around Thanksgiving.

I stopped just inside the dining room as I heard Alec say that the trip hadn't exactly been the sort of Hawaiian vacation he'd dreamed of taking with me. He what? Oh, my! The part of my mind that wasn't too upset by the entire idea thought that was just *so* nice. I couldn't hang back forever, though, so I made my grand entrance. It was spoiled when Sasha stepped on one of my flip-flops and almost tripped me. Oh, well.

The dogs' dishes were sitting on the counter drying, and pizza boxes showed what we were having for supper. Apparently they'd started eating without me. I wonder who brought the pizza in? Probably Alec. I sat on the last chair and tucked the robe between my legs. I didn't need to give Alec a show. They both smiled to welcome me, but Alec was by now giving Becky the long version of what had happened to us in Hawaii, and I saw no need to interrupt them. I got back up, picked a piece out of each pizza box and carried my plate to the table. Alec kept talking while he

191

got me a beer from the fridge, opened it and gave me a light kiss on my cheek as he set it down. Lovely breakfast. It'll never replace hot cereal with salsa and cheese, I must say. Or chili.

By now, Alec was up to the motorcycle that came close to running us down. He did seem to over-inflate my...brilliance?...in putting the rock in place. By now, I'd finished the first piece, saving the crust for the dogs. They were lying on either side of me, waiting, tails wagging expectantly, piglets that they are. I shouldn't feed them at the table, and if we'd been in the dining room, I never would have. But this was the kitchen, and both were lying on the floor, waiting calmly—well, sort of calmly—for their treats. Okay, guys, you win this time, but not until I'm finished.

When Alec got to the bullet through the car, I thought Becky's jaw was going to bounce off the floor.

"Don't get too worked up about it," I interjected dryly. "It was fired almost exactly down the midline of the car just as we were both getting out. It's another terror effort, nothing more, and certainly not any actual move to hurt either of us. It's really nothing to get worked up about. Just more of the same shit that I am getting way too tired of. No, make that *have* gotten way *beyond* tired of."

I sounded sour and probably looked it as well. I finished my beer and broke up the pizza crusts into small pieces that I fed the dogs as they lay by my chair. So well behaved at these times! Darling piglets. Standing up, I headed for the coffeemaker. I definitely needed to invest something in coffee. Get some of my money back, if nothing else.

Alec said, "I'm with Amy. I am also getting way too tired of this. And I am especially fed up with people shooting at her, even if they're not trying to hit her. If nothing else, accidents can happen. I'm hereby serving notice"—he glanced at the ceiling—"that they are no longer my friends. What's more, I'm going to strike their names off my Christmas card list."

I snorted. "When was the last time you sent out Christmas cards? And were they ever your friends?"

He shrugged. "Doesn't mean I don't keep a list. Get me their names when you can, would you? That way, I can add them just so I can cross them off. And they won't get an invitation to my next soiree either."

Becky laughed.

Suddenly the opening bars of Bond's Viva rang out. That was my cellphone ringing. Where was it? Plugged into the charger in the dining room, of course. I brought it back into the kitchen as I answered it.

"Youngston."

"Ms. Youngston? Fields here."

Oh, boy, another surprise. Only the second phone call I've ever gotten from him, and look what the last one got me into. What joys did this one hold for me? I could hardly wait to find out. I motioned Alec and Becky into silence and put the phone on speaker.

Fields continued. "I, uh, wanted to let you know of something that's come up here."

When he didn't continue immediately, I asked, "Yes, sir?"

"Well, I'm not too sure how to tell you this, but it appears that whoever has been doing all the things to me that I related to you has decided to get serious." I sat down. This was not likely to be nice. "I've been shot at. Not with toys, but with real guns."

Fine time to tell me that. "I take it they haven't hit you?"

"Oh, no, no. I don't know whether they're poor shots or I've just been lucky. But no, I haven't been hit. Not yet. I just wanted to let you know, in case..."

"In case of what, sir?" Alec looked angry. Becky looked horrified.

"Well, in case something of the sort should happen to you as well, I suppose."

Yeah, I'll just bet. "Well, thank you for the warning, sir. I'll be sure to stay alert and try to step up my investigation even further."

"Um, yes. Are you having any luck so far?"

Well, bad luck is still luck, I thought. "Not a great deal at this time. If I find anything I need to pass along to you, rest assured you'll be notified immediately. The routine stuff, I'm giving you each month or holding for my final report when I'm done. Is there anything else?"

"Oh, ah, no, not at this time."

"Well, then, thank you for the heads up, sir, and I know it has to be late there. I'll let you get to bed."

"Oh, you're very welcome. Good night, Ms. Youngston."

"And a good night to you as well, sir. Goodbye." I snapped the phone shut and looked at Alec and Becky. "Well, isn't that bloody interesting?" Alec opened his mouth, but I held up my hand. I tapped my ear. Back to the coffeemaker. "Who else wants some coffee outside?"

I made a pot and the three of us were loading up to haul everything out to the chairs on the dirt when my phone rang again. The others headed outside, with the dogs tagging along. They looked like they were still hopeful. No luck, the remaining pizza was going to be safe inside. The couple of wind chimes left provided some audio cover. I probably shouldn't put the rest back up. Not here and now anyway.

I answered the phone as I walked. "Youngston."

"Amy, it's Carol. It's a lovely pin! You shouldn't have."

I smiled. She and I don't get together much; she lives in northern California and thinks Tucson is beastly most of the year. From her position, she probably has a point. But we remain very close anyway.

194

"Oh, yes, I should have. You're an absolutely wonderful person and you're very important to me."

"Oh, thank you so much, honey. I'll wear it often and think of you. Love you."

"Love you, too."

"By the way, Amy, is anyone doing a background check on you?"

"Me? Not that I know of. Why?"

"Well, I had two nice men come by about two weeks ago and ask me some questions about you. Very nice men. They flashed some badges that I didn't get a good look at and then they stayed around for more than an hour."

I felt an all too familiar chill down my spine. "I hope you didn't tell them anything." Was I in danger on that front too?

Carol laughed. "Amy, sweetie, you know me better than that. We spoke for over an hour, as I said. We had some very nice tea and cookies together. If they boil down what I told them, they will know that I lived with you and your father—how is he, by the way?—for something around two years, that you like hot foods and chili, and I told them a couple of incidents from when you were training Gabriel. That's all. Of course, they think they heard a lot more, but that really is all they heard. Plus some details about Gabe's digestion, intestinal problems and such. Nothing of any significance."

Well, that was certainly safe enough. Gabriel was my second guide dog puppy back when I was in high school. A lovely German Shepherd puppy, although he had some problems processing his food that he eventually grew out of. He's gone now, I'm sure, but he was a spectacular guide dog for a very nice man for many years.

"Carol, you're a dear, truly you are and I love you. Daddy's fine. He's back in Denver these days and I'll be sure to tell him you asked when I talk to him again. I don't know what's going on, but I'll tell you when I find out."

195

"That would be nice, honey. Please give my love to Becky."

Now it was my turn to laugh. "Just a moment and you can tell her yourself." I handed the phone to Becky and settled myself in a chair while they chatted. Alec looked quizzical, but I motioned for him to hold it.

After Becky hung up and I carefully turned the phone completely off, I filled the two of them in on the people who'd been to see Carol and what she told them. They were both silent for several minutes afterward.

Becky was the first to speak. "That was really Mr. Fields on the first call, wasn't it? What do you think his call means?"

Alec looked disgusted. Not a patch on how I felt. "That's the $64,000 question. On the one hand, he could be dealing straight with me. If he is, that means they apparently escalated with me first before starting to shoot at him. With real guns." I snorted. "My God in heaven, what have I gotten myself into?" There was no answer. Not from Alec, not from Becky, and certainly not from God. I suppose the question was rhetorical. Although I'm sure He could have answered if He'd been so inclined.

"And on the other hand?" Alec didn't sound like he really needed the question answered, but for Becky's sake, I did anyway.

"If this is all a setup by him for some reason that presumably he knows and I damn sure don't, then he is probably calling me to divert our suspicions from him. Once again, there is no third choice. At least none that I can see."

Becky's mind seemed to be lacking in traction as my own. She went back to her previous train of thought.

"So now what? You've checked out one more board member, and once again you've found nothing, right?" Alec and I nodded. "They know about me and they know about Carol. I'm not sure I could have carried off what she

196

did anywhere near as well. I'm thrilled the dogs were there with me and I didn't have to." She paused for a moment while seemingly lost in thought. "So where do you go from here? And what, if anything, does Mr. Fields' phone call do to affect that?"

Alec and I exchanged glances before I replied, "I keep going. His call changes nothing, and I'm certainly not going to pay any serious attention to it since we've already been shot at with real guns. And most especially when we're wondering if he's even telling me the truth. There are only three board members left and I can check out the one in Wyoming easily enough. Although I'd rather wait until summer to go there, like anyone asked my opinion.

"I honestly have no idea how to tackle the two in Europe. I've no idea whether my equipment will work there, and I've never driven in Europe. From what I found on Mapquest, McTolland lives near this little town on a Scottish island out in the middle of nowhere, and it's an entirely new set of issues for me to address. I've been hoping I'd find what I needed by now, or at least enough to point me in the right direction before I had to get to them. If I could find something to give me at least a bit of traction in this investigation, I'd be a lot more comfortable with this."

Alec leaned back and stretched. He looked as though he was having an idea. "Can you get to their cellphones? Even if you can't get to their landlines or their computers, that should give you something."

What a concept! I turned to Becky. "See why I keep him around? He has ideas like that." She smiled enigmatically. Mona Lisa Swan, Ph.D.

I thought for a moment. "Yeah, I'll bet I can. The basic circuitry and software of cellphones should be pretty much the same anywhere, regardless of the network, and the recordings are fed back to me through the Internet. It's

197

worth a try in any event, and it'll save our having to travel to Europe, if it works."

Alec looked thoughtful. "What about when you call Fields for that? Will he be suspicious that you aren't actually in Europe?"

I snorted. "Like I have to tell him. Think about this one. We had no problems in Sedona, in Albuquerque *or* in Denver until *after* I called him and told him where we were." Alec's face went blank. "Does this suggest anything to either of you?" I looked from one to the other before continuing. "I mean, Hawaii was the first time we used commercial transportation, *and* I got our tickets online. So anyone with a line into my computers knew ahead of time where we were going, when we were getting there, how we were going, and what car rental company we'd be using. Every other time, we've driven, and unless somebody was actually following us, we disappeared. Until, that is, I called Fields. For Hawaii, I get our tickets on my probably-bugged computer because it never occurred to me to worry about someone looking over my shoulder, and we go by commercial airline. I seem to remember saying that I wanted to avoid commercial transportation as much as possible. Now I see why."

From the angry look that came over Alec's face, it certainly suggested something to him. Becky was the one who spelled it out.

"Fields is telling these people where you are."

"Yep. Give the lady a cigar. Or a cup of coffee." Her cup was empty, so I refilled it. "Of course, that certain somebody might simply have Fields' phone tapped instead." Cautiously, I crossed my legs. The robe held. I'm narrow enough to have plenty of overlap. "I've found nothing so far to dispute our earlier understanding that either his story is straight and we're subsidiary targets, or that he's leading me around by my nose for some as yet unknown purpose, and what he told me was happening to him was really what was in store for me. In that case, this call he just made is more of the same. Way too late, of course. There is still no third choice that I can see.

"We now have strong suspicions that what I say to him over the phone gets back to whoever these people are, either because he tells them directly, or because they're tapping his phone. But, and this may be the nicest part, if I call Fields to have him call either Ian McTolland or Tobias Greibe because I'm listening in on their cellphones to everything they say, and I tell him, or at least strongly suggest to him, that I'm on the scene there, then just maybe these clowns will hare off to Europe to find me and leave us the hell alone here for a while. Assuming they haven't already gone because they've seen me make our reservations. Or they may be following me more closely and see that I'm still here, but either way, it offers a bit more information, info we can certainly integrate into our so far fruitless arrangement. I can't see that it does us any harm under any circumstance." Both of them were nodding at this. Good. It's a plan. I love it when a plan comes together. "Do either of you speak German?" Becky put her hand up slowly. "Scottish?"

Alec looked indignant. "Amy, they speak *English* in Scotland."

I laughed. "Have you heard the way they talk there? It's not the Queen's English, or if it is, it's Mary, Queen of Scots. Daddy and I sat with a nice Scottish couple one evening over drinks. We were having a very pleasant conversation, I was cautiously tasting my first real Scotch whisky and I absolutely loved listening to their accents. At one point, he turned to her and said something utterly undecipherable. And she understood him, or so it seemed, because she responded in kind. So yeah, they speak English. But it's entirely possible that at least some of what we pick up will be something completely unintelligible to people who speak American English. Which, the last time I looked, included all three of us."

Alec waved that off. "Let's worry about that if and when we have to. I, for one, don't see any point in worrying about it until we absolutely must. German is another story."

Becky waved her hand again. "I speak German. Not perfectly. I'd never pass for a native, but I can usually carry on a slow conversation and I generally understand what's said to me. Give me a dictionary and I can manage just about anything, as long as it's not too technical and I don't have to talk to someone about it in depth."

I smiled at her. "Not to worry. If it's too technical about investing, we should know that we've hit pay dirt. If he does nothing, then I can guarantee you it won't be technical. And we're going to be eavesdropping, not conversing, other than to tell him sorry, wrong number—for which we don't need to use German." She thought that was funny. Good. I wanted to keep things light where I could. I cocked my head as I looked at Alec. "Well, there you are. We don't even have to go off the reservation. Oh, and speaking of reservations, what day will you be free to fly to Europe? Reasonably speaking."

He looked completely baffled. "I thought you just said we weren't going over there."

I lowered my voice, just in case. "We aren't. But if my call to Fields suggests that we're there, and I make reservations on the computer, which I then cancel with, say, the netbook through some wi-fi hotspot that I've never been to before, then whoever is watching us should, with luck, conclude we're going, shouldn't they? Especially when we take our bags in a cab to the airport at the appropriate time." I beamed. Their expressions didn't suggest unbridled admiration so much as sarcasm. Oh, well, no matter. I thought it was a pretty great idea.

Besides, it was my case, so we'd do it my way. I love doing things *my* way.

I got out the laptop. Sure, it was bugged. That was just fine at the moment. I *wanted* someone to know what I was doing. I did a few searches before I found what I wanted.

"Okay, then, we're flying Northwest. Tucson to Minneapolis, Minneapolis to Amsterdam, and Amsterdam to Glasgow on a Northwest-numbered KLM flight." Alec looked puzzled. "Look here." I spun the computer around and pointed at the screen. "We fly to Glasgow with two stops. We can argue about where we want to stop, but there's apparently no way to get from here to there with only one stop. Maybe there is somewhere, but since we're not really going, it doesn't matter anyway. Once we're hypothetically in Scotland, we check out McTolland. We then, still hypothetically, take the Chunnel to France and drive to Oberwesel. We bag the tickets from Glasgow back to Amsterdam, the tickets we will have cancelled long before, of course, because we drive without telling anyone. There we check out Greibe and then drive back to Amsterdam and hypothetically fly home, hopefully leaving whoever is looking for us trying to not-so-hypothetically get from Glasgow to Oberwesel while we're hypothetically going the other way and actually here all along." I looked from one to the other. They both seemed to approve. I turned to the dogs. "How about you guys? You okay with that? Huh?" Their tails wagged. They were happy just being noticed and fed bits of pizza crust. I grinned. Maybe later.

Alec still looked a bit uncertain. "We're not really going, right?" I nodded. "Well, since we're not going, I suppose I could leave in two days or so. Hey, wait a minute. Do you want to make the reservations first? Or do you want to hit their cellphones first, just in case they get notified that we're supposedly coming?"

"Oh, good point. Let's see." I tried to count on my fingers and failed. I called up a world time zone web page. "Aha! It's eight hours to Scotland, and nine to Germany." I checked my watch. "It's now 6:30 tomorrow morning in Scotland and 5:30 in Germany. Okay, then. I can call McTolland in an hour and a half and Greibe an hour or so after that. Then I can make our reservations."

Alec looked skeptical. Becky just looked worried. "Do we need to wait around? I do have patients tomorrow morning."

I remembered my manners. Mom would have been proud. I hope. "Oh, heavens, no! I'm sorry, Becky. No, I figure I'll call him and talk to him in English. Whether he speaks it or not, the only thing I really need to do is connect to his cellphone. The computer does the rest. Even if he only speaks German, he'll understand a contrite apology, if only from my tone. Then I hang up. McTolland can't be that difficult. I'm sure he understands standard American English. Even if he doesn't speak it." I glanced at Alec who tried to look innocent.

Becky stood up. "Then I guess I'll see all of you in a day or two. Let me know if you need me to bring a dictionary, will you? Oh, and call me before you don't leave."

Alec and I stood as well. "Of course. Besides, we have to drop off the dogs if we're going to make it look real. At least for the day." She smiled as we sandwiched her with kisses on both cheeks.

When she was gone, Alec and I sat there in silence, sipping more coffee. Sasha got up and began sniffing around the yard. "What is she looking for?" Alec asked.

I smiled. "Probably the right place to pee."

"And what makes it the right place? As opposed to some place a foot away, say?"

I laughed. "I haven't the faintest. Ask her. Maybe she'll tell you."

202

Alec laughed in return.

I gave myself plenty of time to quarantine the spyware program on the laptop. It was, unfortunately, the only computer I had configured to transmit this software. Equally important, I didn't want what I did to be seen by whoever was watching us. It would look to them as though the computer had been turned off. Well, I could make reservations in the morning. I figured it wouldn't look as curious as it would if I turned the machine off and then immediately turned it back on at this hour, and that was exactly how it would look to them if I removed the quarantine now.

Alec was beginning to droop by the time I could call cousin McTolland. "Do you need to head to bed?"

He waved me off. I was sure he wouldn't wait around until I could call Greibe. I was almost right. He was still there. He did move to one of the recliners to snooze a bit, but asked me to wake him before I made the call. I did give a moment's thought to letting him sleep—the poor man needed his rest—but woke him as I'd promised. He went home afterward.

By the time he came back in the morning, I'd been up for almost an hour. He poured himself a cup of the ever-present coffee and joined me and the dogs in the study. I was already setting up the reservations.

"Okay. Let's make it three days from today. Let me put the dates in here, two people there, and viola! We have our reservations. Alec, please remind me tomorrow to cancel them. And now for a rental car. Think I can get a left-hand drive car in Scotland?"

He didn't look completely happy. Why was that? "You got it. As for the car, does it really matter if we won't be using it?"

I chuckled. "Would you believe my reservations if I didn't have a rental car too?"

Dryly, he pointed out that renting a left-hand drive car in Scotland, or trying to, might give away the plan to drive to Germany.

"Good point. Okay, then, I'll make the reservation and let them worry about it. Can you drive on the other side of the car?"

"Still hypothetically? As long as there are controls there, I expect so. But it's likely to be a bit hard from here. My arms are only so long."

"Touché."

Somewhere among all of the 'other shoes' that have dropped so far on this case, there was room for another one. I entertained the cheery thought that by leaving Kauai as abruptly as we had, we might actually have made our getaway and been able to have a day or two of peace. But that begged the question of, what then? I'd find out soon enough, I was certain.

* * * *

TO: D
FROM: HB
After arriving home, Youngston and Trevethen had extensive discussion with Swan. The portion of discussion recounting events in Hawaii was conducted inside; recording and transcript attached. Youngston received phone call from REF; recording and transcript attached. She received phone call from Carolyn Morgan, recording and transcript attached, previous resident lady friend of Youngston's father during her early teen years subsequent to death of her mother.

Investigation had previously been attempted unsuccessfully on Morgan, recording and transcript attached. Morgan informed Youngston of team's efforts. Further discussion between targets outside Youngston's house. Many noisemakers removed, making acoustical screening much less effective. Recording and transcript attached. Youngston and Trevethen intend to spoof traveling to Europe to investigate board members McTolland and

Greibe while actually conducting electronic investigation from Tucson. Continuing efforts as previously planned.

TO: HB
FROM: D
Excellent work. Unfortunate about the interview of Morgan, but I am satisfied by your efforts. Continue with Plan B.

Chapter 19

I now had something to do besides read about investing for a few days. I busied myself with constructing new units from the parts I already had. I took advantage of my experience with them during this investigation and didn't do them all like identical granite rocks. One looked like granite. Another was broad and as shallow as I could make it, kind of like a small gold pan or pie tin turned upside-down and painted grass-green, although I fully intended to take up a bit of turf and hide it under the sod whenever possible. The third was done like a phone company box, just like the one I'd cobbled together in Hawaii.

On that one, I made a few minor improvements. I gave some thought to using magnets to hold those to the pedestal, but they wouldn't hold to a plastic pedestal, and magnets strong enough to hold it securely to the metal ones were likely to play hob with the unit's memory anyway. Using big zip ties had worked just fine in Hawaii, and I had plenty of them, so I figured I'd just go on using them. As long as nobody from the phone company came by, I was in good shape. And if they did, what sort of box I was using probably wouldn't matter, as my surveillance would just have come to an abrupt end anyway and I'd be out another unit. The damn things aren't cheap, but...oh, well. They'll go on my bill, at least the ones I've lost.

It must have been two nights after I'd made the reservations. Canceling them had been a piece of cake. But that night...well, it was actually early morning, in that dim time when you can see just slightly more than at night, but still hard to make out anything in detail.

I was expecting another shoe to drop. What I got was more like a size fourteen steel-toe work boot.

This time nobody bothered with pebbles against my window; a burst of automatic weapons fire through my newly replaced picture window, my brand new blackout curtains, and into the far wall. Once again. Something broke in the living room. The dogs were barking, but luckily a bit too scared to go running out of the bedroom. Good sense on their part. If I'd been smarter, I'd probably have gotten down on the floor with them and stayed there. I'm not that smart. I also wasn't as scared as I expected to be. Excited, yes, but I didn't have the shakes. Not yet anyway. That particular problem could wait until this was all over.

If they still weren't trying to kill me, I was probably safe as houses. Ironic thought; this *is* my house. Doesn't feel very safe at the moment. If they've decided to take me out, then I probably won't fare any better by being terrified and it'll make it a lot harder to try taking someone with me.

I rolled out of bed with the .45 in my hand. To hell with the flashlight. I yelled at the dogs to go down and stay. Another burst of shots through my window. Some part of my mind, that tiny part that never lost its rational outlook, wished I'd kept the window glass so it would have shattered completely by now. I low-crawled out to the front door and paused before suddenly reaching up to jerk it open, flinging myself to the other side of the doorway as I did so. I saw the same damn jacked-up pickup parked in front of my house, and then abruptly another burst of shots shredded the top of my doorframe. Splinters rained down on my bare back. I tried, still unsuccessfully, to burrow under the carpet and wished that I hadn't gotten rid of the low wall around the front porch to open up the front of the house some years ago.

As I dared to raise my head for a look, there was another ripple of fire from the passenger-side window. I steadied myself in the prone position and put three quick shots into the passenger door before rolling to the opposite side of the doorway. My heart was beating a tarantella in my chest by now and it was all I could do to hold the gun steady. All the training and adrenalin drills I'd done over the years were paying off. Not as well as I could wish, though. Then yet another burst. It was a goddam war zone in my front yard.

Reaching cautiously around the door, steadying my hand against it, I put another three rounds into the truck door, slightly behind my first aiming point. Three shots left. I'd better save them. This was ridiculous. Why was I using three shots each time instead of the double-tap I'd been taught over and over? No answer to that one other than stress and adrenalin. Probably as good an answer as any. Another magazine was in the bedroom, unimaginably far away. The way my heart was pounding now, I'd have been hard pressed to hit anything anyway. I guess all my training and drills can only do so much compared to the real deal.

I kept the gun trained on the pickup, fearing that the worst was yet to come. Had they finally decided to escalate from merely terrorizing me to seriously trying to kill me? If so, I fervently hoped I'd already taken one with me. Were there other ones to get? If so, how many? Could I get them with only three more shots? Especially the way I was now trembling?

Another burst from the truck—but this time, I noticed that there was no impact sound. Wait just a goddam minute! There's something fishy here. Nobody just keeps shooting like that when they're being shot at. They shoot more frequently, more carefully, and they'd shift their aim to shoot back at me instead of shooting blindly. Besides, six rounds of .45 through the truck door and I guarantee that there was nobody behind it alive and healthy. I waited.

Another burst, and again no impact sound. Then Alec came running from his house shirtless and crouched to my front porch where he slid into a prone position in front of the door—interposing himself between me and the truck. Dear Alec! Thank God too, that I'd replaced the weathered wood porch with synthetic, or he'd have been a mass of splinters. He glanced at me and turned his attention to the truck. When the next ripple of flashes and bangs came, he put several rounds through the back of the truck close to the passenger door.

"Easy, Alec." He didn't take his attention from the truck. "It's a ruse. There's nobody there, and they're not really shots. The first ones were, but now it's just some sort of device that sounds like shots." I got to my knees.

Alec kept watching the truck, although when the next burst of sound and flashes came, he merely twitched and didn't add any more holes.

"Amy, for Christ's sake, go put something on. A robe or something. The cops will be here any minute." Oops, he was right. Nude woman with gun, redux. Carpet burns redux as well. And this time out on my front doorstep. Oh, well, enjoy the show, neighbors. We're not even charging admission. Oh, my, what must our neighbors think? How did I look to them? Well, screw it. I had no time to feign embarrassment. Or interest, either. I had bigger and far more important things on my mind, like surviving this. I'd worry about my dignity later.

"Thanks, dear. I'll be right back." It took longer to get back to the bedroom, if only because I had no idea what I might be walking into. I wasn't about to be surprised. The dogs were waiting nervously, tongues lolling and tails wagging as soon as I came into view. Good dogs. Not threatened all that much, although understandably upset. Jeans and T-shirt were on the chair where I'd left them last night. I gave each dog a quick pet, then jumped into the jeans and pulled the T-shirt over me. Thank God for small breasts. I could go without a bra. I grabbed a full magazine off the nightstand and replaced the one in the gun, dropping the partial on the floor. Worry about it later. Next time, you damn idiot, if you're not going to grab the flashlight, at least grab more ammo! Extra magazine into the jeans pocket.

By the time I made it back to the front door, dogs in tow, where Alec was waiting, the cops were arriving, all right. Not just cops either; the SWAT team. Oh, joy. Yes, there were other cops behind them, but the SWAT team got my complete attention. We were pinned by searchlights as we stood there on the front porch brandishing our pistols. Thank you, Alec, for having told me to get dressed. I wouldn't feel half as...well, I wasn't comfortable at all anyway, but I'd have felt a lot worse in just skin and gun. Certainly would have had much more explaining to do then, since I would have appeared to them to be one totally crazy lady instead of just partly crazy. I raised my left hand, put the safety on with my right thumb and slowly set my gun down on the doormat, pointed in a safe direction. No concrete for this baby, not if I could help it.

To make sure nobody would feel an overpowering need to kick it out of my reach, I edged slowly away from it down the steps to ground level. The rational part of my mind was puzzled. Tucson doesn't have a dedicated SWAT team; that's collateral duty for officers with other job assignments. They normally get to the scene and then gear up if they're needed. Of course, I supposed they might have been geared up for a meeting or drill of some kind.

The dogs came to the door and started barking. I turned and told them to stop and down. Wonder of wonders, they obeyed, although Bruno never took his eyes off the officer approaching me, except to occasionally glance at the one nearing Alec. I kept my hands far away from my body.

Alec had already gone down the steps. He carefully set his gun down on the dirt by the walk and edged slowly the other way until he got yelled at and told for the second time to stay where he was. Then, as the team members approached, we got onto our hands and knees as we were told and then flat on the ground, spread-eagled. I did ask the cop coming toward me to please not kick my gun, it was quite expensive and I couldn't even begin to reach it

210

from where I was anyway. He looked at it, and I could see the debate he was having with himself. Finally, he seemed to decide that I was being a good girl and he could take a chance.

Thank you, officer. He seemed equally worried by the dogs, and I told him that they'd behave. I'm not sure he believed me on that one. I had my own questions, at least about Bruno, and especially if someone went after the pistol lying right in front of him. But I told him I was okay and he needed to *stay*. I hoped he was listening. I certainly didn't want them shot. I'd had enough trouble today already. Losing one or both of the dogs that way would completely break my heart.

Just then there was another burst of imitation gunfire from the truck. Had I blinked? Suddenly, all of the police had disappeared—until I lowered my gaze and saw the two who had come up to us were now flat on the ground with their guns—9mm submachine guns, I thought detachedly, although I'm not enough into squirt guns to know exactly which ones—trained on the truck.

I said, "Those aren't really shots. It's some sort of diversionary device."

They ignored me and kept their guns trained on the truck, although nobody returned the fire from the truck. When there was another flash-bang series and still no impact noise, the one who had been on Alec slowly got up and advanced carefully toward the truck from the rear. Reaching the passenger side, he yanked open the door. Nobody there. Something fell off the door, hit the ground and smashed. He straightened up and relaxed. Somewhat.

"All clear," he announced. I noted a look of exasperation on his face. He shook his head in dismay. Everybody else reappeared from behind their cars. Amazing how fast you can move when you think you're being shot at, isn't it? This was probably the most excitement any of them had had in quite some time as well. At least I hoped so for their sake.

Then another cop walked up to me. He had his attention split three ways, between me, Alec and the dogs, but he seemed less tense than the other two had been. He smiled. Well, that was certainly a surprise.

"Should I say good morning? It is morning, although I realize it may not seem all that good to you at the moment. Go ahead, both of you. Stand up, please." Alec and I exchanged glances as we stood. I looked at my gun on the doormat, then at the dogs just inside the door watching the whole thing. He followed my eyes. "The dogs should be safe if they just stay where they are. Please leave the guns as they are too. I'm Sergeant Tom Windlows, Emergency Response Section of the Tucson PD. Could you please tell me just what's been happening here?"

I have to admit that I wasn't completely reassured by his polite manner. Having cops come to my front door was bad enough, but I'd been there before. Not all that long ago either. Having the SWAT team arrive before sunrise was worse. There'd been way too many cops in this whole investigation anyway. Now it looked like half the department was holding a convention in front of my house. Such stories my neighbors would tell. Probably about me too. No, strike that 'probably'. I'd be the topic of conversation for some time to come. But I'd return politeness for politeness with this fellow. Couldn't hurt. Might even help.

I explained about the previous incident, the shots fired this morning—his eyes flicked up to my window and doorframe before coming back to me—as well as what had happened to us on the way home from Denver. Did it sound as bad as it had felt? Should I be reacting more than I was? I was a lot more angry than frightened. I'd been through this sort of crap way too many times by now. The more I related, the more he seemed to relax. Not a lot, but noticeably, at least if you're seriously into body language. I've found it's always important to keep track of the total person I'm seeing, and as I've said, I'm more observant than the average bear.

The team member who'd checked the truck came over. "Hey, boss, you should see the groups on the truck." The sergeant turned just enough to pick him up in peripheral vision. "Four 9mm's in about five inches behind the door. Two groups of three .45s each in the door, both of them about two inches."

Was the sergeant impressed? I couldn't tell. He wasn't that easy to read for such a subtle thing. I began to wonder if I'd really seen him relax before. Then he blew it. He looked at Alec and said, "Nice shooting, sir."

Alec had the decency to look embarrassed. "I had the 9mm, sergeant."

Now the sergeant looked properly abashed. Again, briefly. He looked at me again. "I'm sorry, ma'am." Damn. Would I always be 'ma'am' now? I didn't feel that old. Maybe tomorrow.

Sasha began to cry quietly. He turned a bit more of his attention to her. "Is the dog worried?"

"She probably is. I expect both of them are. It's been...difficult for them. And they probably both need to relieve themselves too."

He thought briefly. "Are they going to be okay with us out here?"

At last a normal sort of question. I wanted to laugh. I didn't. "They'll be fine. Sasha! Bruno! Come on, guys. Come to mama. Come!" They got up and trotted to me. Well, Sasha trotted. Bruno ran. Their relief was evident. I gave each one a pet and a hug. "Go do your stuff." I pointed away from the team. Sasha went. Bruno had to sniff each cop in turn first, delicately, but although they watched him carefully, nobody moved. Satisfied, he went off to empty his bladder as well. Afterward, both came

213

back. Sasha went over to Alec, who was still standing on the other side of the walk. Bruno came to me and sat.

One of the cops looked interested. "Is that a Malinois?"

I nodded proudly. "You bet. Damn good guard dog too." I saw no need to tell him of Bruno's other abilities.

The sergeant spoke again. "You know, this is a first for us. We get a certain number of calls about gunfights in the streets, but this one is, at least for me, unique. I don't think I've ever before been called to one without anyone on the other side. At the same time, I can certainly see what happened. And I've confirmed the other incidents"—I noticed his earpiece for the first time—"so I'm going to take a chance here. Clarkson!" One of the team members trotted up. "Go clear these people's guns and place them—carefully—on the carpet inside the door." He turned to me. "Will that be all right? Good. I'll ask you to leave them there for a few minutes more. I don't think anything is going to happen while we're here." He smiled just a little. "You're a private investigator, is that correct?"

He had clearly found out a great deal of information in a few minutes. Good team, I guess. Very thorough. They'd better be, it's why they get paid the big bucks. The detective who'd been here the other morning walked up behind him and nodded to him without speaking.

"Yes, that's right." Okay, where was this headed? As though I couldn't figure it out.

He turned to Alec. "And you're a lawyer, sir, correct?" Alec also nodded. "Ma'am, does this...incident...have anything to do with any investigation you're pursuing? To your knowledge?"

I thought furiously. Should I admit it? What had he found out about the truck? He wasn't telling. Bite the bullet, girl, no irony intended. "Yes, sergeant, I believe it does. I have no proof at this time, but I'm fairly certain that it does."

He looked thoughtful. "Tell me about the investigation, please."

Oh, boy. Now what do I do? Alec stepped in to rescue me. "Sergeant, I'd like to put an end to this line of questioning. I'm very sorry, but Ms. Youngston is not at liberty to disclose information about her investigation, which is confidential. Unless she is being accused of a crime?"

The sergeant seemed to be at a loss for words, but for just an instant. I was watching for it, or I'd have missed it. He exchanged glances with the detective before turning to Alec. "Is this an investigation she's conducting for you, Counselor?"

Oops, now it's Alec's turn. He made it look easy. "It's an investigation in a case she and I are working on together, yes."

Well, that's an interesting way to put it, I thought. Not inaccurate, I suppose, although I'd never have thought to describe it quite like that. But whatever works. Alec certainly knew his stuff. Inwardly, I smiled with delight. Outwardly I wore my best poker face. I think I could have given Becky lessons. I would at least have made her proud.

The sergeant thought some more. "Well, you both understand, I'm sure, that we'd really like more information on people who go around shooting up houses in our city. Can I prevail upon either of you to consider this your civic duty and tell me more?"

I stood mute. Alec simply shook his head.

"Very well." Another glance at the detective. "There's no suggestion that either of you acted improperly, although the initial report of a nude woman in a gunfight in the front of her house certainly, ah, got our attention."

I could feel my face getting hot. I guess I can still blush. He went on as though nothing had happened, although I wouldn't bet that he'd missed it.

"I'm sure that the detectives will wish to speak with you more about this. But I believe that we, at least, are done here. And for me, I think I can turn the two of you over to the tender care of Detective Jackson." He nodded at the detective with him. "I would like to ask both of you to minimize the gunfights if they start again."

I looked at him quickly. He smiled. Okay, that was sort of a joke. I can handle that. All this would probably have a bit of amusement value when I backed away from it and gained some perspective. That was going to be a bit easier now that bullets weren't flying any more, although gaining that much perspective could take a couple of years, or so it felt. My heart rate was down to only about one and a half times normal, I thought. It could go entirely back to normal if these bloody cops would just go away and leave us alone.

Alec thanked him. The sergeant turned away, took two steps before turning back to face us. "Oh, one more thing." Good lord, another Columbo. I snorted. "A word of advice. Don't make each other angry. That was some very impressive shooting by both of you."

Now I did smile to myself, I have to admit. It's nice to be recognized for your skills. Lord knows I'd worked hard enough to get them to the point that I could do that well when my bloodstream hold more adrenalin than actual blood, even if I had just learned that the most stressful drills I'd been able to dream up had their limits.

By now, a forensic team had appeared to work over the scene and a wrecker was waiting to hook up the truck. It seemed like half the neighborhood had come out to watch the proceedings. Well, why not? It was probably more excitement than most of them had seen in years, and a free show to boot. I could have enjoyed being like that, I thought. No worries, nobody shooting at me, nobody hitting my car or setting off fireworks under ir. Ah, well, no rest for the wicked. Or for Alec and me, either.

"You do seem to attract trouble, don't you?" Detective Jackson said.

He was sort of smiling, so I guess he wasn't trying to be offensive. It also seemed somewhat accurate, unfortunately. Behind him, a technician was photographing what was probably the brass around the truck. Another one circled around behind us to check out the doorframe and probably photograph and gather up the brass from me and Alec.

"I'm going to have to ask both of you to come down to the station with me. We have some questions we need to ask. And we're going to have to bag and tag your guns so we can get ballistic exemplars."

I was becoming distinctly unhappy about this. I could say that I needed some coffee. I did, but that was so far down on the list that it wouldn't have occurred to me at that point.

* * * *

TO: D
FROM: HB
Highest level of Plan B reached. Youngston and Trevethen returned fire effectively. One team member sustained slight injury, not serious. Police response extensive, including elite team.

TO: HB
FROM: D
IMMEDIATELY TERMINATE ALL USE OF PLAN B. REFER AGAIN TO INSTRUCTIONS AND CAUTIONS. PROCEED TO ALTERNATE PLAN C. REPEAT: IMMEDIATELY TERMINATE ALL USE OF PLAN B.

Chapter 20

Alec got there first. "Detective, we can certainly come down to answer your questions. But we have some issues here first."

I didn't say anything at that point; I was watching one of the techs bag and tag my pistol.

"Hey! Be careful with that gun!" I didn't want it scratched, or worse, damaged by somebody being careless. The tech merely glanced at me before finishing what he was doing. Damn.

Detective Jackson followed everything with his eyes. I turned to him. "And when will we get our guns back? We weren't doing anything wrong. We were just trying to protect ourselves."

He held up a hand. "We're not filing any charges, but we need to get to the bottom of whatever is going on here. These guns were involved in a shooting, even if you weren't doing anything wrong, and we need to get exemplars. Think of it as getting a handle on which bullets we recover and which brass from the scene we can safely ignore. Since you'll be free to go once we're done, I'll personally haul the guns to the lab and expedite their taking of whatever evidence they think they need and then see that they're returned to you after we've had an opportunity to talk at the station. Will that work for you?"

Well, okay, that was probably the best I was going to get. I nodded somewhat sullenly. "I do need to warn you, if I'm overruled here, then the guns will have to remain as evidence." He glanced at Alec. "You understand, sir?" Alec nodded, although he didn't look any happier about it than I was.

Detective Jackson was actually fairly nice. I needed to feed the dogs before we went. My own stomach and its sounding alert could wait, but they were babies and didn't deserve to be treated this way. Maybe he was a dog lover.

He and his partner came with us into the house and watched while we fixed the dogs' meals, let them out for a quick spin in the backyard afterward and then escorted us to the station. At least they were trying to be nice and accommodating. To a degree anyway, although it didn't escape my notice that neither of us was ever out of somebody's sight.

I had to let Alec wear one of my T-shirts since they wouldn't let him go back to his house, except to lock the door. There seemed to be a limit to the slack they'd give us. Luckily the techs were done with the living room when we left. And despite the damage at the top of the doorframe, I could even lock the front door. The alarm system wouldn't set, but I figured that was probably because the doorframe sensor had been destroyed in the firefight. Not likely to be a big issue with the dogs there.

The interrogation room was small and stark, to say the least. I accepted the coffee they offered—I needed the caffeine—but not only was it pretty piss-poor coffee, I also had to assume that bladder pressure would be used against me. That weighed in favor of going very easy on the liquid intake. I took a few sips, amounting to about one good mouthful or maybe a tad more, before setting the cup down.

Jeez, you'd think that Alec and I had conspired to shoot up the neighborhood ourselves. They kept coming back to me with the same questions time after time, just to see if my answers would change, I guess. Or if they could break down the resistance they clearly thought they felt.

"No, I don't know who did the shooting. Either time."

Would I tell them if I knew? Well, sure. Like hell! If I knew, I'd be tracing them back where they came from, not that I wasn't beginning to get a damn good idea of where that was. I don't *like* being shot at.

What was my investigation about?

219

"No comment."

"Why were you being shot at?"

Now that's an easy one. I have *no frickin' idea* whatsoever. Goddammit, I wish I did. It might make it just a bit easier to take.

"Why would someone go to the trouble of not only shooting up your home, but rigging a diversionary device to simulate gunfire?"

"Hey, buddy, if you can figure that one out, tell *me*, because I'd be thrilled to treat you to dinner. Or cook it for you myself. Think about this rationally. I have no idea who they are, where they come from, why they're doing this or any of the other issues you detectives kept bringing up. If I don't know any of these things, what in hell gives anyone the idea that I would then know why they bothered with such a device? I mean, come *on*."

Even I knew that one was ridiculous. Yes, it seems to be connected to the investigation I'm currently pursuing. No, I won't say more than that and I won't tell you what the investigation is about. Thirty-eight times each, or so it felt.

There were moments when I swear the only thing that kept me silent was the way I'd had it drilled into me since I was a kid: you do *not* talk about the Family. Not to any outsider, ever. Which led to the question of how Alec would be doing on the same issue. He didn't have that lifetime of training. Yes, he seemed a bit cooler under most stress than I was, but these guys were very practiced at breaking people down. No, not rubber hoses and bright lights, just question after question at a very wearying pace. And over and over, in different order, just to confuse me and get me to spit out the truth.

I could have had four or five cups of coffee before I finally got a bathroom break. I still had my first cup in front of me, long since cold, that I'd been sipping as often as I needed to wet my tongue. No more. It tasted even worse than it had to start with, and it had been pretty bad then. But it was liquid, sort of.

I wanted this to be over so bad. I managed to control my thoughts just enough to maintain the mindset, that I didn't know anything beyond what I already told them. If I hadn't heard Alec's response at the house, I wouldn't have thought to bring him and his confidentiality issue into it. I think that helped, and every time I could bring him up in my mind, it helped settle me a bit. Oh, yeah, that was important. But I needed him by me. Being with him felt comfortable. It felt safe. I needed both feelings, badly. It was lonely in that damn room. And I was so tired of having all these questions fired at me that I could barely keep my thoughts straight. I could have asked for a lawyer, but I wouldn't have gotten the one lawyer I needed. He was in another interrogation room, naturally. Going through the same sort of grilling I was.

It was almost mid-afternoon before the detectives finally decided they weren't going to get anything more out of me and were willing to turn me loose. I have to admit that I was surprised when Detective Jackson showed up to not only offer us a lift home, but held up two evidence bags with our guns in them. I wanted to throw myself into Alec's arms, pull him close and shut the world out.

Changing the subject, and more emotionally comfortable for me, I wanted to ask him about his interrogation. Had he said anything I hadn't? Had he mentioned the Family? I wasn't all that worried for myself now, and he didn't look much the worse for wear, but I'd been in that little room for something like six hours. While I was certainly grateful that we would be driven home, since neither of our cars were there, I couldn't say much of any consequence to him until the cops were gone. God, it was as bad as trying to talk in my bugged office!

By the time we got back to the house, the forensic team was long gone and the neighbors were nowhere in sight.

Detective Jackson dropped us off at the sidewalk, and as he drove off, Alec came over and stood by me. A tentative hand on my shoulder and I leaned against him, snuggled right into his side. It felt comfortable. I felt safe. I *needed* to feel safe. We stayed that way until the detective was long gone. It felt so good to be there with Alec like that. That sort of vulnerable feeling was at odds with how I am and how I thought of myself, but I liked it anyway.

The front door was still locked, precisely as we'd left it. The dogs weren't exactly frantic, but they clearly hadn't been happy with us gone for so long. Bruno jumped up on my chest and for a change, I let him before getting down on my knees with him. Sasha would have climbed onto Alec's lap if he'd been sitting down. Well, she would have tried. Instead, Alec just knelt by her and hugged her. After several minutes, she came over to me and sat quietly, leaning into me and occasionally licking my face. The right side; Bruno had already claimed the left. When I could finally break free, I gave Alec a quick peck and headed for the bedroom. Ripping open the evidence bag, I checked the pistol. No scratches worth mentioning, no scrapes or other damage that I could see. I loaded the gun and put it carefully back under my pillow, the one spare magazine back on the nightstand, and I topped off the other.

I pulled off my T-shirt. I sniffed the armpits. Pretty ripe. Tossed it toward the hamper, got a fresh one and re-equipped myself. Not the best without a shower, but I'd been through a lot already today. It could wait. At least I was once again ready to face the world. It had better be ready to face me, because I was by now major-league pissed.

Alec had already given the dogs a chewie each and was pouring fresh coffee. Good coffee, for a welcome change. He was really *the* most thoughtful and caring person. And he felt so good to lean against. Immediately, I stuffed that thought back into the depths of my psyche. Taking my cup of coffee, I thanked him and walked into the living room. This was definitely getting way beyond old, I thought. The bullet holes weren't quite as high this time. But they still would have missed me, and anyway, the shooters had no reason to think I'd be in the room when they fired smack dab through my brand new window and my brand new blackout curtains. Damn. This was getting...no, make that *had gotten* very old and very expensive as well. I knew the glass company was going to absolutely love my business.

Alec came in after a few minutes. "Penny for your thoughts."

I shook my head. "Nothing worth mentioning, actually. Mostly, I was thinking that this is getting way too repetitive in a number of ways. Oh, and aren't you chilly? Why'd you take off the T-shirt?"

He took a moment before responding. "Yeah, it is much too repetitive. And while I could have kept the shirt, it *is* yours. I don't know about you, but I'm hungry. Make that starved. Want something to eat? Here or out?"

I had to admit that I hadn't really thought about food. I'd been too upset by the interrogation. "Okay, there's a container of chili in the fridge. Put the shirt back on."

He laughed. "Some things are back to normal, I see. Okay, that's for you. Aren't there some English muffins in there? That's more my speed."

My turn to laugh. I hadn't done enough of that today. "I finished them yesterday. It's chili or eggs, that's all I've got."

We wound up with eggs scrambled with chili. Workable compromise, especially as it was the first food we'd had all day, and as late as it was, I doubted we'd have much in the way of supper. Alec got more of the eggs, and I got most of the chili. I was happy. Well, as happy as I was going to be. At least some portions of my life were good. Hold onto that thought.

Over breakfast, whatever you wanted to call it in mid-afternoon, he started to bring up the interrogation. I shushed him immediately. I really didn't want to give anything to our unseen listeners. I tapped my ear and he nodded. We finished eating in silence, refilled our coffee and walked out into the backyard. Once we were seated in the middle of the yard, he started again.

"So tell me about your day. Mine was pretty rough."

I kind of slumped in my chair. "God, mine was absolutely horrid. I thought they'd never stop pounding away with the same questions. And they kept doing it over and over." I looked at him. "You know, I've never been interrogated before. I always figured that it was pretty much like being deposed, just a bit worse." I stretched and rolled my shoulders. "I was wrong. It's a *lot* worse. God, I hope I never have to go through anything like that again." I finished my coffee and poured another cup. The unasked question still hung there in front of me, so I asked it. "And what did you say?"

Alec shrugged. "Not much. I let them go a round or two with their questions, then I told them I wanted a lawyer. They asked me who, so I called Rick from the office." Why hadn't I thought of Rick? I knew him well enough. "When he arrived, I told him that this shooting was connected with some work I was doing with you and I had to keep it confidential as a condition of the work. That there had been no accusation of wrongdoing on either of our parts, and could he possibly make all this go away? I don't know what he did, or who he spoke to. I sat in the room for a long time, but at least I wasn't being badgered. Then he came back and they tried again with him there until he called it off. At that point, I sat in the hallway and waited for you. We both tried to get them to stop with you, but since you hadn't lawyered up, they wouldn't pay any attention to either of us trying to insert ourselves. Why didn't you ask for a lawyer?"

I probably had a very sour look on my face. I'd been so fixated on Alec as my lawyer that it never occurred to me to call for one, get someone else and tell him that I couldn't talk about what I was doing. Shit!

"I hadn't thought of it. I figured that my lawyer was in the next room and I wouldn't be allowed to have you come in to rescue me. I really never gave any thought to getting someone else just to make them stop." Alec came over to my chair and got down on one knee. He held me against him for long enough to make me feel much, much better. God, what a day it had been! And he could be so comforting.

That evening, we sat around Becky's patio and told her all about our day. I could see her shudder. She isn't used to shootouts in front of her house. Who am I kidding? I wasn't either. Who is? I only handled them better than she probably would. I'd done some learning how to react to them too. I did ask if she wanted to learn how to shoot. No. Well, I hadn't expected anything else. The idea of being interrogated by the police for hours on end, that was so foreign to her that there was no relating. I did get the distinct impression that she was sort of glad that she and I didn't live together anymore. At least at the moment. I didn't blame her one bit.

One other thought occurred to me and I didn't like it. "You know, there is a certain amount of what I suppose I'd call escalation here, and I have to wonder if they're actually going to cross the line and try to kill me."

Becky looked shocked and horrified. Alec was more thoughtful. "I doubt it," he said. "I can't argue with your assessment that matters are ramping up, but at the same time, they've been very carefully directed at you and seemingly focused enough to avoid collateral damage, as well as being done in a manner to avoid actual injury to you. We all know that if they want to go lethal, you're a goner. I probably will be too. Trust me, if they don't kill me, I will find them. And when I do, they will pay."

Becky had to break in, which stopped me from thinking about what Alec had just said. "This is terrifying. I mean, it's absolutely horrible."

Alec and I looked at her very sharply.

I spoke first. "Let's not even go there. Trust me, my friend, you do *not* want to go there."

Alec smiled, just a little. "Trust Amy on that one, Becky. It's difficult, but we're managing. Being able to say with at least some assurance, if we have any, that they *won't* step up whatever they're doing doesn't answer the question of what they *will* do. I have to admit there would be a certain nice feeling to be able to at least predict what they're likely to do next."

I pondered this for a few moments. "You may be right. Of course, if they figure out some other way to get at me..."

As we were getting ready to leave, I told Sasha and Bruno to keep Becky safe. Bruno cocked his head like he was trying really hard to understand me. Both dogs stayed very close to her as we gave her pecks on the cheek and headed for the car. I chose not to make eye contact with Becky as we left.

The next morning, we loaded our bags, one suitcase and two carry-ons into a cab and went to the airport. I didn't know how far we had to carry this little act, but I certainly wasn't going to blow it on a small detail like looking like we weren't really heading for Scotland. That would have made somebody's life far too simple. Not mine, of course. I did *not* want them to have anything easy at all, whoever they were. I was beginning to wonder if life would ever be easy again, or for that matter, if anything would be the way it had been back when I thought life would be so wonderful if I could merely get more shares and a seat on the board. Little did I know. Didn't somebody say to be careful what you wished for, that you might get it?

What could possibly happen next? I was sure I'd find out. I was also quite sure that I wouldn't like it. I didn't know what was coming, but I also felt sure that someone would enlighten me. Probably way too soon.

* * * *

TO: D
FROM: HB
Youngston and Trevethen taken into police custody for extensive questioning following previous incident. No direct surveillance of questioning possible, but subsequent discussions between targets, and then targets and Swan, offer substance of police questioning. Recordings and transcripts attached. Preparing for Plan C.

TO: HB
FROM: D
Much better. Remember all instructions and cautions. Continue with Plan C.

Chapter 21

We ducked into our respective airport bathrooms and waited for exactly forty-five minutes. We then met by the ticket counter and went to the lower level to grab another cab back to my house. Standing on the sidewalk, we gave some thought to what we were going to do next.

"I'd love to go inside and relax for a bit, but since we figure both our houses are bugged, that would be the biggest dead giveaway that we haven't gone anywhere," I said.

Alec nodded. "Yeah, we considered that point when we planned this out. Let's put our bags in the garage and head for the coffee shop. You did say you were going to bring your garage door opener, didn't you?"

"That was indeed the plan, and I am *so* ready to get some coffee, and maybe a chili doughnut. Then we can plan our next move."

Alec picked up the suitcase and his own carry-on and followed me into the garage. "A chili doughnut?"

I grinned at him. "Remember on our way to Albuquerque? I thought I heard that on the radio? You told me he'd actually said 'jelly doughnut.' Ruined my whole day." He laughed. "Although I bet a chili doughnut would taste really great." He snorted.

Our usual coffee shop was a lot more crowded with students from the U of A than we normally found it, but then we were usually there relatively late in the evening, not in the middle of the morning. We were on the verge of hauling ourselves out to some handy bench when a fellow sitting at one of the outside tables stood up. Alec made his way through the maze of tables and chairs to grab the table while I went inside for our coffee.

There were too many people too close around us to talk about anything in depth, not that we had much to talk about regarding the case anymore. Mostly we sat in companionable silence and absorbed more caffeine.

By the time mid-afternoon rolled around, my butt was quite numb. We'd both taken in—and gotten rid of—a huge volume of liquid. Any more and we'd be sloshing, I figured. By now we were probably safe. Our plane had been gone for several hours and anyone trying to follow us should be long gone, unless they hadn't been fooled by our efforts in the first place. In that event, we were wasting our time anyway. I stood up.

"Let's head for home." All bets were off. We'd have to find out for ourselves. "As far as I know, there's only the two of them we've seen so far. If they think we're on our way to Glasgow, they aren't watching our houses. If they're still watching our houses, they already know that we haven't gone anywhere and they aren't going to be fooled by our sitting around here any longer, if they were at all. And if there are more than two of them, we're probably covered no matter what we do. Either way, I figure we can go back by now."

We had about an hour before we had to leave for Becky's to pick up the dogs. I spent my time going through the mail, both at the house and at the office. Would our watchers pick up on our not having stopped our mail? I never thought of that. Oh, well, it's too late now.

On Becky's patio that evening, I played our first cellphone recordings from McTolland and Greibe. McTolland is an interesting fellow. He began his career as a junior analyst in British Intelligence, MI-6 specifically, and moved up the ladder there. Eventually, he left government employ and became an analyst for a private intelligence firm. On the board, he appears to be primarily responsible for international relations and the impact of political, military and religious factors. He does some international trade analysis, but appears to have more interest in foreign exchange, just like Casaday. McTolland was actually fairly easy to understand. He had a delightful Scottish accent, of course, but at least in my recording, it never descended into the thick accent and slang that I had found so incomprehensible with the other couple.

Greibe was a different matter because he spoke German. Becky had to listen to his conversations several times, dictionary in hand, to make complete sense of them, but only two of them dealt with investing, and both were simply straightforward analyses of the day's news and how it was likely to affect his personal and his friends' investments.

I checked my watch and did some math in my head. Our hypothetical airplane would be landing in Glasgow in about two hours.

"So what do you think? We get in around four p.m., local. Do we call Fields immediately or do we fall into bed and try to shake some of our jet lag first?"

Alec looked thoughtful. "Personally, I vote for the latter. You need to be on your toes for a proper investigation. But how far is it from Glasgow to wherever this fellow lives?"

"Oh, good point. Let me see." Good old Internet. I couldn't pull up exactly what I needed, but I was able to find a map and sort of wing it. "As near as I can figure, it's on the order of 120 miles or so. And those don't look like the best of motorways either."

"We should probably allow at least three hours, possibly four, to get there," Alec said. "It's your investigation, but I think we should spend our first night somewhere in Glasgow and head up there the next day when we're rested."

"I want to get moving when we get there. Hypothetically, of course. I want to call Fields fairly early in the morning their time, and we should be near the target when I do."

230

"Since we're not really going, it probably doesn't matter," he responded dryly. "The same goes for Germany."

"If the plane lands in two hours, allow another hour for retrieving our luggage and getting the car, that's already about one in the morning here. Another four hours to get to wherever this place is, that's five. It's now early afternoon there. Wait a minute. You said we get in around four in the afternoon local. That's more like eight in the morning here, isn't it? That's not two hours from now. In any event, I think that late the following morning is the soonest you'd be calling. You need some time to set up, after all, as well as getting over your jet lag even if we do it there, and then you certainly wouldn't call Fields in the middle of the night."

I did some calculations in my head. "Okay, then. I can call Fields around five a.m. on Friday." Becky just looked lost. "That's a reasonable time, I figure. That it's not reasonable here doesn't matter, since we're not really here."

She now appeared to understand. "Oh, that's good. If you were here and had to get up that early to call him, then it would be a problem. But since you're there, not here, it should be easy enough." The gleam in her eye said she was just yanking my chain.

That left us with a full day to kill. We wound up hiking through Tucson Mountain Park, which isn't all mountains. It covers a fair amount of comparatively flat land on the far side of the Tucson Mountains west of town. It was thick with cactus and ocotillo. Lovely plants to look at, but nothing you want to get close to. Some of them were starting to show buds, but none of the saguaros were blooming yet. There were some hedgehogs and prickly pear in bloom, but they were not overly spectacular.

I'd given some thought to the Desert Museum, but if we'd gone there, the dogs would have had to stay home. In the park, they could go with us. On their leashes, of course, which really helped when we found a good-sized rattler that told us in no uncertain terms to go away. Both dogs wanted to take him on. We wouldn't let them. A handy stick let us prod him gently until he reluctantly vacated the path and allowed us to go on without further incident.

Five o'clock the next morning came far too early. Actually, it was more like 4:30 when my alarm went off, because the dogs needed a shot outside first. I poured myself some coffee so I could sound as if I had been up for hours when I called Fields. I also needed to check the weather in Sligachan, because I didn't feel like being tripped up by a simple question like 'how's your day going?'

And the question did come. Luckily, I knew the temperature there was chilly even by Scots standards and a light rain was falling. Of course, I told him that it was damn cold and wet. But that was just the desert rat in me speaking. I actually lucked out in one regard when I told him I'd be checking on Greibe next and could he call Greibe next week, or did I need to call him again when I was ready? Oh, no, he would remember, no problem. Sir, I cannot emphasize enough the importance of your being really, really adamant, forceful, in fact, in turning down their investment ideas. He assured me he would. I'd heard that before.

Alec came in just before I hung up. It was my turn to do breakfast, and I'd even gotten him some English muffins. I actually surprised him with my southwestern take on eggs benedict. A toasted muffin, some nicely browned slices of chorizo sausage, then a layer of chopped green chilies, topped with a fried egg, jack cheese melted a bit under the broiler and salsa. I was in seventh heaven. Alec enjoyed it, I believe. I needed to keep working on him, but I had made progress. He didn't even need extra water.

I excused myself to take a shower. Some small part of me thought how nice it would be to have someone, Alec specifically, come do my back. Quickly, I packed that thought back into the depths, but I did notice that doing this was becoming a regular experience for me. Too regular.

I wasn't sure how I felt about it. Screw that. I was entirely sure that I wasn't willing to look at those thoughts now. I'd look at them later. Much later. The depths of my mind were getting plenty crowded enough. Sooner or later, I might not be able to cram quite so easily. I'd worry about it tomorrow. Tomorrow is another day and I'll look at things then. Sure you will, Scarlett. I knew that Alec had feelings too. For me. That I knew rationally. Becky had told me so, too. Emotionally, it scared me. Scared me beyond belief. There. I admitted it. Let's put this away and get dressed. I've got work to do.

Listening to the phone tap, Fields was still far more conversational than I would have liked. After six tries, I'd probably have to live with it.

Somewhere around 8:30, the dogs and I headed over to the office to see if there were any fires I needed to put out. Alec was doing the same thing at his office and we were going to meet later for lunch. As I headed for the front door to check the mail, Bruno suddenly passed me and began digging energetically through the pile of today's mail on the floor. When he found the envelope he wanted, he pulled it clear and stood over it proudly.

I picked it up and released him, praising him lavishly. It had clearly been hand-delivered. It was quite thick and simply had my name written on the front. I gathered up the rest of the mail, most of which was junk, and carried it to my desk. I slit the envelope open and found a stack of hundred-dollar bills; fifty-two of them, to be exact. There was a note explaining that this was in payment of a bill, signed by a client I'd written off two or three years before. Well, that's a nice surprise. Found money. Obviously drug money from Bruno's reaction, but beggars and all that. I hadn't ever expected to hear from this client again, and I'd

233

certainly never expected him to clear his bill. I'd take it to the bank right away. A quick call to Alec—left a message on his voicemail when he didn't pick up—and put the dogs back in the house first.

I gave a moment's thought to simply putting the money into my safe and using it as ready cash. It would have avoided any IRS issues, if they didn't find out about it anyway. The thing about doing that is that I avoid IRS scrutiny at all costs. Uncle Jack and Aunt Lori got audited one year—I must have been about ten or so, and Becky was eight. One of those prove-every-line-on-your-return sorts of audits. It was not a pleasant experience. I swore right then that I would cross every i and dot every t to avoid having such a lovely experience. Being Family doesn't exactly help matters either, since it's significant outside income.

All of our checks come from the Bank of Golondrino. I'm sure there are some people who leave their dividends to accumulate there and don't declare them, at least not until they draw them out. Their choice. We're given 1099s, but only on whatever is paid out to us. Trust me, Becky and I take all of our dividends and declare them in full every year. We're not taking any chances. Either of us.

The other issue was that this was, from Bruno's reaction, clearly drug money. Not simply from drug-related enterprises, but probably seriously contaminated. Now I understand that most bills, twenties and up anyway, will test positive for cocaine. Be that as it may, Bruno doesn't alert to money as a rule. If I deposit it, then these bills are gone and it's not a concern to me any more. That suited me just fine, and since I wasn't going to hide them from the IRS anyway, it seemed like the best way to handle it.

The bank is a bit too far to walk conveniently, so I had to drive. I walked in with my envelope full of money and went to the teller. Handing her the money and a deposit slip, I turned halfway around to scan the room. Always be aware of your surroundings. The teller cleared her throat and I turned back to her.

"Is there a problem?"

"No, I don't think so, but I've, ah, I have to go check with a manager about accepting this much cash. Could I ask you to go have a seat in that room for a few minutes?" She gestured to one of the offices that opened onto the corridor extending from the room. The only one open was way down at the end of the corridor, and while it struck me as an odd request, I saw no harm in it and went. She came with me, and after she ushered me in and asked me to have a seat, the door shut behind me. I heard the lock click. What was this? I tried the knob, but it wouldn't turn. Alarm bells were going off in my head, but that didn't do me any good. I already knew something was wrong...very, very wrong. Aware of my surroundings, my ass! I'd been suckered. Shit!

I dug out my cellphone. Alec could, I felt sure, come get me out. But the screen held the dread words: Searching for Service. Shit!

* * * *

TO: D
FROM: HB
Youngston and Trevethen spoofed departure for Europe. Proceeded with investigation of board members McTolland and Grebe from Tucson. Plan C under way.

TO: HB
FROM: D
We could not allow their deception to appear to work. You are doing very well indeed. Continue with Plan C.

Chapter 22

I was sure there had to be some mistake. I rapped on the frosted glass of the door. Nothing happened. I rapped harder and still nothing happened. I tried to look at the situation logically. I'd been knocking on the glass hard enough that I should have been heard throughout the lobby—well, all along the corridor anyway. If nobody is going to respond, that suggests that nothing short of breaking the glass would accomplish anything. And since I can see the fine wires within the glass, breaking it wasn't likely to do much to improve matters either, nor will it endear me to the bank. Not that they're exactly endearing themselves to me at the moment. If I make enough fuss, any customers will hear me. Would that help me? I don't know, so I'll table that for later consideration.

I looked around the room, but there was little I could use to actually break reinforced glass. Apart from a desk, a chair, a file cabinet and a bookcase, the place was damn bare. I could hammer the glass with my pistol, I suppose, but the butt and the entire frame is plastic, so I'd just as soon not do that. If I had the .45, with a metal frame, it would be a different proposition. The only part of this pistol that is definitely strong enough was the steel slide and barrel, and I don't care what you see in movies. You do *not* go beating on things with the business end of your gun. Not unless your life is in the balance, and I hadn't gotten to that point. Hell, I could probably toss the chair through the window, if I got to that point. I'd rather not do that.

Not yet anyway.

Two people came to the door. Not to open it; they just stood on the other side. I stood stock-still on my side of it so I could listen to them as best I could. They were talking about me. One of them was gesturing in my direction. I was barely breathing. I couldn't make everything out, but one of the two was a Secret Service agent! I saw him show his ID folder to the other man. I strained to hear even more. Counterfeit? Yes! Funny money? My money? Oh, *shit!* Funny money my ass! I whirled toward the desk. I really, really needed to talk to Alec. Like right now. Like about five minutes ago.

But there was no phone there. The desk was completely, utterly bare. I was truly screwed, blued and tattooed. Now what? The agent took an object from the other man, apparently he wanted the fake bills to take with him, and told them—I *thought* I heard him say—that he had to get something from his car and he'd be back shortly. They should hold me until then, but under no circumstances whatsoever should they let me out. He emphasized that. Son of a bitch!

My heart was pounding. I was in federal custody on an accusation of counterfeiting; no phone, no cellphone, and Alec had no idea where I was. He'd probably check every bank in the neighborhood—there weren't all that many— but would they even tell him I was here? If he even called here? I felt I was totally out of control with no ability to change the situation.

Shit!

I tried to take stock of my situation. Federal custody! I kept coming back to that. Frankly, I'd rather have someone outside my house shooting at me. Not a huge preference, true, but that was just scary and something I could cope with. This could mean going away for a long time. A very long time. And not even for anything I'd done! Not to mention when they search my house—the poor dogs!—and find my wiretap equipment. I was hyperventilating. My heart was pounding. Alec!

Help!

Finally, I could take a couple of deep breaths and really calm down. Relaxing was out of the question. Probably no harm done, although after everything I've been through in the last couple of months, my heart might never settle down completely. I was still locked in, still waiting for the Secret Service agent to return, and nobody had come to look in on me.

I checked my cellphone. Still no service. I checked the time on the phone. I'd been locked in here...good God, had it already been three hours? It was a little after one p.m., so yes, it had been. My bladder began sending out some urgent signals. I tried rapping on the glass again. Still no luck. I told my bladder firmly to bother me later, I was busy. I was also getting angry, which was at least better than worried.

Let's see. I haven't been formally arrested, so technically, this isn't federal custody. Yet. I haven't been Mirandized. I haven't gotten to make my phone call. I've been locked in an office and left there. Kidnapping or false imprisonment—like that distinction mattered right now— the bank could be buying themselves a major lawsuit. Of course, that would take time and I wanted out *now*. This whole episode smells to high heaven. I don't know what else the Secret Service agent might have told them, or threatened them with, to get them to hold me like this, but the basic facts remain. I'm stuck here, I've got no way to get hold of Alec, and short of physically breaking out of here, or raising such a stink that they have to let me out, I'm still stuck; if the latter option would work at all.

I have no frickin' idea what the Secret Service is doing with me, and frankly, I'd just as soon not find out. They can have the bloody money. If it's not real money it hardly matters to me anyway, does it? They can have my fingerprints—come to think of it, somebody already has them, since they got them for my concealed weapons permit. Several times, since they're taken at every renewal. Like they're going to change. *Let me the hell out of here!*

Time to take a closer look at the office. The only things in the drawers were a couple of sheets of blank paper, an empty file folder, a pad of sticky notes, three paper clips and a staple puller. The bookcase was empty. No phone, no phone book, not so much as a wastebasket.

What can I do? I can't pick the lock with paperclips. Maybe somebody else could, but I can't. The office has no windows other than the one in the door, so I can't spell out 'HELP' in sticky notes on the window to get some passerby to call the police. Would I even want the police coming here? Oh, shit! Out of one frying pan and into another, since they'd defer to the Secret Service.

Damn. Not even a potted plant to pee in. It would have served them right.

People came and went outside my door, but nobody stopped. I tried rapping when they went by. I could see them turn their heads and hesitate, but nobody stopped. Nobody said anything. Pounding harder didn't help and I still hesitated to break the glass. For all I know, there's someone outside just waiting for me to do that, and I won't like the result. Three o'clock came and went. Now my bladder was really getting upset.

So was I. I even gave some thought to trying to shoot my way out. No, that would be tacky. It would get me talked about, and there was probably a security guard somewhere outside who would shoot back. And then the police would come and take me away. No good solution there.

It was a bit after three when somebody unlocked the door. I almost rushed him. I stopped in my tracks when he showed me his ID folder. Secret Service. Shit. I'd hoped they'd forgotten about me, but no such luck.

"Hi. I'm Agent Miller. I understand you've been in here for some time."

I probably sounded even more indignant than I was, but I was going to do my best to take charge of this situation *right now.* "Damn right I have. I've been in here for absolutely *hours*, and I need to go to the goddam bathroom! Do I get to go or do I just do it right here on the floor?"

He turned to the woman behind him. "Agent Gomez, would you be so kind as to accompany this young lady to the bathroom and then bring her back here?"

"Thank you, Agent Miller!" I snapped. Both for letting me go and for calling me a young lady. I'd kiss you if it weren't so serious. And if I weren't in such a hurry, and if I weren't so pissed, no pun intended.

Oh, God, the relief! I thought I'd never stop. Having the stall door open didn't bother me. Having the agent leaning against the sink watching me didn't bother me. Well, not as far as my being able to pee anyway. What the hell. She was a woman. I didn't have anything she hadn't seen before. And even if I did, I didn't care. Finally, I was done. I washed my hands and we walked back to the office. I managed to lead the way. Small triumphs.

Agent Miller was seated behind the desk. I looked at him closely. He had that same sort of slightly skeptical look, at least to my eyes, which seems common to most people in that line of work. I probably have it myself and you probably got it from having started to figure out how many times you've lied to by people. But I had something more important to worry about.

"Agent, you should know that I'm armed. I have a CCW, and I'm carrying."

He actually smiled. I couldn't have been more astounded if Alec had shown up.

"Please understand that we're only here to try to find out what happened today. Something very odd has been going on, and I'm simply trying to get to the bottom of it. We're not going to hold you. We've got no reason to. The bank said something about counterfeit money, but there's no sign of it here, which leaves us nothing to hold you on even if we wanted to. So we'll make you a deal. You don't draw your weapon and Agent Gomez and I won't draw ours either. Deal?"

He wasn't going to hold me? He wasn't going to haul me off to jail? No Leavenworth? Nobody searching my house? Thank God! If only I could call Alec.

"Deal. Can I call my, uh, my boyfriend?" *Boyfriend*! There was that word, the word I'd never used to describe Alec before, and I had used it. To a total stranger. Will wonders never cease? "He hasn't heard from me all day, he doesn't know where I am, and he's got to be concerned."

Agent Miller waved me to his partner, who escorted me to a phone.

Alec answered on the second ring. "My God, Amy, where have you been? I've been worried sick. Your cell didn't answer, I don't know which bank you use, but I called half of them in town and none of them were even willing to say they'd seen you. I've been here with the dogs, and Becky's here also, and we've all been climbing the walls."

I took a deep breath. "Alec, dear, I'm...a little tied up at the moment. But I'm fine and I'll be home as soon as I can. It shouldn't be too much longer. The Secret Service isn't going to hold me. I'm not entirely sure what's going on here, but I'll fill you in when I get there. I think I've been...messed with again. Kiss the dogs for me. Becky, too." My heart hadn't quite settled down, but it was working on it.

Oops. I probably shouldn't have mentioned the Secret Service.

"Secret Service? Amy, what in the hell is going on? I'm your lawyer, remember? Tell them you're lawyering up and I'll be there in just a few minutes."

I almost laughed. I really did. Not from amusement. I think it was mostly from the release of tension. Need a lawyer? Trust me, dear, you would be the first person to know. Well, the second, as soon as I figured it out.

"No, no. No need for that. Everything's fine. They just want to ask me some questions about what happened here today, but they've already said they have nothing to hold me on and no reason to. I'll be careful and I'll holler if I need you. Otherwise, I'll be there as soon as I can. Just hang tight."

"Dammit, Amy—"

"Trust me, Alec. I'm a big girl. I'll call if there's any problem."

Agent Miller was most kind. I did tell him how much it had reassured me when he smiled as he offered me his 'deal'. He simply smiled some more and said, "We're not the FBI. We're allowed to have a sense of humor."

Anyway, when the previous 'agent' hadn't come back, the bank had finally called the local field office, and since they didn't know anything about it, these two had been sent out to see what was going on. No, I hadn't seen the 'agent' who had asked them to hold me. I described the envelope and money. The note, naturally, was still inside the envelope. Apparently, this was something Agent Miller had gotten from the people at the bank; the fake agent—there is evidently nobody in the Secret Service named Coddleston anywhere in the western U.S.—had warned the bank that I'd be coming in with some counterfeit money. Fairly good bills superficially, but only three or four serial numbers in the entire stack. Who looks at serial numbers? Then he'd waited around for me to show up. Anyway, after he had them lock me up, he took the funny money and said he would be back shortly, he had to get something from his car. That's the last anyone saw of him.

And I'll bet he used to drive a jacked-up white pickup too. I didn't mention any of that. Agent Miller did ask whether this could be connected to an investigation I was pursuing. He got the same sort of response as the SWAT team sergeant had. Agent Miller did indicate that the Secret Service was seriously concerned about someone impersonating a federal agent with, apparently, excellent forged credentials, but since I hadn't seen him, spoken to him or had any personal interaction with him, I had precious little to offer and they were done with me until they found him, if they did. At that point, I might have to testify about the counterfeit money, but unless and until then, I was free to go. God, what a relief!

By the time I dragged myself into the house, it was after seven. Alec had given up on anything serious for dinner and had hamburger buns out and a couple of nice heirloom tomatoes to slice. Honestly, I didn't care.

It took me well over an hour to detail my day. Becky was simply astounded. Well, I suppose I was too. Alec was absolutely furious. He started muttering about a lawsuit. I stopped him.

"We know who did this, Alec. It wasn't the bank's fault. Apparently the fellow's Secret Service ID was just as good as the real thing. That's according to the people who not only saw his, but saw the IDs from the two real agents who came later. I'm not happy with what the bank did, and I'm not keeping my accounts there any longer. Well, not much longer. But I also can't completely blame them. They were doing their jobs. Probably wasn't much of a good day for them, either."

Now that I was calming down from the panic that had ruled most of my day, I was getting just as furious as Alec. No coffee now. I had a stiff Scotch. So did Alec. Watered, Becky's looked a lot weaker. I sat and listened to the wind chimes for a few minutes.

"So now I've got another experience to hold against those bastards. I suppose it could have been worse. At least you didn't bring in the FBI."

Alec looked sheepish. "I did call them. I thought maybe you'd been kidnapped. They wouldn't get involved. Not yet anyway."

It was just too much. I started to laugh hysterically. Alec got worried, but Becky stopped him from coming to me. Finally, I ran down.

"Oh, God, this is way too much. We've seen most of the Tucson PD, then the Secret Service, and that would have brought in the FBI." Another burst of laughter. "Who's next. The IRS? BATF?"

Becky looked concerned. "Are you going to be all right?"

I waved her off. "Oh, yeah. It's just"—another burst of chuckles—"it's just too much for one day. Somebody owes me, big time. I don't know if it's Fields or someone else. But somebody's going to pay. Alec, have you ever heard of anyone getting involved with more law enforcement agencies in such a short a time? When they haven't even *done* anything?"

He shook his head.

* * * *

TO: D
FROM: HB
Youngston confined at bank for most of day in accordance with Plan C. Added benefit that she was completely unable to communicate with Trevethen or anyone else until arrival of Secret Service several hours later. Youngston, Trevethen and Swan discussed event later. Recording and transcript attached. Preparing for next incident.

TO: HB
FROM: D
Very well done indeed. Continue with Plan C. Discontinue use of Secret Service credentials to avoid potential further interactions with them.

Chapter 23

If there was anything I could conclude about the whole bank episode, it was that our little charade about heading to Europe hadn't worked, at least in any way we imagined or hoped it would. Weekends presented their own problems during this whole process, since there was less I could do, and that left me with way too much time to brood.

Things picked up on Monday, unexpectedly so. The first thing was a knock on the door at 8:15. I opened the door—cautiously, I didn't need any more surprises, even if it didn't seem likely to be their style—to find a delivery service driver. The same company, coincidentally, which had 'misplaced' my unit on the way to Hawaii. He wasn't delivering my unit.

He did, though, have an overnight letter for me. I signed for it and he left.

I carried it into the kitchen and pulled the tearstrip. Then I looked carefully for any sort of wire or thread. It did occur to me, much too late, of course, that I should probably have done this outside in case it was booby-trapped, but it seemed to be a standard overnight letter packet. I flexed it open. It held one sheet of paper. Cautiously, I eased it out and looked at it. Heavy, off-white, with an engraved letterhead: Raymond Escarton Fields.

I tilted the sheet and looked at the lettering on the letterhead more carefully. Yes, it was engraved, not thermographed. The raised ink was absolutely even and perfect, precisely what you'd expect from someone with Fields' money and position. The letter itself was quite impersonal, and it said, in essence, that he no longer had a need for my services and that I should terminate my investigation forthwith, billing him for my expended time to date.

What the hell? I called Alec. He was on the verge of leaving anyway. When he walked in, he asked me what was up. I handed him the letter. He was as nonplused as I was.

"Why? He doesn't say a word about why he wants you to stop. I think that given the number of things that have happened to you, if nothing else, you deserve an explanation."

"You're right." I picked up my cellphone. My regular one. Fields picked up promptly. "Mr. Fields?"

"Ms. Youngston. What can I do for you today?"

"Well, sir, I just got your letter, and to say the least, I'm a bit at a loss for words. Has my service been lacking? Is there some sort of problem?" There was a long silence on the other end. Finally, I had to say something. "Mr. Fields?"

"Yes, I'm here. I'm just trying to figure out what letter you are talking about."

"The one that was delivered this morning. It was sent overnight—well, last Friday—from"—I checked the envelope—"your office in Greenwich, Connecticut. According to the shipping label anyway."

"I've sent you no letter."

"You're sure, sir?"

I couldn't be certain, but did he sound as though he was a tad irritated at being questioned like this?

"Of course I'm sure, Ms. Youngston. I believe I would know if I'd sent you such a letter. It's nothing I sent. If you've nothing else, and you'll excuse me, I have things I need to do."

"Uh, no, sir. That's all I had. Thank you for your time, sir." He'd hung up before I could get the last three words out. I looked at Alec.

He said, "They're screwing with you again. Cheer up. This isn't going to make you replace your picture window."

I shook my head. The letter looked genuine as could be. I'd never seen Fields' letterhead, but I had no reason to doubt it. The signature looked real, as real as the one on my contract, and I'd watched Fields sign that one himself. I had less faith in the shipper's label, but that matched too. I didn't bother trying to pull up a directory to see if his office really was on East Putnam Avenue. I couldn't imagine anyone being that sloppy, given everything they'd done so carefully up to this point. And since Fields had denied sending the letter, it didn't really matter if they had been.

The way they'd gotten past my alarms and security system, they could certainly have lifted a sheet of letterhead from his office. I suspected that he didn't have half the security I did, and mine certainly hadn't slowed them down. All I was doing was second-guessing myself. I only had his word that he hadn't sent the letter to me. But if he hadn't, then who had? If he had actually sent it and now denied it, *why in the hell*? And come to think of it, I'd never given him my home address. So far as I knew, all he had was the office address—but the letter came here, to the house!

* * * *

TO: D
FROM: HB
REF letter ineffective. Preparing next interaction.

TO: HB
ГПОМ. D
Some failures are to be expected and have been allowed for. Continue with Plan C.

Chapter 24

Late that afternoon we were loading up the car for our trip to Jackson, Wyoming the next day. I'd put it off as long as I reasonably could. If I could still carry off the fiction that we were in Europe, I'd wait another week or so. But since the watchers obviously knew we were here, there was no reason to stick around. We had the garage door open and were busy putting our suitcases into the back of the car when Bruno gave a warning bark. I turned around to see a reasonably well-dressed fellow standing on the sidewalk looking at us. He was armed. It didn't show much, but it was something I'd learned long ago to look for.

"Excuse me, but I'm looking for Mr."—he checked a note in his hand—"Alexander Trevethen. I was told I might find him here."

Alec straightened up. "I'm Alec Trevethen. And you would be...?"

He pulled an ID folder from his inside jacket pocket and flipped it open. "Special Agent Enrico Gonzales, Justice Department. I'm following up on a report of a possible kidnapping."

I muttered quietly, "Yeah, right." I don't think he heard me. I also didn't care. Alec heard me.

He stepped up to Gonzales and took a closer look at the ID folder. "Amy, this claims he's from the FBI." He indicated it to me. "Would you please go call the field office and check on him?"

Gonzales, of course, had no idea of the things we'd been going through. He seemed to bristle a bit at the suggestion, but responded most politely. A lot more politely than his body language suggested he felt like.

"Mr. Trevethen, I'm following up on a call you made to us last week. If I weren't genuine, I wouldn't know about that call and I wouldn't know your name either."

Bruno simply watched the agent intently. So did Sasha, but she hadn't moved from where she was lying in the yard. Such a slug. Lovable but lazy.

Alec said nothing for a moment. I could guess what he was thinking—that this fellow, assuming he really was FBI, literally had no idea what sort of a mess he was intruding into.

Alec simply said, "Let's just say that we have an excess of caution, okay?"

The agent tried, very reasonably, to convince him otherwise. He also pointed out that the field office wouldn't say anything. Yeah, right. They hadn't had to cope with me before.

It took a bit of work, quite a bit of misdirection, and some acting, but by the time I'd made several phone calls on different lines, the field office had, without realizing it, confirmed that they really had such an agent, and what physical description I could worm out of them matched.

It turned out he was looking for me. Not in the fashion that he was asking after Alec; he was following up on my possible kidnapping that Alec had called them about on Friday. Satisfied that everything was fine, he left. I didn't tell him about my run-in with the Secret Service. I remembered what Agent Miller had suggested about the FBI's sense of humor. When he was almost back at his car in front of Alec's house, I shook my head.

"I'd have bet a good chunk of change that he was another fake, you know. I mean, we've had a fake Secret Service agent already. There's no reason on God's green earth not to expect a fake FBI agent too."

Alec had a wry smile. "True. But there is a point beyond which a healthy paranoia becomes dangerous. Blowing him off because we didn't believe he was real wouldn't have been the best possible idea. Checking on him was legitimate."

After steak, salad and baked potatoes that evening, the three of us hauled our coffee outside as usual. Becky was not surprised by the letter.

"Actually, I'm a bit impressed by them. They've tried the physical approach and it hasn't worked. You could make a case that it's backfired on them, inasmuch as it's made you angry, determined not to be scared by them any longer and even less likely to stop your investigation. Then they tried the official approach. This is more the psychological tactic. Interesting. It really doesn't tell me anything substantive about them, but it's interesting. You're sure it's a fake?"

How could I answer that? "It's as much a fake as Fields is being honest with me. What does that tell you? And factor in, of course, that I never gave Fields the address of this house. To the best of my knowledge, all he has is the office address. I gave the Family that one when you and I first moved in, and I've never bothered to change it. All my Family mail comes there. Fields came to see me there. On the other hand, he was awfully cavalier about someone sending out a fake letter on his letterhead over his signature. You'd think he'd be more upset by the idea, and he just brushed me off. Does that help?"

Alec put in his two cents worth. "I compared the signature on the letter to the one on Amy's fee agreement. As a layman's opinion, I'd say the signature appears to be genuine. The originating address checks out. The letterhead looks genuine. But if Fields is lying from the beginning, then he could very well have done this letter himself just to deny it and yank Amy's chain some more."

Becky looked lost in thought. I waited a moment before interrupting her. "Penny for your thoughts."

She shrugged. "I simply don't know. It really comes down to his honesty, doesn't it? If he's dealing straight with you, then the letter is a fake, pure and simple, and he may just have been too engrossed in something else to react more. If he's not, then you're both right. He could very well have produced the letter and then lied about it. Is there anything we can do to check his story out?"

That made me think. I'd never really given any serious thought to trying to double-check Fields' story. Had that been a mistake? One problem was that he specifically told me that he'd avoided involving the police after the initial incidents. What about his being shot at? I'd never been to Greenwich, but Fields has more money than God, I think, and I suspect that there were some big estates out there, probably plenty big enough for a couple of gunshots to go unremarked by the neighbors and consequently unnoticed by officialdom. How could I check?

Alec ducked inside and came out several minutes later with our law school class directory. He had to hold it at an odd angle to catch the light from the patio, but he finally determined that we had no classmates anywhere in lower Connecticut. No major surprise.

Becky said, "How about Port Chester, New York? It's just across the state line. Or most anywhere else in Westchester County." Nope, nobody there either. Then she spoke up again. "I have a classmate in Stamford. That's just up the road from Greenwich."

Alec saw one potential problem. "Family?"

Becky shook her head. "No, she's not. I do know of two Family members in Riverside, but I figured you'd want to avoid them."

I was relieved. And it could give us the opening we needed. "See if your classmate can locate a good PI, and/or a line into the Greenwich PD while we're gone, would you? I don't think I can do much before then."

We decided not to push ourselves getting to Jackson. Straight through, it's something like an eighteen-hour drive and over a thousand miles. We could have driven in one stretch if there'd been a need, but there just didn't seem to be any real reason to push that hard.

I found a nice little B&B in Panguitch, Utah, about halfway between Tucson and Jackson and only a block off the main drag. Panguitch is also the last town before you have to go over the mountains and hook up with the interstate after coming up US 89 from Flagstaff. I'd made the reservation before I got a good look at Panguitch and realized that at a block off the main drag, the B&B was almost halfway to the city limits, or so it seemed. It only had one room available with one bed. Luckily it was a king.

I must have been tired. Very tired. I have a vague memory of feeling Alec's back against mine through the long T-shirt I again wore in lieu of the nightgown I don't own. The next thing I knew it was morning. No dreams, no thoughts of him next to me...well, that at least didn't make me uneasy, and wonder of wonders, I awoke rested. I was able to duck into the bathroom while he was still asleep. A quick shower, new panties and bra, and by the time I came out, he was awake. A quick peck for the morning, then I hopped into my jeans, put on the holster with the pistol I'd retrieved from under my pillow, clipped on my knife, slipped on the T-shirt, zipped my bag and carried it downstairs. Had my very restful sleep anything to do with being next to him? Once again, my mind was hard at work on things I'd just as soon not look at. Stay tough, stay on track.

North of Panguitch, we cut over to I-15. The interstate going north through central Utah tended to remind me somewhat of I-25 going through central New Mexico, or southern Colorado, for that matter: long stretches of up-and-down hills, not much to see except grassy plains and mountains off in the distance.

We took advantage of the emptiness to do the by now usual routine of ducking into exits, waiting briefly and then jumping back onto the freeway. Nobody seemed to have any interest in what we were doing. I even got out at one of these out-in-the-middle-of-nowhere exits and spent some time scanning the sky. Also nothing, except for a couple of turkey vultures hoping for a meal. But at least we were looking. I'd like to say I was done being sloppy. Hopefully I was right. Being the target instead of the investigator, even after all these weeks, was still a new and unsettling feeling, and the reactions weren't completely automatic yet. Give them time.

This held us all the way to Salt Lake. The stretch east of the greater city was clearly mountain sports territory. Crowded with condos, very pretty, and exactly the sort of place I'd love to see—in a travelogue, not first hand. At least there wasn't all that much snow left. Shortly before we crossed into Wyoming, the scenery changed to prairie country and stayed that way for a long time. We climbed into hills again before eventually heading into a river gorge—magnificent if you like that sort of thing. Mountains rising up out of sight on either side, thick pine woods all around—definitely not to my taste. When we came out, we were significantly higher in altitude and it was bloody cold outside. Alec suddenly pointed at a moose off the left side of the road. I couldn't resist. I pulled over and we watched the animal for a while. It didn't move. We eventually realized that we'd been suckered by a statue. Who puts a moose statue out by the road? We drove on.

Coming into Jackson from the south is, to say the least, not impressive. As I eventually figured out, all the pretty snow-covered mountains are to the northwest of town, and you really can't see them when you come in from the south. Finding the resort where we had a condo reserved was no problem. I'd spent quite a bit of time debating whether to go ahead and make our reservations online, or on the prepaid cell. I settled on the cell so maybe nobody would know where we'd be staying.

The resort, Snow King, was on the southeast corner of Jackson, and it was easy enough to find. We finally got a tiny bit of a view of the mountains from there. It was suppertime when we got in, but they had a nice Mexican restaurant in town to recommend. I could at least find some decent food. Alec ate it, before admitting that it was quite good. I think I amuse him when I'm not cauterizing his taste buds, as Becky would say. The condo itself was quite nice. One side was a complete suite and the other much the same except it only had a partial kitchen. I took the bigger side.

George Rogerton was the final board member for me to check, unless I actually went to Europe and took a close-up look at McTolland and Greibe. Rogerton was the senior board member; he'd been elected in a special election shortly after David Brixton became the CEO, more than twenty-five years ago. Cousin Rogerton had worked all his life in various parts of the retail industry, and he rose to the level of managing divisions or portions of stores and even chains, but never held overall command of any store or chain.

Some of his career moves seemed to suggest to me that he was deliberately avoiding the topmost slots. He eventually left the retail business to become an analyst for a major mutual fund family, specializing in retail industry securities. He retired from there about ten years ago.

Hm. I should have asked Jim Briteman about him, since they had served on the board together. Oh, well, a bit late for that now. His address took some finding. It didn't seem to be in my nav system, which wasn't exactly what I wanted to have happen. I finally had to break down and buy a local map. Enough looking around and I eventually found the street I was searching for south of the highway near Teton Village. If I'd known that, I might have stayed out there instead of in town, or so I thought at first. When I got a look at Teton Village, I decided that no, I was happier where I was. It's not a great choice between one ski resort and another, but the town proper didn't seem to be quite as dedicated to winter sports. Oh, well, we were there, unpacked, and we now knew where we were heading.

Finding a phone pedestal was a lot harder. The roads were empty, which was good. But the only pedestal I could find was about a half-mile from the house. I had my doubts about whether it was even the one I needed, but we'd been driving aimlessly around the sparsely populated neighborhood for close to an hour, and this was the only one I'd located. I figured I'd take a chance, and given the total lack of traffic, I would try to set up right now. I'd have a problem if someone showed up, but I hoped I'd hear before any car came into sight so I could duck into the woods.

Nobody came. I used the rock; it was that or the phone company box. I'd left the other two home. My luck couldn't be running so bad that I'd need four units to carry out one surveillance, could it? Hush, girl, don't tempt fate. I could almost hear Grandmother Alannah telling me that. Good advice, though.

My unit was gone the next day when we went back for my initial recordings. Shit! I took even less time to set up the phone company box. Luckily my wire harness had just been disconnected from the unit, not from the pedestal, which saved me some small amount of time.

That one worked. Or perhaps it just fooled whoever was doing this long enough that they didn't remove it. I didn't know and didn't care. I had it in place and was getting good clear recordings off it. Yes, it was the right pedestal. And cousin Rogerton had a cellphone, so I uploaded my software during the usual 'sorry, wrong number' call.

Once more the obligatory call to Fields, asking him to call Rogerton. I was no longer surprised, or even annoyed, by how casual he was when I specifically asked him to be emphatic. By now, I expected it. And since this was the last time, it just didn't seem worth the effort any more even to be annoyed.

255

I also expected the reaction I got from Rogerton, that is, zippo. No follow-up phone call, no email, no talking to himself about his failure. Not a goddam thing. I was pissed when I retrieved my box. Very pissed.

Alec and I walked into town for supper. I wasn't sure what I wanted, but I definitely wanted to get out and move around. I hadn't been to the gym anywhere near enough lately, I needed my exercise, and I kept hoping to stimulate my brain, or perhaps his, to notice something we'd overlooked.

There was a place facing the square on the west side that claimed to have excellent hamburgers. We had to wait quite a while, and then eat sitting at the counter in what looked like a 1950s diner, even down to the linoleum floor and the swivel stools with the red vinyl cushions, but it was worth it. They really were first-rate burgers, with waffle fries, not french fries. Then we walked back to Snow King. No new insights came while we were out except the realization that Jackson was way high up and didn't have a lot of oxygen available. Or warmth either, but that was something we were more prepared for.

Back at the condo, I poured us some stiff drinks before sitting heavily on the sofa. "I just don't get it. No, back up. If there is one thing that I now feel entirely safe saying about this *shitty* case, it is that we have been deceived from the start." Alec motioned with his hand for me to continue. "It is certainly possible that one, or even two, of the board members might be involved with some group acting for nefarious purposes and not have any immediate reaction to being told that their efforts don't mean squat. But let's look at it analytically. One or two members can't do anything by themselves. We know that at the very minimum, practically speaking, there could not be fewer than four involved. I'd go with four as a lower limit because four of them could almost certainly sway one more to vote their way in filling a vacancy in the CEO's chair. Not fewer than four. But it absolutely beggars belief that *not one* of those four would react in some fashion to give themselves away after being foiled or blown off completely by Fields."

Alec was nodding. He drained his glass and got up. I handed him mine for a refill. "You're right, I think," he said as he headed for the kitchen. It's only separated from the living room by a low partial wall, so he kept talking. "But that makes it essentially certain that Fields has been lying to you and leading you on from the very start. Even if we accept that, it doesn't answer the prime question it raises. Why? What's his reason for putting you through all this?"

I took my glass and had another swallow of my drink. What sort of reason could there be? And why agree to such a major payment if I found something? Especially since it didn't even look as though there were anything to find? I mean, a hundred shares and a board seat, whatever that seat might be good for, or worth, with a total investing dufus such as me in it, was still one hell of a payment. Shit, if he tossed me off the board the very next day, I'd still have my hundred shares. That was pretty major all by itself. And was his reason, whatever it might be, serious enough to be worth putting me through all this? Was it enough for *me* to be worth going through it?

Tentative answer: yes, to him it was. Obviously, because he had done it. And yes, it was to me as well. That hundred shares made it so. I said as much to Alec.

"Well, if we're correct, then you've found who's behind all of this," he said. "He is. You weren't tasked with finding out why, just who. I'd suggest that you cannot, on the one hand, go to him and tell him that you can't find anyone behind everything that he told you was happening. There obviously *is* someone, since it's happening to you too, whether it's actually happening to him or not. But it really appears more and more that the responsible party is

Fields himself, if only because he's the only one left. I wish I knew why."

He took a good swallow of his drink. I didn't think he felt any more certain of this than I did, but he was right, at least to the point that there seemed to be only the one answer.

"So what happens when you tell him that?" he asked. "And by the by, if none of the board members are involved in this, whose seat are you going to get?"

"Both are excellent questions, and the only answer I have for either one is, I don't know." I drained my glass. "Oh, hell. I'm going to sleep on it. Maybe I'll have a dream that will give me all the answers." I patted his shoulder on the way to the kitchen.

He stood up. "Me, too. Are we leaving in the morning?"

I shrugged. "No reason to stick around."

* * * *

TO: D
FROM: HB
Youngston, Trevethen and Swan discussed REF letter, began planning to investigate REF for possible involvement. Recording and transcript attached. Youngston and Trevethen traveled to NW Wyoming to investigate board member Rogerton, but lack of results have caused targets to focus on REF as primary responsible party. Recording and transcript attached. Taking immediate steps to disrupt return trip.

TO: HB
FROM: D
Reaction unfortunate, but not unexpected. Continue with Plan C, redoubling efforts as possible.

Chapter 25

I'm sure that Jackson is an absolutely beautiful place in summer. It's probably also beautiful in winter, if you appreciate that sort of thing. The Tetons are magnificent, although I have to wonder about the Frenchman who purportedly named them. If I understand correctly, he named them as what they reminded him of: big tits. No, according to the couple of translations I've seen, that's not being vulgar, that's really how it translates. Well, when I look at them, I figure their proper name should probably be Grand Dents, because they look one hell of a lot more like teeth to me. He'd probably been away from women for way too long. I can also assure you that they look nothing like my—well, my breasts. Not that I have grand ones.

As for the rest, suffice it to say that being a devout desert rat, I don't appreciate snow-capped mountains, big lakes, rivers, pine woods and so on. I also don't go around comparing rugged, rocky mountains to boobs. If you do either one, more power to you. Of course, if you appreciate this sort of scenery, you probably like winter too. Frankly, I think it's frickin' *cold* here. Here it is, the end of April. I mean, I understand it's not going to be shirtsleeve weather. This is northwestern Wyoming, after all. It's too far north and too high up for that. But damn! It shouldn't be down jacket and wool scarf cold now, I shouldn't be seeing my *breath* at this time of year. Oh, Lord, why can't I just have some decent three-digit temperatures? In the plus category, that is? I probably couldn't work up a decent sweat while exercising. As cold as it is, I'd probably have to work out for an hour just to be warm.

Enough bitching about the temperature. We were getting ready to leave town and go home to Tucson. I'm not sure whether we were discouraged for being skunked once again or if we felt optimistic that we had ruled out yet one more uninvolved board member, narrowing the field of possible malefactors down that much more. Like to only one. If there really are any bad guys at all here; I still didn't know what to make of all this, given what we'd found about the power structure of the Family corporation. Assuming, of course, that 'power structure' was the best term to use in this regard. But 'suspicious as all hell' came to mind rather quickly, and my suspicions weren't directed at any of the eight board members. The CEO, now...that was a horse of a different color.

One of the nicest things about the Love Ridge condos at Snow King in my book, and even more at this time of year, is that they have parking underneath the buildings. We carried our suitcases down the narrow stairs, stowed them in the back of the car and got in. We were leaving early, so Alec was driving first, as he's generally more of a morning person than I.

We'd moved just inches when there was an extended bl-bl-bl-blam! as four explosions went off virtually at once, sounding almost like they were in the car with us. Alec jammed on the brake and threw the car into park in one single motion as we both bailed out in record time. This was getting beyond old. As I drew my pistol while leaping out of the car, I saw that both tires on my side were flat and the wheel wells showed minor scorching. The parking area was small enough that there really aren't any dark corners worth worrying about, so we advanced on the stairway for the other side of the building and cleared it together before we inspected the car further.

When we did, I went through the roof. Not just the tires on my side, but *all four* tires were blown and there was the same sort of scorching n all four wheel wells. Alec thought, as he said later, that it looked like it might have been the small explosive charges they use in movies to blow tires on command.

I screamed. I couldn't help it. One long incoherent scream of utter rage that probably echoed down the length of the Wind River Range we could see off to the east. When I was done, I looked at Alec as he was pulling his fingers out of his ears. He shook his head sharply as though to clear it.

"Done?" He asked, and I nodded. "Then I'd suggest you put your gun away. Somebody's likely to be here soon."

Several people arrived within minutes. One of them was the manager, or perhaps he was the owner. I never really got that straight. At any rate, he told us not to worry, we could have the condo as long as we needed to stay while we got the car taken care of.

By the time I'd dropped my suitcase in the bedroom and come back into the living room, Alec had already begun making coffee. I threw myself onto the couch, plopped my feet on the coffee table and waited for him to bring me a mug.

I sat and fumed in silence. Mentally, I ran back over the entire investigation, but no matter what I looked at, who I considered, I kept coming back to the same conclusion. Alec was right last night. We'd looked at everybody, every board member, and *not one* had reacted as we knew someone involved in these supposed attacks on Fields *had* to have reacted. By sheer elimination, Fields himself had to be the person responsible for everything that had happened. There was no other possibility left.

And there was Alec...

The one constant through everything that had happened to me during this entire investigation was Alec at my side as though he belonged there. When I knew what to do, he supported me. When I had a problem, he was there to help me. When I was lost, he was my rock. When I'd been lied to, he was straight with me. When I was in danger, he did everything possible to protect me. I could always depend on him.

Oh, come *on*, Amy. You know where this is headed. Becky's been trying to tell you for ages and now you've finally gotten to the same place. Just *do* it.

Screw Fields, so to speak. I stood up. Alec stood up too, a puzzled look on his face. I reached for his hand, then turned and led him towards the bedroom.

Once in the room, I turned to him and slid my hands under his T-shirt.

"Amy, are you sure?" His face showed concern.

As he raised his arms, I pulled the shirt over his head. "No, I'm not sure. But it's the right thing for us to do at this point. Now just shut up, okay? If I think too much, I may not go through with this, and...and I want to."

It felt good to let the tough girl front go for a bit. Just relax and give in to him for a while. And damn! If I'd known it would be like this...

Obviously the one time we'd tried having sex before, we'd both been far too messed up by our marriages and not over our various traumas. I do have some memory from that episode of cringing inside, waiting to be so badly hurt once again, and being utterly convinced when it didn't happen right then that it was just building up and it would be that much worse when it finally came. Much as I hated to admit it to myself, Alec has always been inside my defenses, and that had made him too dangerous to risk having that deep a relationship with. I couldn't make that adjustment from listening to my mind to feeling with my heart. So I wouldn't—*couldn't*—take the chance and I shut that avenue down completely. I was desperately trying to mitigate my losses in the relationship department. So much so, in fact, that I wouldn't even consider that forming a new relationship takes time and care. I had plenty of care, but I wasn't willing to give it the time it needed. I could see that now, although it hardly matters any more.

262

I'm sure Becky could come up with some fancy explanation, but the truth is that she probably knew long ago, at least the critical portions of what was going on within me and, just like Alec, knew that if I were left alone long enough, I'd figure it out and get beyond it if I could. There was no rushing this progression. No, knowing me, if anyone had tried to rush me, I'd have dug in my heels and headed in a different direction just to prove them wrong. I had to do it in my own way, in my own time. I finally did, when what had been done to me finally pushed me over the edge and I needed somebody so badly.

No, not *somebody*; I needed *Alec* that badly. It took such a very long time. Probably way too long, but at least the waiting was over now. It had definitely been worth the wait, at least for me, and while I'd wasted a good deal of possible time we could have had together, it had certainly given us the opportunity to become absolute best of friends first. Long lasting relationships need that as a cornerstone, I'm utterly certain. Mentally, I snorted. Hear me talking about long-term relationships! But I think I'm not scared anymore. No, I know I'm not. Not at least, that is, of being with Alec. Truly *being* with Alec. And ain't that just the most incredibly amazing thing?

It had been about seven in the morning when we had originally tried to leave, but once back in the room, we stayed. Hunger finally drove us out of the room by mid-afternoon. I guess you can only have so much sex on the fuel you have stored. Whatever had gone wrong on that abortive attempt Alec and I had years back was, as I now realized, a total abreaction. He probably didn't have enough separation from his ex, and I certainly didn't from mine. Instead of being patient, I had erected a wall of truly unbelievable proportions. It was gone now, utterly shattered by the explosions this morning.

The next day when we returned to the reality of the moment, I realized we couldn't simply remain here with the car sticking a foot or two out from the parking place and four flat tires. The wheel well scorching turned out to be cosmetic, but the tires were another matter. I sat down and began calling around. Not all that many tire shops in town, and apparently there had been a lot of demand for that size tire lately. The one shop that was willing to come get us without my having to arrange a separate tow couldn't have four tires of the right size until the next day, or maybe even the day after. Jackson is a long way from almost anywhere. But they would not only bring us to the shop with the car, they'd even bring us back or drop us wherever in town we wanted. Good. I was getting tired of the Snow King food and needed a change of scenery. Not Alec, but I wanted something other than the condo to look at. He was going to be around for a long, long time and I loved looking at him, loved being with him. I was beginning to love everything about him. More than I had before, that is.

I hated to leave the car with them, but I also had to admit that it wasn't doing us a whole hell of a lot of good where it was with four flats. After I signed the paperwork and got the shop manager's promise to call us when the tires were in and then collect us when the work was done, we had them drop us off at the Snake River Brewery. Pub food was something I hadn't had in a while and it suited my mood. Beer brewed on the spot to wash it down with was even better. This place had simply terrific food. We'd have to come back in the unlikely event that we ever returned to the frozen northland.

We both probably had a beer or two too many by the time we left. The sun was low in the sky over the mountains to the west, but we had a fair amount of light left to walk home by. We also probably shouldn't have been armed while we were drinking, but neither of us is the type to brandish a weapon unnecessarily, and after what we'd been through, I was damned if we were going to be functionally naked simply because we enjoyed a beer or two. Or three. Each. Big ones. Luckily they had nice rest rooms.

* * * *

TO: D
FROM: HB
Plan C appears to have caused Youngston and Trevethen to progress into a more involved relationship. Please advise.

TO: HB
FROM: D
Somewhat surprising, but not entirely unexpected. Do not worry about it. Prepare for shift to Plan D.

Chapter 26

Snow King Resort is easy to find. Snow King Mountain looms over the south side of town, and the first thing is to walk toward it until there are no more streets. Then you head left and keep going. The road runs right up into the Snow King parking lot. Even with a bit too much alcohol, we could find it just fine. The altitude was punishing, and we'd already had a good walk and were breathing heavily by the time we got up the hill of the parking lot. Most of it, not all, was from exertion at altitude.

With the door locked and chained behind us, we could have ripped each other's clothes off and gone at it, right there on the hardwood floor. But no longer being teenagers, we spent a bit more time and genteelly got into bed first. Oh, hell, there was nothing genteel about it. We leapt into bed. Most of the time was spent cuddling, but not all. Eventually we dropped off to sleep in each other's arms. The night was too short and morning arrived with the car issues and our departure still hanging over us. However, I must admit, that once again, I had a good night's sleep. A *very* good night's sleep. I also gave Alec one hell of a wake-up call. How wonderful! Especially when he returned the favor.

I figured that we were probably better off leaving directly from the tire shop rather than bringing the car back here, unless we were just coming in to load up and go. I was not about to leave it for another night in that garage, supposedly operable, and then have to wonder what sort of surprises would be in it the next morning. This put our leaving a bit later than we had wanted, but by 10 o'clock or so we were driving down US189 through Hoback Junction, heading for I-80 as it made its way toward Utah. The moose still hadn't moved an inch.

We'd switch off driving now and then, and while neither of us slept all that well while riding, we both could do so adequately enough to let us drive on instead of stopping overnight somewhere, like when we came home from Denver. I suspect both of us were more than a little paranoid by now. I know I was.

It was late afternoon, approaching suppertime, when we saw the signs for the exit to Utah SR 20, which would take us over the mountains to US 89 that went down through Panguitch, Kanab, and eventually into Flagstaff. We'd come up that way, and I presumed that we would go back the same way. Alec drove by without slowing.

"Okay, dear, you've obviously got some devious plan in mind. How about letting me in on it? You can trust me." I chuckled. "You're not dropping me off in the desert somewhere, I hope. Remember, it's my car."

He chuckled in return. "I'm not trying to get rid of you. Quite the opposite. We're going into Las Vegas and we're getting married by the Elvis of your choice. I let you go once, and when I realized what a mistake it had been, I vowed that if I ever had a second chance, I wouldn't make that mistake again. Then, I only had to wait for you to realize what I already knew. Helluva wait. But well worth it."

My eyes seemed to be leaking. I brushed the tears away. "What if I don't want to marry you? I've done quite well on my own, I think."

He snorted. "Uh huh. Yeah, right. First things first. Are you turning me down?"

Silence reigned in the car while I thought furiously. Was I turning him down? Of course I was! But every time I started to think that, yeah, I was turning him down, I came back to the last two days. Not only had I come frighteningly close to going over the edge and losing it completely, only to be rescued by him, and nobody else could have managed that particular trick, I realized that I had been truly happy for the first time in years. He really was the one dependable rock in the maelstrom that had been my life ever since Raymond Escarton Fields stepped into my office. I simply could not have managed to conduct this investigation with its associated experiences without Alec by my side. Not to mention that he had already been my partner in virtually every other way for years. I depended on his presence at least as much as, if not even more, than I did Becky's.

I opened my mouth to say that, yeah, I was turning him down. Instead, I heard someone saying softly in my voice, "No, love, I'm not turning you down."

I chewed that over in my mind for a minute before deciding it was the right thing to do. I'd get over my issues later, if they were still there. "But honey, does it have to be Elvis? I don't *want* to be married by Elvis."

Alec laughed. What a sweet sound! "No, it doesn't. You can choose whomever you like. But we can be married tonight." He glanced at the dashboard. "No, let's make that tomorrow. I don't think we'll be there before midnight."

I stretched. "Need me to drive?" I asked.

* * * *

I'm sure that driving I-15 through the Virgin River Gorge as you go from Utah to Nevada in a really good road car in daylight is loads of fun. Driving it in the dark in an SUV, even a BMW, isn't really my idea of a good time. Luckily, I had several semis on the road to not only show me where the road was going, but also give me a good reason to take it a lot slower than the usual highway speed.

We were out of the little chapel as husband and wife well before lunch. For much of Las Vegas it was probably still breakfast time. I was incredulous, ravenous and exhausted. I needed a good pinch, food and sleep, in about that order. Oh, and a ring, I guess. On request, Alec supplied the first right away. Nope, I was still me, awake and still married to him. Good. We found a nice jewelry store by the simple expedient of driving by it and finding a parking place.

Twin gold bands, no decoration. I asked Alec if he really wanted to wear a ring. He responded that he'd worn one for years, it just hadn't showed. I left him there for a quick minute while I ducked into the store next door for a surprise for him later. We then drove to the Wynn and checked into the Bridal Suite. Alec protested that it was too expensive.

"Raymond Escarton Fields is going to pay for it, love, so just simmer down. He owes me big time." Alec shut up.

Several hours later, he said, "I've heard there's a casino around here somewhere."

"Tired of me already? Or is the lure of losing money that great? Aak!" He'd grabbed me, hard, proving that he wasn't at all tired of me just yet. Or that tired, either. A while later we resumed our conversation.

"No, my love, I am not tired of you. I never will be as long as I can draw breath. Maybe beyond as well, but I can't say for sure about that. Losing money holds no particular allure for me either, although I admit that winning it has a certain attraction. But can you imagine any better place to have a private strategy session than in the middle of a bunch of noisy slot machines, just like we did in Albuquerque?" His grin was a mile wide. My eyes grew as wide as I saw what he had in mind. Nodding, I pulled him out of bed as we headed for the shower together. We even spent most of our time there getting clean. And yes, it's *very* nice to have him wash my back.

Before we left the room, there was one more thing I had to do without a backdrop of slot machines. I pulled out my cell and called Becky. Taps and bugs be damned, I wasn't going to say anything that a listener would find of value anyway. I got her machine instead.

"Becky, honey, it's me. How are the dogs? Hey, we're going to be a bit longer than I'd planned. I can't say yet when we're getting back, but I'll let you know as soon as I can. If it's a problem, call me. Otherwise give the puppies a hug and a kiss from mama and tell them I'll see them soon. Sorry to do this to you, but it's important. Real important. I'm sorry I missed you. Love you. Bye. Oh, and I've got something real special to tell you. See you soon. Bye." I flipped it shut and dropped it back in my fanny pack as we headed out of the suite.

It was midmorning the next day when we rolled out of Las Vegas on our way south. This time, I started the driving. I had the radio on. We were almost to Kingman when the breaking news came on about the bomb in the luxury suites at the Wynn. It didn't have anything to do with us.

Or did it?

Several hours later, we turned off I-10—thank God the reconstruction was done and we could use the Speedway exit once again!—and drove to my house. My house? Our house now. Alec turned to me.

"Should we get Bruno and Sasha back now before it's too late to call Becky?"

"No, they're comfortable with her. Let's let them stay another night and get them tomorrow." I turned off the alarm with the remote, picked up my suitcase and unlocked the door from the driveway. Alec reached around me to hold it open and we stepped inside. They didn't hit us until the door had shut behind us.

* * * *

TO: D
FROM: HB
Youngston and Trevethen were married in Las Vegas this morning. Please advise.

270

TO: HB
FROM: D
I shall arrange further actions in LV personally. Return to
Tucson immediately to prepare Plan D.

Chapter 27

I don't know what they used on us, but it knocked us right out. We'd gotten home somewhere around suppertime, but I had no idea how long we'd been unconscious. I was blindfolded and tied up in a chair when I came to, and I had to operate on the presumption that Alec was in the same situation. I certainly hoped he was, but I had no way of knowing for sure.

Well, since my options are limited, let's take stock. No special pain, so while the position I'm in isn't all that comfortable, I don't think I've suffered any particular injury. I may have bumped my head when I was knocked out, but that's minor. The holster under my left arm—I tensed my muscles imperceptibly—felt empty. That checked with the lack of weight. I concentrated. I thought I felt the Hideaway knife below my bra—I still had my T-shirt on—but I couldn't be sure. Might just be the sheath. Amateurs! It's a lot easier to throw your subjects off if you strip them naked. That puts them off balance. Helps you find any weapons they may have hidden too. Shut up, girl. It's to your advantage that they didn't. Don't complain about it.

How about the knife at the back of my waistband, the Hideaway claw? I concentrated on that one. The problem is that I've worn them so long that I no longer feel them under normal circumstances. I thought I could feel it. Maybe. I hoped. The one at my ankle I had no chance of checking on while I was tied up and trying to fake being unconscious, so I wouldn't worry about it for now.

I finally figured out that we were in the kitchen. The chairs were right and I could occasionally hear someone moving about on the floor. It was the only room without carpeting, other than the bathroom, which would have been too small, so that made sense. Finally, I heard a thump and someone said, "All right, you've got to be conscious by now. Make a noise."

Oh, I was gagged, too. Funny I hadn't noticed before. A muffled noise—that had to be Alec. Dear Alec! Then I felt a rough tap on my shoulder.

"How about you. Awake yet?" If nothing else, Alec needed to hear me. I said something that came through the gag as a muffled mumble. Good enough.

We sat in silence for what seemed like a long time. Without some way to tell, it could have been minutes, it could have been hours. It merely seemed like days. If nothing else, my bladder would give me some objective indication. Based on that, I figured that it was probably less than an hour. Finally the same voice I'd heard before spoke again. I think he was addressing me.

"You just don't take hints, do you? We've been trying to tell you to quit your investigation. You could have gone and done something else, but you wouldn't do that. We tried to show you that we could kill you at any time, and still you persisted. What shall we do with you?"

I have to admit that I was really worried. I still didn't know who this was, although obviously these were the people who had been responsible for what had been happening to us over the past several months. One more small piece of the puzzle, just still not enough to show me what the picture looked like. Now he was on the other side of me.

"Yes, what shall we do with you? With your husband here too, for that matter."

That statement really concerned me a lot. Where was the SWAT team when I really needed them? Or the Secret Service? Or anyone, for that matter.

Another piece. They knew Alec and I had gotten married. How? It had been less than thirty-six hours ago and we hadn't told a soul. Even Becky didn't know yet. Of course, as closely as they had obviously been following us for the past several months, and without my being able to see or find them despite repeated efforts, they probably knew what brand of toilet paper I bought, much less anything as obvious as our getting married. We hadn't publicized it yet, but we hadn't exactly hidden it either.

I strained to hear better. I had the distinct impression of not one but two sets of footsteps. In rubber soles, which made my hearing them that much harder, but I was sure that—yes! A scrape of a foot while there were footsteps on the other side of me. Definitely at least two people. Three? I don't know. Not yet, but we've never seen any sign of more than two.

Whap! A slap came out of nowhere and hit my left cheek. Not all that hard, but my head rocked.

"What shall we do with you?" The same voice, more demanding this time. God, it's horrible being blindfolded like this. I have no idea what was happening when there is no sound involved and I can't see anything. Whap! Another slap, but not against me this time, the same demanding question. Obviously hitting Alec. Damn him! I'll rip his throat out. I'll cut him into little pieces and feed him to the dogs. For just an instant, I was glad the dogs hadn't been here; at least they were safe.

Whap! Another slap, on my right cheek this time. Then the same voice, back to a more conversational tone.

"Don't worry, I am not expecting a response. Yes, I know you're gagged. But it does seem extraordinarily difficult to get you to take a hint."

Hm. Some sort of faint accent. Had I heard it before? Maybe. Hispanic? No. Russian? Possibly. European of some sort? Equally possible. What sort of native language? Can't tell yet. If it was anything I'd even recognize.

He went on. "I would really rather not kill you. Dead bodies are so...inconvenient. But if that is what it takes to stop you from continuing your investigation..."

What did he want me to stop? And *why*? I had already checked all the board members who lived in this country and found zilch. From what little I'd been able to get on the two in Europe, they weren't dirty either. Then why try to scare me off now?

If one or more board members were dirty, then something—*something*—should have shown up already. Some hint at least, even if not anything concrete. There was absolutely no way in hell that there wouldn't have been a hint of *some* kind from somebody. But I had absolutely nothing to show for my efforts so far. So why try to scare me off of nothing? It makes no sense. I hate it when things make no sense.

"Think on it for a while," the man said. "Remember that nobody else knows you're here now. If we kill you, nobody will discover your bodies for days. Not until the smell gets out. By that time we will be long gone where your police cannot reach us. Is that what you want to have happen? We'll be back."

I heard both sets of footsteps leave the kitchen.

He was right. Becky knew we'd be home 'soon', but that covered a multitude of sins. If they turned up the air conditioning, it could be a week or more before anyone noticed. The thought of imminent death tends to focus one's thinking like almost nothing else. And the most likely person to discover our bodies when she came to get more dog food would be Becky. Oh, God, what a horrible thing for her to go through! At least Bruno and Sasha would be in good hands. Calm down. Stay rational. Panic solves nothing. Don't let it take me over. I'm tough. Let's use that.

'Long gone where your police cannot reach us'? That suggests somewhere out of the country, which fits with the accent, whatever it might be.

I found I could wiggle my fingers now that I wasn't quite as concerned with what was going on around me. Suddenly, I felt some other fingers—Alec's! Just a touch of fingertips, but oh, how comforting. I wasn't alone. Neither was he. I inched my chair backward just a tiny bit, but the scraping noise sounded louder in the silence than it could possibly have been. Or maybe not. It was only moments later when I again heard footsteps approaching.

"I see you have moved your chair. We cannot have that, now can we? You must think alone. You, after all, are the problem. Your husband will follow whatever you decide, I feel quite sure."

Rough hands hauled me away from Alec and turned my chair. Judging from where the footsteps came from, I figured I had to be near the dishwasher, to the right of the doorway into the dining room, for what good that did me. I needed a plan. First and foremost, I needed to think and consider my options, if I had any.

As frightening as the situation was, I knew that giving in to my fears would only hurt me. Plenty of time for that later, if there was a later. If there wasn't, well...No, damn it! I don't give in to being terrorized. I was done with being terrorized. I'd sat in one of these very chairs and hollered defiance at these people, at their bugs anyway. Hadn't I? Of course, that was before I was at their mercy. Before they had Alec at their mercy too. The defiance faded away, leaving me feeling very small, insignificant and scared. Very scared.

There has to be a way out. There *is* a way out, and all I have to do is find it. Oh, Alec!

* * * *

TO: D
FROM: HB
Youngston and Trevethen immobilized in her residence according to Plan D. Team is proceeding according to plan. Updates will continue.

TO: HB
FROM: D
Excellent. Keep all warnings and cautions in mind. Complete Plan D.

Chapter 28

Whoever he was, he came back. He said something about wanting to hear from us, but he didn't ungag me. Then I heard Alec gasp before asking what they thought they were doing? Oh, my God! A thump and a grunt from Alec. They had to have punched him. Oh, God! A couple of slaps. *Oh, my God! Alec!* Then it was my turn.

I hardly noticed the physical assaults. I was too busy trying to find some moisture in my mouth. They didn't spend any more serious effort on me than they had on Alec. When I could finally move my tongue without it sticking to the roof of my mouth, he heard from me. I tried to sound tough.

"Okay, fella, whoever you are. You've proven that you can beat up a couple of people when they're tied up and blindfolded, and you can generally try to terrorize them. Big fucking deal. Hit the poor woman when she's all tied up and can't hit back. Makes you feel like a real man, I bet."

He chuckled as he strolled around the kitchen. "Oh, I think we can do more than that. Look at that simply as an introduction. We have a lot more things we can do. And we will."

Then I heard a sound that made my blood run cold. He lit one of the burners on the stove.

"Perhaps we'll heat this up"—metal clinked—"and see what this does for you."

Oh, *God!*

"Perhaps we will try it on you." He moved around the kitchen. "Or perhaps we will try it on him instead."

Oh, God! Not Alec!

Then he shut the burner off. I let out a long breath. I didn't know I'd been holding it. I didn't think I was half as quiet about it as I wanted to be.

"That frightens you, does it? Good." His footsteps receded into the dining room.

When I had my heart rate under control, I spoke quietly. "Alec?" Nothing but breathing. "Alec, honey?"

Finally he responded. He sounded winded. "Amy." Several deep breaths. "Amy, love, what's going on here? I'm scared for you."

"Oh, God, Alec, I'm terrified for *you*." A shuddering breath. "I've got no idea what's going on, except that these are obviously the people who've been pulling all the shit that's been happening to me. To us." Another breath. "We've got to find a way out."

"Yeah. I'm trying to work on it, but I'm a bit short on ideas. These ropes are pretty tight and they don't feel like they were tied by amateurs." He sounded awfully calm for someone as terrified as I felt. I forced myself to subordinate my terror. I almost succeeded.

I flexed my muscles. No, the ropes didn't feel loose at all. They felt like whoever had tied them had known exactly what he was doing. Why they hadn't used duct tape, I had no idea. I had the idea that rope might be easier to get out of. Does using rope tell me anything? I don't know.

"Yeah." I paused. "I'm fresh out of ideas myself."

I lost count of how many times he came back, how many different threats he made. It seemed like every fifteen minutes or so, he'd be back. The threats: metal shears. I could hear them clack. The stove burner, several more times. One time, he drew the point of a knife slowly down my arms. Over and over. Another time it was down my cheeks. Over and over. I didn't dare move my head. He seemed to do the same things to Alec. We didn't break down and scream. Why we didn't, how we resisted the urge, I have no idea. Alec was stronger than I would have expected. I know I wasn't. There were times that the only reason I didn't scream was because I was too terrified.

279

Other times, I resisted only because Alec was there and I wouldn't, *couldn't* do that to him. Some time later they gagged us again.

Then the footsteps came back and the stove burner was turned on once more. Metal clinked from the stove. We sat for several minutes in silence, broken only by the hissing of the burner, until suddenly there was a faint sound, kind of like the sound of slapping a steak on the barbecue, and almost simultaneously a pair of pincers closed on my knee. I was taken completely by surprise and couldn't help myself. I screamed into my gag. I have a vague memory of the odor of burning meat, but my knee hurt so bad being squeezed, I continued to scream whenever I wasn't gasping for breath.

Alec went berserk in his chair behind me. Despite the pain, I could hear the noise as he tried to holler through his gag, struggling against his bonds and rattling his chair against the floor. Finally the pincers let me go and the pain stopped. Well, sort of. My knee throbbed for the longest time. I whimpered. I sobbed. At that moment, I thought that I'd have happily quit the investigation, given them all my notes and never cashed another Family dividend check if they'd just go away. They never made the offer. I couldn't tell them through the gag anyway.

The footsteps receded into the living room once more. Again we sat in silence, well, almost. Alec was clearly still straining at the ropes. I was quietly sobbing from the residual pain. As it abated, so did my sobs. They were largely muffled by the gag, but not completely. I could feel the moisture on my face where the tears had run down behind my blindfold. I hadn't known how much pain a grip like that could cause.

Some time later the footsteps returned and the burner was turned on again. By the time I could smell the heated metal of whatever they had over the flame, I was almost insane. Then Alec screamed into his gag and the smell of burning meat once again permeated the room.

Oh God! *Alec!* I sobbed into my gag as I struggled with what little strength I had left against the ropes binding me.

"I'll quit," I said. It didn't get beyond the gag. What else could I say? What else could I do? "I'll stop." It also didn't get beyond my gag. *Alec!* By now, I'd have been whispering if not for the gag. Not because I didn't want to be heard, but simply because that was all the energy I had left. I was crazy with fear for Alec. Worried for myself as well, but much more for him than for me. If they'd have taken my gag off right then and there, they'd have won. I'd broken. I'd have given them everything they wanted, whatever it was. Anything to keep them from hurting Alec.

Perhaps I fainted. I never noticed them leave the room. Once again we sat in silence. I had a chance to reconsider my surrender. The always rational part of my mind had nothing to say. The rest of my mind was too frightened to say anything. I was simply trying to see if there was any reserve of strength left somewhere, anywhere, deep inside me. I had this horrible fear that there wasn't.

Then the footsteps came back. They went to Alec and did something. I strained to hear.

"Come along. It's time you had a bathroom break."

Something exploded in my mind. *Fucking amateurs!* If they're really trying to break us, then force us to break toilet training! This is *crap!* The footsteps receded and I strained to hear again. No such luck. The bathroom was much too far away. After a while the toilet flushed and they came back. It sounded as though Alec was almost thrown into his chair. Some grunts and a gasp; I guess they were retying him. *Damn them!* Then it was my turn. I was untied from the chair, then my legs were untied from the chair legs. Not my hands. I was pulled to my wobbly feet. I was halfway across the dining room before my legs became

281

reasonably steady. My knee still hurt, but it was manageable.

I expected to be taken directly to the bathroom. Stupidity on their part, but I'll take what I can get. It sounded like only one person came with me. No talking. Is this the leader or the stooge? I stumbled against the wall, then against the hallway doorframe. Mentally, I reviewed the layout of the house. I should be nearing the bedroom, with the door to the bathroom another six or eight feet down the hallway on the right.

Suddenly, I was pushed to the right, short of where I figured the bathroom would be. Rough hands pushed me through the doorway and shoved me face down onto the bed. I fought to turn over onto my back. He actually helped me turn over. Then I realized why as his fingers began to struggle with my waistband. I tried to kick out, but he wasn't where I could reach him. Then he unbuttoned my jeans and unzipped the fly. For just a moment, I thought about the tiny black thong I was wearing. I'd put it on it as a surprise for Alec. It would have been a good day to have worn some nice thick tidy whities. No such luck. At least I hadn't gone completely without just to give Alec a thrill when we got here.

The rational part of my mind thought that he's probably getting more thrill right now than he'd bargained for anyway. Not necessarily a good one, of course. Then the reality of the situation hit me. By now my jeans were open and in a minute they'd be off. I'm about to be raped! In my own home! In my own bed! I was wild with fear, panic and rage. No! This can't be happening! The terrorized part of me was screaming, but the rational part told me to shut up. Giving up is not on my list of options. Not for me, and absolutely not for Alec's sake. Now that I've found him, *really* found him, I'm not going to give up without a fight. This son of a bitch is going to rue the day he decided to mess with me!

* * * *

TO: D
FROM: HB
Plan D essentially complete. Will depart Youngston's residence pending return to base as soon as HR returns from final stage of Plan D. Youngston and Trevethen temporarily immobilized.

TO: HB
FROM: D
Excellent work. My personal thanks to everyone. Transportation will be furnished shortly.

Chapter 29

The phone rang. Sorry, I can't pick up. I'm a little preoccupied at the moment. Tied up, actually. But the stooge pulling my jeans off stopped what he was doing for a moment. By now, he was down by the foot of the bed to get better leverage. This may be my chance. My hands were trapped under me, but I had managed to get my fingers into the handle loop of the Hideaway claw from inside the back of my waistband as the jeans came down. By now my right leg was free and the jeans were hanging from my left foot.

I took advantage of his distraction by the ringing phone and drew back my right leg before kicking out suddenly as hard as I could. Twice. I'm quite strong. I connected where it counted. He gasped and I heard a thump as he fell. I rolled onto my side so I could get the knife onto the rope holding my wrists. The rope was tough, but the claw is very sharp and it gave way soon enough. Adrenalin and fear are a potent combination. As soon as my hands were free, I ripped the blindfold and gag off and kicked my jeans the rest of the way off. I wasn't completely surprised to see that I had nicked myself while cutting the rope, but it was minor, only a little blood. Least of my worries.

He was lying curled up on the floor next to the bed, clutching himself where it hurt. I hopped off and delivered the strongest kick with my heel that I could to the side of his head. When he rolled slowly onto his back, I got him again in the crotch as hard as I'd kicked his head. He must have been unconscious by then, because he didn't twitch. I didn't think he'd be going anywhere for a while. Then I looked more closely at his face and recognized him as the supposed cop in Los Ranchos who had pulled us over. I kicked him once more for good measure.

I was panting from the exertion and the stress, but not so hard or so loud that I couldn't hear the footsteps as the boss—that's how I was thinking of him by now—began walking from where he'd probably been watching Alec in the kitchen, toward the bedroom. I scuttled to the doorway and crouched at the side away from where the stooge was lying. As the boss stepped into the doorway, distracted by his pal on the floor, I leaped onto him and began hammering him with my hand and both feet. He couldn't do anything but try, not very successfully, to fend off my blows.

I still had the knife, but I was so furious by then that I never even thought about it. Right at that moment, I would have very happily cut his throat, but that would have made a horrid mess on my bedroom floor and I'd have had another visit from the police. Not to mention a lot more to explain. I certainly was in no mood for another visit to the police station. I was just beginning to slow down and give some thought to how I was going to take him down, when suddenly, Alec came and hit him from behind, knocking both of us to the floor. I was now sandwiched between the boss and the stooge as Alec hit the boss over the head again, harder this time, with a cast-iron frypan that I kept hanging on the wall as a decoration. Decoration, hell. It was actually hanging on my wall to remind me not to spend any more money on hokey crap, which it was. Suddenly, I could not believe how thrilled I was to have bought it. I slithered out from between the two still bodies.

I couldn't stand up straight yet. I stayed there, stooped over with my hands on my knees, breathing heavily as I gave Alec my best lopsided grin.

"Honey, as much as I've ever loved seeing you in the past, I don't think you've ever looked better to me than you do right now." He grinned back.

"Are you all right? Does the burn hurt?"

"No burn, just a sore knee. I'm fine otherwise. They were sloppy when they retied me after my bathroom break. I gave them a bit of help in that regard too. I was trying to find the opportunity to slip the rope off my wrists when this clown"—he gestured at the one I'd tagged the boss—"left the room. That was all I needed. And thank you for having this frypan so handy."

I looked at it. It had had a crappy still-life food scene painted on the bottom, and that was now smeared beyond repair. I began to laugh.

"Here." He handed me the pan. "I'm going to get the rope."

The boss started to stir. I tossed the pan and jumped on him. I wasn't gentle about it. I stuck the knife in his face just as he opened his eyes.

"If you want to see out of these eyes ever again, you will hold very, very still." I must have sounded even more menacing than I felt, because his entire body went limp.

The stooge on the bottom of the pile stayed unconscious. As Alec came back, I realized I was kneeling on this guy's stomach with my bare ass hanging out for God and all the world to see. Well, for Alec anyway. He was the only one in any position to see much of anything at the moment.

Alec had a couple of ropes and had his pistol besides. He said, "Your gun's on the buffet, along with one of your knives. They've unloaded the gun like they did mine, but the magazine and chamber round are right there with it. You can get up now if you want."

I stood up slowly, keeping the knife pointed at the boss. "Roll over onto your face."

Reluctantly, he did as I directed. Touching my chest, I confirmed that the knife I kept clipped to my bra was the one they'd taken. The sheath was still there. I knelt on his butt and gave him a quick pat down before reaching out my hand behind me.

"Let me have a rope. No, two."

Alec put two into my hand. I spent some extra time tying the boss's wrists together most carefully, then I used the second rope to tie his feet and pulled them up hard so I could tie his feet to his wrists. I stood up and considered my handiwork before reaching down again. I stuck the knife into the back of his waistband, sliced his belt in two and cut his pants open for at least six inches. Alec looked perplexed. I didn't take my attention off the boss.

"If he gets loose and tries to go anywhere, he'll have to use both hands to keep his pants up. I have had it up to *here* with these clowns. *Beyond.* I may not be able to bug them, shoot out their windows and blow out their tires, but they are going to rue the day they crossed me."

I pushed the boss off the stooge, then pulled at the still-unconscious stooge until he was lying on his face. I wasn't very gentle about it.

"Gimme the rest of the rope."

I patted him down and tied him the same way, delivering another kick where it would count when he finally woke up. Then I slit his belt and pants before I stood up and looked at Alec again.

"Watch them for a minute. I want to get my jeans back on."

As I've said, I'm not particularly body shy, but there is a time for underwear and a time for pants. Being without my jeans right now was leaving me feeling a bit more vulnerable than I liked, and this was definitely a time when I wanted to have my pants on and as much of a feeling of invulnerability as I could muster. There was also absolutely no need to treat them to a view of a black silk string up my ass and around my waist with some pearls at the junction for trim. Alec could see it again later. I turned my attention back to the boss.

"Okay, fella, give. Who hired you and what were you doing? You said you wanted me to quit my investigation."

As I questioned him, I was doing everything I could to get him onto his back. Having him tied as he was made it lots harder, but I was not about to be balked by something as simple as having his feet and hands underneath him. My surrendering days were over. They'd left me gagged when I would have happily given them everything they wanted, everything I owned or ever hoped to own, just to save Alec and me. Especially Alec. Now the shoe was on the other foot and they were at my mercy. I didn't have much. I suppose I can be bent to the breaking point, but I recover quickly, given the opportunity.

He said nothing. Okay, I can manage the strong and silent type. I knelt on him again. Not gently. He had a very muscular build, not at all what you'd expect from a garden-variety hoodlum. I stuck the knife in his face before laying it alongside his throat.

"Listen up, chump. You have been on my case for months. I am *so* done with your shit. I can do to you what you threatened to do to me." I drew the knife lightly along his throat. It was distinctly sharper than the one he'd been using. It left a hair-thin line of blood where it passed. Not much, just a scratch. But it bled a little. Enough. I held the knife up in front of his eyes. A drop of his blood gathered on the point and threatened to drop into his face. He had good control, but the slight widening of the irises gave him away. Love those involuntary muscles.

Kneeling on him that way was not exactly comfortable. Probably not for either of us, although I had absolutely no concern for his comfort. I came back onto my haunches and reached into his crotch.

"Or we could do something else that you might truly regret." I squeezed. "Care to sing soprano?" He closed his eyes. "Alec, go heat up something on the stove. We've got us a stubborn one here."

Alec had been quiet through all this, but he didn't exactly look like he disapproved of what I was doing. He

288

handed me the pistol as I stood up. I covered the two until he returned.

"You know, we could just check their wallets. I mean, it might be simpler than torture. Inherently less satisfying, I admit, but also a whole lot faster and easier to explain if there's ever a need." He had a wry grin.

I looked at him for a minute, my jaw hanging open. "You're right. That is *so* simple. And we can always torture them later, can't we?" I grinned at him.

Handing the pistol to him, I bent over to haul the boss onto his stomach again. He didn't cooperate, but he couldn't really fight me the way he was tied. Between pulling with my hands and pushing with my feet, I finally turned him over. When I could, I tried to pull his wallet from his hip pocket. It wouldn't come. Okay, I can manage that. I slipped the claw into the pocket and slit it down one side. Obligingly, the wallet popped out. I hauled the sides of his jacket open and checked the inside pockets. Hm. A passport and some identification folders with badges. His pants pocket yielded another badge. I tossed everything onto the bed and repeated the process with the stooge, who was beginning to stir. I leaned over him again.

"Lie still or I'll remove some of your body parts. Starting with ones that probably still hurt. I'm sure you'd prefer to let them try to heal. Lie still and they might have that chance. Move and they're *mine*." He lay still.

His pockets yielded the same count of wallet, passport, ID folders and a stray badge.

I turned to the bed. First were the ID folders. I started flipping them open. FBI. BATFE. Secret Service, in the name of Herbert Coddleston. Gee, what a surprise. IRS. All very official-looking, very authentic-looking, with proper badges and all. Nice heavy badges too, not some cheap stamped crap. All with the right pictures of these clowns. All with different names. I checked the two loose badges. I looked at Alec who was going through the wallets.

"Recognize either of these two?" He shook his head. "Look at this one." I indicated the stooge. "Harder. This might help." I flipped him the badge from Los Ranchos de Albuquerque.

Alec got a sour look on his face. "Goddam son of a bitch! Honey, if you decide to remove those body parts of his, I'll help hold the bastard."

I jerked my head toward the boss. "This one we saw in Denver being ticketed by the cop up by the Richtofen mansion. Remember?" Alec nodded slowly, comprehension dawning. "I'll also just bet that if we put sunglasses on them, they'd look exactly like the pair in that pickup that kept hitting us outside of Denver." Alec kept nodding. "You remember, the one we shot up out front that morning the SWAT team showed up? The name on his Secret Service ID just happens to match the name the bank had for the fake agent the day I got suckered into trying to deposit all that funny money."

I tossed the folders back on the bed and turned my attention to the passports. Their design struck a chord. I turned the top one around so I could read it. A goddam *Golondrino* passport! And an official one at that. It dropped from my nerveless fingers. What the *fuck* was going on here? I checked both passports. They were the same, except for the personal data inside. Absently, I noticed the claw still on my fingers. I dropped the passports again, wiped the knife on the boss's clothes and slid it back into its sheath inside the waistband of my jeans. It's a two-handed job, unless I want to risk stabbing myself in the lower back. Then I picked the passports up once more. The one I'd tagged 'the boss' was listed as Stefan George. The stooge was Roland Kreisler. Or so their passports claimed. I smelled a rat. Two of them, in fact.

Chapter 30

Just as an aside, something surfaced from the packrat recesses of my mind. There are three basic kinds of passports. Any normal person who gets one gets a 'passport'. It's an official document, but it's not an 'Official Passport'. Those are reserved for government personnel and anyone else traveling on government matters. That's sketchy, and probably not one hundred percent accurate, but it'll do for this. Suffice it to say the passports these two had weren't ordinary tourist passports, they were government official-type passports. There are also diplomatic passports, but they don't matter for this account. Official passports don't confer any immunity, and the United States doesn't have any diplomatic relations with Golondrino anyway.

Alec sat on the bed and continued rifling through the wallets. He pulled out their identification cards, glanced at them and handed them to me. I sat heavily on the bed next to him. Surprise of surprises, they were Golondrino military IDs. Beside the shock of realizing that Golondrino even *had* a military, the names didn't match the passports. Big surprise. These, at least, were names I didn't recognize. Nor would the historians. Without a word, I motioned Alec to get up and move toward the kitchen. I looked at the two on the floor as I stepped into the doorway.

"Gentlemen—and I use the term *very* loosely—be here just like this when I get back. Or I assure you, you *will* regret it. I won't say you'll *live* to regret it. You likely won't. But you *will* regret it. Trust me on that."

Grabbing my gun on the way through the dining room, I reloaded and holstered it. In the kitchen, I looked at the counter. There was a big beef brisket on it with a couple of badly charred spots.

"What's that? And what's it doing on my counter?"

291

Alec gave me a strange look. "That, I think, is us. Or so we were supposed to think when they were making us think they were burning both of us. I don't know about you, but they squeezed my knee until it hurt like I couldn't believe. I couldn't stay quiet. I'm sorry if I worried you."

"Don't be. They hurt me just as bad. I would have...I really didn't even notice the burning meat when it was my knee. When I heard you scream, I was frantic. It's okay, love." I gave his cheek a brief caress. He didn't need to know the rest. Not yet anyway.

We pulled our chairs together so we could talk quietly about the two in the bedroom without being overheard.

"Forget the meat," I said. "Done is done. Anyway, the IDs may be genuine. The passports are unquestionably fake. I mean they may be real Golondrino passports, but those names are definitely fake, and those two don't seem to want to talk." I glanced at the stove. Nothing was on. "I thought I said to turn on a burner."

Alec smiled. It wasn't a nice smile, but I didn't think it was meant for me. "I didn't think I really needed to. Yet."

"Oh. Well, you were probably right. Anyway, now what?"

He took the passports from me. "How do you know these are fake names?" He seemed puzzled.

"I told you that your historical education is lacking, dear. Like I said, Daddy got a lot of plot ideas from history. I worked my way through most of his library as a kid. Stefan George was a German poet—sort of a mystic poet—in the years leading up to World War II. Had quite a following of young men, including at least two of the von Stauffenberg brothers. Roland Kreisler—you remember the old joke about ninety-five percent of attorneys giving the rest of you a bad name?" He nodded cautiously. "Well, Roland Kreisler was a judge in the Nazi People's Court. Think about the sleaziest, scummiest and most unethical lawyer you've ever known. Kreisler would have given *him*

292

a bad name. Don't worry. It's just my packrat memory acting up again." I thought for a moment, then handed him the IDs. "Here. Go look these two up on the Internet. Probably pointless, but you never know what you'll find."

"I'll have to turn the computer on. What's your password?"

I smiled. "I need to change it now. It's your birthday. The day, spell out the month, four-digit year. No spaces." He grinned and headed for the study.

I went back to inspect our captives. They hadn't moved. Good boys. Alec came back about fifteen minutes later.

"Well, you were right. The IDs are apparently genuine and those are their real names. There were photographs of both of them online. This one"—he toed the boss—"is really Colonel Helmut Beindorf, and he's the ranking officer in the Golondrino Defense Force. The other one"— he nodded toward the stooge—"is Lieutenant Colonel Henry Rachison, and he's the second-in-command of the GDF." He looked at me. I simply sat there with my jaw hanging open. Eventually, I closed it.

What was going on? Obviously this was an official assignment. It had better be, at any rate, with their ranks and official passports. And genuine official passports with fake names suggested even more government involvement, and we know who *that* meant. Fields himself. Well, there was certainly no reason not to go directly to the source for confirmation. I looked at Colonel Beindorf.

"Okay, sucker, start talking. If you think you can tough this out, you are *very* mistaken. I'd really rather not resort to heated tools and electric shocks, but don't think for an instant that I'll hesitate. Or even worse. As you said before, dead bodies are *so* inconvenient. Trust me, if it's *your* body, it's not going to be half so inconvenient for *me*. And"—I dropped my voice and let it get as gravelly as I could manage—"you will not be in any position to care. Understand me?" He said nothing.

I gave in somewhat to my rage. I kicked him on the side of the knee, not in his crotch. I simply wanted to hurt him the way he'd hurt me. Judging from his wince, I succeeded.

"Now listen to me, you son of a bitch. If you think you can break into my house *and* my office, bug me, shoot at me, shoot up my house, set off fireworks under my car, generally terrorize both of us *and* our friends, and then have your stooge try to rape me on *my own bed*, I'll show you just what happens to shits who try to do things like that to me!" My voice had gotten progressively louder and more shrill as I spoke, to the point that I was yelling at the end.

Finally, he spoke. "You were not going to be raped."

I yelled at him. "That's easy for you to claim now, you motherfucker!" I'm generally a lot more restrained in my language, but this seemed like a special occasion when nothing else would quite do. "Your buddy here had me down and was busy pulling my pants off. You weren't even in the room!" Waving my pistol around like a crazy woman probably helped convince him that I was one at that point. Maybe I was.

It seemed that he just needed to be started to be willing to talk.

"No, you were not going to be raped. Henry was under very strict orders. You were to be convinced that you would be raped, but he would not have done it. Our instructions were to do everything possible to make you turn away from your investigation, as well as finding out everything you were doing, but that we were not to harm you, your husband, your friend or your dogs in any way. The way it was put to us was that while the effort was exceedingly important, we must not do anything which would cause actual injury. I specifically asked about making you think you would be raped if the occasion arose. I was told that letting you believe that, so long as nothing actually happened, was not forbidden."

Alec and I looked at each other in shock. Their *instructions*? I turned to Colonel Beindorf.

"Whose instructions?" He said nothing, so I gave him another kick in the knee for encouragement.

"We were given our orders by the Director."

I thought I knew what he meant. The Family CEO used to be called the Director, a century or more ago. We'd had suspicions and beliefs, yes. But I needed to be sure.

"Give me a name. Who gave you your orders?"

"The Director, Raymond Escarton Fields."

Holy fucking shit.

Alec had some other questions. I didn't. I was still too stunned by his revelation. Well, as I told him more than once, it's been my experience that things always make sense if you look at them from the proper angle. I was still having some trouble making complete sense of it, but there was enough that at least the general angle was now clear.

Alec straightened up. "It seems that both of these boobs are distant cousins of yours. Of course, if you want to repudiate the relationship, I'd definitely understand. Anyway, all the GDF officers are Family members, although the enlisted may or may not be. He's been constantly reporting back to Fields on the results of his bugging and all the efforts he and Rachison were making. Fields is as up to date as he can be. In fact, the last report Beindorf filed was after he and Rachison had gotten us tied up here."

I had a very bad taste in my mouth. Obviously, I had been lied to, manipulated, suckered and sucker-punched at every turn in this whole affair. Why me? I mean, why the *fuck* me? I was also so mad, I could barely see straight, although lots more keenly rational now than I had been before. I had a purpose now.

"Look, Amy, let's get these two out of here. If they leave their shoes behind, along with what you've done to their pants, they're going to be a while getting anywhere.

Oh, and we'll keep their car keys too. That should make things very interesting for them and give us some time to plan our response."

I nodded and waved at him to go ahead.

Our visitors hadn't been gone more than fifteen minutes before I jumped up and began throwing clothes into a suitcase. As I packed, I said to Alec, "The monthly board meeting is in three days. Fields will be there. So will we."

Ten minutes after that, I had arranged tickets and Alec and I were heading to his place so he could pack his own bag. Becky and the dogs would just have to wait a bit longer. Clearly, we had some more work to do.

* * * *

TO: D
FROM: HB
ALERT! Youngston and Trevethen have discovered our identities and are aware of your involvement. Targets are in possession of our passports and all identity documents we had with us. Targets are proceeding to base immediately via Munich. Unable to track or pursue further. Off the record: Youngston is one tough cookie.

TO: HB
FROM: D
Excellent. Job very well done. Target was expected to be good, even if she turned out to be better than expected. I shall assume all responsibility from here. Transportation will be arriving at TIA for you 1400 local tomorrow; your own passports and replacement ID cards will await you on board. Please report to me ASAP upon arrival. Thank you. Again, job very well done.

Chapter 31

I had plenty of time to think during the flight to Europe. The only problem was, the more I thought, the more I smoldered. How dare he! That son of a bitch! He'd sat there in *my office* and *hired* me to get into the middle of this. I had many more choice thoughts, but they were more colorful and got to be quite repetitive. Suffice it to say that I didn't sleep a wink on the plane. I don't do much of that anyway, but this time, I didn't do any at all. I was simply way too agitated and just too downright furious.

Alec did sleep, but luckily for me, he wasn't snoring. I was also far too conscious of the emptiness under my left arm where my little Kahr usually rode, not to mention the knives I always wore. Way too reminiscent of the time we'd spent tied up and helpless in the past two days. The knives, at least, I could get as soon as we cleared our checked bags through customs in Munich. The pistol was safe at home. Most places in Europe take a dim view of going armed, which I thought was horribly narrow minded of them. They didn't care what I thought.

The reinforced pen and the couple of fiberglass-reinforced plastic knives I had on me that could all go sailing through the metal detectors and security screening would have to do, if there was a need. Somehow, after we'd cornered the colonel who had been screwing with us all this time and gotten him to spill his guts, I doubted that there'd be any real need for weapons, at least on quite the scale there had been so far. But I don't carry concealed weapons because I knew there'd be a need for them. I carry them for the times when the need appeared without warning, as I'd just been forcibly reminded. If I knew there'd be a need ahead of time, I'd be carrying something far too big to hide conveniently, but also far better able to settle matters before they got out of hand, like a shotgun, a rifle, or whatever the situation called for.

Before the sun caught up with the plane again, just as the sky was beginning to turn a brilliant pinkish-salmon, I nudged Alec. Then I nudged him again when the first one didn't wake him. He glanced at me before stretching as best he could in his seat.

"Jeez, honey, didn't you sleep at all?" He came awake fairly quickly, a good trick without either coffee or adrenalin, in my book. We caught the stewardess as she went by and snagged cups of coffee. That still seemed to be the primary lubricant on this case.

"Nope. Not a wink. I'm too enraged. *Way* too enraged. I want to take out that son of a bitch. Permanently. I want to watch him suffer a very slow, agonizing death for what he's done to me. I can't even detail what I want to do to him. Maybe I could remove body parts and frame them. Maybe I could...no. It'd take far too long to figure out a suitable form of torture, and even then it still wouldn't be enough. I'd have to resurrect him and kill him again. And again. You get my drift."

I let out a shuddering breath and allowed myself to run down. I doubt I could or would do any of the things I've considered. Well, maybe I wouldn't. By now, I certainly wasn't going to take any bets that I couldn't. Doing any of them would get me talked about, that was for sure. The way I was thinking and talking was definitely anything but ladylike. No, I don't put much effort—any, really—into being a lady. But that was the degree of rage I felt. Besides, doing any of them would feel so *good*.

I recalled thinking at the very beginning of this case that it was going to be interesting to see if there was anything more going on than what Fields had been telling me. Well, gee, that was certainly an understatement. 'Interesting' hardly began to describe what had happened over the past several months. In fact, it ranked right up there with 'mildly upset' as a way to describe how I felt at the moment. I could have done without this whole job, all things considered. But the lure of respect, a board seat before I knew how little a board seat was really worth, intrinsically, and the extra shares were just too much to pass up. Well, they had been. I had a different take on them now that it was too late. Isn't that always how it happens? So much for foresight.

"Okay, you're angry with him," Alec said. "Furious even. I can see that, and it's hardly any surprise. But do you have a plan, or are we just making it up as we go along?" He swirled his coffee and looked into the cup, not trying to meet my gaze. "One thing I'd like you to keep in mind. You have every right to be furious with what we've been put through. As long as I've known you, you can rage with the best of them. But remember this. Don't let your fury with Fields get so out of hand that it hurts *us*."

That hit home. Not that it made me any less angry, but it put a limit on how much I was going to let myself give in to the fury I felt. When push came to shove, that was probably going to be a good thing.

"The monthly board meeting is scheduled for two days from now," I said. "I plan to crash it and accuse him right there in front of all of them. That's my plan, such as it is."

I believed it would be the right thing to do. So why didn't it make me feel better to think about doing it? Sure, it would expose him, but it just didn't *satisfy*. Dismembering him in front of the entire board, that might. Oh, sure, it would definitely get me talked about. And if it got me talked about, well, it'd be a long, *long* time before anyone did anything like that to me again. The way I felt right now, that suited me just fine. No, I wouldn't really do it. Not after Alec's last remark. But the thought sure was enjoyable.

Clearing German customs in Munich was easier than I'd expected. We didn't bother trying to explain that we were married; our passports were still unchanged. So it seemed simpler to go through the way we appeared on paper, as just good friends who lived close to each other. They didn't care anyway. I took my suitcase into the restroom and retrieved my serious knives. Alec got a rental car as I sat on the bags and fumed some more about the way that Fields had treated me. I hadn't gone through the same circular line of thought more than three or four times before Alec drove up and I had to haul the bags to the car.

We'd been lucky with a hotel. We'd gotten a room at a little place a couple of blocks off what I guess is the town square, the pedestrian area in front of what I think is City Hall. No real point to that; this wasn't a sightseeing tour. The nicest thing was that the hotel had underground parking, although I doubt that any American hotel would have called it parking. I'd call it tight, but that would give the impression that it was a lot bigger than it was. We did manage to get the car into the slot, and Alec didn't have to back out and adjust more than twice to get it completely between the lines. I think Americans are spoiled by the size of our parking lots.

There was a big Mercedes in one slot. It looked as though it could never have made it into the space without a forklift, but obviously it had. I wondered who owned it. It was check-in time when we dragged in and made our way up in the tiny elevator. I needed a shower before I moved any further. After I felt reasonably clean, I lay down for a few minutes to clear my head. The next thing I knew, it was close to midnight. Jet lag is a bitch. Alec was beside me, breathing softly and regularly. I turned over to snuggle next to him, put my arm over him and went back to sleep, comforted immeasurably by his presence.

When we came downstairs for breakfast the next morning, we both felt rested and something close to human again. We sat out in a little courtyard among the flowers and sipped excellent coffee. Free refills. Yay! If it hadn't been for what got us here, it would have been the absolute best combination possible.

"Golondrino is tucked into the corner where Switzerland, Italy and Austria meet," I told Alec. "Normally, if you were headed there, you'd fly into Zurich. But if we'd gone there, I think we'd have been noticed for sure. Hopefully, by coming here instead, we've avoided being seen."

"I take it we don't have a reservation when we get there?" Alec looked unconcerned.

"Correct. If nobody knows where we're staying, they can't set up a surprise for us. I want to do the surprising from here on in. I've had it with being on the receiving end of whatever mischief Mister Raymond Escarton Fields has in mind. Or might decide to have in mind."

"So just how big is this Golondrino place? I couldn't find it on any of the maps I looked at."

"I've never actually been there, you understand. But from what I've heard, it's real tiny. It's probably measured in acres, or, since this is Europe, in hectares. Hell, for all I know, it's only a building or two. But it's real, and it's where we're going. That's all we need to know."

He got a sour look on his face. "Amy, if it's that small, then it's entirely possible that going there isn't going to be the easy part. We've got to *find* it. At that size, we could go right by it and never notice. But there's no time like the present, I suppose." We stood up and headed for the desk to check out. No, there didn't seem to be anybody paying any attention to what we were doing. Of course, we'd never seen anyone doing that, even when we knew we were being followed.

As it turned out, Golondrino wasn't really all that hard to find. It's measured in square kilometers, not hectares, even if only a handful of them. There's even a sign on the highway indicating the turnoff. We didn't take it, but turned around and headed back into Austria. A night spent in a small but tidy gasthaus chosen at random seemed like a workable way to foil any potential watcher, and it didn't take us very long to find one that also offered a pleasant, if plain, supper. The bed was on the small side, but after a lengthy and pleasant interlude making up for the night before, we wrapped ourselves together like a pair of happy puppies and dropped off to sleep.

The next morning we drove into Golondrino. Crossing borders in Europe is, for the most part, very easy now that the European Union covers most countries. The EU isn't recognized in Golondrino; they actually have border checkpoints. Other than the border guard, presumably another member of the Golondrino armed forces, who had a pistol, there were no armed guards, at least none that I saw. I have a lot of experience seeing things that people don't expect or want me to see. Of course, that didn't mean they didn't have them, just that if there were any, they were very well hidden. The guard took our passports into his little shack and returned a few minutes later.

"Thank you, Mr. Trevethen. Welcome to Golondrino. Ms. Youngston, are you here for the board meeting?"

I'd like to say I was nonplused, but dumbfounded was probably closer. How did he know I was Family? That was my US passport! Were they expecting me? It didn't matter. I thought for a moment. He would probably let Fields know I was here, but maybe I could throw him off a tad. And if it didn't work, no harm done.

"No, we're just sightseeing." Let the son of a bitch chew on that.

He smiled in that sort of official manner that means nothing. "Of course. If you'd like some refreshment while you're here, there are a couple of very nice restaurants on the square. The meeting, if you have any interest, will be in Government House on the north side of the square. If you're spending the night, the hotel opposite Government House is quite nice, and their restaurant is probably the best

302

in all of Golondrino." He checked his watch. "The meeting begins in twenty minutes."

Chapter 32

"Where is the square?" I hated to seem like the yokel from out of town, but I had very little choice, especially since I was exactly that. With the meeting about to begin, I couldn't afford to waste a lot of time.

This time his smile was real. "Just on the other side of that building." He gestured down the road ahead of us. You'll have to park on this side of the building; the square is a pedestrian mall. No cars allowed. But show them your passport at the parking structure and they'll allow you to park for free."

I thanked him and we drove off. If, as seemed likely, the square was in the middle of Golondrino, then the whole thing was something around four square miles or so in size. Hardly any size to the place at all. I wondered if it had any function other than being the family seat, and maybe keeping stamp and coin dealers happy. Probably not.

Alec finally spoke up as we got out of the car. "I guess they know who you are." He seemed mildly amused, or maybe I was just projecting. I was most definitely *not* amused at all.

"Yeah, I guess they do. Shocked me, I can tell you." I looked around as we entered the square. "I wonder what happened to this place during the war?"

Alec chuckled. "I doubt the Germans had any real interest in the place. It's not like the Family keeps its money here, I suppose, and the place isn't really big enough to inspire a lot of interest otherwise. They probably just sent in a company or two of troops and let it go at that. The money's probably in Zurich, you know. Or maybe they treated the place like a little bit of Switzerland and left it alone."

One way or the other, he was probably right. I stopped for a moment and faced the building. I needed to get the two passports I'd gotten from the colonel and his stooge out of my fanny pack and slide them into my hip pocket before I went in.

In better times, I'd probably say something about how picturesque Golondrino is, in a postcard sort of sense. This time of year, the buildings, every one of them in a Swiss chalet sort of design, even the largest ones, had their boxes under every window filled with cascading flowers, making for a riot of color on the white buildings. My own thoughts were of a very different sort of riot, and given the way I felt at the moment, the window boxes simply struck me as cheesy.

There was another uniformed guard at a desk outside the meeting room. He stood courteously as we approached and I saw the Glock holstered on his right hip. I held my own passport out in my left hand, not getting it quite into his reach, while my right hand went to the back of my waistband. As he came within range of the passport, I 'accidentally' dropped it.

"Oh, I'm so sorry." He was bending over to pick it up as my right hand came out with the Hideaway claw in it.

I really, really love that knife; it's earned its keep many times over in the past couple of days. I laid the knife gently alongside his jugular.

"Don't move or you'll make a mess all over the floor as you die," I told him quietly. He froze. Good choice on his part. I drew his pistol with my left hand. "Now straighten up, please," I told him as I stepped back and transferred his pistol to my right hand. I let the knife stay where it was, sticking out from my fingers like the nasty claw it resembles.

"Sit down, if you would, please." I gestured to his chair with my left hand. "Push back from the desk all the way to the wall." He did as he was told, but he didn't look all that worried now that he didn't have to face the knife up close and personal. I handed the pistol to Alec. "Honey, would

305

you watch him? I have some business to attend to inside." I tucked the knife back into its sheath inside my waistband.

The guard still didn't seem all that concerned by being covered with his own gun. "You can simply go on in, Ms. Youngston. You're expected. Mr. Trevethen can go with you, if you'd like. It really isn't necessary to go through all this."

Oh, that now all-too-familiar accent!

I looked at him for a moment. He seemed far too relaxed for someone who could be shot at any moment.

"Check the gun, Alec." Alec squeezed the slide back fractionally before letting it slip back into battery. He dropped the magazine out with a disgusted look. I glanced at it; other than the black baseplate, it was blue—a practice magazine. He and I exchanged looks of bewilderment. "Toss the gun out the window. He might have real ammunition on him."

The guard ignored Alec and looked at me. "I'd really prefer that you didn't have Mr. Trevethen do that, Ms. Youngston. It's a good pistol, and there is no need to do anything so drastic. If you're concerned about what I might do when your back is turned, then please feel free to take the pistol into the boardroom with you. As I said, you're expected."

What did he mean, I was expected? By whom? Why? Who knew we were coming? How? I looked at Alec again, jerked my head toward the doors and simply said, "Come on."

I marched to the doors, braced myself and put my back into it as I shoved them open. Hard. They hit their stops with an almost satisfying boom that reverberated through the room.

Inside, it looked like what I imagine a fairly typical high-end boardroom looks like. Elegant chairs surrounding a magnificent conference table, all sorts of provisions for visual aids, coffee, tea and pastries on the sideboard, it all seemed so *normal*. The board members seemed startled by the suddenness of my entrance. All except one. There at the head of the table opposite me sat the devil incarnate himself, Raymond Escarton Fields.

"You bastard! You son of a bitch! This was all your doing! None of these people were involved at all, were they?" I'm afraid my voice was loud enough that it was on the verge of getting shrill. I flipped the two confiscated passports onto the table so they'd slide down to Fields' end. One slid off onto his lap. Nobody noticed. Then I tossed the two IDs after them. They slid just beyond the center of the table. Fields was smiling. Not broadly, but unmistakably.

He stood up and stepped behind his chair. The passport fell to the floor unnoticed. It was a nice, fancy high-backed leather swivel chair, probably horribly expensive and comfortable as all hell, but it wouldn't *begin* to shield his ass from what I was going to do to him. I took a step toward him before I stopped as he spoke. Looking around the table, he sounded quite relaxed.

"Ms. Youngston, I believe you know everybody here, although you haven't actually been introduced to them formally. Let me remedy that." He looked down one side of the table. "On my immediate right is Roger Mouleton of Albuquerque, New Mexico. Next to him is John Barnsfather of Santa Fe, also in New Mexico. Beyond him is Tobias Greibe of Oberwesel, Germany. Finally we have Ian McTolland of Sligachan, the Isle of Skye, Scotland. On my immediate left is Gregory Casaday of Sedona, Arizona.

"You should know that he and Mr. McTolland seem to have a constant difference of professional opinion. I've found it advisable to keep them well separated during business occasions, although they're fine together socially. Next to him is James Parkinston of Kileaua, Kauai, Hawaii. Next up is William Morristone of Denver, and finally we have George Rogerton of Jackson, Wyoming."

307

I nodded to each one automatically as they were introduced. I knew their voices, now I had faces to put with those voices. They nodded back, still looking puzzled.

"This is a bit cursory, I know, but there will be plenty of time for you to get to know them," Fields said. "Gentlemen, this young lady"—I snorted, but at least he hadn't called me 'ma'am'—"is Family member Ms. Alannah Meav Youngston, known to her friends as Amy. I strongly doubt that I qualify, as you can probably surmise from her, um, *dramatic* entrance."

How could that son of a bitch be so calm? Especially when he was on the verge of being ripped to pieces? Small ones!

"The gentleman with her, who is not himself a Family member, although he is very well informed about the Family, is her new husband of less than a week, Mr. Alexander Forsythe Trevethen, known to his friends as Alec. You're also probably wondering why she is here, along with why she is so...upset with me. Let me assure you that her upset is entirely normal and expected."

Normal? Expected? Huh?

"Ms. Youngston, I promised you a seat on the board if you found whoever was 'behind all of this', as you put it so succinctly. You're quite correct that it was a put-up job, as I believe you would characterize it, just as you're correct that it was all my doing. You found me out, and as promised, you will indeed get a seat on the board. This one." He gestured to the seat in front of him that he had just vacated. Then he looked at the rest of the board. "Gentlemen, it is time. I hereby resign the position of CEO of the Family and name this young lady as my successor."

I was completely at a loss for words.

"But you can't...I don't...it's not..." I looked at Alec for help, but he seemed just as astounded and lost as I was.

His smile got broader. "Trust me. As hard, or even impossible, as that must seem to you at the moment, I am now being quite honest and completely above board with you in this matter. Gentlemen, this meeting is adjourned. You all may leave until next month's meeting. It has been a pleasure, I assure you." He turned to me again. "Please, Ms. Youngston, come with me. You too, Mr. Trevethen. Oh, and you can leave the pistol on the sideboard. You won't be needing it, and I'm sure the guard will appreciate getting it back in good order."

Chapter 33

Fields led us out of the boardroom into a very nicely appointed private room reserved for the CEO. It's large enough to seat the entire board with room to spare, but it was now made up like the typical, or perhaps stereotypical, Hollywood image of a British gentlemen's club with small tables and three sinfully comfortable chairs. Fields motioned the two of us to seat ourselves while he went to the bar along one wall.

"What can I provide for you? I have drinks of almost every kind, and if there is anything else you'd like, including a meal, I can certainly order it in for you."

Alec and I were still gawking at the room and looking at each other at regular intervals. Finally he broke the silence.

"I could use a drink. Actually, I *need* a drink. Scotch if you have it, please."

Fields opened the bar and looked inside. "Certainly. I can offer you your choice of a twenty-one-year Balvenie Portwood, a twenty-five-year Talisker or a twenty-one-year MacAllan, if one of those would be acceptable. With water?"

I was impressed; those were all very pricey scotches, and the selection showed some definite good taste. Like any of that was going to save his ass.

"I'll take the MacAllan, with water on the side, please," Alec said. "Oh, and one large ice cube. Thank you."

Fields looked at me with those bright blue eyes and arched his eyebrow. I still hated that, mostly because I couldn't do it myself.

"Just coffee, please. I don't think alcohol would be such a good idea for me right now."

Damn right it wouldn't be. I wanted to be stone cold sober when I ripped him to shreds. I was going to *enjoy* doing it, and I didn't want anything to interfere with the experience. And yet...I couldn't seem to quite muster that level of anger any more. My rage seemed to be fading away. It was almost more a memory than a feeling, and my reaction more reasoned, which I found a bit puzzling after the way I'd felt coming into the boardroom.

Fields fixed himself something that looked like Alec's drink and seated himself across from us. We sat in silence for a moment, sipping away, before he spoke.

"I could say something like 'I suppose you're wondering why I've called you here', but I think I can skip the trite small talk and get right to the point. Ms. Youngston, I really am retiring from my position. I've held it for close to fifteen years. Not a record by any means, but it's not an easy position, even if it doesn't take up a huge amount of time. It can be quite wearing, and frankly, I'm tired of it. I want to move on with my life. To do that, I need a successor, and you're it."

I looked at him over the rim of the coffee mug I was holding in both hands before setting it down on its coaster.

"How do you know I'll do it? For that matter, how do you know I'll do it well?" And just what do you really know about me to even make such an offer? While we're at it, how about the hell you put me through over the past several months? My mind was churning, but I thought it was better to keep those thoughts to myself.

He smiled warmly. "I knew you'd do it when we met in your office in Tucson back in February. You wanted a seat on the board, remember? By now, I'm sure you know"—he glanced at Alec—"that really, there is only one seat on the board that matters, that of the CEO. Which seat you now have. Your husband also explained to you—in the sense that you had all the pieces—that mine is the only board seat that I have the power to fill. We actually had to intensify our efforts then to try to keep you too busy to stop and thoroughly analyze what you'd been told, so you would

311

have that much less opportunity to figure out what was going on. As for the suggestion of a special election for a board seat with just one candidate, you will find out—it is not exactly public knowledge even within the Family, although it's hardly a deep secret—that while the CEO can name candidates for the board, it is utterly unacceptable for the CEO to name everyone on the ballot. And to the greatest degree possible the CEO should never name more than half of the candidates.

"There was literally no way that I could get you onto the board except into my own seat, which was what I had intended doing all along. As for doing the job well, you've had at least the beginning of a crash course of your own devising in investing and investments since then, and you have the entire board to advise you and do whatever research you deem necessary. That's their function. None of them is qualified to hold your job; they're not action people, not decision people. I don't say this to denigrate them in any way, because they're all very good at what they do, but they're desk people. Taking the helm of an investment machine of this size would most likely leave any of them paralyzed and incapable of doing anything. You go out and *do* things. You know enough to get going, and they will help steady you while you get your feet under you. You don't have to do much of anything for a while; the Family investments have, for the most part, a sort of inertia.

"You see, most people think that the CEO is, and should be, first and foremost, an investor. There is naturally a kernel of truth in that. What the job really entails, however, as I eventually came to realize, is being able to make decisions, often very hard decisions, at a time when they need to be made, without dithering, and then taking the responsibility for those decisions. Being willing to accept the blame for bad ones and take the credit for good ones. That is really the most vital qualification for the position. The times when a CEO has concentrated simply on investing expertise in selecting his successor have often resulted in poor choices. When the ability to make and stick with hard choices in the proper timeframe has been the primary criterion, we've had extremely good CEOs, even when they came in knowing little or nothing about investing. Some of the poorer ones grew into the job. I'd like to believe that I have. But what is really needed in this position, in my opinion, is someone like you. You see, I know a great deal about you, a great deal indeed. The Family keeps extensive files on all of its members, and frankly, it would surprise you how much we know about everyone in it, especially those we choose to focus on, such as yourself. When I decided I needed a replacement, I did a lengthy search and your name popped up."

I snorted. "Along with how many others?"

He smiled. "Honestly, none. Oh, there were several who trailed you, generally by a significant degree, but you stood alone. Let me explain why. Being the Family CEO is the sort of job that you would normally expect to go to someone with a lifetime of experience. The Family has plenty of those. A number of our doctors and lawyers in particular, could probably handle the job, although I would submit that nobody in the Family is initially able to essentially wager several billion dollars on a single investment, for example, without spending several sleepless nights. Eventually, you either learn to do so with the best information you have, and accept and learn from the results without beating yourself up over your mistakes, or you pass the job on. But the paradox of the position is that the truly successful CEOs have always been relatively young. Not, perhaps, as young as I was when I first took office. But the sort of people who have grown into their own jobs until they reach the level at which they could handle this job are, as a rule, quite a bit older than I feel the position needs, or that Family experience demonstrates the position requires.

So, age was one of the first criteria I used." He paused to take another swallow of his drink.

"Next was something of the history of the people I was looking at. Most Family members go through some sort of graduate school. In the usual course of events, after getting your degree and professional license, you would join a practice in your field and work your way up the ladder to eventually become a senior partner. At that point, such a person might be capable of doing the job. But following that sort of career track and working up the ladder step by step suggests a certain need for having someone look over your shoulder and provide hands-on education for some time. That sort of mentoring doesn't happen here. There simply is nobody to look over the CEO's shoulder while he or she learns the job. It's strictly sink or swim.

"Those who strike out on their own were more in line with what I was looking for in a successor, but even then they had to be at least reasonably successful. Those who are merely eking out a bare living were not in contention. What I was looking for, in essence, was someone who was relatively young—you were, in fact, near the upper end of the age range I considered—and who was independent. The actual professional field of a contender was not important, but striking out on his own was particularly important. Your willingness to go into another field than the one you had been trained in was a significant plus, because it showed that much more independence, in my assessment.

"But one of the biggest factors was finding someone in a position to accept the challenge of the ordeal. A senior doctor or lawyer, as a rule, simply has no incentive, nothing to lure them into whatever ordeal I might construct to suit their situation. They believe they have already proven themselves to their satisfaction. Someone who is exceptionally successful in their field at a younger age is often even harder to entice. To gloss over some of the less relevant issues, I needed someone young enough to handle the job, who had shown the requisite streak of independence and been successful at what they did, but who was not so comfortable that he or she could not be intrigued by something I could dangle in front of them...bait, if you like...to get them involved in their ordeal."

There was that word again. What *was* that about? I got the feeling that I needed to know.

"Add in the decisiveness that I understood the position absolutely had to have, and out of the eleven thousand, four hundred and three Family members you fitted the parameters better, indeed *far* better, than any of the rest.

"When you asked for a board seat when I hired you, that confirmed it for me. I know I didn't look happy at the thought, but that was mostly acting. I had this most elaborate plan to try to offer you a board seat if you succeeded and to convince you to take it even over your objections. You surprised me and quite took the wind out of my sails by asking for it instead. You know"—he glanced at Alec—"that as the CEO, I name my own successor. I know you do; your husband explained it to you. You truly are my choice for the position."

He knew about those conversations? The rat bastard! How? Probably some sneaky son of a bitch with a parabolic or shotgun mike.

"What if I refuse? What if I don't want the position? What if I want to go on being an investigator?" I was still in shock over everything.

He was still smiling. "Tell me another. You wanted a seat on the board back when you thought it was worth nothing more than prestige and some additional shares, and that it only required an occasional meeting and vote. Trust me, there is, as I said, only one board seat that matters, and that is the seat you now have. You will have plenty of shares, over and above the hundred extra we agreed on, and all of the authority there is. Prestige like nobody else within

315

the Family. No, you'll take it. If you want to continue being an investigator..." He shrugged. "That would be your choice. There's a fair amount of free time in this job, although I can't think of any previous CEO who's held a second job. You'd probably...no, you *would* be the richest PI in history before long, but that would be entirely up to you."

The real aggravation was that he was right. I would take the job. I'd do well at it too, or die trying.

"Do I have to use these same selection criteria you used on me when I want to pass the job along?"

He laughed. "Absolutely not. Once you take the reins, the job is yours. You can do almost anything you like and nobody can gainsay you. Here's what you can't do. You can't name anyone to the board other than your successor. You can't name all of the candidates for a board seat, and if at all possible, shouldn't name more than half. You also can't take a salary or set your own compensation. You and the board are specifically paid simply in shares, and the nine of you vote on the number of shares awarded each year. Eight of you vote, I should say, on the shares to be given to the ninth. The person whose compensation is being voted on must be out of the room and will never know the vote, simply the outcome. So they will decide how many shares your performance is worth each year. Outside of those, you're like royalty. You literally *are* royalty. As for passing the job along, you can choose according to literally whatever criteria you like. It truly is up to you and, of course, whatever you feel is right and best for the Family."

That gave me some food for thought. Of course, in the current maelstrom of my mind, it might take a month before I could get to it. Then something else occurred to me.

"What about my $50 an hour? You still owe me for the last two months' billing!"

He laughed again, deeply and honestly. I had to laugh as well. Here I was, being taken up to the top of the mountain and given literally everything I could see, and I was worried about a measly couple of thousand dollars. But he *owed* me, damn it, and I wanted my money. I'd earned it, worked awfully damn hard for it, and generally gone through a lot more than I had ever expected for it.

"I'm sorry," he said as he wiped his eyes. "I don't want to seem as though I'm laughing at you. I'm really not. It's just that it's such a trivial amount under the circumstances. But I still remember what it was like when I was handed the job and how I had thought before. There is certainly a principle involved as well. Just submit your bill to me personally, not to the Family, as you've been doing, and I'll make sure it's paid promptly. But there is something else you need to understand."

I tensed. What was coming now?

"There is a book that comes with this position. It was started by James Escarton, the founder of the family. No, he wasn't really a pirate, although as I read between the lines of what he wrote, I come to think that he would have found the reputation amusing. Many of the Family's young people, when they have other Family children to talk to, appear to come up with the same idea. He was, in fact, a merchant and a trader, a highly successful one, although Family history shows that he did deal with a number of pirates by buying into their ships. He also bought interest in ships of a number of respectable merchants, in both cases for shares of the profits from their voyages.

"He was not originally named Escarton, by the way. He was an orphaned boy of the London slums in the 1480s, and managed to apprentice himself to a merchant and trader named William Escarton. After a number of years working for Escarton, James took his last name. Anyway, subsequent CEOs have, as they saw fit, added to the book. One thing that every one has done is sign in to the book on taking the seat and, except for a few who died before passing on their office, sign out of it when they left."

I noticed a good-sized, well-aged, leather-bound volume on the table by his side. He lifted it and opened it to a spot just over halfway through.

"I shall sign myself out of the book and then you may sign yourself into it. There is a vault in the CEO's office in this building for the private use of the CEO alone, and it's perhaps best to keep it there. I've scanned it so that you may take an electronic copy with you—don't print it out, please—but I emphasize that nobody except the CEO and his, well, *her*, spouse ever sees the book or even knows about it beyond rumor. I should warn you that some of the earlier language is very archaic.

"When James died, Chaucer had been dead less than a century and a half, and it was close to half a century before Shakespeare was born." He looked at Alec meaningfully. "There is one proviso in the book, a charge, a geis, if you will, on the Director, or what is now usually called the CEO, that the successor must successfully undergo an ordeal before ascending to the position. This is specifically intended to show whether the next Director will actually be a fighter, someone with the persistence and drive needed to fill the seat and fill it well. Additionally, the ordeal cannot, *must* not be revealed to the candidate until he or she has successfully completed it."

My jaw dropped. "You mean that this was all a *game*? Just some sort of cockamamie *trial* I had to go through for a job I didn't even know about?" I could feel my face getting hotter. So all this had been nothing more than one hell of a job interview?

Fields held up his hands. "Please, Ms. Youngston, it's not like that. This is literally a charge upon us, the CEOs, from James Escarton himself and, as you will see from the balance sheets, in the main it has served the Family well. Especially when you contrast the few Directors who took the position with no ordeal because they were stepping into dead men's shoes. Although you may not believe me, I actually have a very good idea how you feel. I came close, *very* close, to wringing David Brixton's neck when we sat in this same room and had much this same sort of conversation. I certainly wanted to, just as much as you want to harm me now. Trust me, I quite understand.

"As you may remember, I was already well versed in investing, at least on an individual basis. At the time, my personal fortune was probably the most important thing in my life to me. By the time I was selected by David as his likely successor, I had already parleyed my initial shares into what was, for me, a fairly respectable fortune. But for my ordeal, I was challenged into some related activities in which I had no expertise and, as I found to my...dismay, no knowledge either, so I had some real hurdles to overcome. I actually saw my net worth drop to a point where I feared I could not hold out until my next family dividend check. I was devastated, all but destroyed. Then I turned it all around, primarily by sheer force of will, and by the time I arrived here to brace him, I had twice what I had started with.

"David had literally driven me to the brink of bankruptcy for no better reason, or so I thought then, than to see if I could recover. I shan't bore you with more details than that now; you'll find them in the book. Most of us have spelled out our ordeals in there. Suffice it to say that I had to put you through something that would challenge you sufficiently to show that in fact you belong in that chair.

"My instructions to Helmut and Henry were very explicit. You, Dr. Swan, Mr. Trevethen and your dogs were not to be harmed in any way, but you were specifically to be pushed as close as they could to the breaking point. I should add that I gave both of them quite a talking-to about the second time they shot up your house. They had not realized, although I did instantly, that the potential threat to

319

your dogs was well beyond the acceptable level. As I was saying, though, it was not that they *wanted* to break you, and it would not have mattered to the outcome if they had, but I needed *you* to understand how much stress you could manage, what would potentially break you if you reached that point, what form that breaking would take and how you would feel within yourself. You see, in this position, there are at times some very serious stresses, and they will all fall on you. *All* of them. Those stresses have become worse over the years. I have seen a noticeable increase during my own tenure. You have to know how much stress you can handle and you are well served by knowing within yourself the signs of impending disaster. Your husband will help you, I feel sure. But while you can delegate authority, the responsibility will be yours. Always, until the day you designate your successor and step down. I wanted—I *needed* you to be put through the most intense test possible, and I would have to say that you surpassed my expectations."

Well, nobody knew what had gone on in my mind during my time tied up at the house. Nobody, other than Alec and possibly Becky, if even they, ever would. But he was right that I'd certainly never forget it, and I now knew things about myself that I had never known before.

"How so?"

"Frankly, I had expected you to investigate the entire board, as you did—that investigation may assist you in deciding whom to keep on the board and whom you might choose to replace—and then report back to me that there was no outside influence being exerted, that all the board members were simply acting on their best judgment as far as you could discover. Which they actually have been all along. That would have been sufficient for my purposes. Incidentally, the board members were entirely unaware of what was going on, and still are.

"One of the more difficult, or perhaps simply interesting, parts of the entire ordeal from my perspective, was convincing Steve Wynn to let us place that fake news bulletin about the bomb in one of his luxury suites. It would have been so much easier were he a Family member and I could have been more...up front with him. I shall have to, at some point. It turns out that he'd heard rumors about the Family, and the price I had to pay was a promise to meet with him in person and explain it all to him in the very near future. He may set something like this up for his own descendants. Since we weren't talking about actually destroying the interior of one of his suites, we were able to reach an accommodation.

"Incidentally, you would be most welcome to accompany me if you so choose. At any rate, when I heard that you had turned the tables on my people and discovered, or perhaps I should say confirmed, my own involvement from them, I was shocked. When I was told that you and your husband were on your way here, I presumed that you would do essentially what you did, although I expected you to merely storm by poor Gustav instead of taking his gun and threatening him as you did. As you discovered, however, we were prepared for that eventuality as well. You have definitely done more, far more, than I had expected, and I am truly impressed."

I was still a bit nettled, but he had pretty well defused most of my anger. He opened the book and wrote something in it before handing it to me.

"Sign and date there, and it's all yours." He stood up. "With your leave..."

Chapter 34

I couldn't take over quite this easily. "Wait just a God-damned minute. I mean, this ordeal seems so damn *stupid*—and believe me, I'm still plenty *pissed* about what I had to go through."

He sat down. "As I've said, that's entirely understandable, and I expected it. Now that we are all here, I can honestly say that I am truly very sorry for what was done to you—to both of you, even as I would continue to maintain that it was utterly necessary. However, to answer your question—in addition to establishing your ability as a fighter, to overcome obstacles"—I waved that away, annoyed. I'd heard it before—"There is actually a brief discussion of it in the book, where Escarton places the charge upon his successors. He is sparing of words, but it is not difficult to read between the lines, shall we say. You need to understand that he himself came up from the gutter, largely taught himself to read and write and made his entire fortune on his own. Nobody handed him anything. William Escarton gave him a chance, nothing more, and made it clear that while James would have to learn to read and count beyond his fingers in order to continue working for him, he, William, didn't have the time to actually teach James.

"James could read, but only a little, when he first began working for William Escarton. From there, James taught himself with only the smallest occasional bit of help. William merely taught him *how* to be a successful businessman, and then James had to do the rest himself. For a successor, though, James had to give the matter of succession a great deal of thought and consideration.

"He could have designated one of his children to become the CEO and then had the office going from one descendant to the next. That would, for all intents and purposes, have created what amounted to a royal line within the Family. For reasons you will see from his own account, he was very unimpressed with royalty. No matter how well they start, eventually the line deteriorates and it would have put the remainder of the Family at the mercy of that lineage. He envisioned a Family and a Family fortune, which would last and grow much as it has and continues to do so. He was not willing to grant that sort of power to one part of the Family and shut out the remainder.

"Second, he could have set up a procedure for choosing a successor by some sort of Family plebiscite. That, of course, would have led to the rise of a political class within the Family. He was shrewd enough to realize that the sort of courtiers whom he despised almost as much as he did the royalty they served would then become the ruling class and in much the same fashion, concentrate the power and the money in themselves, again to the detriment of the remainder of the Family.

"So he decided to let the current CEO name a successor from the entire Family. Not a perfect solution, but we all know that there are no perfect solutions. There are simply better ones and worse ones. This method has, overall, resulted in many very good CEOs, a few poor ones, and a certain number who have been merely undistinguished. What it definitely does do is avoid the pitfalls he knew about and allow for the potential to choose the best successor CEO out of the entire Family pool, subject that person to a severe test, and if successful, entrust the office to someone who, hopefully, realizes and appreciates the importance of the office as well as the importance of passing it along to the next CEO who will have similar qualities. In short, he took a chance on a system carefully structured to avoid systems with more pitfalls. Now"—he stood again—"by your leave..."

I looked at him. My voice was a lot softer now. "Can I call you when I need to talk to someone who's been there?"

"Of course. Although I suspect you'll find that your husband is going to be more helpful than I before long. Oh, and do give your dogs my best. Both of them. They're both most attractive animals."

My jaw dropped. "You knew?"

"Oh, yes. I told you that you'd be surprised at how much we know about Family members. I admit that I don't know where Sasha was the day I saw you, but I've seen pictures of her. She's a very pretty girl, and while my role that day required that I act like a stuck up prick, I'd like to think I'm a much better and more human person nowadays, and I am very much a dog lover. I have Belgian Tervuren myself. Rather like Bruno, except perhaps with a bit less intense personality and with longer hair. Of course, I don't live in a place anywhere near as warm as Tucson can be, as you know. Needless to say, I was sweltering in my overcoat even in February, but I was acting a role." He turned to leave. "Stay as long as you like. This is your room now. Gustav, the guard outside the meeting room, will be happy to show you to your office. There's a document on the desk that will explain how to access everything you will need and how to do the basics of the job."

Gustav really was very nice, especially when I wasn't holding a knife to his throat. He showed us to my new office, and after helping us get some coffee, he disappeared. Alec and I sat on the couch together, opened the Director's book and began to read the beginning part. Well, we tried. I couldn't make complete sense out of what had been written, so Alec, who'd had some exposure to English of that era in high school, puzzled his way through and put it into more modern English for me.

"The eighteenth day of May in the year of our Lord, 1530. My name is James. In truth, that is all the name I grew up with. My mother never told me who the father was that quickened me within her womb, and the only item of the pitiful few she passed on to me on her death that came

324

from him was a button with an eagle on it. I have no interest in discovering to whom it once belonged."

As Alec read it, I was fascinated to hear how James grew up and began working for William Escarton. William eventually gave James his name, but James, being always aware that it was not a name he was born to, decided to simply call his descendants the Family.

I sat back against the back of the couch and looked at Alec. "You know, I often wondered about that. You even asked about it, back when. Why the Family was simply called the Family, I mean, and not with a name attached like the Rockefellers. Now I know."

Alec nodded. "James must have been quite a fellow, especially for his time."

In its own way, it was utterly fascinating. To hear the actual words of a London slum lad, orphaned before he was even in his teens, relating how he'd made his way and became so successful that he could actually found the Family—I was in awe of him. And to send his oldest son off to find the land that became Golondrino? I had never heard this before, and while we didn't go any further that evening than Will's 'prodigal son' return in 1532 and James' handing Will the reins of the Family, I got enough to set my mind churning and make me eager to go through the entire book when I was able.

"I sure hope Fields put the combination to the vault into his letter, because I'm going to put the book away for the night," I said. "I've had more than enough for one day, and I'm sure you have too."

Alec nodded. "Let's go see what we can do about dinner and a place to sleep." By the time we finally left the building, it was getting dark. Gustav suggested we try the hotel across the square, and it turned out that they wouldn't even take my credit card. Just knowing who I was, they got our luggage from the car and gave us the Director's suite. I guess it was now my suite.

For breakfast the next morning, they weren't even fazed by my request for grits with salsa and cheese. In fact, they offered me a choice of salsas. I suppose the change really struck home, though, when I went to call Becky that first night. I was sitting in the suite late in the evening, well after midnight actually, so I called down to the desk to ask about paying for an overseas call. I was told simply to make the call. When I persisted, the manager on duty pointed out that since the hotel was a Family business, there was absolutely no way for them to charge the CEO for anything that happened in the suite and I should just go ahead and make the call. Okay...

When I got her on the line, I couldn't bring myself to tell her of the change; that would have to wait until we were face to face. I simply apologized for not calling sooner, told her I'd see her in a couple of days and sent hugs and kisses to Bruno and Sasha. Before she could hang up, I changed my mind and asked her to meet us at the airport in three days. I named a time and told her to make it the executive terminal, which seemed to puzzle her, but she agreed. I told her good-bye before she could ask me any questions and hung up, feeling insufferably smug.

It was somewhere around ten in the morning the second day when Alec and I were in my office—my office!—trying to work our way through the letter that had been left for me, along with making some sense of the Family holdings and everything that the CEO did, when the intercom buzzed and Margarete, my secretary, came on the line.

"Colonel Beindorf and Lieutenant Colonel Rachison of the Defense Force to see the Director."

Alec and I looked at each other. This was going to be...interesting. Alec got up from his chair and walked to the far side of the office, taking a seat on the sofa facing me. Then I responded to the intercom.

"Please send them in, Margarete." I have to admit that I wasn't certain what to expect. Of course, I still wasn't certain of much in my new position. But this was even more unnerving for me than most of the things had been so far.

The two of them, quite resplendent in their dress uniforms, shoulder boards and all, actually marched into the office, stamped and braced to attention before my huge antique desk. They wouldn't look me in the eye. Both of them stared fixedly at a spot well above my head on the wall behind me. They also looked a little the worse for wear. Well, I'd put them through a lot. It made me feel a bit better on some level to know that it still showed. Of course, they'd put me through a lot too. Payback's a bitch.

Beindorf finally spoke. "The Commander and Deputy Commander of the Golondrino Defense Force reporting to the Director," he announced. I waited. After what was probably not all that long, he produced two sheets of paper and laid them on the blotter before stepping back and resuming his brace. Rachison never moved. "Would the Director accept our resignations?"

I picked up the papers and looked at them. That's what they were, all right. Identical except for the names and ranks, both citing 'personal reasons' for the resignations. I considered my possible responses before looking at Alec. He shrugged slightly, said nothing. I supposed it was my call, after all.

I looked up at Beindorf. "Sit. Both of you." I gestured at the chairs in front of the desk. They both sat at attention and still would not meet my gaze. I let the silence drag out for a few more minutes. "Well, Colonel, I presume you realize that the two of you are not exactly my favorite people at the moment." No response. It wasn't really a question, after all. If I had the responsibility, I'd have to make the decision, wouldn't I? "Colonel, I understand why you did the things you did. I also understand the orders you

327

received from my predecessor and why he gave them to you. I'm not going to pretend that I was thrilled to be on the receiving end of those orders. At the same time, however, and without discounting the potential abuse of the excuse of 'following orders', I realize that you were given a very difficult assignment and carried it out in a most... conscientious and even exemplary fashion. If I refuse your resignations, will the two of you serve me and this office with the same loyalty and diligence that you have in the past?"

The two of them leapt out of their chairs and braced again. "Yes, ma'am!" they chorused.

I took their resignations and put them near the front edge of the desk. "Then take these back. We'll revisit the issue in a year. Dismissed."

They came to attention and marched out.

When Alec and I got through the entire list of Family holdings, we both thought back to the time he was doing his thumbnail math and coming up with what seemed like a reasonable per-share income level. Trust me, the per-share income is *way* more than he had figured. But the letter Fields had left me directed me to the Book as it also explained his own reasoning. The dividend paid out is entirely at the discretion of the CEO. I could order dividends and more, actually returning some or even all of the principal of the Family holdings to the members. I had the power, if I so chose, to completely liquidate the Family fortune, the entire country of Golondrino, and split it all up among the Family shareholders. Drastic, eh? It'd make all of the Family members suddenly richer than hell too, although it would be the end of the Family as an entity.

I could, at the other end, order no dividends to be paid at all, which would certainly make me no friends. There are three basic considerations, or so Fields' letter said. First, the Family needs a certain amount of income for its own expenses. These include the Family plane that regularly picks up the board members for the meetings, the salaries for every one of the employees of the Republic of Golondrino, the maintenance of the state of Golondrino, and more. Second, the Family supports a number of charities—it actually runs several. I added a couple to the list for future contributions, primarily the NRA and the Desert Museum. Finally, the Family pays its members dividends on their shares. But the considerations—this was Fields talking in his letter—include being reluctant to make them so high as to encourage Family members to sit around and just enjoy their dividends, and yet also reluctant to make them so low as to reduce the net income to the members to the point that it was simply pocket change for them.

He also kept it from being a specific repeated number so as to leave us all a bit uncertain about exactly how much we would receive, although it tended to vary with, not against, the market. In the Book, James Escarton had made sure that we understood that maintaining and increasing the Family fortune was a priority, even a significant part of *the* priority.

I was given an official passport. Whenever the CEO travels on Family business, it's official government travel. It turns out that the CEO's spouse, if any, gets a Golondrino passport, an ordinary one, for the duration of the term or marriage, whether Family or not, so Alec got one too. I had some announcements printed up. They were very elegant, with the Golondrino eagle on the front, and inside they simply said: "The Republic of Golondrino is pleased to announce the retirement of Chief Executive Officer, Raymond Escarton Fields, and the accession to the office of his designated successor, A.M. Youngston."

All sorts of fancy printing, engraved, cover tissue—the whole bit. Just three copies. I hand addressed one to Daddy and another to Aunt Lori, and sent them off by mail. Becky's I'd hand deliver.

When we finally left to catch our flight home, this time on the Family jet from Zurich, everything felt just about the same as it had when we drove into Golondrino. But it was an entirely different world for us. We went by limousine; our rental car was returned by somebody else. Needless to say a much different world indeed for us as I noticed when I stopped at a particularly elegant jewelry store in Zurich to spend a truly extravagant amount on a gorgeous necklace for Becky. Oh, and traveling by limousine is simply... wonderful.

Epilogue

I was cleaning out some things the other day and ran across the flash drive that held all my notes on my board member surveillances. As I reread my notes, it seems as though it happened a lifetime ago, although in actual fact it's only been about six years since Alec and I went through those experiences that would change our lives forever.

It's been an interesting six years. For a change, Alec and I have no more money concerns, needless to say. Quite the opposite. He closed his practice—never resumed it, actually—and took me on as his sole client, and Becky and Jeff, another Family member, as needed, of course. He also became my alter ego within the Family, although as a non-member, he's always stayed behind the scenes. Margarete, my receptionist/secretary in Golondrino, knows he speaks with my voice, but she's the only one. I've kept my investigation business going, as it seems to be in my blood, but I've been able to turn down some of the hinkier cases that came my way without worrying as I used to about turning away a fee.

I engaged a process server to take that minor and unenjoyable load off me. The business became 'A.M. Youngston and Associates' as soon as I realized that I was better off presenting to anyone calling from the Family as Amy Trevethen and letting "A.M. Youngston" stay unseen. When my time became too full of Family matters to handle some of the investigations, it became "A.M. Youngston and Associates" for real, as I hired a beginning investigator to join my practice.

Jeff is another Family member, which should probably be no surprise. It certainly makes it easier to talk about things in the office. I'm beginning to suspect that I'm on the downhill run as an investigator, but if I can get several more good years at it, I'll be happy.

A little over three years ago, we moved into our dream home overlooking Tucson Mountain Park—well, my dream home. Alec's dream home, so he says, is wherever we live and Becky is just glad to be out of her old house. We had a very nice housewarming too. Becky was there, of course, and Daddy, Aunt Lori and Carol all came. I had planned to put Aunt Lori and Carol in one of our guest suites and Daddy in the other, but when Daddy arrived, he and Aunt Lori took one and left Carol the other. That was...a bit of a surprise. I tried to keep my mouth from remaining wide open for too long. But since they're only third cousins, they're adults, and hardly likely to have more children now anyway, I guess I have no problem with it, at least once I recovered my composure. Becky seemed bemused by it, though she admitted that her mother had never said anything to her about it either.

We eventually discovered that they'd been an item for about two years at that point, ever since Becky's time in jail, but that's a whole different story. A much bigger surprise was when Carol arrived. Becky was cooking, so Alec and I met her in the driveway and we hugged all around after I'd introduced them. Then she held me at arm's length and told me just how thrilled she had been to hear that I'd become the new CEO. Once again, I was utterly flabbergasted and speechless. After a moment I regained control of my vocal cords and said, "You're Family? You never told us!"

She laughed. "How could I have told you and your father when I didn't know *you* were? You of all people should remember, 'you don't talk about the Family'. I did check into the relationships after I heard about you taking the position. You and Becky are my sixteenth cousins, twice removed, which is pretty remote by most people's standards. It's actually just about as distant as we can get within the Family, since you two are descended from both Will and Robert Escarton, and I'm descended from their sister Deborah. I might have figured it out if I'd ever needed a doctor in Lori's specialty, but since I was young and healthy, I never bothered to ask which doctors in Denver were Family, and you have to admit that there isn't a lot of call for consulting authors." She looked at me again. "Just look at you now. Boy or girl?"

I smiled. As much of a shock as this was, it certainly removed the one problem I had had no idea how to resolve, which was having her as the only person not informed about the Family here for the weekend. She had meant far too much to me growing up to ever leave out, and I would have had no idea how to explain how I came into the very substantial money for such a magnificent house and property.

"Girl. She's due in six weeks."

Carol had always loved children, but now I understood perhaps a little better why she always seemed to love someone else's rather than having any of her own.

"And a name?"

I couldn't help blushing, such a rare event for me. "Elizabeth Carolyn. For both of my mothers." That got Alec and me another hug. There were simply no words to express her utter delight and pride, but then none were needed.

We all spent quite a bit of time in and around the nifty swimming pool on the west side of the patio, one of those edgeless pools overlooking the parks west of the house, although I didn't get into the water much. Since I was almost eight months pregnant and felt like a whale, I really didn't want to complete the resemblance by doing much floundering around in the water in front of everyone. But it was a wonderful time.

After reading the Book, I came to understand that previous CEO's had a wealth of accumulated knowledge about the position, and that observing the usual practice of letting them go without any further contact with the new

CEO wasted that knowledge. I resolved to be different in my term. Reading about some of their ordeals, as well as the CEOs no longer with us, was absolutely fascinating. At least two of the earliest Directors took their seats as the result of duels! It also turns out that Ray Fields, when he's not acting, isn't half the asshole I had remembered him as being. We've been on a Ray and Amy basis since, I think, the second time I called him to help hold my hand over what I felt was a rough spot. He now has a plaque for his house, a gift from me, rather like the ones I have at my doors, that also says "House of Dog Hair", although his is in Algonquin instead of Yaqui like mine.

I do think I'm more accessible than he was as a CEO, but that's probably just personal style. Well, not really all that accessible, at least in person or on the phone. But I always respond to any letter, note or email that comes in; it's a point of pride for me. I am the first female CEO after all, and at least sometimes my gender shows in my work, especially when I don't keep it firmly hidden the way I generally do to the Family at large and will continue to, at least until the novelty of having a new CEO wears off, which it pretty much has now.

I still don't work at being ladylike, but that's just me. However, I do curse less, at least in public. I've also had more than one board member tell me how much more interesting and comfortable it is to have the CEO trying to build a consensus on a given investment, rather than simply having the board members attack each other's ideas. I don't know...I like it, even though it's only a guide to me, not a directive, and it seems to work. That's probably enough. The Family balance sheets certainly seem to suggest that it does work, and the bottom line is what really matters.

Bruno is getting along in years. Now twelve, he's starting to show clear signs of arthritis and general old age. We know he will leave us before too much longer, and we dread the day. He does very well with our daughter, Betsy, who is now three and adores him as much as he does her. When Betsy came home from the hospital, we started her out in a bassinet in our bedroom. Bruno lay beside it whenever Betsy was in it. When she moved into a crib in her own room, he went too. When she left her crib for a real bed, he not only stayed with her, but he slept on the bed with her every night.

I swear he taught her how to walk. He's now more comfortable with a step to get up onto the bed, but we also credit him with helping her learn as early as she did to make it through the night without wetting the bed, and he and she are too inseparable to attempt to keep them apart unless it's absolutely necessary. We don't even try.

We lost Sasha quite unexpectedly about two years back when she just crashed one day, and even after all the tests that could be done and then a postmortem, we still aren't sure why. Hard as it is to accept at times, money can't buy everything, and all lives must come to an end some day. We miss her still, Becky especially, and likely we always will. But Bruno has a new friend now, almost as hairy as was Sasha. Callie—her registered name is Callista Of The Fields—is one of Ray Fields' Tervuren puppies, a long-haired version of Bruno. But she isn't being trained to guard or find drugs. Other than the basic sort of obedience training that we feel she, or any dog needs to have in order to be a good family member, we are raising her to be a happy dog and friend to all of us. If she stops leaping on Bruno, biting at his legs and learns to come when she's called, she'll be an absolute doll. Well, puppies have privileges, or so Bruno's tolerance of her behavior suggests.

Alec and I go back to Las Vegas from time to time, mostly to remind ourselves of getting married there. We don't gamble much. There's really very little point now. But I admit that we do like to cash in a couple of hundred bucks or so at the lower-level blackjack tables once in a while. It's not the money, of course. But there's always a thrill to winning, and even losing a completely inconsequential amount of money hurts for a moment or two. Certain personal beliefs remain no matter what, I guess. Alec and I have both started playing occasionally in some cheap local poker tournaments. Not for the money, but simply for the chance to act normal with normal people from time to time. That is, if you consider poker players normal. Also for that thrill of winning every once in a while. Some day, I may even learn to shuffle chips. I keep trying.

Although I'm not actively looking for a successor yet, I do have several family members I'm keeping tabs on. Unlike some of the CEOs in the past, I not only recognize that I could die in office, but if that were to happen, I don't intend to leave the office simply vacant. I fully intend to leave the board with several serious potential possible successors, any of whom would be ready to step into it, even if they don't undergo an ordeal. There is now a surreptitious training program to prepare—without their knowledge, just steering them in the right directions—not just one, but a couple of potential CEOs, so that there is *always* going to be someone ready and able to take the reins as I can manage.

When it comes time, if they haven't sorted themselves out for me by then, the ordeal will likely include an actual competition, even if the participants aren't aware of it when it's going on. I'm still trying to fashion just the right competition, and I'm coming to understand how much a good ordeal must be tailored to the person undergoing it. Ray was right; the Family does have an unbelievable amount of information on its members. Not as detailed as some of the things Ray had on me, but as that showed, it can be stepped up on request. I've got an incredible amount of information on my potential successors, because, having identified them, I am having them monitored very closely indeed.

Speaking of ordeals, I did eventually break down and tell Alec and Becky about what went on inside me during our time tied up in my house. Becky was horrified and supportive. Alec seemed to want to wrap me in cotton batting, hold me close and make it all go away after he took care of the men who had done it. No problem. I've come to understand that I am, for myself, as unbreakable as I can be. My real weakness, my vulnerability, is others: Alec and Becky, Betsy and the dogs, even as they are my strength. Threats to me I can cope with.

Threats to them, my relationship with them and my inability to respond to those threats were what did me in then and would likely do so in the future, should it ever come to that. But learning that helped me grow, and it was the missing link in my being able to tell the two of them about it. I can, and do, open up a lot more to them now than I ever could before, although I'm still private with others as ever. I understand now that it's simply a choice, and it's one that I elect to make. I just do so now with my eyes wide open instead of simply turning away from things I didn't want to look at the way that I used to.

It's not easy, but it's been both interesting, endlessly so, and fun. When it's no longer fun, then we'll see who will take over and I'll retire, probably as abruptly as Ray did. Hopefully with a bit less animosity between me and my successor at that moment too. But time will tell, and if that's what it takes to get the right successor, then so be it. Which, I see through the Book, has often been the CEO's response to such an often-repeated situation between them and their successors. Good CEOs have always put their responsibility to the Family above such petty concerns whether their successor will come to take over the office in a pleasant, or at least civil, frame of mind. It also appears that this is rarely the case.

Oh, one other thing. Nowadays, whenever you buy a cup of coffee or a package of coffee beans, at least a tiny bit of that goes to the Family. You could go direct to a grower for your beans, but even there, some of them will tell you they're family-owned. What a couple of those will never tell you, of course, is that they're Family-owned. Some investments just make perfect sense. Don't they?

About the author

Insurance sales, collections and even the practice of law get old after a while. A.J. Kohler did all of those, but is mostly a retired attorney who practiced law in Denver before heading south for a warmer climate. Winter sports were never an interest, and shoveling a driveway, not to mention careening around town on ice- and snow-covered roads got real old, real fast, so the desert beckoned and a love affair blossomed (with the desert; the partner was already a commitment).

A.J. is not Family, but since long drives out to the gun clubs west of Tucson gave plenty of time to invent and refine the concept, perhaps the Family would consider adoption?

A.J. lives on the outskirts of Tucson with a partner of the opposite sex and two long-coat Akitas, also of opposite sexes.

Acknowledgments

First and foremost, my thanks go to my publisher and the entire team working on this book, for all of the work and help to finally bring it to publication.

I also have to thank those long-suffering friends who read various versions of this book and provided feedback that made it better, made the characters more believable and more real, found typos that everyone before them had missed, or even just gave me the encouragement to keep on going. In no particular order, Chrisan Smith, Joi Pettigrove, John Stevenson, Jan McGonagle, Sean Gerritson, Dave Livingston, Ann Pollard, Barbara Ellis, Susan Berger, Cathleen Moore, Greg Cranwell, Jerry Dixon, Keith Moyer, Pat Felker, Rick Waite and Scott Thrall. If I've overlooked anyone, my deepest apologies.

My thanks, too, to the people at Hideaway Knives (www.hideawayknife.com), whose innovative designs inspired most of Amy's weaponry.

Finally, there is a special place of honor for my partner, CEO, who not only gave me the encouragement and impetus to start this book in the first place, but who gave me the change of direction I needed when I ran into a wall, and then suffered through not only version after version, question after question, conversation after conversation, but has also listened to me tell innumerable other people about the same things that have been heard over and over. I couldn't have done it without you.

Other crime fiction from Solstice Publishing

Two thrillers by Alan McTeer:

ESCAPING CUBA

Ace pilot Alan Richards has taken a job ferrying Greenpeace scientists in a seaplane to identify freighters and cruise ships that are pumping waste overboard. But when an engine glitch forces him to land in an area of Mexico known for drug smuggling (and for which he has not filed a flight plan), he opts to abandon the plane and take his chances living on the beach rather than run the risk of being mistaken for a smuggler.

This gives the CIA the chance to make their move. They know that Richards is always running away from his past, and they need a rogue pilot like him to fly into Cuba, land, pick up two baseball players, and get back out before the Cuban government knows what hit them. But when Richards and his co-pilot (Cuban American Mario Rodriquez with secrets of his own), eventually begin their descent, they see on the field below not only the two ball players they were expecting, but also more than fifty men, women and children waiting for transport to America. And that's only the beginning of their problems...

Escaping Cuba is a thriller teeming with aggressive CIA agents, Navy Seals, merciless Cuban Army soldiers, beautiful women and ordinary Cubans trying to get by without making waves... It's an absolute must read for anyone who likes their adrenalin rush mixed with authenticity, historical detail and great company.

RED ZONE

"A hell of a journey into the heart of darkness. McTeer inherits the keys of the high adventure novel from the likes of Wilbur Smith, Desmond Bagley, and Hammond Innes."
-- Paul Bishop, author of *Chalk Whispers*

"A riveting, white-knuckle read, with writing so vivid you'll believe you are sitting right there in the plane's cockpit with these unforgettable characters. McTeer is a natural-born storyteller who writes with the authority of a real adventurer. He doesn't just talk the talk-he has actually walked the walk."
-- Tess Gerritsen, author of *The Sinner*

"McTeer walks the reader into a treacherous maze where entanglement and evil wait at every turn. This is a journey where there are no right moves, no one is to be trusted and there are no clear exits. A spine-tingling novel from beginning to end."
-- Steve Zettler, author of *The Second Man* and *Double Identity*

Two books in the Atrophy series by Sean Danker-Smith

ATROPHY

Velvet Valmont doesn't ask for much: just a quiet existence apart from her past. When one of her colleagues goes missing, Velvet only wants to make sure she's safe, but she's barely started her search when she uncovers conspiracy, murder, and too many questions. Her life has never been simple, but now she's bitten off more than she can chew. If she wants to survive, she'll have to reconnect with the killer instinct she's been working so hard to lock away.

Friends and enemies, outlaw bikers, pathological killers, buried secrets – and she hasn't even scratched the surface of the real threat.

This is how it begins. Welcome to Silver Bay.

HARBINGER

All Frank wants is a quiet investigation, but what he gets is four blown tires, a stowaway in his trunk, and a community going insane.

He's on the trail of Wainwright Multinational, a global conglomerate that may be responsible for hundreds of deaths, and he believes they have an interest in Condon Falls, Washington. People have been going missing, the remaining citizens aren't themselves, and there's something loose in the valley he can't explain. Things turn desperate when a Wainwright clean-up crew appears, all too happy to add Frank and his stowaway to the rising body count.

Frank has to deal with crazed locals, contagions, friends and enemies from his violent past, and worse. Monsters and mercenaries are just the beginning; Frank's mixed up in something bigger and more dangerous than he realizes.

TEN-A-WEEK STEALE

Stephen Jared

Returned from the Great War and living in 1920s Hollywood, Walter Steale is hired as muscle by his politician brother while a platinum blonde, renowned for playing empty-headed nymphets in the flickers, rekindles his faith in the world. But before long, lies stack up around his work, and Steale finds himself on the front lines of corruption. Steale's dirty work is used against him to protect powerful state leaders.

Forced into the life of a fugitive, it's only the secret love of a film star that keeps him sane. But the former GI won't give in, as he's determined to expose the state's true enemies. No easy task while he's hiding in the shadows of a thriving new metropolis where everyone is dancing fast, chased by sorrow, drugged by the dream of change.

BLOOD, PURE AND SIMPLE

Stuart Chesterfield

André Warner is a professional killer. Thirty-nine contracts have made him a wealthy man, and his fortieth is to be his last. The hit goes smoothly enough, and the victim - son and heir of a vicious drug baron - is eliminated with minimal fuss, though the man's mistress gets caught up in the crossfire: regrettable collateral damage. Warner drives off into the sunset to hang up his gun and retire to a Mediterranean idyll. Then into his life comes Gina, a stunningly beautiful divorcee with a bad experience of men. Despite her initial resistance, she and Warner eventually fall in love, upsetting his plans for a footloose existence. Simultaneously, his past catches up with him, putting Gina at risk.

Vengeance is in the air.

His retirement plans in shreds, his new love in jeopardy, Warner strives to regain control of his destiny in the only way he knows.

MURDER DOWN UNDER

Nancy Curteman

When corporate trainer Lysi Weston attends a conference in Sydney, Australia, g'day turns into a very *bad* day after her Harlem-born colleague, Grace Wright, stumbles on the battered body of a childhood friend. Determined to sniff out the murderer, Lysi embarks on a labyrinth of trails that lead her to suspect a womanizing cop, a suave Black businessman and a voyeur who videos his victims.

Handsome Detective Maynard Christie tolerates Lysi's meddling in his case until it jeopardizes his investigation. He orders her to stay out of his way, a directive she ignores. Both irritated with and attracted to her he begins to long for the quiet life on his Outback sheep station.

What Lysi does not anticipate is Grace succumbing to the charms of the prime suspect. A second homicide leads Lysi to an unexpected rendezvous with the murderer who is set on eliminating the last piece of incriminating evidence–Lysi Weston.

MURDER ONCE, MURDER TWICE

B.J. McMinn

Detective Julie Hartman must solve a high-profile murder while she combats the chauvinistic attitudes of a small, Oklahoma county's, all male sheriff's department.

She wonders why the sheriff gives her the case until she overhears him and the undersheriff, whom she's nicknamed the 'pissin' buddies', plotting to sabotage her case and use her failure to rid the county of its only woman detective.

Her prime suspects include the husband, his business partner, an ex-lover, a wife abuser, and the undersheriff. When Detective Malloy attempts to integrate himself into her investigation, she suspects him of spying for the sheriff. When she learns of his secret relationship with the victim, he becomes another suspect.

She follows a trail of corporate greed and lust and discloses a thirty-year-old secret. As she her investigation leads to the discovery of the murderer's identity, she becomes the killer's next target...

Reviews

"B. J. McMinn hooks your interest on the first page, with shiver-inducing prose and vivid characters. I hope this is the start of a series."
- William Bernhardt, New York Times bestseller

"B. J. McMinn has done an intriguing job with this tough mystery. Don't miss getting your copy."
- Dusty Richards, Award winning author

Made in the USA
Middletown, DE
15 April 2019